PRAI
CHERI

"*The Drowning House* is deliciously eerie, atmospheric, and impossible to forget. The setting, the friends, and the washed-up house itself combine together to create one of this year's best horror stories."

—Darcy Coates, *USA Today* bestselling author of *Dead of Winter*

"*The Drowning House* has taken up permanent residence in my subconscious alongside the briniest haunted houses around. Be forewarned: there's an undertow to this novel. Once you start reading, it'll suck you right in."

—Clay McLeod Chapman, author of *What Kind of Mother* and *Ghost Eaters*

"Propulsive, exciting, often terrifying, *The Drowning House* effortlessly threads compelling mysteries and horrors into a supernatural thriller, drawing readers in from the first heart-stopping pages and not letting go until the end. Priest once again proves she is a masterful storyteller promising secrets and revelations. She delivers on all counts."

—John Hornor Jacobs, author of *A Lush and Seething Hell*

"Cherie Priest has made something truly special with *The Drowning House*, a haunting story of ghosts, family, friendships, and horror. This is one of her best."

—Stephen Blackmoore, author of *Dead Things*

"Cherie's Priest's *The Drowning House* is a haunted house tale of a totally unique order. I consider myself a hard reader to surprise. Priest's thrilling and heartfelt novel will keep surprising you."

—Nick Cutter, author of
The Handyman Method

"Fiercely original and bone-deep chilling, *The Drowning House* is as satisfying as it is unsettling."

—Carter Wilson, *USA Today* bestselling
author of *The Father She Went to Find*

"Cherie Priest can be counted on to tell a bang-up tale with engaging characters and exciting twists. She is one of our most underrated horror authors."

—Poppy Z. Brite, author of *Lost Souls*

"Cherie Priest is our new queen of darkness, folks. Time to kneel before her, lest she take our heads."

—Chuck Wendig, author of
The Book of Accidents

"Cherie Priest is one of our very best authors of the fantastic. Brava!"

—Jonathan Maberry, *New York Times*
bestselling author of *Ghostwalkers*

"There are few writers I'd rather have keep me up half the night than Cherie Priest."

—John Scalzi, author of *Starter Villain*

THE DROWNING HOUSE

THE DROWNING HOUSE

CHERIE PRIEST

Cover design by James Iacobelli
Cover images © Brian Volk/Getty, Elena_Alex_Ferns/Shutterstock
Internal design by Laura Boren/Sourcebooks

Published by Poisoned Pen Press, an imprint of Sourcebooks
P.O. Box 4410, Naperville, Illinois 60567-4410
(630) 961-3900
sourcebooks.com

Cataloging-in-Publication Data is on file with the Library of Congress.

Printed and bound in the United States of America.
VP 10 9 8 7 6 5 4 3 2 1

This one goes out to Kat Richardson—
for indulging the impromptu field trip
that made this book happen.
Next time, let's write about someplace warmer, eh?

1

WEDNESDAY

A fat harvest moon hung low over the beach the night Tidebury House washed ashore—over the wet, packed sand and ragged black rocks, all the way past the edge of the high-water line. It dripped with dirty foam and seaweed, and it rested crookedly, draped with rotting nets, crusted with barnacles. Tiny clicking creatures with small sharp claws climbed the teetering two-story structure and then—finding nothing at the top but a collapsed roof and the ghosts of broken chimneys—retreated again to the shelter of briny pools, where they waited for the waves to return.

Tidebury House never sheltered anyone. That's not what it was for.

The brutal, late-autumn storm had not quite receded when Charlotte Culpepper grabbed her house robe and slippers. "It's not possible," she muttered as she crammed her naked feet into the soft satin shoes. She threaded her arms into the robe's sleeves and cinched its belt around her waist. "Not possible, no."

She stumbled at the edge of the hallway runner and caught herself against the wall. Must be careful. Mustn't fall. Not again. She'd never recover from another one, not at her age. Where was her cane? She'd left it behind, beside her bed, leaning against the nightstand. No matter. She wasn't going far.

Her heart thundered in her narrow chest. She clutched it, and she fought for balance. One hand against the wall, her fingertips sliding down the textured grasscloth wallpaper. One foot in front of the other.

"It won't be there," she lied out loud. "I hid it from the world. I sent it away."

A sleepy, confused voice called out from the bedroom down the hall. "Grandmother?"

She shouted back, "You heard it too, didn't you? It was loud enough to wake the dead!"

Simon opened his bedroom door and yawned. "Did a tree fall on the house?" Then he noticed that the elderly woman was hustling toward the front door in her night clothes. The realization woke him much faster and more thoroughly than the crash outside. "What are you doing? Are you all right?"

Beside the front door, a wicker basket offered three umbrellas. She ignored them. The coat rack held two of her raincoats—one for lighter weather, one for wetter and colder. She left them both behind and reached for the dead bolt. She twisted it hard and then released the chain above it. She did not so much open the door as yank it inward.

Rain blew sideways into the foyer. The sharp, wet wind clutched at the dangling light fixtures and flapped through the raincoats. It rattled the umbrellas, the pillows on the parson's bench, and the philodendron with the long green tentacles and heart-shaped foliage. The sprawling old houseplant swayed and fluttered; its loose leaves fell free. They bounced and lurched in the spiral gust that circled the elderly woman like a spell.

"Shut the door, please!" Simon begged. "Stop it, Grandmother. I'll go check. I'll find out if there's any damage. I'll go see how bad it is, you stay here."

"The damage," she muttered.

She already knew it was no tree. Not even the hundred-foot alder behind the house would've made such a racket. She'd heard that sound before: the violent crunch, and the teeth-splitting scrape over the peculiar thunder that shook the night in a rumbling, protracted roar. It could be nothing else.

Except it wasn't possible. It was too cold for thunder. Far too late in the season for this sort of storm.

Wasn't it?

Leaning hard against the weather, she launched herself onto the porch. Her feet hit the cedar boards; she slipped, she steadied herself.

The air sizzled with ozone and fire. A flash too close, too hot and sudden.

The power went out.

All the ambient light in the big old house disappeared in an instant. No glowing clock numbers from the stove in the kitchen, no soft night-lights in the hall to guide the way to the bathroom. No lamplight spilling out of her grandson's room.

No moon. Nothing, except...

She wiped wet hair out of her eyes and saw the flash of lightning in the distance, silent and bright. Sparks flying from the power lines. The lighthouse at the north end of the island, its lamp burning a streak of white that swung back and forth across the churning water in the shipping lanes—powered by its own emergency generator.

Everything else was black.

Charlotte scrambled down the three short steps to the ground, clutching the rail all the way. Her feet hit the brick walkway and slipped, but she still had one hand on that rail. Against the odds, she stayed upright. Leaned against the wind. Squinted against the driving rain that still spit hard off the water.

It was hard to see. Impossible, if you didn't know what you were looking for.

Charlotte knew, and when the sparkling edges of the night's wee hours showed something enormous resting at the beach's edge, she almost stopped breathing.

Instead, she started running.

Her joints ached and her chest burned. She was closer to a hundred years old than most people ever come, but she had never been as fragile as her grandson believed. Once, she'd stood against a bigger storm than this, and she'd wielded the earth itself against the ocean, against a house, against a man.

But the cost had been great, and she could not pay it twice.

She stopped running. Her lungs screamed and her ankles popped; her ribs ached and her eyes stung. Simon was calling out, but she couldn't hear what he was saying. When she checked over her shoulder, he was only a flailing shadow. He stumbled forward, feeling his way from the house in the trees to the edge of the water. When the lighthouse lamp swung her way for the briefest instant, she saw him struggle toward her in sock-feet.

Before her: the terrible square block of darkness, somehow blacker than the night that surrounded it. She could see nothing past it. Not the thrashing waves, not the swelling tide, not the horizon line, or the land on the far side of the Sound.

Slowed by age but propelled by terror, Charlotte pushed forward.

She knew every boulder, every driftwood log, and every grass-covered dune at the edge of her property. She knew where to step and where to avoid, but there might be new debris. There could always be fresh obstacles between Charlotte and the beach.

None of it was half so dangerous as the thing that couldn't have *possibly* come back onshore.

All the same, there it was: a structure carved out of a black hole, with all the same inscrutable gravity.

Charlotte hadn't seen it in seventy years. Apart from a faint outline when the lightning flashed, she couldn't see it now. It absorbed the reality around it. It consumed everything. Everyone.

Simon came running up behind her at an uneven pace that half slapped, half stomped.

"Stay there!" She held out her hands. "Don't come any closer!"

Years before, she'd stopped worse things that way. A lift of the hands. The raising of a horn. Old words in the old family tongue, carefully pronounced. Old words, shouted. Given to the earth. Thrown at the water. Now forgotten. Old.

Words. Lost.

Charlotte gasped. Her vision went white and spangled. She dropped to her knees. Something inside cracked. She heard it, but she did not feel it. She opened her mouth in case the old words would come falling out. In case they still lived inside her head and might be summoned.

Nothing came out. Not even air.

Hands reached her. Touched her back, on her side. Lowered her to the ground, where it was rough and wet and the sand squished beneath her shoulder blades.

"Simon," she tried to say. "Run," she would have added. "You have to run, before he. Before. Before." Her lips shaped the words, or maybe they only moved because her teeth were chattering.

"Grandmother," he wheezed. "Don't move, hold still. I'm calling 911."

He was a stranger now, some unknown party with unclear motives, and she would have fought him if her arms worked at all. If her legs could kick. If she didn't taste pennies and salt. If she could see anything through the stars that filled her eyes—except for the uncanny shape that loomed large over the beach and the movement within it,

and the light within it, and the shadow within it

the man within it, sliding back and forth between then and now

here and there

now

2

1985

LEO

All three children sat on the sand atop a series of towels they'd borrowed from Mrs. Culpepper. The towels were entirely too fancy for an oceanside lounge, with fringes and velvet trim; they were cotton/silk blends that were mostly for show in a rarely used bathroom. But Simon had begged. As he'd vigorously reminded his grandmother, the weather was uncharacteristically warm and there wouldn't be many days like it. The kids could either take advantage of this happy boon… or play inside the house—where they would surely drive the old lady batty.

On purpose, if necessary.

"Don't go any deeper than your ankles," Mrs. Culpepper had warned. "Wading is fine, splashing is acceptable, and damp knees are to be expected. But *no swimming*. I know it's hot outside but the water is too cold for swimming, and the current is stronger than it looks." Then she'd given them the towels and kicked them out to do their worst.

Now these pasty Pacific Northwesterners had sun, they had time to kill, and they had a beach.

Or if not a beach, they had a coastline—and it stretched along the eastern side of a slender, minimally occupied island on the western end of Puget Sound. Sure, this coastline was covered in gravel and crushed shells, and yes, it was pocked with volcanic black boulders that were too sharp to climb without bloodied elbows, knees, and palms. But it was long and narrow and private, just out of sight from the Culpepper house on the other side of the tree line.

The ocean hovered around forty degrees most of the year. In August, maybe as high as fifty.

It was only the end of June.

All three children sprawled in a row, wearing their smallest clothes. None of them owned bathing suits, but they all had shorts and Melissa had a tank top rolled up to cover little more than her nonexistent boobs.

Simon was eleven years old. He had hair and freckles the color of carrots, and the lanky, pale body of a boy who wouldn't hear from puberty for another couple years at soonest. His eyes were the color of the sky past the horizon line, mostly blue with a bit of gray. He'd lived with his grandmother since his parents had died in an accident when he was eight.

Melissa was also eleven. She'd been a towheaded baby and now was an ashy blond child. Mrs. Culpepper had offered her tousled head a spritz of lemon juice to let the sun brighten those dull, unruly locks. "It'll give you highlights," she'd promised. Given time and no further lemon juice intervention, her hair might eventually catch up to her eyes, rich and golden brown.

And then there was newcomer Leo, seven years old. Small and round. Darker in complexion than the other two, with black wavy hair and eyes that matched it perfectly, until you saw them in the light. He was chatty and excitable and eager to please—desperate to fit in with Melissa and Simon, who were the only other children on the island. Despite his efforts, he remained a third wheel wherever they went—even if they were only going down the walkway, past the big driftwood tree that was as long as a truck, and through that narrow gap in the seagrass-covered dunes, onto the rocky sand beside the ocean.

Regardless, Leo was happy, especially when the sun was out. Even if the big kids didn't include him in every conversation, even if they talked over his head. He had a baby blue towel with a faux-Persian velvet pattern around the hem. It was very soft between his fingers when he fiddled with it.

He wished for sunglasses, but he didn't have any. Neither did Simon, but Melissa was wearing a pair of Mrs. Culpepper's that were comically oversized on the little girl's face.

Simon pointed out, "You'll get funny tan lines, if you don't take those off."

She shrugged. "I don't care. I like them. They make me feel rich." Melissa was not rich. Her parents sent her to stay with her grandparents every summer because they couldn't afford daycare when school was out.

Leo said, "I like the sunglasses. They make you look grown-up and important." Leo's family wasn't rich either. He was living with his aunt and uncle part-time for the same reason as Melissa. Their house was through the woods on the next lot over.

"Thank you, Leo. See? He's little, but he's not stupid."

"He's not *that* little," Simon said, with a friendly elbow to the younger boy's shoulder. "One of these days, you'll be bigger than both of us, I bet."

He liked that idea. "Then I shall have vengeance!" he declared, as close to the tone of his favorite Saturday morning cartoon character as he could manage.

Simon and Melissa cackled. They knew the show too.

Their laughter pleased the smaller boy. But he still added, "I'm just kidding." He sat up and then reclined on his elbows, staring off into the ocean. He liked the unusually hot day. It didn't often crest eighty degrees that far north and west, and nearly ninety was a rare thing indeed. The ocean breeze made it feel wonderful and pleasant; it smelled like salt and cool, wet things—but it *felt* like summer and soft, warm things.

"Look at me," said Melissa, not for the first time. "My skin is already getting kind of..." She poked her shoulder, and then gave it a pinch. "Pink. I'm getting a tan."

"So am I!" Simon announced. He pressed his hand to the top of his thigh and removed it, leaving a white impression in the sunny blush.

Leo jabbed at his own thigh, his own shoulders. "I'm not."

"You're not as pale as us," the girl informed him. "It'll take more sun to make you darker."

Simon patted his arm. "I bet Melissa and me will get a burn. But you're lucky. You probably won't."

Melissa said to Simon, "Maybe *you'll* get a burn, but not me. I'm going to look like Brooke Shields."

"Does she have a tan?" Leo asked. He wasn't sure who she was.

"She did in *The Blue Lagoon*. I saw it on video. We rented it from the gas station down the street from my parents' place."

Simon asked, "Was it good?"

She shrugged. "Sometimes Brooke Shields is naked, and her skin is really gold. Mine will be gold soon."

Leo didn't argue, but he knew what sunburn looked like, and his friends were definitely getting some. His uncle owned a company that did construction work around the Sound and he'd seen his uncle's shoulders, bright cherry red on top of his usual bronze. He knew what a farmer's tan was, and how brown skin can singe and peel, just the same as pasty skin with freckles.

Melissa sighed at the waves. "I want to go for a swim."

Simon said, "No, you don't; it's freezing."

"I don't care about the cold."

"You will when you're wet," he insisted.

Leo was just as tough as Melissa, he was pretty sure. "I don't care about the cold either."

Melissa was less confident. "Then why don't you dive in?"

"Mrs. Culpepper said we shouldn't. It's not just cold; the water is strong. It'll take us out to sea if we go too deep."

She rolled her eyes. "Mrs. Culpepper says a lot of things. It's only water. It's not that cold, and it's *really* hot out here. You'd be fine."

"No, Grandmother's right about the water. There's an undertow. It'll grab you by the feet and sweep you away. You'll go out to sea and drown, if you don't freeze to death first."

As if she had any idea what she was talking about, Melissa dug in. "You can't freeze to death if it's not even cold enough to make ice," she said with confidence. "Don't be a chicken," she told Simon. Then to Leo, "Don't be a baby."

Now the little boy could feel the pink. It crawled up his neck and settled into his cheeks. "I'm not a baby."

"You act like one." She adjusted the sunglasses and settled back into her towel. "If it looks like a baby and acts like a baby, it must be a baby."

"I'm *not* a baby," he protested through gritted teeth.

"Prove it."

Simon didn't like it. "Melissa, don't. Come on. He'll get hurt, and we'll get in trouble."

"He won't go out there. He always does what he's told, because he's a *baby*."

"He's just...not as old as us. We weren't babies a few years ago either. Don't listen to her, Leo. Stay here on your towel. Simon says: *Stay*."

"I *don't* always do what I'm told," he grumbled. But he felt very hot now, and he was sure he was finally getting a sunburn. Cold water would feel good on a burn, wouldn't it? That's what the school nurse said, the one time he came to kindergarten after he touched the stove.

"If you get hurt, Grandmother will kill us," Simon said, meaning him and Melissa. "We're supposed to look out for you."

"Because I'm the baby." He sulked a little harder. Then he stood up. A corner of the towel stuck to his foot, and he kicked it off. "But I *can* get in the water. Mrs. Culpepper said we could go wading."

"That's...true," Simon said warily.

"Then I'll wade." Up to his knees, at least, would be safe. "I'm not afraid of the water."

"Maybe you *should* be," Simon said, watching the younger kid stroll with feigned confidence toward the edge of the tide. "No deeper than your knees!" he called.

Leo waved without looking back.

He was barefoot and wearing only a pair of jersey shorts that weren't really swim trunks, but how often did he need swim trunks, anyway? The sun blazed down dry and hot and so bright that he wished he had a pair of Mrs. Culpepper's sunglasses to wear too. Even if they looked silly. Even if they wouldn't stay on his face.

His toes and heels sank into the sand as he trudged past half dried tide pools, oddly shaped shells, limp seaweed, and the scuttling crabs that he'd already learned not to pick up for closer examination. He wasn't afraid of them, but he knew not to touch them. They pinched.

"Seriously, Leo—don't go deep!" Simon commanded from his towel.

Simon said something to Melissa, and she said something sarcastic in reply, but Leo was far enough away that he didn't hear what it was; he just recognized the tone.

His toes hit the water. It foamed up around his feet and retreated, then returned—the little waves at the edge of the sand creeping onshore. The tide was coming in, but it wouldn't reach the towels for hours. It was rolling up cold, as frigid as anything he might take from a jug in the fridge, or a can of soda freshly cracked and fizzing. His body lit up with goose bumps, despite the toasty warm sun on his back and shoulders.

It was a strange and thrilling contrast, being too hot and too cold at the same time. He wiggled his toes in the chilly, wet sand and let them sink.

The waves were not so scary. They crawled up short and shallow around his ankles. Their current did not pull him anywhere. Their coldness did not turn his toes blue or make him want to run and put on socks.

He went out a little farther. Now the waves came up to his shins, and his goose bumps got goose bumps.

The sun was brilliant and the sky was perfectly clear; the air was so warm that it almost made him forget the cold. It made him think that the cold was not so bad, and he could—perhaps, if he was careful and slow—take some more of it, and that would be fine. The water was not strong. The water was not frozen. The beach was right here, under his feet. The sands might shift and the water might sweep in and out, but it wasn't going anywhere.

And neither was Leo.

He took another few steps, another few yards.

A wave crested at his knees and he jumped, startled. It was the skin behind those knees, so sensitive to the cold. He hadn't expected it—the frigid wash that foamed and bubbled around his legs.

He hugged himself and went deeper.

"Leo!" Simon called from shore. "That's far enough. Come back, please?"

He pretended not to hear.

Melissa chimed in. "Come on, I was just messing with you. Don't do anything stupid." When he didn't answer, she added, "Please?"

Leo smiled. And he kept walking.

Until suddenly, he wasn't. He was falling, backward into the surf.

It happened suddenly, almost instantly. The water had gone over his knees, up his thigh, and then something had grabbed him. Not with hands, not with claws or tentacles. (He'd learned about octopuses just a few weeks before, from a show on TV.) It'd been a force, something aggressive and hard and so fast that he almost hadn't felt it; he'd been upright, looking through the clear, cold water at the sand and tiny fishes…and then he'd been on his back, staring at the sky, being pulled along by his ankles and shoulders, his back and his elbows, everything dragged away, toward Whidbey Island on the horizon.

At first, he was too surprised to breathe. He only floated away, astonished by his circumstances.

It felt like lying on a conveyor belt, the kind that brings the bags into the airport—he'd seen one, last summer, when he and his parents had flown out to meet his grandparents in California. He'd been fascinated by the unending flow of bags, resting motionless and moving swiftly at the same time, down the metal conveyor, around and around until they were collected by their travelers.

Now he felt like one of those suitcases, along for the ride to heaven knew where.

Leo knew how to swim, but that's all you could say about his skills. He wasn't a strong swimmer, or a fast swimmer, and he wasn't coordinated enough to swim in a straight line. But he should be able to hold his head up and breathe. Why couldn't he hold his head up and breathe?

It must have been the cold.

He'd never been so cold, so completely, in his whole life. He was so cold that he could feel nothing else, not even fear. Not even confusion. He knew what was happening: he was cold. That was enough. That was everything.

At the edge of his awareness, Simon and Melissa were screaming his name, screaming for Mrs. Culpepper, and just plain screaming. But what good would screaming do? What action could Mrs. Culpepper take? She was very old, hideously old—sixty years old, at least. Decrepit and helpless against the ocean. What could she do if, if,

how could she even

but what if

His thoughts curdled.

He smiled, thinking of ice cream firming up in the crank tub, getting thicker and slower as it chilled. He heard a noise. Something far away. No, not very far? It was hard to tell with the water in his ears and the cold in his bones. He did not recognize the sound. It was very low, very loud, and rather musical. He could hear it under the water, when his ears dipped below the surface. The vibrating rumble, the roar of something being called, followed by the crash of something answering.

He couldn't hear Simon and Melissa anymore. He must be very far out to sea by now. Probably halfway to Seattle, which was over there somewhere, on the other side of the water. He'd been there once—to the Pacific Science Center, where the nice ladies in matching blue vests had let him touch the tornado's fog as it spiraled from the machine in the weather exhibit.

The fog had been cold too. It had been a vapor, more seen

than felt. It was nowhere as dense and not nearly as cold as the all-consuming darkness when he closed his eyes.

Under the waves, something moved.

He didn't feel it so much as sense it—not the pull of current on his limbs, not the rush of water...but the awareness that far away something very large was alive, and awake, and moving.

Toward him.

He could feel the noise through the water, the echoes and vibrations of something pitched lower than bass. He almost enjoyed it. He could almost appreciate it. Something large was coming, coming for him, coming to help.

Something would. Someone would. If not Melissa or Simon, who were not strong swimmers themselves then maybe

no not the old lady either, could she even swim

probably not

proba

pb

He sighed, and the last of the air in his lungs floated up in bubbles. So that was which way was up. If he followed the bubbles, he could see the sky above. Cold and blue. Cold and white. The sun was only a sparkle.

But something rushed toward him.

It washed him away; it pushed him deeper into the tide. Only for a moment. Then the jerking and pushing stopped. Something enormous rose up beneath him, and in front of him. Something hard that scratched up his back when it hit him and knocked against the back of his head.

He tumbled in the tide, upside down and right side up and

rolling, now that the world was full of rushing bubbles and blinding sky.

Up through the water he came, borne on the back of something he couldn't see, but when he looked toward shore, to the right, to the west, he could see her coming. Mrs. Culpepper was walking across the water, coming right for him.

Not rushing or running, for she seemed to lack the footing.

But coming.

Splashing and struggling all the way out into the surf, past the spot where the waves broke into foam and puddles. Walking on water, just like Jesus, or that's how he'd heard it in church.

Mrs. Culpepper was there, balancing on something just below the water, standing wet and ragged and fierce. He'd never seen her look so fierce before, so angry and so frightened and something else, something he wouldn't put his finger on for another forty years, almost.

She shoved her hands through the surface and seized Leo Torres, age seven. Beloved nephew of Marco and Anna Alvarez. Temporary resident of the house on the next lot over.

She got him by his shoulders, and then she heaved him up out of the water by his armpits—and hung him over her forearm like a dishcloth while she pounded the heel of her palm against his back.

After the fifth or sixth smack, water burped up out of his lungs and he began to cry.

His lungs emptied, he coughed and sobbed and dangled over Mrs. Culpepper's arm as she carried him back to the shore. He stared down at the water, not fighting it, not fighting her, not fighting anything. Just wondering, really, as he gazed down at the long line of big black boulders that reached all the way back to the sand. He'd never noticed them before.

All the way out to where Leo had almost drowned.

3

WEDNESDAY

MELISSA

Melissa absolutely hated "first thing in the morning" conference calls with corporate in Philly. The worst part was schlepping all the way downtown to her office in order to take those calls—because nine in the morning on the East Coast meant six in the morning for Washington State.

To hell with Philly. Why couldn't they use Zoom like everyone else?

She'd rolled in barely awake, contributed virtually nothing to the call, and been sent home as soon as everybody hung up. Now it was only a little after 8:00 a.m., and on the one hand, she could work from home in her pajamas for the rest of the day like usual. On the other, she felt like she'd already pulled a ten-hour shift in the graphic design mines. Bleary-eyed and grumpy, she stood at the bus stop and pulled out her phone to kill a little time.

Truly, she needed more caffeine.

And she needed to check her messages more often. She'd missed both a call and a voicemail overnight. She hit play and held the phone to her ear, but she heard only silence, so she pulled up the call details: Simon Culpepper had left fourteen seconds of audio at 2:16 a.m.

She turned up the volume and listened again. There was static, maybe, and some distant noise that sounded like the ocean. Or a car's engine. Or thunder.

A butt-dial, she concluded.

Her bus arrived. She climbed on board and took one of the only seats that remained, across the aisle from a homeless guy who looked like a Victorian fisherman's ghost—complete with retro yellow hat and angry gray beard. He belonged on a box of frozen fish sticks.

When the bus began to move again, she settled in to check her nonwork email. It was as good an excuse as any to avoid eye contact with spooky mariner, and she had twenty minutes to kill before the ride would take her home to the other side of First Hill. Pill Hill, everyone called it. Tons of hospitals and doctor offices.

The bus paused at a stop.

Melissa glanced up, then scooted over to make room for a blue-scrubbed nurse in a black puffer jacket. She looked ready to cut a bitch at the first opportunity, so she must've been fresh off a shift. Best to leave her alone. Best to keep her eyes on her phone.

"Oh, hey. Here we go." Simon had sent an email too. To herself, to the phone, and to a distant friend who couldn't hear her, she said quietly: "Hit me, handsome. What's shaking on the island today?"

Did a boat sink under mysterious circumstances? Did a strange fish wash up, prompting talk of cryptids again?

I don't know how to say this but Grandmother is dead, she just dropped dead, and everyone will say it was a heart attack or a stroke—and it probably was. I think something on the beach scared her to death. Can you come to the island for a few days? Take some time off work? Stay here at my place. Rent a car if you have to. I'll pay for it, if you need help. Just come out here, please. I can't do this alone.

That was it. No sign-off except "sent from my iPhone."

"Oh my God." According to their respective time stamps, the email had arrived about three minutes before the nonstarter of a voicemail. A dark sour feeling twisted in her stomach. "Oh my God," she said again.

Mrs. Culpepper had let the kids play at her house every summer, for the sake of her orphaned grandson; and she wasn't always warm, but she'd always been kind. The combination made for many fond memories but few intimate ones, and in the great matriarch's advanced old age, it had seemed ridiculous that Simon remained on the island to look after her. That poor woman should've gone into assisted living years ago.

Still, it was the end of an era, and an enormous loss for her old friend...never mind the added grim intrigue of a woman being frightened to death on a beach. Why hadn't Simon elaborated? Melissa didn't like it when he didn't elaborate. It was usually on purpose, and he was usually leaving out the most important part. Sometimes she feared she didn't really know him as well as she thought she did, but she knew how much she cared about him.

So of course she'd take some time off to go out there. Of course, whatever he needed.

What *would* he need help with? Funeral arrangements? Paperwork? Shoulders for crying upon? Maybe he wanted more practical help, since the end of one era always heralds the beginning of a new one—and maybe *this* time, he'd leave the island for good. She could definitely help him with *that*. In fact, she was positively embarrassed by how excited the prospect made her. She'd started to think the day would never come.

Melissa didn't like making calls on public transportation and she didn't like it when anybody else did either, but surely a dead grandma was grounds for an exception. Nobody needed to know it was someone else's grandma.

But Simon's phone rang, and rang, and rang.

He didn't answer. She didn't like it when he didn't answer. As far as she knew, that was never on purpose.

For the rest of the ride, Melissa held her own phone in her lap.

When her stop rolled around, she hopped down off the bus's bottom step and tried to call again. The sidewalk was crowded with the rush-hour crowd of nine-to-fivers beelining to work from the light rail station or the parking garages; she weaved between them, a salmon headed upstream, her phone plastered to her ear once more, even though it was starting to rain.

Simon's phone rang, and rang, and rang.

She was about to give up again when someone on the other end of the line answered.

"Hello?"

But it was not Simon.

Startled, Melissa stopped in the middle of the sidewalk. Someone behind her clipped her shoulder. She retreated out of the flow of pedestrian traffic to lean against a tall stone building. "Hello?" she replied. "Who is this?"

"This is Deputy Dave Svenson," he said. "Jefferson County sheriff's office."

"Where's Simon?" She pressed her back against the wall and shivered. "Why are you answering his phone?"

"We found it in the living room. Now, ma'am, who am I talking to?"

Her answer came out in a stutter. "This is, this is, I'm... Melissa Toft. Simon left me a message overnight, and I was trying to call him back. Is he all right?"

"What kind of message? What time did he send it?"

She'd just checked. Why couldn't she remember? "Something like two in the morning, I think?"

"What did it say?"

"It didn't?" she said, pulling her coat a little tighter around her shoulders. The rain was coming down harder now, a proper shower instead of the drizzle of the damned—but she was sheltered by an overhang. "It was blank. I thought he butt-dialed me. He...he does that sometimes," she finished weakly. She was rattled and anxious, and that's why it took her a minute to remember. "But he sent an email. He said his grandmother died. He thought something scared her to death?"

The deputy did not react to this bit of information, a fact which confused and alarmed her further, and she couldn't say why. He asked, "Ma'am, where are you? Right now, I mean? It sounds like you're outside. There's a lot of background noise."

Maybe that was it. He just hadn't heard her. "I'm in Seattle. I just got off a bus. It's raining. But did you hear me? Simon said

Mrs. Culpepper was scared to death. Please, could you tell me what's going on? Is Simon okay?"

The deputy was quiet for a few seconds. Then, rather than answer her, he asked another question. "Are you a family member?"

"I'm...an old friend. I've known the Culpeppers since I was a little kid."

"What'd you say your last name was? Toft?"

"That's right. My grandparents were Amelia and George. They lived on the island for decades."

He made a "hmm" sound. "I remember George. Used to have that little blue fishing boat, tied up at Mystery Bay. He'd sell you bait, if you were running low."

"That was him," she confirmed. "Always had a bucket with a lid on it and something gross inside it."

Even now, there weren't a thousand full-time residents on the island. Back in the eighties, it hadn't been more than a few hundred. Everybody knew everybody. To a surprising extent, everybody still did.

The deputy said, "I remember when your granddad sold that house, after his wife died. My dad was thinking about buying it, but someone else got to it first." He cleared his throat and tried to get back on track. "Look, we aren't sure where Simon Culpepper is, but we're trying to find out. When's the last time you saw him?" he asked.

"A few months ago. He came into the city, and we got dinner and drinks like we always do."

"Is there any chance you know the passcode to his phone?"

She shook her head, then felt silly because he couldn't

see her. “No, I don’t have any idea what it is, I’m sorry. We weren’t…we weren’t that kind of close.”

He sighed. “Well, it was worth a shot.”

“Have you searched the woods? He might’ve gone to the lighthouse. We used to do that, when we were kids…” Her voice trailed off. It was a silly thought. This wasn’t the 1980s. Cell phones meant nobody needed the lighthouse radio anymore, in case of emergency.

“All I know for sure is, Mrs. Culpepper died out on the beach, during last night’s storm—presumably of natural causes. We think maybe Simon found her, then ran back inside to get his phone and call 911. But he wasn’t there when emergency medical personnel arrived.”

The feeling in Melissa’s stomach was hotter and heavier than lava. “Simon would never… He wouldn’t just leave her there. I don’t understand.” She floundered, seeking some explanation. “He might’ve gone to Nordy’s.”

“Nordy’s burned down.”

“What? No. No, it didn’t.” She couldn’t wrap her head around it. The little store had been the island’s hub since before Charlotte Culpepper was born. Almost everyone’s mail arrived there, via general delivery, or at least it had when Melissa was young. It was an emergency hub, a lifeline, a community center.

Deputy Svenson said, “I’m afraid so. An electrical fire took it, a little while back.” His tone shifted. “Look, I’ve been here since about three in the morning, and I called another deputy, who joined me around four. Neither one of us has seen hide nor hair of Simon Culpepper, but we’ll keep our eyes open. Thank you for your time, ma’am.”

Quickly, she asked, "Hey, do you know where they'll take Mrs. Culpepper's body? Simon might turn up there to claim it. He won't leave his grandmother for very long. He never does."

No reply. The deputy had hung up.

A large drip of water splashed down from the overhang to hit her phone. The overhang was no longer protection enough, and Melissa didn't carry an umbrella. She wiped the phone on her jeans, pulled up her jacket's hood, and headed back to her apartment as fast as the morning crowds would allow.

Ten minutes later, she was wrestling with a vintage doorknob and its 1960s dead bolt. She lived in a building that had gone up in thirty minutes or less like a goddamn pizza, just before the World's Fair, and it felt like living in a plywood doghouse—even though rent was a fortune and it didn't even include parking.

She threw her bag onto the table beside the door and tossed her coat onto the rack to drip-dry. For a moment, she stood in her living room/dining room/kitchen, catching her breath and thinking.

Mrs. Culpepper was dead. The authorities were investigating. Simon was missing, and he didn't have his phone. It was not quite nine in the morning on a Wednesday.

First things first.

She went to her laptop and flipped it open. It only took a couple of minutes to fire off an email to her boss, something about a dead grandmother and a funeral. She kept it vague. She was pretty sure she'd never mentioned that her own grandparents were all dead, and forty-six wasn't too old to still have a grandparent walking the earth. After all, she and Simon were the same age, and Simon's grandmother was alive and kicking until a few hours earlier.

Melissa didn't ask for time off; she merely informed her bosses that she would be out of the office. She'd been their lead graphic designer for several years. She was reliable and trusted, and she had no expectation of pushback.

Next, an email to Simon. She pulled up his message and replied to it.

> I tried to call you back, and some cop named Svenson answered. He said he found your phone in the living room? They've picked up your grandmother, but I don't know where they'll take her and I don't know what happens next. I'm so sorry, Simon. I don't know what happened or where you've gone, and I'm hoping you just freaked out and took a long walk, and that you're fine, wherever you are, and that you'll reach out when you get home and find your phone. Or your laptop, or whatever. I don't know if the cops are keeping your phone or not.
>
> One way or another, *please* reach out when you can. I'm worried about you.

Her fingers hovered over the keyboard. She wasn't sure what else to add.

> I know you said something scared your grandmother to death, but we both know she was very old and sometimes things simply happen when you're that age, so don't you dare blame yourself. I won't have it.
>
> Please be okay. Please let me know.

She stopped again, thinking about that email. The deputy had mentioned a storm. It was possible that a bad one might've scared her to death. Thunder and lightning were rare around the Sound. A loud crack, a bright flash, an ancient woman with a fragile heart…it wouldn't take more than that to end almost a century's worth of life.

Right?

Melissa didn't quite believe it, but she couldn't think of anything else Simon might've been talking about. Well, she could ask him in person when she got there. He'd be home by then, definitely. She'd make him some coffee and toss in some whiskey. They could sit on the driftwood tree at the edge of the property and stare out to sea while he told her what happened.

She added one last note.

> I'll call Leo and see if he'll meet me out at your place. I don't know anybody but you on the island anymore, I don't think. So if you can't reach me for some reason, please try Leo. We've always got your back.
>
> I've taken some time off work. I'm free through the weekend, so I'll drive out there today, okay? Whatever is going on, hang in there. The cavalry is coming.
>
> Lots of love,
> Melissa

She hit Send and stared obsessively at her sent message, willing an immediate response to manifest. None arrived.

But it would. Eventually. He wouldn't leave her hanging. They'd been too close for too long.

She and Simon first met the summer they both turned ten—two little Cancers only a few weeks apart, and two of only three children on the island. Most of its inhabitants were the solitary sort, and many of them were older. The majority had Scandinavian family origins, having settled in the region via careers in the fishing industry, or shipping, or trade. When Melissa thought of the island, she recalled a place occupied by gold- or silver-haired people who didn't talk much, didn't get out much, and didn't like kids much.

By now, that probably wasn't fair. When she'd been a child, it'd felt like the gospel truth.

She closed her laptop and picked up her phone again. She dialed, she waited, and she got the voicemail inbox of Leonard Torres.

"Leo, it's me. You might already know this by now, but Mrs. Culpepper is dead. Simon left me a message overnight, and when I called him back, some cop answered his phone. It was weird, and I don't like it, and I think something's wrong. Extra wrong, you know. Not just...wrong because Mrs. Culpepper's gone. I'm heading out to the island..." She pulled her phone away from her ear to look at the time. "In a few minutes. I'll be on the road by ten, and at the house by lunchtime, if I'm lucky. You want to meet me there? We can all get lunch together in Port Hadlock or something. Call me when you get this, would you? I'd really appreciate it. If not I um...I guess I'll see you at the house."

She hung up and wiped the phone screen on her jeans to clean off the last of the rain and a smudge of cheek sweat. She'd need to stop for gas. She rarely drove, and her car rarely had more than a quarter of a tank. As the crow might fly, the island was only fifty-odd miles away, but a crow could fly across the water without waiting for a ferry.

Melissa chucked her phone onto her desk and went rummaging in her closet.

Where was her suitcase? The little rolling one that always fit under the airplane seat in front of her? She wouldn't need anything bigger.

The sour feeling clenched in her belly, hard and fierce. Something was wrong. *Really* wrong. She should hurry. She retrieved the suitcase from the closet and filled it in less than a minute, even with her hands shaking.

One more pass around the apartment.

Leave the laptop. Smartphone would be fine. Extra cable and charger? Yes. Makeup bag? Already crammed on top of her extra socks. Shoes? She switched into a pair of sneakers then changed her mind and stuffed her feet into her favorite thrift-store Timberlands.

Cash. Wallet. Passport? Nah. One more pair of extra socks, though, because you could never have too many. Sufficient underwear. A spare bra. She grabbed her messenger bag and slung it across her chest. Made sure she had her keys. Picked up her suitcase, locked the door, and ran to her car while pulling up the ferry schedule on her phone.

The next one left for Bainbridge in forty-five minutes. If traffic didn't keep her, and if it wasn't too crowded, she *might* get onboard in the first round. Then it was just a half hour ride and an hour's drive northwest, give or take.

Over the river and through the woods, to Marrowstone Island we go.

4

1985

MELISSA

"Go get Grandmother!" Simon shouted from knee-deep in the surf. He gave up on any rescue efforts of his own and started splash-trudging back to the shore. "Go get her!" he hollered again as he stumbled over a half buried bit of driftwood. He fell forward and landed on his hands; they sank into the wet sand and left deep palm prints when he stood up straight again.

Melissa was speechless and useless, and she knew it.

This was all her fault. Every moment of it.

She shouldn't have called Leo a baby. She shouldn't have goaded the little guy into the water. Now he was washing out to sea. He could swim, though. He'd told them all about the classes he took, and if he could swim, he might be okay...until he froze to death. She was absolutely paralyzed by the horror of what she'd done.

"Melissa!" Simon grabbed her by the shoulders and shook her. "Get Grandmother!"

"Oh...okay..." she sputtered, still straining to see Leo—who retreated farther into the surf with every second.

Simon let go of her and darted north across the shoreline.

"Wait, where are you going?" she screamed after him.

He did not look back when he called, "Lighthouse!"

"The lighthouse, okay, yeah, good idea..." The lighthouse would have Official People who could get Real Help, she knew that much. It wasn't so much a lighthouse anymore as a research station for the Geological Society, but even so...useful folks. Useful folks with emergency medical supplies and access to a radio that'd reach help faster than a phone call, probably. Melissa had gone there once on a summer field trip, sneaking into the little oceanside station with a group of kids from the RV park who were taking a tour. There'd been computers and science equipment and people in uniforms, or at least matching jackets.

Melissa started running back to the house. "Mrs. Culpepper! Mrs. Culpepper! Leo went in the water, and he's washed away!"

Rationally, she had no idea what she expected Mrs. Culpepper to do. The woman was small and old, and she probably couldn't even swim. If she used the phone in the kitchen to call 911, who would even come? There were no cops or firefighters on the island, and no ambulances that she knew of. No lifeguards. No *nothing*, as she'd often complained upon being dropped off at Grandma and Grandpa's for three months.

Anyone who might come would surely come too late. She knew it, and the thought made her sick to her stomach because this was entirely her fault, and she knew that too.

"*Mrs. Culpepper!*" she shrieked at the top of her lungs, running past the driftwood log and up the walkway to the porch.

Mrs. Culpepper flung the front door open and raced outside. She was holding something in her hand, and Melissa couldn't tell what it was—she'd never seen anything like it before. Something long and slender and softly curved; it made her think of a stretched-out steer's horn or a very peculiar trumpet. "What have you done?" she asked the girl.

"I didn't mean to do—"

Furiously, and with fear, she said, "He's just a little boy, and you should've known better!"

Melissa started to cry, embarrassed and ashamed that Mrs. Culpepper had figured out everything so easily. "I know, I'm sorry, I'm so sorry..."

"Sorry won't help anything, now get out of here—run for the lighthouse, go!"

"Yes, ma'am," she sobbed, and she turned back the way she'd come. She didn't say that Simon was way ahead of her, and she didn't ask if she shouldn't run for the road instead, and flag down a car. She didn't do anything except run and cry, barefoot, back down the trail, back to the sand, back to the shoreline—because that was the easiest way to reach the lighthouse. If the water was out, she could run along the pale strip of beach and skip the trails, the trees, and the inevitable wandering deer who'd get in her way and maybe even chase her.

Behind her, a loud indescribable song moaned a single low note. It was louder than anything Melissa had ever heard before, louder even than the fireworks at the stadium in the city—the ones that blocked out the sky itself, and every other sound in the universe. She almost stopped, buckled, and covered her ears, but she couldn't do that.

Because she'd fucked up, and she had to get help for Leo before it was too late.

But it was already too late. Everything that happened now would be a useless gesture because, God help her, she'd killed little Leo Torres. She would probably go to jail, maybe forever. She probably *deserved* to go to jail, maybe longer than forever. Melissa was absolutely, no question, the worst person on Marrowstone Island.

The terrible sound faded into nothing.

Melissa shook it off, pulled herself together, and kept running. At least no one would say she hadn't tried.

Simon was nowhere to be seen, and that meant he'd already rounded the outcropping to the north. He'd reach the lighthouse soon. Any minute, surely. It was only half a mile away, and Simon could run like a cheetah. Melissa was only following in his wake. This was silly. There was no point to this at all, but she didn't know what else to do, so she followed behind him anyway, as fast as she could.

But something strange was happening.

The sand was shifting beneath her feet, wobbly and loose like it might swallow her. She jumped up onto a dune covered in tangles of sea pickles and tall scratchy grass—something firmer than the loose stuff by the water. She fell to her knees and grabbed clumps of grass, and she held on tight.

It wasn't enough that Leo was drowned and blue and floating out to Seattle; no, there had to be an earthquake too.

Not a bad one, she hoped. She'd been in a couple already, none of them bigger than this. If she were still lying on her borrowed towel, she might have even enjoyed it—nothing to fall on top of her, nothing to run away from, only the vibrating bounce of tectonic plates shifting past each other (or that's how her science teacher had explained it).

Now it was a terror.

Now it was slowing her down, and slowing down Simon too, wherever he was.

When the quaking stopped, Melissa ran again. She didn't stop until she made it all the way to the lighthouse.

No one was there.

The front door was hanging open, but there were no cars parked in the lot beside it. Usually she'd see at least one or two. Simon must have outpaced her by quite a lot, and she was glad, because it meant that Leo might have a chance—if there was someone with life preservers who knew first aid or CPR or whatever drowned people needed, if you wanted to make them undrowned.

Melissa doubled over, her chest cramping with exertion. She had lost her breath halfway there and kept running regardless. Now she saw static even when her eyes were open, a slow, spreading sparkle of glitter and light.

She sat down. Her legs weren't working right anymore. She listened to the water rushing forward and retreating, the seabirds squawking, and the ship horns blowing across the water in Port Townsend. When she'd rested enough to stand and think at the same time, she made her slow, grudging, miserable way back to the Culpepper property and the little private beach with the borrowed towels.

It was empty. The towels were scattered and Mrs. Culpepper's sunglasses were half buried in the sand.

For a moment Melissa was confused. There was no sign of

Simon or his grandmother, or of drowned and frozen Leo, who was surely a Popsicle by now, having bobbed too long in the frigid ocean.

But when she listened hard, she heard commotion back at the house.

Still too exhausted to run and barely strong enough to stagger, she lunged across the sand, through the gap in the dune, past the driftwood log, and back to the walkway that led up to the Culpepper house, where there was an extra car and a lot of talking going on inside. She heard voices but couldn't make out most of the words, even with the door cracked open.

Melissa climbed the porch steps and froze at the top, unwilling to push past the door or go inside. Leo had washed out to sea. She would have to explain what had happened to Mr. and Mrs. Alvarez, who had never been anything but nice to her—and now she'd killed their sweet little nephew. She would go to jail, and she would deserve it. And worse.

But she heard a soft little cough. Then a louder, more ragged hacking that went on for a few too many seconds before it ended with a burp that sounded like water coming up and splashing down.

Now she pushed the door, and went inside. "Leo?"

There she found Mrs. Alvarez and Mrs. Culpepper, and Simon, and someone from the Geological Survey Team—or that's what their jacket said. And Leo, who had in fact thrown up a great gush of water all over the living room rug. He was wrapped in a blanket, not a towel, and his lips were still a little blue around the edges, but he was alert. He looked confused, and not entirely unhappy to be the center of attention.

Mrs. Culpepper sat beside him on the couch, rubbing his back and telling him not to worry about the water; she'd clean it up later. She was every bit as soaked as Leo, and her hair was perfectly wild, blond streaks in a silver waterfall, and much longer than Melissa usually thought of it. It was typically pulled up in pins or a bun, tied up tightly. Now it hung down well past her shoulders, crusty with drying saltwater. Across her face was a streak of something red, like she'd been slapped across the nose with a paintbrush.

Melissa wanted to ask what that red stuff was, and what had happened, and how was Leo sitting right there, alive and more or less well?

But Leo saw Melissa first. His face lit up, and it made her heart clench. "Melissa!"

"Hey, Leo. Are, um...are you okay?"

He nodded. Happily, he announced, "Mrs. Culpepper pulled me out!"

Mrs. Culpepper did not look happy, either about the wet clothes she was wearing or the exclamation made by the boy—which prompted plenty of questions. None of which she answered with more than, "He got stuck in an eddy that pulled him close to shore. It was fine. He'll be fine."

Leo looked like he wanted to argue, but he wanted the old lady's approval more. He nodded again. "She saved me."

"Your teeth stopped chattering," Simon noted helpfully. "You must be warming up!"

"Leo, I'm sorry about what I said." Melissa said it fast, in front of everybody—even though everybody probably didn't know yet that it was all her fault. Simon wouldn't have said anything. Leo was still recovering. Mrs. Culpepper knew, but she wasn't the kind to announce it, Melissa didn't think.

The geologist was wearing a badge that identified him as Dr. Helms. Melissa knew from experience that he was probably a doctor in something weird like "fancy rocks" and he wasn't a physician, but "any port in a storm," as her grandfather always said. Dr. Helms declared, "I think he'll be just fine, Mrs. Alvarez. He was breathing on his own by the time I got here. He's a lucky little guy!"

He gave Leo a quick pat on the shoulder and excused himself, wishing everyone well as he left.

Mrs. Alvarez and Mrs. Culpepper retreated to the kitchen to have one of those half whispered adult conversations, and Melissa halfway thought maybe she'd be sent home, and she wouldn't be able to come back and play with Simon or Leo ever again, and she'd be stuck in her grandparents' house for the rest of the summer—or worse yet, for the rest of *every* summer until she was old enough to stay home alone during the day, whenever that would be.

Her eyes filled with tears, and she sniffled. She sat down on one side of Leo, and Simon sat on the other.

"It must have been so scary. I'm so sorry, I didn't mean to call you a baby. You're not a baby. You shouldn't listen to me, anyway," she added, trying to add a little lightness to the apology. "I don't know squat. I'm practically a baby myself."

"It's okay," he assured her, then followed that up with a couple of hiccups. All three kids waited to see if there'd be more, but that was all. He added, "Nobody's mad at you."

"*I'm* mad at me."

Simon said, "I'm...not mad, but I'm not really happy. But I'll get over it."

Melissa hoped so. She didn't think she could stand it if Simon stayed mad at her forever.

When the women returned from the kitchen, it was to give all three kids a very stern lecture about safety, and responsibility, and the importance of doing what they were told. All in all, the talking-to was a tremendous relief to Melissa, since she'd been bracing herself for hard time in the clink.

A few hours later, her grandfather called to say he'd come pick her up at the main road and bring her home for dinner. That's how they always did it. The access road to the Culpepper property had never been paved, and Grandpa didn't want any extra dirt or dings on his Buick. It wasn't even a quarter of a mile, short enough for a kid to walk alone if it wasn't dark.

Melissa told Leo she was sorry again for good measure, hugged Simon goodbye, and went to thank Mrs. Culpepper for her hospitality (as her grandparents always insisted she ought to), but the older woman was nowhere to be found.

She gave up and told Simon to pass along her goodbyes; then she left the house.

Evening wouldn't land for another few hours, so the way to the main road was bright and clear. Summers in the northwest meant sundown didn't come until nearly 10:00 p.m., and the sky was bright blue without any clouds. Only the big old trees loomed above her, shading her from the blinding, too-warm sun.

The woods were quiet, but not silent. A few birds, some

squirrels. Something larger—maybe a raccoon or a groundhog. No deer to stare her down with their big black eyes and soft brown faces.

But some other sound caught the edge of her attention and she stopped. She looked back at the Culpepper house. It wasn't far behind her. She could see it through the trees.

From her angle, she faced the house's southwestern corner—the side of the two-car garage and part of the building's rear wall. She'd been back there once or twice before, but no more often than that. There was nothing to see back there, and nothing to do.

Well.

There *was* a hatch. But the hatch was locked.

It made her think of a tornado shelter she'd seen in a movie, with two big doors mounted flat in the ground against the bottom of the house, steps leading down underneath it. Mrs. Culpepper always told them not to worry about it, that it was only a back door to the basement.

That was enough to keep the kids out of it. None of them liked the basement. It was cold and smelled like damp and mildew, and the light always flickered, and sometimes there were rats so big you could hear them gnawing inside the walls, if you listened close. You could hear their teeth grinding the bricks into dust.

Or that's what Mrs. Culpepper *said* the noise was. If it was something even worse than rats, Melissa didn't want to know about it.

But today, the old woman was back there behind the house, opening one of the heavy hatch doors. It was so big, Melissa couldn't imagine how she had the strength, but she lifted it like it was easy, if unwieldy.

Mrs. Culpepper was carrying something under her arm—whatever she'd been holding on the porch, when Melissa had come running up, screaming for help. What was it? Some kind of tube? Could it be a spyglass, like from an old ship? Something that let her see Leo bobbing around in the surf?

Whatever it was, it wasn't shiny. It didn't look like metal.

Melissa was curious, but nowhere near curious enough to run up and ask her. She was treading on thin ice with Mrs. Culpepper, and she'd probably feel that way for the rest of the summer.

It was strange, though. Melissa didn't even know the hatch doors opened at all. She'd had an idea that they were fused or rusted into place.

No. One was open now.

Mrs. Culpepper looked around, almost like she sensed that someone might be watching her. The streak of red across her nose and cheeks had partly rubbed off, but not completely. When she saw Melissa, she held very still.

The girl raised one hand and waved. "Goodbye, Mrs. Culpepper. Thanks for everything. I'll see you again soon."

Mrs. Culpepper didn't respond right away, but then she nodded. "Goodbye, Melissa. I hope you learned a valuable lesson today."

"Yes, ma'am. I did."

"Good. Give your grandparents my regards." Then she returned to the hatch and descended down the stairs into darkness—pulling the door shut behind her.

5

WEDNESDAY

LEO

Leo Torres was finishing up an early showing when he got the call. His picky prospective buyers were standing in the kitchen, arguing over whether or not they could live with the rooster-themed decorative tile for a few months, or if it'd have to go immediately, or if it meant the whole house was tainted with chicken cooties and they should return their attention to their first choice—a new build on a hill overlooking the naval port. When Leo saw Melissa's name on the screen, he let her go to voicemail.

She left a message.

He fully intended to ignore it until he was free of his clients, but some faint intuitive worry wouldn't let him.

"Excuse me," he said to the fortysomething couple, looking to buy a place big enough to move into with a mother-in-law. They barely glanced at him. "I've gotten an important message." He looked around for someplace relatively private. "I'll be…on the back porch. Give me a moment, please."

He stepped outside. The ringer was always off when he was working. He prided himself on never taking calls when he was showing a house, but this was Melissa, and it almost certainly wasn't a social call.

It wasn't that they weren't friends; they'd known each other since childhood. It wasn't that they'd never been close; he'd once considered her and Simon to be his very best friends in the world.

But in truth, he'd always felt like the third wheel—every summer on the little island to the north—and these days, he and Melissa never really hung out if Simon wasn't present. When the three of them were in the same town, the same bar, the same restaurant...it was just like the good old days, with better booze than the Zimas or Seagram's they shoplifted from Nordy's as sneaky teens.

When it was just Melissa and Leo, things got awkward. They'd never spent much time alone together as adults, so they defaulted to their weird childhood dynamics. Idle teasing, back and forth. Critiques disguised as questions and silly, pointless competitions.

In short, they fell back into big kid/little kid stuff.

It annoyed the shit out of him, even when he could see it clearly for what it was and knew it wasn't personal. The fact was, the only thing they had in common anymore was Simon—and that meant her call was probably about him.

Leo hadn't heard from Simon in a few weeks, not since they'd met up in Port Townsend the month before. It'd been great, like always. He'd looked good, but he forever looked good—tall and ginger, a more Nordic version of Prince Harry, sans the facial hair.

Leo had eventually come into his own, but it was hard for a broke kid from Tacoma to pass for upper-middle class. A heavyset, baby-faced Latino who wanted to sell houses to wealthy Scandinavians in rural western Washington had an uphill climb ahead of him. He'd known it from the start, especially in a profession where appearances could be everything.

But he was making it work.

One of these days, he'd level up to the promotions and bonuses of his more established peers, he just knew it. All it would take to haul him up the next rung of the career ladder was the sale of a million-dollar house—and it was only a matter of time before he'd become one of those guys with a portfolio of seven-figure listings. He'd already come close, once or twice. Next time, maybe.

But not today.

Today he stared out at a half acre's worth of steeply sloped yard and a tree line of cedars and pine and a house that probably wouldn't go for more than $700,000 if he was lucky, goddammit. He tried not to think about it as he held his phone to his ear and played Melissa's voicemail.

Of course it was about Simon…and Simon's grandmother, the great old dame Charlotte Culpepper.

"Holy shit," he breathed. "Mrs. Culpepper's dead." That news was shocking enough on its own, never mind the bit about the police. Or the sheriff's office, that's who would've been on the scene—but Melissa either didn't know that or didn't care. As Leo had explained to a prospective home buyer or two, the island was unincorporated and it lacked city services of any kind, but it was still part of Jefferson County.

It probably wasn't a red flag if law enforcement was on the scene. Uniformed folks usually turned up when someone died and it didn't happen in the hospital—if only to run paperwork and corpse retrieval.

Then why did it feel like a red flag?

And why did his mind already wander to the grand old midcentury house, which now belonged to Simon? Or so Leo had to assume. He wondered if this meant Simon might leave the island at last and set up a household of his own, someplace else. He wondered if Simon might need or want an agent to sell the house.

Back inside the two-story Cape Cod that needed a little cosmetic work but not much else, the couple was still discussing the merits and pitfalls of a gut job or a facelift. Leo joined them again.

"I beg your pardon for the interruption, but I'm back now. That call was...something I can take care of later." He might've been worried and impatient, but he was also an hour closer to the Culpepper property than Melissa was, over in Seattle. While he was eager to get over there and find out what the hell was going on, he was also a professional and he was refusing to speculate. Declining to freak out.

Appearances were worth keeping up. Simon would understand.

Leo plastered a smile on his face. He asked his clients if they wanted to go see the other house on their wish list, a sweet little bayside number a mile away. Smaller house, tidier yard, better view—farther up a hill, overlooking the main shipping lane that brought the big military ships in and out of Bremerton.

Instinct told him they'd turn up their noses on sight, because he already knew that the wife half of the fussy couple wouldn't even go inside when she saw the front porch. Somehow, she wanted a porch that both wrapped around the front for better outdoor space...and yet didn't make her feel "exposed" with too *much* outdoor space immediately outside her windows.

No, it didn't make any sense. Buyer whims often didn't.

But half an hour later, he was free of them both. They never even made it to the house on the hill. They'd opted to fight in the car instead.

Alone in his own vehicle at last, Leo pulled out his phone and almost called Melissa back. After all, she'd asked him to. But something stopped him—some strange, dark feeling that burned in the pit of his stomach. He changed his mind and called Simon directly instead. Even if someone else picked up, he might learn something new about the situation. He was better at asking questions than Melissa, who tended to get flustered or frustrated if she couldn't get immediate answers. Leo was a natural born salesman, or so he'd often been told.

No one picked up. When the voicemail inbox kicked on, he left a message.

"Simon, it's me. Melissa told me about your grandmother, and I'm so sorry. I'm also worried, if I'm honest. Melissa said something about the police having your phone or something? She's headed your way, but she probably won't be there for..." He glanced at his watch. "Another hour and a half, if she's lucky with the ferries. She said to meet her at your place, so I'm leaving work in a few minutes."

He wasn't sure what else to say.

"Again, I'm sorry about your grandmother. She was a great lady, and I always appreciated her kindness. More than that, we both know I owe her my life. I just... When you get your phone back, or when you find another one, please call me? Let me know you're all right. Melissa sounded worried, and you know me. I'm *always* worried, haha." Did it sound pleasantly self-deprecating? He hoped it did. "So...yeah. Hopefully, I'll see you soon. But seriously, give me a call."

He hung up and checked his email. One closing scheduled for next week, everything on track. One closing slated for the end of the month, also cruising right along. The paperwork snafu from last week, all sorted.

He was free and clear.

Should he stop at home first? Nah, he could day-trip it just fine. He had an overnight bag in his car in case of literally anything. Leo left his phone in the cup holder and tried to keep from glancing at it every five seconds.

It never rang.

He reached Port Hadlock in forty minutes, and by then he was hungry, so he hit up a drive-through and sat in his vehicle. He didn't honestly think Melissa would show up in time for lunch, and if she did, she could get food without him.

While he ate, he stared at his phone. But all his new emails were on the subject of real estate.

He wondered if Melissa would swing by the sheriff's office to raise a stink. Sometimes she had a whiff of the ol' white lady Karen about her—and sometimes she even used it for good. Sometimes it could be useful.

Sometimes it drove him crazy.

When he finished eating, he hit the road again, eventually driving over the causeway and past the estuary or swamp or whatever it was that ran under the bridge, stretching out north and south, soggy and gray and flat between the green island hills. He liked the mist. He even liked the fog. Fog was quiet and safe. Fog was another layer of privacy.

Leo turned on his low lights and kept going, up the eastern road to his aunt and uncle's place, the next lot down from the Culpepper property. His aunt and uncle were on a Caribbean cruise, having a blast. Leo knew this, because he was the one who sent them off and paid for it.

A fiftieth anniversary called for a mighty big gift, and he was proud that he'd been able to offer it.

The road to their house was paved, which wasn't such a novelty on the island anymore, but last time he'd been out to Simon's place, the Culpepper access road was still dirt, and he didn't mind walking. If the tide was out, he could hike all the way there across the sand. It wouldn't take ten minutes. If it was in, he'd take the trail through the woods, and it might take fifteen.

The weather wasn't great but it never was this time of year.

Water spit and splatted against his windshield and wind whistled between the trees. The rain would get worse before it got better, if the local weather forecast could be believed—and it often couldn't. But he was always prepared for the worst. In the back seat rested a long black raincoat that would keep the worst of the wet away.

A little salt and sand would only do a little damage. Not the end of the world.

He parked and locked the car with a beep of his key fob, out of habit and reflex more than necessity. The island didn't have a thousand residents, and at least a third of those were seasonal. He'd only passed one other vehicle on the way to the house, and it'd been an RV that was undoubtedly headed out to the old military base—since Fort Flagler and its camping offerings were the only tourist attractions to speak of.

He shrugged into the raincoat and pulled up its hood before too much of him got too wet. The tide was headed out, but it'd left behind a firm strip of sand to walk on.

He didn't walk on it. Not yet.

He was too distracted by what he saw a short way down the coastline, maybe a quarter of a mile out. It was sitting on the sand, lodged there right outside Mrs. Culpepper's place.

"What the hell is *that*?" he asked the universe at large.

At a distance it looked almost like some kind of vessel had washed on shore. But that wasn't quite right, was it? No. He squinted. It was a building, he was nearly sure of it. Large and pale and teetering, lodged in the sand at a slight angle.

"Fuck me, is that…a *house*?"

After all this time, Marrowstone could still surprise him.

6

WEDNESDAY

MELISSA

Melissa caught the next ferry by the skin of her teeth. At first, she was thrilled to have made it onboard; but ten minutes later, she was wishing she'd skipped the boat and driven the long way around the Sound instead. The trip would've taken longer by an hour or more, but the remnants of the previous night's weather made for a rough shortcut across the waves. The big craft rocked and swayed, rising and dipping, threatening to ditch its passengers and their cars into the Sound.

Melissa never liked taking her car on a ferry. There was some odd dissonance to the idea of driving on water; it felt unnatural and upsetting if she thought about it too hard. And of course, now she was thinking about Simon—which made her unease even worse. Simon's parents had died on a ferry. Or rather, they'd died when they were thrown from one into the icy surf during a "surprise weather event." That's what the news had called it.

She'd never met Simon's parents and had heard only a little

about them over the years. His father, some kind of inventor—like his own father before him. His mother, a homemaker. Then his whole life, after they were gone, was spent on Marrowstone Island with his grandmother. First out of necessity. Later from some mix of affection for and obligation to the woman who'd raised him.

She needed him in her old age, that's what he always said.

By the time Simon was in his forties, he was helping run a nonprofit that moved vaccines and life-saving medical equipment to serve developing countries and disaster zones. He'd traveled for the sake of his job at times, but for quite a while, he'd done most of his work remotely. Decent internet didn't arrive on the island until the twenty-first century, but when it did, it'd seemed to seal his fate as a permanent resident.

Much to Melissa's chagrin.

God knew, she'd begged him to move to the city for years, and maybe this was her chance to drag him out of there at long last. Seattle was an expensive city with a chilly social scene unless you plugged directly into one of the established subcultures, which Melissa had never fully managed to do. She had a few casual pals among her neighbors and fellow wage slaves, but she wasn't really a tech worker, a nerd, an outdoors enthusiast, a progressive activist, or any of the usual regional suspects. She would absolutely *love* to have a close friend nearby—someone who didn't expect her to conform to a greater group aesthetic or cause.

And maybe...now that Mrs. Culpepper was gone, Simon would consider it. Maybe it was time for him to join the rest of society, get out of that sprawling old house, and set up a life for himself that didn't revolve around his grandmother. His devotion had been admirable, but it was time for him to get a life of his own.

Ideally, near Melissa. She wasn't sure she believed in second chances, but she could cross her fingers.

Finally the midmorning ferry bucked against the Bainbridge dock and swayed to a stop. Workers in bright yellow raincoats with reflective silver stripes struggled against the wind and rain—tightening ropes and pulling levers, dragging the craft into position. All the passengers who'd left their cars returned to them. One by one the engines started up, and headlights blinked on. It was dark inside the ferry—and not much brighter outside it.

She drove off the boat with relief, and just a touch of guilt that she chose not to examine very closely.

Now she was home free: just a hop, skip, and jump to Marrowstone.

She crossed the causeway to Indian Island, past the naval battery and around the southern end to the Marrowstone bridge. There was no other way to get to the Culpepper house; the island connected to nothing else.

No other islands. Not any point on the mainland.

You either took the two-lane bridge from Indian, or you swam—since the island didn't have any ferry service either.

Just over the bridge, the road split. She took the eastern fork and rode it north. The dark tree-lined road was paved, but it wasn't marked, and technically the asphalt strip was wide enough for two vehicles, but you wouldn't necessarily want to be one of them. Good thing there weren't any other cars coming or going, much less one of the massive RVs that could run you off into the grass without even trying.

But Melissa hadn't seen another soul since she'd left the mainland.

Here and there, brand-new mailboxes stood sentinel at the ends of dirt driveways that disappeared through the trees. Most of them were also accompanied by "NO TRESPASSING" signs, but those had always been there.

On the left, she spied a shiny black receptacle at the end of a road she knew very well, and she wondered who'd bought her grandparents' place. Her parents had never told her.

Almost there.

She needed the next driveway off the main drag, up ahead on the right, and yes, there it was. She'd know it anywhere and she couldn't forget it if she tried, though Mrs. Culpepper's ancient roses looked considerably worse for wear.

Melissa flashed her blinker, even though there was no one else on the road to see it. She turned right and the paved road ended immediately, leaving her with sandy mud and gravel. She thanked her lucky stars for four-wheel drive and prayed there wouldn't be any downed trees or other debris to stop her, because she knew there was nowhere to turn around until she reached the house.

The remainder of the trip to the Culpepper home felt like driving through a tunnel, with giant evergreens looming on both sides—their dark canopies shading everything below, their trunks as straight and strong as soldiers. Then, at the end of the tunnel, a light. A clearing, at least.

A house, sprawling three thousand square feet across a single level.

Mrs. Culpepper and her husband had lived there together for ages, until he died of emphysema in 1981. Not long afterward, Simon had moved in. Of course, there was no school on the island, so his grandmother had to make arrangements when it came to his education. In the end, he was homeschooled with a series of tutors—each one older and more decrepit than the last, to hear him tell it. From ninth grade onward, he went to boarding schools. After college, he'd decided to come home and regroup…and he'd never left.

Melissa pulled up next to the house, into the wide, empty concrete driveway. She climbed out and shut the door behind her, not bothering to lock it.

With her hand over her eyes to cut the glare, she squinted through the small garage windows. Simon's green Volvo was parked inside, next to his grandmother's classic white Cadillac, which no one had seen her drive in years.

Melissa felt a wave of relief. His car was right there. He hadn't gone anywhere—or he hadn't gone far. He'd be back any minute, probably.

A sharp, scraping tickle in the back of her head didn't believe her. She ignored it.

A tug on the garage door said it was locked, so Melissa made her way around the side of the house to the front door, stepping carefully. The path was covered in brown leaves and branches, and when she looked up, she saw that a big bough from the cedar by the porch had landed on the roof. It looked like it hadn't done much damage. It rested there securely, lacy green edges blowing in the wind.

The porch had three short steps, with a secure old iron rail beside them. Its paint was peeling and the metal beneath was rusting. It flaked off onto Melissa's hand when she touched it.

"Time to repaint again," she muttered. Simon wasn't much of a home improvement or DIY guy, and hiring people to come all the way out to the island was sometimes easier said than done. She hoped it wouldn't be too difficult to find somebody to clear the roof and clean up the storm debris.

She stayed where she was, one foot on that bottom stair, and called out, "Hello?"

A couple of seagulls squawked, flapped, and flew off.

"Hello? Is anybody here? Simon, where are you? Officer... deputy? Any chance you're still around? Sir?"

A set of gurney wheel tracks in the sand pointed back toward the drive. The cop and whoever had picked up Mrs. Culpepper's body were long gone.

She tried to picture that tiny old lady leaving the house in the middle of the night in a terrible storm. The woman hadn't weighed a hundred pounds last time Melissa had seen her, and there wasn't much light on the island at night in the best of circumstances—without even the porch lamp, how far could she have gone? Had she taken a flashlight? A candle? There was a stash of candles inside the record player, where Mr. Culpepper's vinyls used to rest. They smelled like plumeria and ylang-ylang, English roses and French jasmine. When all of them were lit, the house smelled like a store in a mall.

She thought about glass jars from Yankee Candle Company and ran her fingers over the rusted rail. It was slick and gritty, a gross combination that made her want to wash her hands.

"Hello? Is *anybody* here?" she tried again. It felt like

trespassing, even though she'd spent every day of so many summers on this very same property. Scrambling over the thick grassy dunes with Simon first, and later Leo. Climbing trees and rocks, building forts and poking at tide pools with sticks. Using homemade slingshots to fire at cans, lined up one-two-three on the big driftwood tree at the end of the path.

Once she'd blown out Mrs. Culpepper's taillight with a piece of beach glass she'd found in a tide pool. Everyone had freaked out except for the woman herself, who'd only rolled her eyes and told Melissa to aim away from the house next time.

It wasn't the *worst* way to spend summers growing up, even if it'd often felt boring.

Mostly, the house and its acreage still looked the same. The thinner trees between the house and the beach were thicker now, and the more established trees out back were taller. The house's roof needed a good cleaning; moss and pine needles had collected in the eaves and coated the shingles. The walkway was covered in mildew and needed power washing, but Simon probably wouldn't bother until spring. There was no point. The grime would only come back in a week.

The low sprawling rancher with its open-gable design and hipped wings could have looked boxy and flat against the tall wild flora of the rural island—but the architect's keen eye for exterior details and a lot of expensive landscaping almost let it blend in. Most of the original landscaping was either mature and impressive or long gone. Two or three times a year, Mrs. Culpepper paid the grandchildren of various assorted friends to attend to what remained.

"I wanted it to feel like part of the beach itself," Mrs.

Culpepper had told her once. "Light and smooth and flat, like a piece of driftwood after a calm tide has receded. I told him, it should feel close to the ground, like it's part of the landscape."

Simon had bluntly called it a "bunker." But it was familiar and comforting to Melissa all the same, or it would have been if Simon were present and his grandmother wasn't dead.

One more time, so no one could say she hadn't tried. "Hello?" she shouted. The word bounced between the trees and echoed off the house's stacked brick siding.

"Hello, Melissa."

She spun around so fast that she forgot to let go of the porch stair rail and almost wiped out. She caught herself at the last second, stood up straight, and wiped her hands on her jeans. "Jesus Christ, Leo. Scare me half to death, why don't you?"

"I didn't mean to sneak up on you." Leonard Torres stood at the bend in the walkway, with the wind blowing up behind him off the water. It ruffled the hem of his dark raincoat and hit him with a spritz of ocean spray. He pulled down his glasses and wiped them on his shirttail, then restored them to their usual position. That's when Melissa noticed that his hands were shaking. "I, um...I got your message about Mrs. Culpepper. Sorry I didn't call back. I was in the middle of a...thing."

She thought he might come in for a hug, but he didn't. He stayed where he was, quivering and cold, an expression on his face that she couldn't quite read. She asked, "Where were you?"

"I was working. In Bremerton." He looked back toward the ocean, to a spot she couldn't see. "I got here as quick as I could, but I haven't been here very long."

"Leo?"

"Yeah?"

"Are you okay?"

He didn't answer that question. She wasn't sure he was able to. He looked shell-shocked and confused, like he was staggering away from a plane crash and wasn't yet sure if he'd broken any bones. Once again, he checked over his shoulder. "Did you just get here?"

"Yeah, a minute ago."

"Then you haven't looked around yet?"

"No," she admitted. "Simon's car is in the garage, though, so he's around here someplace. Leo, what's going on? You're being super weird."

"The cops didn't tell you about it? I thought maybe you were holding out on me, but I guess not. Did you hear from Simon yet?"

"No, sorry. Tell me *what*?"

Motioning for her to follow him, he turned away and walked toward the beach. "You should...you should take a look at this."

"Okay, okay. I'm coming." She pulled a pair of sunglasses out of her jacket pocket. It wasn't that bright, but the mist was driving her crazy, collecting on her eyelashes and spilling down her cheeks when she blinked. She fell into Leo's wake and caught up to him with a quick sprint. "Hey, happy birthday soon, right? It's—" She tripped over a raised crack in the walkway and collected herself again. "It's just before Thanksgiving, I remember that much."

"Next week," he said absently.

"That'll make you...what? Is this your big four-oh?"

"That was two years ago."

"Oh shit, I'm sorry. I forgot. But you could…if you could just talk to me, please? Tell me what's going on. Did *you* hear from Simon?"

He was only halfway listening, and he only halfway answered. "I haven't seen or talked to anybody." When he got to the end of the concrete path, he stopped and faced her. "And you'll act weird too, when you see it."

"When I see *what*?"

He stepped aside, clearing her view. The path behind him dead-ended onto the beach, cutting a thoroughfare through a long thick dune that was covered in seagrass, shells, and half eaten crabs discarded by seagulls. You could see all the way out to the water from that spot, even at low tide.

Or you usually could.

Today, something blocked the view.

"What am I looking at?" It was an honest question. All she could see was a large dark shape blocking the foamed white waves and the flat gray sky. "Is that…a shipwreck? Did a boat wash up on shore?"

"No," he said tightly. "It's not a shipwreck."

Melissa gave it a wide suspicious berth, approaching from the side. The giant salt-crusted object was festooned with seaweed and battered by ocean debris; it was covered with cracks and broken glass, and it had a teetering lean that said at least two of its corners were buried in the sand. It towered over the old driftwood log where the kids used to sit, and it ground up against the trail of boulders that lay in a straight line, pointing toward the Culpepper property.

The tide had not quite finished retreating, and the last of its rolling waves slapped up against the side. They splashed against the ruined remains of a porch, still clinging to a front door that hung open and dangled on a single hinge, and against the fallen bricks of a shattered chimney.

"Holy shit," she breathed. "It's a *house*wreck. I didn't even know that was a *thing*."

7

1986

MELISSA

Simon Culpepper and Melissa Toft tiptoed downstairs. "Are you sure they're still down here?" she asked, following in his wake.

"Nope, but we might as well check. If we can't find them, I guess we'll just...have to play something other than Yahtzee."

"I'm tired of Monopoly, and Life takes too long to play."

"We've lost most of the little pink and blue people-pegs from the Life box, anyway," he agreed. They'd lost most of the dice for Yahtzee too, but his grandmother said there might be a stash someplace in the basement.

The kids were only a month into summer, and they were already desperate.

The stairs were creaky, faded wood, and the handrail existed mostly for show; even the two children, neither of them quite twelve years old, would have relied on it by choice. But there wasn't much in the way of light, down below the house—where the concrete floor and exposed brick walls bounced every small noise from corner to corner—so they clutched the rail regardless. It strained against the bolts that held it against the wall. Dust trickled down where the screws were loose and scraping against the bricks.

Simon said, “There should be a bucket or something. Grandmother said she never threw them away after he died, but she tossed them into a bucket.”

“Did you ever meet your grandfather?” she asked.

“Yeah, but I don’t remember him very much. He died when I was a little kid.” He hopped down off the bottom stair, and his feet slapped loudly onto the rock-hard floor.

Melissa dropped down beside him, leaving one hand on the rail for a few extra seconds before letting go. “Well, if he collected games, I bet he was pretty cool.”

“He was an inventor.” Simon wandered over to the nearest set of shelves and started poking around. “He made up safety equipment for, like, elevators and escalators.”

“I saw the pictures in his office. The drawings with tiny numbers on them.”

“They’re *schematics*,” he informed her.

The basement was an unpleasant place with too many shadows and a weird smell. It made Melissa think of an old swimming pool with just a little bit of dirty water lingering at the bottom, though she couldn’t explain why. It might have been the humidity or the faint whiff of mud. “Schematics. Whatever.”

“They’re different from drawings.”

“No, I get it. They’re schematics.” She did not get it, but if it was important to him, she’d let him have it. “I don’t see any buckets, though.”

“Maybe they’re in a box. Or a bowl.”

"Something that starts with a *B* anyway," she muttered. She ran her hands over holiday decorations, boxes of moldering romance paperbacks, gardening tools, and a toaster that was probably older than her parents. She peeked inside boxes full of spare light bulbs, batteries, and small bits of hardware like screws and nails.

Behind them, though, on the wall, through the gaps where there weren't any boxes or books or Christmas wreaths, she could see something strange. Or part of something strange. She took a step back. "What's that?" she asked out loud.

"Found them! Look, it's...it's about a dozen. They're all different sizes and stuff," he concluded uncertainly. "But I guess that's okay. They must be from a bunch of different games, but they all have the same numbers on them... Hey. Hey, are you listening?"

"What's behind these shelves?" she asked.

"Nothing? The wall, I guess."

"It looks like something's painted on it, back there." She pushed a box over to get a better look, but all she could see was a curved streak of black paint, part of a larger image.

"So what? It's an old house," he said with a wave of his hand. "There's all kinds of weird stuff down here."

From the top of the stairs, Mrs. Culpepper called down. "Did you find the dice? Or the cards?"

Simon answered her at the top of his lungs, even though it wasn't strictly necessary. "Yes, Grandmother! I found them."

She descended the top few stairs until she could crouch over and see the kids below. "Then what are you still doing down here? It's not the safest place to play."

Simon held up the bucket in triumph, or to demonstrate his pure intentions. "We were just looking around for more game stuff."

"Hey, Mrs. Culpepper?"

"Yes, Melissa?" She came down the rest of the stairs, her low heels clicking on the planks and then settling on the concrete floor.

"Mrs. Culpepper, what's that on the wall over there? Behind the shelves?"

Mrs. Culpepper smiled without showing any teeth, and the corner of her eye tightened into something like a wink. "Paint, I suppose. We used to store paint up there." She indicated the top shelf. "But during the last earthquake, the cans fell and leaked. See?" Now she pointed at some dark splashes on the floor, alongside some putty-colored ones, and a few dribbles of yellow.

"Oooh," Melissa said. It made sense. Spilled paint. No mystery.

But.

She looked back at the wall anyway, and at the marks that showed between the boxes and bins.

"Melissa, dear." Mrs. Culpepper's voice was smooth and strong. "I'm sure the dice and Uno cards are much more exciting than some old paint. Let's go upstairs and set up a new game for you two to play while I watch my stories."

Why couldn't she tear her eyes away from it?

It was nothing more than a dark streak, as wide as her foot was long. But something about it snagged her attention and wouldn't let go. Some faint sound pinged at the far edge of her hearing, and for no good reason at all, she thought the two things must be related.

A hand on her shoulder. She jumped.

It was only Mrs. Culpepper. Her face was gently amused. "My girl, you must be careful. Some people in this world...they catch a glimpse of something they don't understand, and they let it eat them alive. Don't be one of those people."

Melissa's eyes slipped back to the shelves. "It looks like... but it looks like something's painted on the wall back there."

Gently but firmly now, Mrs. Culpepper took the child's face in her hand and pulled it toward her own. "It's only what I told you. Don't do anything silly, please, and pull things off the shelves or move things around. The basement is set up in a very particular fashion these days—to keep things securely in place, should there be another earthquake."

She released her and stepped back, still keeping her eyes locked on Melissa's. Melissa's were amber brown. Mrs. Culpepper's were a vivid ocean blue.

"I'm sorry. I won't."

The woman smiled more warmly now. "There's nothing to apologize for. You haven't done anything except notice something, and there's nothing wrong with noticing things. Not yet, at least." She returned to the stairs and put her hand on the rail, then paused. "It's a funny thing, that's all. I've seen it myself a time or two: a single idea gets into a single head, and what once was an innocent inquiry goes sideways. It consumes that person from the inside out, and then it destroys everything he loves."

The children stared at her, wide-eyed and confused.

Melissa understood that Mrs. Culpepper wasn't talking about her anymore, but she did not understand why. "Like...a fire?" she tried.

Mrs. Culpepper gave this some consideration, then discarded it. "No, now that I think about it...it's more like a flood, or a giant wave. A *tsunami*, that's what they call them—when they're big enough to wipe a whole island off the map." Then she shrugged off the strange little moment and opened her arm, sweeping it up the stairs. "Come along, now. Take the dice and go play. If there's one place on earth you don't want to be when the water comes...it's down here in the basement."

8

WEDNESDAY

MELISSA

The housewreck was two stories tall and once it had a sloped roof, perhaps. It was hard to tell, from Melissa and Leo's angle on the sand. Had it fallen inward? Had it been peaked or sloped, or flat and gabled like Mrs. Culpepper's place?

Leo nudged Melissa with his elbow. "Have you ever seen anything like it?"

"I'm not even sure what I'm looking at—I mean, it looks like a house that just...washed up on the beach. I'm not crazy, right? That's what this is? *That's* what we're looking at?"

"If you go around to the other side, you can see the trail in the sand where it just..." He made a long swooping gesture. "Dragged itself up onto shore. Look, come over here. It left a skid mark behind."

She tagged along behind him, too dumbfounded to protest. Sure enough, even with the last of the waves retreating, she could see a deep trench in the sand as wide as the house itself—leading all the way back to the water. There was no question: the house had washed onto shore.

"Like a plaster-covered whale," she murmured aloud.

"What? Oh. Yeah. I don't think that's plaster? Looks like stucco to me."

She shrugged. "It isn't brick, and it isn't vinyl siding. Beyond that, I have no clue. Where do you think it was built in the first place? It must've washed out to sea in some other storm, maybe a long time ago."

"Or it could've been an earthquake," he proposed. "Sand does weird things in earthquakes. It swallows whole buildings, whole neighborhoods."

That sounded familiar. "Fair point. Do you think it came from Marrowstone, or do you think it just showed up here?"

"I can't imagine anything coming all the way across the Sound from Whidbey Island, and we're facing the wrong direction for Port Townsend or the ferry docks. That's where most of the houses are. If you forced me to guess, I'd say that if it's *not* from Marrowstone…it came from somewhere close by."

She consulted her mental map of the island. Marrowstone wasn't a big place; it was barely more than a sandbar—long and narrow, with only six square miles of earth in total, and most of that was coastline. You could explore the whole thing in a day or two on foot, if you had to. "I don't know, man. Ocean currents can be pretty powerful. It could've come here from anywhere."

"Maybe," he granted. He kicked at the bottom of an old glass soda bottle that was sticking out of the sand. "But I bet it didn't."

"*This* must've been what Mrs. Culpepper came outside to see." Melissa tore her attention away from the ruins and returned it to Leo. "She must've heard it. I bet it woke her up."

"I would *totally* run outside in the middle of the night to take a look at this."

"You know what? I believe that." She slipped him a grin.

He was already walking away, up to the wreckage of the porch. The tide was headed back out. In another few minutes, the entrance would be dry, but Leo didn't look like he wanted to wait. He tested the edge of the sand with his shoe, let it sink a little, and made the jump onto a concrete landing that had broken into three large jagged chunks.

"Jesus, Leo. What are you doing?"

He stopped and looked back. There it was, the little-kid smile she remembered. "Don't you want to see inside?"

"Yes? But also…no?"

He grabbed one of the squared porch columns and held fast, securing his footing. The columns were decorated with a few lumpy stones that looked original. The rest had fallen off, leaving craters in the masonry. "It's held together this long. What are the odds that it falls apart now, with us inside? It's been in the water for…years? Decades? This isn't a new build."

Melissa didn't know much about architecture, but something about the angles and the stonework and the oversized windows made her say, "Maybe it's a mid-century modern? Not like Mrs. Culpepper's house, obviously. But it might've been built around the same time."

Leo let go of the column and carefully walked across the broken concrete, peering at details. "Yeah, it's that kind of ugly. It must have killer bones, though. Can't believe it's still in one—" A chunk of stone fell off the column and splatted onto the wet sand. "In *mostly* one piece. Come on, before it gets too much later and darker. Let's check it out while we can still see what we're doing."

"Fine. Give me a second." Her boots were supposed to be waterproof, but she felt a squish in her socks when she stepped across the soggy threshold and caught her heel in the water. She sighed and shook off the excess sand.

Leo extended a hand. "Watch out, it's crooked."

She let him help pull her onto the craggy remains of the porch. He was still a heavy guy, but he'd been a little taller than her for years—and his grip, the lift from his arm...he was stronger than she'd expected.

Up on the porch, there wasn't a right angle in sight. Even where the walls hadn't warped or split or collapsed, the house had been tumbled smooth like a river rock—bleached and rounded at the edges. The walls were so opaque and so pale, they could have been made of frosted glass. It had to be an illusion, the way they glowed as if the light passed through them, but in the afternoon haze, they were luminous.

They were the color of the sand beneath them and the driftwood that scattered around them.

Leo walked up to the front door like he meant to knock and ask if anyone was home, but his footing was unsteady and he fell against it instead. He caught himself and pushed the door. Its sole remaining hinge was rusted out, as frail as a crust of bread. It cracked at his touch. The big wood slab collapsed inward.

He smiled at Melissa and waved her forward. "Now or never."

"Now or never," she repeated. "Okay, I'm right behind you."

"It's my job to clear the way?"

"Like a goddamn gentleman, yes, it is," she said. "You can do it. I believe in you."

"Now you're just being silly." He stretched out his right leg, held onto the doorframe, and stepped inside—over the fallen door and then beyond it.

Melissa followed him closely. "Hello?" she called to the house at large, but she called it softly. She didn't shout it, not like she'd shouted at the Culpepper place. This was different. This house was the opposite of that one, in a way she couldn't explain. If anyone was inside, she wasn't sure she wanted to hear them reply.

"Who are you talking to? Those guys?" He nudged a couple of bickering crabs out of the way with the side of his shoe. It was not an exploring shoe. It was the kind of shoe a man wears to an office. "There's nobody here but us chickens."

"What if Simon's in here?" she asked as suddenly as it'd occurred to her.

Leo stopped. He looked back and caught her eyes. "I can't imagine him coming inside here, while his grandmother was lying dead on the beach. Can you?"

"No," she confessed. "No, you're right."

Then he said out loud exactly what she'd been thinking. "We can keep a lookout, though. Just in case. I wonder where the hell he is."

Every corner of the place dripped, and every tiny noise echoed in the cavernous interior. Every click and scuttle of every small claw, every wheezed breath that fogged and sparkled in the dim light bounced from corner to corner of that big hollow space. "This place doesn't *feel* empty, Leo."

"Oh, come on. If it were a shipwreck, you wouldn't be worried about running into random sailors just…hanging around inside, would you?"

"No," she said. "But it's *not* a shipwreck. I wonder how many people even know it's here, besides the cops." Her feet were now soaked, waterproof shoes be damned. The water was bitterly cold. She could feel her toes going white. "Well, Simon probably knows about it. Wherever he is."

"Maybe he didn't even see it. It was dark. It was storming."

She shook her head. "No. He was here, at the beach. He called me, but he didn't leave a message—just silence and static. But a few minutes later, he emailed from the phone. I think he started to call me, and *that's* when he saw the housewreck. I think he blanked. I think he just didn't know what to say." She paused. "Wait, you're not going upstairs, are you? Those steps won't hold. They're not even attached to the wall anymore."

"What? No, I'm not an idiot." He gave the staircase a little shove. It swayed and creaked. He looked briefly disappointed but shook it off with a change of subject. "What exactly did Simon say in his email?"

She stepped over some object that was so crusted with barnacles, she couldn't say what it'd ever been in the first place. "He said his grandmother was dead, and he thought something on the beach scared her to death—and now I guess we know *what*. When we're someplace dry, I'll pull it up on my phone and show it to you. Jesus, this place is huge," she marveled.

"There's a nonzero chance that *I* would die of shock, if I saw this place in the middle of the night." He glanced out the nearest window. Its glass was so long gone that not even tiny shards remained stuck in the wood casing. "Wherever it came from, I don't think the whole thing made the trip, so scratch what I said about it being in mostly one piece. Over here, out the window. You see this?"

Watching every step, choosing every landing spot for her soggy feet, she crossed the entryway to join him and share the view. "Huh. There's a door over there. A door to no place."

"See the outlines around it? Where some walls and a ceiling used to be?" He leaned out the window and craned his neck. "And I see a couple of stairs, still hanging on. Possibly a basement door. Daylight basement, I bet."

She followed his stare and saw what he was talking about, but it was all lines, shapes, and shadows to her. "Being a Realtor must teach you a lot about houses." She pointedly eyed his shoes. "Speaking of which, did you come out here from a showing? You seem awfully dressed up for climbing around in here."

"Yes, I told you. I was working."

"You dress up for work?"

"I dress like an adult. I need to be treated as an expert and authority. Appearances matter."

"Hey..." She was wearing jeans with a couple of holes in them, thrift-store boots, and a T-shirt with a cartoon cat that read "Creature of the Night." Leo couldn't even see the shirt because she had her raincoat over it, so she knew it wasn't personal, but she couldn't help reacting. "Some of us work from home a lot. Most of the time, I only have to look like an adult from the waist up."

"A lot of Zoom calls?"

"*So many* Zoom calls," she said. "With a little mascara, some tasteful lipstick, and a sweater set, I usually don't even need a bra."

"Too much information." The grin was back.

"Man, you've seen me in my underwear."

"Not since you were old enough to need a bra. And it's not like I was paying attention." He abandoned the staircase altogether and pulled his phone out of his pocket. It was inside a plastic bag. With a few seconds of fiddling, he had the flashlight app up and running—if watery-looking like everything else. The bag warped the vivid white, but it brightened the scene considerably.

"Good call. I need one of those. That's just a zipper baggie, right?"

"Correct. Never play an ace, when a two will do." Then he gave her a vaguely appalled look. "Wait, you didn't bring a naked phone in here, did you?"

"Hell no. I left everything in the car."

"Okay, good." He hiked over a trail of crunchy seaweed tangles and slippery rocks, deeper into the house. He held his phone out in front, leading the way. "Let's go see what's back there. Look, it's drier."

"Yeah, the tide's going out." She fell back into line behind him, and together they walked at a precarious lean, trying to stay upright and level across the sloped and crumpled floors.

"That, and the way the place is lodged in the sand at an angle. It feels like we're walking uphill."

He wasn't wrong. She strained and struggled to stick close, falling to one knee. A broad damp spot spread across her jeans, joining the soaked bits around their hem. "Ugh."

"You okay?" he asked without looking.

"I'm wet and gross, but unharmed."

Leo had pulled ahead. She scrambled to catch up.

He aimed his phone light to the left. "Bathroom," he said. "The remaining tiles are green and black. If we find any with pink tiles, we'll know this place was built after 1953."

"Mamie pink? Like the one in—" She tripped and collected herself. "You know."

He nodded. "Mrs. Culpepper's en suite. But she did that in the sixties, years after the house was built. I don't know what it looked like originally."

"Me either. It's strange, right? I knew that woman most of my life, and I barely knew her at all."

His head bobbed. "I know exactly what you mean. Oh look, this must have been the dining room? Office?" He shined his light into another room, then aimed it at the ceiling. "Eh…the ceiling medallion suggests a dining room. I don't see any fixtures, though. They must be long gone."

"Then the kitchen is around here somewhere."

With a twist of his wrist, he flashed the light toward her. "So you *do* know something about houses."

She held up a finger. "I *have* been inside a few."

He flipped the phone around again. "Very good, you are correct. Over here, there's…well, you can see it used to be a kitchen."

"Oh my." Her nose flared at the smell. The air was full of rust and salt and dead things from the ocean. "This place has been underwater for a while."

With caution, he proceeded inside—dodging a series of

gelatinous globs that might have been jellyfish. They occupied the floor like land mines. "No kidding. I wonder how long it takes for barnacles, mollusks, and shipworms to do so much damage."

"Shipworms?"

He gingerly picked at the edge of a countertop, and then pulled at a cabinet door. It didn't move. "These were old laminate countertops with plywood underneath—and the cabinets were maple, probably. See this damage? Where it looks like a wizard waved a wand and turned the doors into sponges? That's what shipworms do."

Along the wall where a window used to be, a large glassless square faced the lighthouse to the north. The sink below it was still recognizable.

Overhead, something large and unseen let out a loud crack.

Melissa hugged herself anxiously. "We should get out of here. That ceiling could come down any second."

He was staring up, running his light along any splits or breaks he saw up there. "Could've been a floor joist giving up the ghost."

She made for the hallway again. "I'm getting out of here. It'll be dark soon anyway." So far north, and so overcast, the sky was grim by 3:30. She didn't have a phone to check the time and she never wore a watch, but it must be coming up on three o'clock.

"Don't be such a chicken," he protested, but it was a weak protest. He had one foot out the door himself; she could see it in his eyes.

"Better a live chicken than a dead...whatever we are, right now. Sitting ducks? I feel like a sitting duck."

He sighed and relented. "All right, I'm coming." But as soon as he was back in the hall, he was shining the phone around again. "Ooh, look at *that*."

"No." She kept walking.

"Just real quick, come on. It's an office. I think? It looks like an office. Melissa, there's still stuff hanging on the walls."

Just curious enough to stop, she kept herself upright with one hand against the wall. "Like what?"

"Like…come see."

The door was only ten feet away. She listened for any ominous cracks. Nothing. She gave up and joined him. "Huh. Framed stuff, but it's all ruined. Can't tell if they were posters or photos or what."

"They could've been valuable paintings, for all we know. But those smaller ones, they're behind glass. Paintings usually aren't." With one finger, he poked at the nearest one. It swung back and forth on the nail that still somehow held it up. "They're about the size of diplomas, aren't they?"

"That's a big desk too. Under all those barnacles." She tapped one and winced. "Shit, those things are sharp."

"Yeah, don't touch them." Thoughtfully, he made a circuit of the room.

Overhead, another loud crack—maybe louder this time. Maybe closer.

"Nope. Nope, nope, nope," she chanted as she turned around and stomped back down the hall. Every step squished drearily, and each footfall left a brown streak on what might've once been a carpet runner.

"No, you're right. That was—"

Another crack. This one from inside a wall. She moved faster, still trying to watch her step. The floors were sloped, the walls were bowed. It was like walking through a very wet fun house, but it wasn't any fun.

She started to run. She tried to run. Her boots slipped and scooted.

Leo was right behind her.

His light only made everything else seem darker, all the other shadows turned black where before they'd been gray. The light flickered and flared from corner to corner as he fought to catch up and keep up. It flashed against the holes where no windows remained, and shined bright for a split second here, a fraction of a moment there. It lit up the empty squares on the hallway wall where pictures once had been, fragments of soggy shag carpet, a fixture that looked like an old thermostat, a face at the top of the stairs, a pair of eyes that blinked and were gone.

9

1987

MELISSA

Simon did not bother to be quiet, discreet, or sneaky when he pulled the big bag of fireworks out of his closet. It'd been buried beneath an assortment of G.I. Joe figures and long-forgotten LEGO sets in a big plastic tub, but Mrs. Culpepper had found them anyway when she was putting his cool-weather clothes into storage tubs.

Lucky for the kids, she didn't care. "Either that, or she doesn't know squat about fireworks, I don't know which," he admitted when he dropped it onto the floor.

"How did you get all this stuff?" Melissa marveled. She pulled out fireworks with wrappers in languages she couldn't read, some as small as nickels, some as large as soda cans. Roman candles, sparklers, and a bag full of cherry bombs rounded out the assortment.

Simon and Leo exchanged a conspiratorial grin. "Leo's uncle did some work out on the reservation, and one of the crew members gave him a whole trunk-load of these things." A change in school schedules meant Leo had beaten Melissa to the island that year. He'd had an extra three weeks of Simon-time without her.

"*You* brought these over?" she asked the younger boy.

He nodded happily. "I had to carry them through the woods, down the trail. They were heavy, but I didn't drop anything!"

"Well done, little dude!" She offered him a high five and he cheerfully slapped her hand. "Looks like we've got the Fourth of July sorted out. Where will we shoot these off? We don't want to burn down the house. Or any trees. Or anybody else's house."

"Grandmother said we could light them on the beach, out past the dune—and nowhere else. She said if we get hurt, it's nobody's fault but ours."

"Simon, I *love* your grandmother," she said, turning an unfamiliar item over in her hands. "What's this one?"

Leo said, "Those are black cats! That's what Uncle Marco said. They're not very flashy, though. They just sort of..." He made a gesture like an octopus rising out of the ocean.

"I don't get it?"

Simon said, "They're this weird, squishy black foam. You set them on fire and they expand like a science experiment—the one where the bubbles and goo come shooting out of the test tubes, you know that one?"

"Yeah," she nodded. She'd seen something like that in sixth-grade science. It was a light blue foam, though. She had a feeling she'd like "weird and black" better. "Let's take some outside now. Just the little ones, not the big ones. We should save those for the Fourth."

The boys agreed. Simon said, "Maybe some of these black cats and the sparklers. And the little pop things—we can throw those against the driftwood log, I bet. I don't think they'll pop on the sand. I think they have to hit something pretty hard."

"We should experiment!" Leo had just started second grade, and he was very excited to be in an advanced placement science class. He'd seen experiments too. Now he wanted to do some of his own.

"If we take notes about what burns and how, and what makes noise, and what just makes a mess," Simon thought out loud, "we could show your aunt and uncle, and even Grandmother when her TV stories are over."

Mrs. Culpepper was watching her stories and was not to be disturbed, at least not until four o'clock—when local channels switched over to other programming.

"As long as it's not too big or too loud," Melissa agreed. "Nothing bigger than a cherry bomb." The earlier summer's incident with Leo washing out to sea had made her cautious. Somewhat.

"I'm pretty sure Grandmother will hear a cherry bomb, but we can do some of this other stuff before lunch. We need matches, though."

Solemnly, Leo said, "I'm not allowed to play with those."

Simon nodded. "But you could go get some, from the kitchen. I trust you not to start any fires on the way down the hall."

Clearly delighted with this little mission—and Simon's faith in him—Leo trotted away.

When he was gone, Melissa asked, "Are you sure she doesn't care?"

"As long as nobody gets hurt and nothing unexpected blows up...she's pretty cool. Unless you interrupt her stories. This year, her favorite one is *Days of Our Lives*."

Together, they took inventory of the brown bag's contents, sorting things into piles: sparklers and other low-impact items like black cats and cones, middling crackers like the Roman candles and Catherine wheels and bottle rockets, and then the big monsters like cakes and mortars and fountains.

After a few minutes passed, Melissa looked up and listened for the sound of Leo's flip-flops coming back down the hall with the big box of kitchen matches. She heard nothing except the faint, tinny television in the living room. Someone named Marlena was in a coma.

She asked, "What's taking Leo so long? He knows where the matches are, right?"

"Yeah, Grandmother lets him help light the fireplace sometimes. He knows they're in the drawer by the stove."

She stood up and stretched. She'd been sitting there too long, hunched over the hoard. "I'll go check on him."

Melissa followed Leo's path out of the bedroom, into the hall, past the living room, into the kitchen...

...no.

Not that far.

Leo was stopped in the living room, the box of matches dangling from one small plump hand. He was several feet behind the couch, where Mrs. Culpepper stared straight ahead at the television, not knowing the boy was present. The TV was turned up too loud. Her hearing was starting to go, that's what Simon said—but she always told him she wasn't old enough for hearing aids.

"Leo?" she whispered very softly, a little sound that was masked by the television. She knew better than to holler. Mrs. Culpepper had few hard and fast rules, but No Talking During Story Time was absolute. Breaking that rule could get Melissa sent home for the rest of the week. She approached and touched him on the shoulder. "Leo? You okay?"

He was staring fixedly at a corner to the right of the television, under the big picture window that mostly showed trees and sometimes, in the dead of winter, a bit of water when enough of the leaves were dead.

"Leo, buddy? What are you looking at?" She kept her voice as low and soft as she could.

He responded in kind, never taking his eyes off the corner. "You don't see them?"

"See who?"

"You don't hear them?"

"*Who?*"

"They *cry*," he said. "Those boys, they hide in the corners and cry."

"Leo, there aren't any other boys in the house. Just you and Simon. Come on, let's go outside and play with fireworks." She gently pulled on his arm.

"I couldn't see them before. Not until what happened in the water." He looked up at Melissa and said in an almost ordinary voice, "Now I hear them all the time. Sometimes, I see them too."

Mrs. Culpepper's head snapped around. "Excuse me?" she said too loud, with her eyes narrowed. "This will be your only warning, Melissa and Leo." She was stern and firm, until she got a good look at Leo, and saw where he was staring and what he was holding. "Leo? Young man, is something wrong? Where are you going with those matches?"

He dropped them, like he'd forgotten he'd been holding them. He bent down and picked them up again. "I'm sorry. They're for fireworks on the beach; Simon said it was okay. But Mrs. Culpepper, you can hear them too, can't you?"

Now she turned and slung one arm over the back of the couch. "Hear who, Leo? What are you looking at?"

The corner, again. "I..." He looked up, as if he was worried that he'd said or done something wrong—in addition to interrupting story time. "It's like they're a long way away, or maybe they're crying in their sleep. They don't understand me when I try to talk to them."

She rose from the couch and walked over to the TV, turning down the volume. "Them *who*?" she demanded. She approached Leo and crouched down to his level. "I need for you to tell me the truth, Leo."

He tore his eyes away from the cursed spot in the living room and tried to meet her gaze. He shifted and fidgeted like this was all very embarrassing, and he wished he'd never said anything. "I hear them better than I see them." He twisted his feet on the parquet floor.

"Go on," she urged.

Melissa didn't like the odd note of worry in the brief command. Leo obviously wasn't seeing anything, or hearing anything either. He was an imaginative kid, that's all. Why did Mrs. Culpepper take him so seriously?

Simon appeared in the hallway, lured by the sudden quiet from the television. "Is everything okay? What's going on?"

His grandmother waved a hand to shush him, and she concentrated on Leo. "Dear, I'm not angry with you. *No one* is angry with you. We only want to understand," she insisted, but Melissa could still hear some tension in the words.

Bashfully, Leo said, "It's two boys. They're usually..." He pointed limply at the corner. "Over there."

"And they're... Right now, you can hear and see them?" she pushed.

He looked away and shook his head. "I did, but now I don't."

She stood up straight and looked at the spot that had fixated Leo. She glowered at it. With her hands on her hips, she said, "I think you're right. They aren't there now."

He shook his head again. But he tugged on her hand, and she crouched down again. On tiptoes, he put his mouth a little too close to her ear and said, "I think they're dead."

Leo had not yet fully mastered a soft voice. Melissa heard his confession and rolled her eyes.

Mrs. Culpepper did not. Instead, she said the strangest thing. "Well. They *are*, you know. But that's all right. Everybody dies eventually, and sometimes, people linger. They're nothing to be afraid of. They can't and won't hurt you. Do you understand?"

"Yes, ma'am."

Melissa didn't know what to say, so just that once, she didn't say anything. She only watched Mrs. Culpepper's face, her smile tight and forced, her eyes darting to the corner where nothing at all whispered, or hid, or cried.

10

WEDNESDAY

MELISSA

Outside the beached house, Melissa and Leo stood together and shivered, tightening their raincoats around their shoulders and adjusting their hoods. The rain was beating down again in earnest, accompanied by a stinging mist blown off the ocean. Their feet were soaked and their teeth chattered. The house did not make any further noise.

Melissa said, "Shit, that was...yikes. It was very, very...yikes."

Leo pulled his glasses away from his face as if he'd like to wipe them, but there was nothing dry to do the job, so he put them back on. "I was really hoping Simon would've come home by now, but it doesn't look like it."

"Yeah, that's what I was hoping too. Let's get out of this rain," she told him. Side by side, they climbed back up the beach and toward the tree line. "We can make a plan and decide how we're going to find Simon—since I guess the cops couldn't, or didn't."

"Where are you staying?"

"Here, I guess. Like always."

"Yeah, that makes sense," he agreed.

When they reached the Culpepper house, Melissa stopped. "Hey, dumb question: Where's your car?"

At first he looked confused. "What? Oh yeah. I parked at my uncle's place and walked the rest of the way."

With a skeptical eyebrow lift, she looked him up and down. "Why the hell would you do that? In this weather?"

A year or two ago, she and Simon had been gently teasing him in a bar when Melissa'd said something about wearing suits like Gordon Gekko, and Leo got all huffy about it. Rationally, she understood. He probably had to work harder than everybody else to prove himself, and hey, clothes were an easy social hack if you knew how to wear them.

Melissa had never had a knack for it, and she wasn't sure where Leo had learned it.

Wait, yes, she was. Simon must have taught him.

Leo climbed the porch steps and tried the front door. It was unlocked, but out of curiosity or habit he lifted the doormat and retrieved the spare key. "The weather wasn't this bad when I first got here, but Uncle Marco had his drive paved last year and my Tesla's a little low to the ground. After all the rain, I knew the Culpepper road would be a shit-show."

"Maybe if you drove a crappier car..." She was only joking, but she stopped herself anyway. "Wait, you have a Tesla?"

"I do fairly well for myself these days." He opened the door and strolled inside.

She knew he'd landed a gig with a brokerage on the west side of the Sound, but she didn't know he'd achieved Fancy Electric

Car money, and she felt a sudden ungracious pang of irritation about it. "But real estate? Out here? In the middle of nowhere?"

He shrugged off the question. "A lot of boomers are moving to the middle of nowhere, and the houses out here aren't *that* much cheaper than the city. It's a good living, if you can handle people who don't have any idea what the hell they want—and yet, they expect you to provide it."

Melissa could relate. "Corporate clients do that to me all the time. I keep telling them, I'm not a mind reader; I can only give you what you ask for, not what you secretly desire but fail to articulate."

She shut the door to close them both inside. It was warmer in here, if not truly warm. Much like her apartment, but for different reasons. Whereas Melissa had no control over her crappy building's furnace, Mrs. Culpepper had always chosen to leave the heat down low, preferring wool sweaters to the furnace. The smell of it did not agree with her, or so she often claimed.

The thermostat was just inside the hall. Melissa walked up to it and kicked it up from sixty-four degrees to seventy-five. "What?" she asked Leo, when she caught him looking at her. "She isn't here to give a damn, and I'm freezing my ass off."

The furnace kicked on, a great gush of air sucking on the filters through the intake vents. A faint dripping noise seemed to come from far away, but it didn't. It came from the puddle by Leo's feet.

"Oops," he said, when he noticed. "I'd better..." Old habits. He took off his raincoat and reached for the hat rack, then changed his mind. "This thing is...it's soaked. Mrs. C would have a fit if I let it drip-dry here on the floor."

"It's parquet, Leo. What are you gonna do, ruin it?" The parquet in her own expensive, mediocre apartment was crumbling around the front door and rotting below the windows. Her loathing of that particular parquet now extended to all parquet in all its forms, everywhere.

"It's Simon's house now, and I don't want to ruin Simon's floors any more than I want to ruin Mrs. Culpepper's." He opened the front door again and tossed the raincoat so that it fell across the sheltered porch rail. Then he came back inside and shut the door again. He flapped his wrists and frowned at the wet cuffs that slapped against them. "Just because something isn't to your taste, that doesn't mean it's bad or worthless."

"Sounds like something a Realtor would say about an ugly floor." She began peeling off her own raincoat. Hers was wet too. She hung it on the hat rack and left it.

"You got me there." For a few seconds he stood still, like he was trying to figure out what should happen next.

Neither of them proceeded inside any farther. They stood stiffly apart, taking in the details.

Melissa rubbed at her arms as if to warm them. "This is weird, right? This is really weird."

"It's too quiet," Leo agreed. "Not a normal kind of quiet."

"It's because Simon isn't here. He's not in the housewreck either."

"Nope."

Still, they did not move. The grandfather clock in the hall ticked too loudly for a place that was too quiet.

Melissa had no idea what to do. Her entire plan had been: come out to Marrowstone to comfort Simon and maybe help him deal with his grandmother's end-of-life situation, plan a funeral, bake a casserole, whatever it was you were supposed to do when your friend had suffered a loss.

But Simon was nowhere to be found. He hadn't called her back, or Leo either. He would've said something about it by now.

She cleared her throat and asked, in case Leo had any better ideas, "What do we do now?"

He cleared his throat too. Something about his voice told her he was winging his reply, which wasn't very reassuring. "I guess we check the woods and see if Simon got lost or got hurt out there. That makes sense, right?"

She thought about it. "Yeah, I'd been thinking he must've run for the lighthouse, but that's stupid, right? He wouldn't do that, not when he had a cell phone."

"Maybe he ran for the road, thinking he'd flag down a car and get help faster that way. When my uncle had a seizure a couple of years ago, it took Jefferson County more than half an hour to get an ambulance out here. He was fine, but if it'd been a heart attack...he might not have made it."

"Good call, I bet you're right—the road's a better idea than the lighthouse. Then again, the email hit my inbox around two in the morning. There wouldn't be any cars that time of night, not unless he was *crazy* lucky. I don't know. He still might've headed for the lighthouse in search of more immediate assistance."

Leo shook his head. "No way. These days, there's nobody out there but geology nerds in windbreakers."

"Same as thirty years ago, but you never know. Let's go through the woods ourselves, between here and the lighthouse, and between here and the road." She glanced at her smartwatch.

"But we'd better do it quick. The weather's so bad, it'll be pitch dark before long."

"No kidding. Let's make a quick pass of the house, just for a sanity check—because if it turns out he's taking a nap on Grandma's bed, I'll feel pretty stupid. After that, I guess we get out there and find him."

11

WEDNESDAY

LEO

After looking around the house and before they left it to take their search farther afield, Leo and Melissa raided the garage—where an assortment of flashlights and other emergency items were stashed in a big metal cabinet. It wasn't long past midday, but the canopy in the woods was as thick as a thatched roof overhead, even in the summer sunlight, and for all they knew, this would take longer than they hoped.

Leo pressed the button on a big old Maglite with a smattering of rust around the battery compartment at the bottom. It came on dimly, then more brightly. He said, "We can check up to the lighthouse point and out to the main road in a couple of hours, right?"

"Right." Melissa had an orange "floating" lantern that was considerably lighter, despite the chunky size. Its beam was wider than the Maglite's, but not brighter.

"Because if we're going to find him…if he's lost out there, or hurt, or…" Leo didn't finish the thought. "That's where he's most likely to be." He followed her down the path and out to the driftwood tree beside the dune. "Anyway, we should split up if we want to cover the whole area before it's pitch-dark out here."

"Obviously." She checked her light again and left it off for the moment. She zipped up her jacket and tugged the hood down around her face. "Do you have your phone?"

He nodded, pulling it out of a pocket—still in a plastic bag. "Right here."

"Mine's in my pocket too; I found a baggie in the kitchen. When we get far enough apart that we can't see or hear each other, we should check in. I swear to God, if I come back from searching through a wet, dark forest, and you've disappeared too, I will absolutely lose my *shit*. I cannot deal with both of you vanishing right now, okay?"

"You and your abandonment issues," he mumbled. He checked the ringer, confirming that it was on and the volume was up. Before she could snipe at him in reply, he added, "I'm joking. Don't worry, I'll pick up. Now...do you want to take the turf along the beach or along the road?"

She shrugged. "You pick."

"Take the beachside turf, then. I'll take the area along the road. Let's touch base every twenty minutes or so."

With this sorted out, they went their different directions—Melissa along the grass-covered dune, and Leo back toward 116 (also known as Flagler Rd), the north/south stretch that ran the length of the island.

He trudged between the trees, calling out for Simon every couple of minutes and jerking his head around at every faint noise, in case it was a reply. At one point, he saw footprints and got cautiously excited, but a few yards later he found a police evidence bag, rumpled and discarded—or maybe only dropped. "Maybe the cops *did* take a look around," he mused. He couldn't decide if that thought was reassuring or depressing.

He pulled out his phone and looked up a number for the nearby sheriff's office. He dialed it. A woman picked up on the second ring.

"Jefferson County Sheriff's Office, Port Hadlock. How can I help you?"

"Hello, ma'am, my name is Leonard Torres, and I'm a friend of the Culpeppers on Marrowstone Island. Mrs. Culpepper died last night, and I know the sheriff's office handles the 911 calls, so is there any chance you know the whereabouts of Simon Culpepper, her grandson? My friend and I came out here to support him in this difficult time, but he seems to be..." He didn't want to say it out loud, because that made it true. He said it anyway. "Missing."

"I heard about that, yes. It was all the fellows could talk about when they got back to the station. I'm afraid they didn't find any sign of him. It's weird, don't you think?"

"Yes, ma'am, very weird," he agreed, because he had no choice. Then something else occurred to him. "I don't suppose you've had any other emergency calls from the island since then? Any injured John Does lying in the woods or found beside the road?"

"No, nothing like that. I've been here since eight a.m. and it's been as quiet as church."

"Hm." Leo couldn't decide if that was a good thing or a bad thing. All it meant for certain was that Simon wasn't unconscious in the hospital out past Port Townsend. Or the one on Whidbey Island? They had a hospital too, but it was farther away and harder to reach. "Well, thank you for the information, ma'am. My friend and I are out here taking another look around the island. Maybe we'll...stumble across him."

"I sure hope you do, Mr. Torres. Best of luck in your search. Now, Svenson isn't here at the moment—he's the one who went out there so early this morning—but he'll be in the office tomorrow. You're welcome to come down and talk to him yourself. You can compare notes, if you like."

"Thank you. I'll do that. Thanks," he said again, and he hung up.

After the click of the call ending, the woods were terribly quiet. Hadn't there been birds a minute before? Squirrels? Big bugs crawling around in the undergrowth? He didn't even hear any breeze through the leaves overhead. It was as if he'd suddenly stepped into a vacuum.

Then, a faint, soft sound from somewhere close by.

He turned around, seeking the source—listening hard to pinpoint the nature of this noise. It was quiet and rhythmic, with a slight whistle. After a few seconds, he realized it was the sound of someone breathing, but doing so with difficulty. It sounded like an allergy attack, or asthma, or a bad cold.

"Hello?" he called out. "Is somebody there?"

He didn't see anyone. But he could hear them—that raspy, hard breathing echoing through the trees. Unsettled, he started moving back toward the main road, just for the prospect of seeing other people, other cars, maybe. Anything other than those empty woods, with the gasps coming and going through the trees.

Two hours later, the sun was down and Leo had scoured all the turf on his end of the search. He dialed Melissa for a final twenty-minute check-in and told her he was heading back. "I called the sheriff's office and talked to the receptionist there. She said they still don't know where Simon is, but it doesn't look like he's been taken to the hospital as a John Doe."

"Is it terrible that I find this information disappointing?"

"No," he promised. He felt the same way.

She sighed heavily and said, "I'll see you back at the house."

12

1988

LEO

Leo was ten years old and in proud possession of his first proper weapon: a slingshot he'd carved himself (with a little help from his uncle). It was made of alderwood that had been sanded smooth, and it was a tiny bit too big for his hands—on the grounds that eventually he'd grow into it. The sling itself was a piece of leather cut from an old boot tongue, and a bit of stretchy medical tubing rounded out the rest. It was simple, it was pure, and Leo was already good enough to knock a coffee can off a log at ten paces. Most of the time.

Simon was impressed. He turned it over in his hands, admiring the skill and workmanship. "That's really clever, using plastic tubing for the elastic. Did you get it from your mom?"

"Yeah, she brought it from the hospital." His mother had been a nurse since before he was born.

Melissa asked, "Where did you learn how to make this?"

"I went to the library and found a book about things you can do and make by yourself. Uncle Marco let me borrow his pocketknife. He says maybe he'll get me one for my birthday, if I promise not to stab myself. I already promised, so...he'll probably do it."

Simon handed it back to Leo. "Well, I love it. You want to take it outside, maybe put some stuff up on the driftwood log and shoot it off?"

"Yeah!" he agreed happily. "I can show you how to use it. It's kind of complicated."

Melissa smirked. "I bet it is. I'll um...I'll see if I can find any soda cans or bottles or anything." She headed for the kitchen to poke around in the garbage.

Simon and Leo headed outside. They went down the stairs and the walkway, back to the edge of the dune with the driftwood tree, and then past it—to the beach, and to the small parking area just beyond Mrs. Culpepper's property. There was a big trash bin there, and tourists or campers sometimes used it—but sometimes they didn't and just dropped their garbage wherever they felt like it.

Before long, the boys had scared up three glass soda bottles, two boxes that once held snack crackers, a couple of unsmushed cans, and a pair of Capri Sun packets that still had enough juice in them to sit up on end. Leo also stashed a series of smooth rocks in his pockets, because he'd gotten a feel for which fat pebbles flew the fastest and truest.

When they got back to the oversized log, Melissa wasn't there yet—so they set up a little target practice, starting with the juice packets. The boys backed up to the spot where the walkway to the house ended, estimating that it was maybe twenty feet.

Leo was the expert, and it was his slingshot. He held it up, explained just where to hold it, and just how far back to pull the sling so the tubing would go tight—but not too tight—and then let a rock fly.

Simon paid very close attention and even asked questions.

Leo stood behind him, coaxing him through the process. "Okay so like that, yeah. Get your elbow a little bit higher. Hold the handle just a little bit lower. Pull back...a little bit more...a little bit more..."

Simon's shoulder and forearm strained and began to shake.

"Now!" the smaller kid commanded.

He let the rock fly far, fast, and true—almost. It winged the left juice packet, rocking it back and forth but not smacking it to the ground. He lowered the slingshot. "Not bad for a first try, if I do say so myself."

Leo smacked him on the back. "Not bad at all! You want to try again?"

"Why don't you show me how it's done?"

Delighted by the prospect, Leo picked a good pebble from his pocket and did all the things the book had said to do, and that Uncle Marco had helped him refine. Elbow level, shoulder tight, one eye closed. The projectile smacked into the top of the juice packet, sending it flipping back over. The straw was long gone, and what was left of the juice drooled down the log.

Simon high-fived him, and Leo felt like a king.

Finally, Melissa appeared, a plastic grocery bag in hand. "I have an idea!" she announced.

"Ah, but do you have more targets?" Simon asked.

Leo wondered the same thing, not least of all because

Melissa's ideas were pretty hit-and-miss from a quality standpoint. "Did you find any soda cans?"

She nodded. "Two that aren't crushed up yet and a bottle of ketchup that's almost empty. Mrs. Culpepper said I could have it."

"She's awake now?" Simon asked. Grandmother had been taking a nap. Her bedroom was in the back of the house, and she usually didn't hear much of what happened in the rest of the sprawling rancher.

"Oh yeah. She said she'd get started on lunch." Melissa set the bag down at her feet, then crouched down to rummage through it. "She asked if we were all okay with turkey sandwiches and chips, and I told her that'd be fine. If either one of you wants something else, go tell her now."

But everyone was good with turkey sandwiches.

Simon asked, "What else did you find in there?"

This prompted a wicked grin that almost worried Leo, but he decided to hear her out. Melissa told them, "I found a few of the cherry bombs we didn't use up last time."

Leo's eyes narrowed. "I don't know if I can hit something that small."

She laughed and shook her head. "I don't know if *anybody* could, but that's not why I brought them."

Simon sighed. "Melly, we can't fire cherry bombs at Coke bottles. Grandmother will kill us."

"Your grandmother already knows that I have them. She asked what was in the bag, and I told her," she said with a casual shrug.

"Did you tell her what you were doing with them?" he pushed.

"She didn't ask. Come on, it'll be fun."

Leo was warming up to the idea. He was a pretty good shot, and he knew it would take a few seconds for the cherry bombs to explode. "It should be fine," he offered cautiously. "They're a good size, and they don't blow up right away."

Simon looked at the bag and looked at the slingshot. He eyed his friends back and forth. "Okay, we'll do...how about one each? We can save the rest for chasing off seagulls next time we have a picnic."

Melissa groaned but agreed.

Leo agreed too—on one condition. "First, everybody has to try it with some rocks. Just to make sure we all know how to shoot, and we won't drop anything or hurt ourselves."

She said, "Sure, that's fair. Here, let me try. You two have already been out here, murdering... What is that, anyway? A Capri Sun?"

Simon said, "We found some by the tourist can. When they still have a little liquid inside, they stand up better."

"I get it. Here, can I try the slingshot, Leo?"

"Sure!" he handed it over, preparing to explain the intricacies of its usage.

She didn't give him a chance. She tugged on the tubing, tested the leather sling, and checked her grip. Then she reached down and grabbed any old rock on the ground—not even a good one, in Leo's opinion—and assumed the firing position.

He said, "Okay, so how you do it is, you—"

With one swift, confident shot, she knocked the remaining juice packet off the log. It landed in the grass on the dune behind it.

Simon let out a low whistle. "*Nice.*"

"Where did you learn how to do that?" Leo demanded. He did not believe for a moment that she'd only gotten lucky.

She shrugged at him. "I don't know. It seems pretty straightforward, and I have good aim. Let's put these cans up there, and the rest of the bottles. We'll all get a little practice in before we hit the cherry bombs."

Leo sighed but fell in line. Of *course* Melissa was automatically good at this. He should've guessed. He'd forgotten how she'd showed him how to fire spitballs through a straw, and how clean her aim had been with those tiny bits of wet tissue. Well, everybody had to be good at something. Right?

He reminded himself that she was older than him, and taller than him, and also a girl. His mom had told him for years that girls matured faster than boys and that Leo should look to them for leadership.

All things considered, he wasn't sure how accurate that was.

All things being equal, he'd rather follow Simon.

But he liked Melissa all right, and sometimes he found that the two of them had more in common than either of them did with Simon. Melissa came from a broke family, like his parents. She knew how good cheap white bread could be with peanut butter and jelly, and how good baloney was when you wrapped it around a piece of Velveeta. She knew how to make friendship bracelets with gum wrappers folded up as neat as origami. She knew how to make collect phone calls, and how to shoplift candy bars when she couldn't cash in enough glass bottles for snack cash.

Simon's grandfather—the late Mr. Culpepper—had been an inventor. He'd made a fortune patenting safety devices for escalators and elevators, or "Anything that went up and down," as his widow once explained it. The original diagrams for his most profitable pieces were framed in his old office, where no one ever went anymore. Simon's father had followed in his dad's footsteps, patenting a mechanical arm adapter for the big robots that built cars in Detroit, and in more recent years, Mexico and China.

Not that Leo knew what most of those words meant.

Mostly, Leo knew that the Culpeppers had money and that they didn't really need to work unless they wanted to. He knew that Simon didn't eat anything that came in bright plastic packaging, and Mrs. Culpepper never bought his clothes on sale. Simon did not like soft white bread. His favorite was a crusty kind that came from a bakery in Port Townsend. Leo thought it smelled weird, and a little like puke. When he'd said so, Simon only laughed and said that's why it was called *sourdough*.

Deep in his heart, Leo wanted to enjoy the crusty puke bread. He wanted to wear nice clothes made from soft fabrics that fit him perfectly and didn't come apart in the wash, only to be stitched back together again. He wanted to drive a Cadillac like the super-shiny one that was usually parked in the garage for its own protection.

Maybe someday.

Today, he'd settle for practicing with pebbles, then reaching for the cherry bombs because Simon said it was okay if they each did just one.

Practice went well. Simon's next shots were better, Leo's were already strong, and Melissa could knock a fly off a horse's butt while it was running, or so she claimed. Leo never saw her hit anything more challenging than those soda cans, but she could hit them one-two-three—even if she backed up another ten feet.

"Now go back even farther!" Simon gleefully urged her.

But she shook her head. "I can't. My arm isn't strong enough," she said, rubbing her shoulder for emphasis. "But we've practiced enough, right? Let's get the cherry bombs!"

"Me first," Simon insisted. "They're *my* fireworks."

She agreed that this was fair and tossed him one along with the kitchen matches. "How about, you aim, and I'll stand beside you and light it?"

"Let's try it!"

He drew back the sling until his hands quivered. Melissa lit the fuse, and he fired the cherry bomb at a glass bottle. He hit it. The bottle clattered off the back end of the driftwood tree, and a few seconds later, the cherry bomb exploded somewhere off in the dune—throwing a puff of sand and a clump of seagrass into the air.

All three kids cackled wildly. It wasn't exactly a success, but it wasn't exactly a failure either.

They each took turns, calibrating how much time the fuses would give them before they took off a finger, and by the time they got to the very last bomb in the bag (because Simon had forgotten about the "one each" rule), Melissa was almost able to explode a can on contact.

When everything was used up, and everyone was sure to have a sore arm the next day, the kids decided to do some quick wading before Mrs. Culpepper called them inside for lunch.

Leo begged off. "I have to go to the bathroom," he informed them.

Melissa laughed and said, "I hope everything comes out all right!" and then added, "We'll be inside in a few minutes."

Leo went back to the house and let himself in. He heard the television too loud in the living room, playing a commercial, which probably meant that Mrs. Culpepper was in the kitchen making those sandwiches. She didn't care for *All My Children* as much as some of the others; that's why lunchtime was at the same time each day. She'd keep one eye on the TV and one eye on the lunch-making...then abandon the television altogether when the commercials ran.

But she wasn't in the kitchen. She was in the bathroom, as Leo discovered when he found the door shut.

That was just fine; maybe he could forage for stray snacks while she was occupied. He checked the counters and helped himself to a couple of pieces of loose deli-sliced turkey, and while he was at it, a piece or two of cheese. An apple slice from the plate with a dollop of peanut butter.

While he waited and chewed, he emptied the rocks from his pocket, sticking them along the windowsill behind the sink. Sometimes Mrs. Culpepper liked pretty rocks, and some of his rocks were very pretty indeed. He would show them to her later.

He heard the toilet flush and jumped, then darted down the hall. He had to pee pretty bad.

"Leo!" she exclaimed as he dashed past her in the hall.

"Excuse me, Mrs. Culpepper!" he yipped as he threw himself inside and shut the door.

Through it, he heard her say, "Next time if you need to go so badly, use the one in my bedroom!"

"Yes, ma'am!" he replied as he unzipped his pants.

When he was finished, he flushed—and then spent a few extra minutes tidying up and washing his hands, carefully selecting which one of the decorative hand soaps in the big shell bowl he wanted to use. Today he chose a starfish about the size of a fifty-cent piece. It smelled like deodorant or maybe laundry detergent, and it foamed up nicely when he rubbed it between his palms. He let the water run in the sink until it was warm. Finally, he rinsed his hands and dried them on a hand towel that had a scratchy lacy border.

He left the bathroom and strolled into the hall, thinking about sandwiches, but he heard something odd—just below the high-decibel blast from the television. He stopped and listened hard, trying to place the sound; it was maybe music, maybe a few notes played on an instrument. No, not that. But it was a song, yes. He was sure of that much.

It came from the kitchen.

He crept down the hall, unsure why, exactly, he was being so sneaky, but sensing the importance of doing so. Around the corner the living room opened up to the kitchen, with a dining room on the other side. Mrs. Culpepper was at the kitchen sink and yes, she was the one singing, low and quiet.

No. Not singing. Humming.

As soft and deep as a foghorn far off in the distance.

He stood up on his tiptoes and looked over the counter peninsula to get a peek at what she was doing. The water wasn't running. She wasn't washing dishes. She wasn't even looking out through the window; she was looking at the rocks he'd put there.

She smiled at them while she hummed, almost fondly, almost like she was cooing over a basket of kittens. The rocks on the windowsill behind the sink rolled around, circling one another imprecisely on uneven edges. When they clattered together it sounded like pool balls colliding on a felt table.

Mrs. Culpepper did not look up when she said, “These are good rocks, Leo. Thank you for bringing them inside. I like them. They’re very obedient.” She turned now and stared right at him, where his head peeked up over the counter.

She winked at him, and the rocks fell still.

13

WEDNESDAY

LEO

An hour or two after dark, Melissa and Leo surrendered to the inevitable fact that Simon wasn't in the woods, and he wasn't on the beach. Guided by their trusty flashlights, they trudged back to the Culpepper house to regroup. There, Leo proposed, "Let's *really* search the house, going top to bottom. Maybe we'll find some hints about what happened or where he went."

She nodded. "You're right, shit. I didn't even think about that, but it's a good idea."

"Really?" he asked, a little surprised.

"Yeah. I'll uh…I'll start in the kitchen. I got Arby's at a drive-through on the way up here—since you didn't call me back—but now I'm starving. I'll check the snack stash for granola bars or something."

Leo rolled his eyes, but nodded. "Okay. You start here at the front, I'll start at the rear. Holler if you find anything interesting or useful. Simon didn't take his car, and he's only been gone…"

He did the math in his head. If Simon called 911 around two in the morning, and he wasn't around when the ambulance arrived, then he'd been missing for… "About fifteen hours."

Not very long, in the scheme of things. Still totally reasonable to expect that he might turn up any minute, wandering into the house, looking tired and sad.

It could happen.

So why did Leo feel, deep in his bones, that it wouldn't? Why did all his instincts scream that Simon was actually missing, properly disappeared? Into thin air?

Because facts were facts, that's why. Simon wouldn't leave his grandmother lying on the beach in a storm, even if she was dead. If nothing else, he would've gone looking for something to cover her with, to protect her body from the elements. A blanket? Maybe. It seemed like the most obvious answer.

He'd check Simon's room first.

Leo pushed the door inward and stood at the threshold. He'd been inside a million times before, to read comics under the covers, nibble snack food while playing Nintendo on the fat old TV Simon used to have, and generally be obnoxious little boys who plotted world domination with G.I. Joes.

Simon's room was different now. It was the room of an adult man with interests beyond video games and toys—though now he had a nice flat-screen TV mounted above his dresser, along with the most recent PlayStation model. Some things changed, some things never did.

His bed was unmade, but none of the covers appeared to be missing. The navy velour duvet was rumpled and kicked to the side, and the throw he always left at the foot in case he got cold was crumpled on the floor. Four pillows, two for show and two for head and neck support. Everything had been recently enough laundered that it didn't smell like Simon; it smelled like detergent. He'd always been a little fussy about that. He liked his linens crisp and his clothes smelling like a spring meadow or a mountain creek—and he never wore cologne. Thought it was too much.

The furniture was dated, but most of it had come around again in style. Mid-century modern was all the rage, and Leo suspected that the chest of drawers and the headboard had been scavenged from storage or the attic, because Mrs. Culpepper never threw away anything. These were well-kept antiques, not secondhand leftovers.

Leo checked the topmost nightstand drawer and found a phone charger, a couple of paperback thrillers, some lip balm, and a pair of wired earbuds that looked like they'd spent some time wadded up at the bottom of a pocket.

He slid the closet door aside and ran his fingers through the clothes that hung there. A handful of nice button-up shirts in pristine condition for all the virtual meetings Simon did for that nonprofit. What did they do again? Something about distributing medical necessities to underprivileged communities. Simon coordinated supply chains and made sure warehouses were stocked. It was good work and he was proud of it, even as he complained about the necessity of looking capital-*P* "Professional" in front of people, even if he was only on-screen.

Leo giggled, thinking about how Simon had bragged about wearing boxers and flip-flops under the desk for his last committee video call.

The giggle evaporated. Something was capital-O "Off." Everything looked normal, but if everything were normal, Simon would be there. He'd stand in the doorway and tease Leo about being a nosey voyeur; then he'd ask what all the fuss was about and explain that he'd gotten lost when he went to look for...help? And everything was fine? Except that Mrs. Culpepper was dead?

Leo was still staring into the closet, with its mostly tidy rows of shirts and a few sweaters, and a terrycloth bathrobe hanging on a hook. His mind was wandering, fishing around for a logical explanation for why Simon wasn't home and why they couldn't find him.

For all that Melissa was clinging to the semicredible prospect of Simon having fled the beach for help, Leo didn't buy it. He didn't think Melissa really believed it either, but they were each coping with the weirdness in their own way. Maybe he'd let her have this delusion, just for now. Maybe he needed it too.

He looked down at the closet floor. Dress shoes, casual shoes, rain boots. And a pair of bowling shoes, so that was new. "Bowling? Seriously? Where the hell did you find to go bowling around here?" Simon had never mentioned an interest, but those were pretty nice shoes. When Leo picked one up, he saw some wear on the bottom. They'd been used enough times to need a good cleaning. "Huh."

In the back corner, Leo spied a big box.

He smiled, already knowing what was inside,—and pulled it out. He sat down cross-legged on the floor and pried open the cardboard flaps. "Some of these look like leftovers..." he mused, running his hands through the contents. "Some of it's new, though. Already stocking up for New Year's and the Fourth, eh, Simon?"

The box was a little more than half full of fireworks in various sizes and assorted loudness. As always, the holidays were going to be *lit* out on Marrowstone.

Everyone came out for fireworks. January and July. Every year.

"Whatcha got there?" Melissa asked, poking her head around the corner. Then she saw the box. "Ooh, fireworks!"

"Yeah. I should put these up." He folded the flaps shut again. "Sorry, I got distracted. Did you know Simon had taken up bowling?"

"Bowling? No, you can't be serious. I mean, I say that, but... did you know he'd been taking yoga classes in Port Townsend?"

He looked at her blankly. "Weird."

"I guess? I don't know. Maybe he sensed that Mrs. Culpepper was on her way out, and he started diversifying his interests."

"She was nearly a hundred years old. It wouldn't exactly take a psychic to guess that she wouldn't be with us much longer," he countered.

"Yeah, but you know what I mean." She leaned against the closet doorframe and folded her arms. "Anyway, I thought you were being awfully quiet in here. Did you find anything useful? Any hints? Clues?"

He shook his head. "No, and I'm starting to think something's wrong. *Actually* wrong, and I don't just mean the bowling shoes."

She took a deep breath through her nose, then nodded. "Yeah, I've had a weird, bad feeling ever since I got his message this morning. Something is extremely fucked up out here. I'm starting to wonder if..."

"Don't say it."

"You say it, then. We can't ignore the obvious. He's *missing*, Leo. He's not responding to us, the police didn't see him when they showed up in the middle of the night, or super early this morning, whatever. He's gone."

Leo shook his head again, harder this time. "No. He's here on the island somewhere. He has to be."

"I didn't say he wasn't on the island." She chewed on her bottom lip while she leaned on the doorframe, thinking. "We need to find him before something really bad happens, and don't ask me what," she said quickly—before he could ask. "But everything about this situation stinks."

"I can't argue with you there." He knew the bad feeling she was talking about. He'd been trying to chase it away, tamp it down, and convince himself that Simon would reappear any second, but his heart said it wasn't true. "Let's not assume the worst, not yet. Let's try to stay positive. We only just got here."

"I'm pouring every spare ounce of energy into hoping for the best," said Melissa, "but this is just bizarre. Everything I've seen looks like they stepped out for a minute and will be back any second."

"Where have you searched?"

"I rummaged around in the kitchen a little, checked through the hall bath—speaking of, when did he start wearing perfume? Cologne, I mean? There's a half empty bottle in the medicine cabinet."

He winced. "Wow. No. He used to rail against the stuff. Said it made his nose itch."

"I remember, that's why I thought it was strange. Maybe he'd been dating more than he let on. Did he uh...mention anyone to you?"

"Nope."

"Wild." She shook her head like wonders would never cease. "After the hall bath, I checked Mrs. Culpepper's room which was...also pretty weird. It all looks normal, except the bed's messed up, like she got up and left it that way. I've never seen it without the fancy pillows with all the shams, lined up like soldiers along the headboard." Her voice was tight, like the sadness of knowing what had happened had hit her all at once by virtue of some scattered decorative bedding.

Leo felt the same grim, grinding sense of wrongness when he pushed the box back into the closet and climbed to his feet. How dare the house feel so ordinary? How could it sit there, so normal, waiting for its residents to return?

When nobody was coming back.

No.

Leo pushed the thought out of his head. Simon had been alive and well—if rattled by his grandmother's death—fifteen hours ago. He was somewhere. They just hadn't found him yet. Leo shut the closet door. "Well, let's check the rest of the place, in case we're missing something obvious. It feels rude, but I think it's important."

"It does feel rude, and it does feel important. Better to ask forgiveness than permission though, right? We still have...a few places to look. Let's finish up together."

The Culpepper house was large, but it wasn't a castle—and searching it didn't take long, even though Melissa and Leo were quite thorough. They checked the dank and smelly basement, the garage, the narrow attic with a low ceiling and nothing inside but cobwebs, all the bedrooms and bathrooms top to bottom, closet to bed underside, and even in the drawers of every chest and nightstand.

No clues presented themselves.

Except for Melissa and Leo, the Culpepper house seemed utterly empty.

14

WEDNESDAY

LEO

An hour later they were sitting on the couch in front of a bright gas log fire, each of them sulking with a glass of brandy—since neither of them wanted wine or vodka. Melissa's shoes were off and her feet were up on the couch's seat, where they'd never been before.

Leo got up and poured himself another slug. He lifted the glass and spun the cherry-amber contents gently in front of the firelight. It smelled faintly sweet and sharp. "Do you think this is good brandy?"

"I can't tell good brandy from bad—but I bet it's expensive. She had expensive taste."

"Simon does too." He dipped out into the hall.

"Well, they can afford to." Then Melissa said, "Just as well their tastes overlapped, though. This place is a heartbeat away from being a museum. Did you see his grandfather's office?"

"What about it? Simon left up the old diagrams, but the rest of the stuff in there belongs to him." A laptop, closed and password protected, as Leo had learned when he took a chance and popped it open. A coffee mug full of pens, a paper desk calendar with nothing of interest written on it: a dental appointment in Port Townsend, a few conference calls, a note about his grandmother's birthday next month. Nothing suspicious or telling.

"Sure, but even with him living here as an adult, and keeping his own spaces…he and his grandmother are both minimalist souls. Or they were. Or she was. I mean…"

"I know what you mean." Leo thought she must've been tipsy. She hadn't eaten much—an alleged meal from Arby's and some random snacks foraged from the kitchen upon their return from searching the woods. It was well after 7:00 by now. The sky was deeply dark, and the rain drummed pleasantly on the roof. "The house is full of color blocking and texture, without a lot of patterns or clutter. Jesus, now that you say so, it kind of looks like an Airbnb in here." Something else occurred to him. He frowned thoughtfully. "Am I just crazy, or did they never have many family photos? I've seen pictures of Simon's parents, but only because he keeps those in an album on the bookcase." He cocked his thumb toward the shelves in question.

"I saw a picture of Mrs. Culpepper's husband once. She told me to take ten dollars out of her wallet for lunch for me and you, one summer when Flagler was running that hot dog fundraiser, remember?" She didn't wait for him to reply. "She had a little picture in there, like, from Olan Mills, with the vague ombre background and staring off into space and everything. Shit, Leo. I can't believe she's gone. I honestly thought she'd live forever."

"She practically did," he told her, starting to feel tipsy himself. "For years, every time I heard from Simon, every email, every phone call…every time I saw his name on the screen, I wondered if this would be the call. If *this* time, she'd finally died."

"*Finally?*"

He shook his head. "Not like, 'Ding dong the witch is dead.' More like, 'Good God, how long can one person live?' And live independently?"

Melissa sulked. "Simon lived here. Every job he's had for years has been remote, so he could stay close—long after he probably should've signed her care over to someone else, some kind of professional live-in nurse, if not a home. But she wouldn't let him leave. *She* kept him here."

Leo wasn't having it. "No way. He chose to stay out here, out of convenience as much as anything else. The nonprofit took up a lot of his time; he was working fifty, sixty hours a week—especially during fundraising season, around the holidays—and he couldn't have kept that up if he was her full-time caregiver. I haven't seen any supportive devices like a special bed, or appliances, or trays full of medication either. I think she had a cane, and that's about it. That almost-centenarian was in *superb* health."

Melissa grudgingly nodded, looking both drunk and thoughtful. "Well, she fell and broke her hip a few years ago."

"Right, but before that, she walked two miles every day, rain or shine. Up and down the beach, out past that line of black boulders that points the way…to the ocean."

"I never noticed those rocks, until that time you almost drowned." She looked out the picture window that ran along that wall of the house, just above the fireplace. Winter was coming, and the trees between the house and the water hadn't dropped their leaves—but they'd thinned sufficiently to leave a partial view of the water. Those trees were younger and slimmer, there between the house and the ocean. The ones that otherwise surrounded the place were older and better established.

"Don't get me wrong, Simon worried about her constantly. Every time she'd leave for a walk he'd sit right there, in that chair"—Leo pointed at the overstuffed leather number to the left of the fireplace—"with a pair of binoculars. He made her carry one of those med-alert necklaces, and a cell phone too."

"She knew how to use a cell phone?"

"At least kind of?" He took another swig. He was two drinks ahead of Melissa. He was bigger than her, yes. Only a little taller, but easily twice her weight. And he was a man, at that. Some things, men weathered more easily than women.

"For emergencies, though," she started to argue. Then she seemed to decide that it wasn't worth the trouble. "She was strange and sometimes she wasn't always warm, but she was good in her way. She put up with us, didn't she? She looked out for us, and she didn't have to."

"That she did." He toasted again. They both drank.

The grandfather clock chimed, startling them both. No one spilled anything, not on that couch. Old habits. Eight gongs. Melissa said, "Holy shit, it's eight o'clock."

He looked at his glass and frowned. "We should clean up and settle in." Then he remembered. "Wait, you said you'd show me the email. I want to see it. I want to hear the voicemail too."

"Sure, hang on. I'll get it." She'd already brought her bag in from the car. It was on the floor, beside the spot where her feet belonged. "But the voicemail, I already told you. It's nothing."

"I want to hear it anyway."

Her phone had sunk to the bottom of her purse. She fished it out and unlocked it, then pulled up her inbox. When Simon's email was front and center, she tossed the phone to Leo.

He caught it with one hand, wiped his glasses out of habit, and held the screen up to his face to read. "That doesn't sound... right."

"How?"

"I don't know. But it doesn't sound right." Since the phone was unlocked, he tapped over to her voicemail, turned on the speaker, and turned up the volume. He heard air rushing past, the patter of rain, and perhaps the sound of someone breathing in the background.

"Like I said, it's nothing to get excited about."

But he held the phone like a talisman, staring down at Simon's name, playing and replaying the short clip in case it could tell him something it didn't tell her.

15

1993

LEO

Simon was eighteen years old and finally home from boarding school in Portland. He'd picked Leo up from the Alvarez house in the new car his grandmother had bought him—one of the freshly redesigned Volkswagen Beetles, black and shiny with rounded edges and black leather interior. "At first I thought it looked kind of…girly, you know what I mean?" he asked over burgers and fries at the Port Hadlock diner, which everyone went to by default. "But Grandmother wouldn't stop talking about how it was so safe, and so reliable. She got it for me when I passed the driver's license test."

"Girly." Leo repeated the word that'd snagged his attention. He nodded and rubbed a fry in some ketchup. "Sure, I guess."

"But once I saw it in black, I decided to give it a try. Turns out, it's like driving around in a little goth bubble, and it's kind of fun. Don't get me wrong: I wanted something fancier, not gonna lie. School is full of psycho rich assholes, and on the one hand, I don't want to look like one of *those* guys. But on the other...life at school might be easier if I did. Hey, you're being awful quiet. How's school treating you, anyway?"

"It's fine," Leo lied. Then he course-corrected to something closer to the truth. "It's...normal? It's not very interesting, that's the important part. I'd rather hear about high school. You want to give me any warnings about what to expect next year, or...?"

"Warnings? It's just the same people, every year, doing the same stuff as the year before. You get more homework, and some of the homework is harder—but some of it isn't. Just be nice to everybody, and you'll be fine."

"Easy for you to say."

"Easy for me?" Simon looked confused. "I'm a ginger orphan who lives with his grandma when he's not in school. You and Melissa are pretty much my only real friends, and now I'm at a school full of freaking *boys* a couple hundred miles away from home. Melissa is literally the only girl I actually know."

"But you're smart and you're cool. I bet everybody likes you."

Simon shook his head and took another bite of his pickle garnish. "I'm not popular. I'm another boring guy in a school that's already full of them. The only popular guys are the ones who play sports, and I don't do that. I'm not smart enough for the nerds, and I'm not rich enough to hang with the *really* rich people, so, I'm in the middle. Not special, not interesting."

"But nobody picks on you."

Now he straightened up, invigorated by the prospect of righting an injustice. "Shit, Leo. Somebody's picking on you? Okay, I may not be the biggest and the strongest guy in high school, but I'm probably taller and stronger than anybody who's giving you a hard time. You want me to kick somebody's ass? 'Cause I'll do it. Say the word."

Leo smiled despite himself. "No, not anybody in particular." For the most part, Leo kept his head down and his nose clean. He was a good student, so he was friendly with the nerds. He even had a few friends, but no one he liked as well as Simon.

"Then what's this really about?"

Leo wasn't hungry anymore, but he bought himself a few seconds of thinking time with another handful of fries. They were tepid and mealy in his mouth. "My mom and dad are splitting up, but before you say anything...it's actually not so bad. All they do is fight anyway."

"Oh man, I'm so sorry!"

He waved it away. "It'll be weird, but quieter. The worst part is word getting around about...the other thing."

Simon nodded. "The other thing? You've got more big news to drop? Bigger than your parents' divorce? Whatever it is, it must be *epic.*"

"It's not epic." Leo could feel heat coming up his neck, creeping up his cheeks. A girl at school had found his Trapper Keeper, and she'd seen what he'd written inside it. "It's just embarrassing."

"Tell me. Come on, you obviously want to."

Leo very much did *not* want to, but the compulsion to say something was stronger than the reluctance to do so. He spit it out fast, before he could change his mind. "Word's getting around that I like a guy, okay?"

Simon sat back slowly in the booth. The look on his face wasn't quite readable, so Leo was relieved beyond measure when he said, "All right, so you like a guy. Who cares? You can like whoever you want."

"Yeah, but it's—"

"School, I know." Simon leaned forward again, earnest and a bit intense. "But here's the main thing I've figured out, since Grandmother sent me to the academy: This 'school' garbage? It's temporary. You can leave it all behind a grade at a time. Year to year, even when nothing much changes…nothing much matters either."

"I don't believe that."

Simon held up the remains of his pickle spear and pointed with it. "You don't believe it *yet*. Simon says: You're going to be *fine*, Leo. People don't care about…about guys liking guys, or girls liking girls. Not like they used to," he said flippantly, but he left his voice low so no one at the neighboring booths would hear him. Leo didn't know if he was being thoughtful or if he was just embarrassed by his little homo friend.

He wanted to ask, but he didn't. "That's what Aunt Anna says. I didn't tell Uncle Marco. I don't know how."

"Tell him the truth. Or don't." Simon shrugged. "It's nobody's business but yours."

"It doesn't change anything?"

"Nah. And for what it's worth, Melissa won't care either. If she tries to tease you about it, she isn't serious. I hear she made out with a girl at Bible camp last month."

"Oh my God, *what*?"

Simon laughed merrily. "Her parents made her go, I don't know why. It was right before she came out here for the summer."

"What? Oh wow, she never said anything. To me." Leo liked the idea of knowing something about Melissa when she didn't know that he knew. "You really think she'll be cool?"

"Sure. Whenever you feel like telling her. If you ever do. It's totally fine, though. I'm serious." Then, as if to demonstrate how very cool it was, he changed the subject. "Hey, are you thinking about college yet?"

Leo grinned from ear to ear. Not because of college, but because he was prepared to believe that Simon truly didn't care.

He hadn't told Simon the whole truth. He wasn't ready for that yet. He couldn't say that Simon's name was the one his biology lab partner had seen in his Trapper Keeper. Maybe he'd say it soon. Maybe he never would.

Either way, he didn't say it now. "I have to get some scholarships if I'm going to do college. I get good grades, though. I can probably get good test scores. What about you? What will you major in?"

"Engineering," Simon answered quickly. "Grandfather was an inventor, my dad was an inventor, and I have some ideas. The internet will be the next big thing, you just watch. I'll take computer science as a minor, combine that with engineering, and save the world. Or something."

Leo nodded along, barely listening.

Simon didn't care. Simon thought he was cool.

16

WEDNESDAY

MELISSA

"Okay, so let's settle in. It's getting late. We should rest up and look around the rest of the island tomorrow." Melissa waved her empty glass and moved it to the sink. She stared at it a little too long, thinking about enamel over steel, rusting into flakes from the drain outward.

Leo said her name, startling her back to the moment.

"Sorry, I'm just really, really tired." This was more physical activity than she'd had in a year, and she didn't even have anything to show for it. No Simon, no clues. Just the sneaky feeling of a blister coming up on one toe, and the raw, scraped feeling on her palms.

"Yeah, we should get some rest." Then he asked, "Do you think Simon would care if I borrowed some socks? Maybe he has an oversized T-shirt or something I can sleep in."

She planted her hands on the edge of the sink and stared into space. "I'm sure he wouldn't." Then she turned her attention back to Leo. "Hey, what room do you want? Simon's room or the guest room? I don't mean to sound like a crazy person, but I'm *not* gonna take the dead lady's room. It just feels rude."

"I'll take Simon's room," he decided.

She delivered a ridiculous curtsy or bow, or some combination of the two. "Perfect. Now if you'll excuse me, I need a shower worse than I've ever needed one in my life, but I'll keep it short and sweet. If you need anything, use Mrs. C's crazy pink bathroom." For no good reason at all, her brain flashed to the house on the beach.

She didn't like it. Didn't want it. Tried to blink it away.

Leo stretched and stood up. "You say *crazy*, but I have buyers who'd say *hooray*. Everything comes around again, and when it does, people will pay a premium for the original. I mean, be honest. You never really *liked* this house, did you?"

"No," she confessed. "Mid-century modern isn't my jam, that's all. It makes me think of my grandparents' place, which I always thought was super ugly. Maybe it was because they didn't have money. I don't necessarily think they had bad taste, for their time—they made use of the styles available to them. It all just feels…"

"Old." He gave her the word he meant, even if it wasn't the one she was looking for. "It feels old to you, because you've mostly known old people who had houses like this. You're Generation X, and in my experience…" He waved his hands around again, and it amused her. She'd forgotten how much he used them to talk. "Gen X buyers don't want mid-century modern. They want something older than that, or they want something brand spanking new."

"I'm not *that* much older than you. You're...okay, if you're a millennial, you're an elder one. Isn't that what they call your people? Elder millennials?"

With a sniff, he said, "I prefer the 'Oregon Trail Generation,' myself."

"Okay, fine. Well, I'm taking that shower and turning in for the night, but I want you to promise me something: don't ghost me, man. If you change your mind about staying here and you want to go home, that's cool, you do you. But say something first. Don't leave me hanging."

Solemnly and just a touch drunkenly, he said, "I'm not going *anywhere* until we find Simon."

"Excellent."

She did not move to settle in.

Leo sighed. He smiled a tired smile. "Good. I'm glad we got that out of the way."

At last, she set off for the guest room. She flipped on the light and saw a quilt covering the bed with a 1970s crocheted granny square blanket folded at the foot. It had been there since before she was born. Same furniture, some peculiar set of antiques that were, as Tim Gunn might say, "a lot of look." The place was a time capsule.

The front door opened. Then it shut again.

For a single thrilling moment, she thought Simon had returned. Her heart jumped into her throat, and she dropped her bag onto the bed before fleeing the room and gunning for the foyer in her sock-feet.

But it was only Leo, holding his raincoat. It was still damp, but no longer dripping.

He looked up at her, confused. Then he realized her misunderstanding. "Sorry. I'm sorry, I just didn't want to leave it outside all night."

"I don't know why I thought...but that's okay, it doesn't matter. Good night, Leo."

"Good night, Melissa. I'll lock up and turn off the lights."

17

1998

MELISSA

Yeah...so," Melissa said, unsure of where to begin. "This is weird, right? Now that we don't spend the whole summer here. And you're already going back to Evergreen in a couple of weeks? That's not even fair, man."

"I need this stupid summer course if I'm going to graduate on time. It isn't personal, believe me. Leo's off at that internship, anyway, so it's not like everything would be the same—even if I wasn't headed back early. We're grown-ups now. Of course it's weird. It'll probably just get weirder from here on out."

He wasn't wrong, but that didn't make her feel any better. "This kind of weird sucks. I love our summers! I don't really have a life the rest of the year. I don't know very many people, and I don't like most of the people I do know. At least with you and Leo..." She wasn't sure where she was going with that, so she stopped. Then she tried again. "It felt normal. I felt like I had friends, and I knew how the world worked. These days, everything's just..."

He sighed and stared off toward the far side of the Sound. He finished her thought. "Everything's different. Which isn't so much weird as normal."

They were sitting on the driftwood log, and the day was cooler than either of them would've preferred. The sky was half-cloudy and half-bright, and the tide was coming in. Three seagulls bickered over the corpse of an enormous fish that Melissa and Simon could smell from a distance.

"Ugh, why do you have to be so…right? Most of the time."

"You act surprised, but this was always going to happen." He swung a mostly finished cigarette around and then decided he was done with it after all. He chucked it into the sand. He didn't usually smoke, but sometimes, on the beach. In the summer. When his grandmother wasn't looking. "We were always going to grow up and leave someday. Look, I'm sorry about your grandparents. Grandfather, I mean. I know your grandmother already passed."

"My dad inherited the house, and he's planning to sell it. He says it'll pay off my student loans, and they'll have some money left over for retirement, probably. But I don't know. After Grandma died, Grandpa didn't really keep the place up, so it needs some work. And who wants to live all the way out here, anyway? I mean," she corrected quickly, "who wants to buy a house out here? Most people want to live closer to the city. Any city."

"Would…um…would *you* live out here, if you could?"

"Seriously? What job could I get on Marrowstone? Countergirl at Nordy's? Come on, man."

Still staring off at the water, he said, "I thought maybe you could live in your grandparents' house and stay here year-round."

She frowned at him. "I can barely afford my car, and it's a total piece of shit. What, are *you* gonna buy my grandparents' place for me? Because you know I don't have the money."

"Jesus, Mel."

"That's what I thought. You're right. We're grown-ups. It sucks, and it's inevitable, and no—I *can't* stay here on the island year-round. I don't even want to. I was thinking maybe it could go the other way."

"What other way?" he asked, and she was almost amused by how clueless he was, except that it meant he hadn't even considered the possibility. Jesus, had it never occurred to him? How badly she wanted him to come to her?

Or did it simply not matter?

"I thought…instead of me coming out to the island, maybe you could come out to the city. Think about it: We both graduate this year. I don't want to live at home, but I can't afford my own place. I need a roommate and I know you. I know you're… reliable," she finished weakly.

For a minute, he didn't answer. Finally he turned to her and said, "You really think that'd be a good idea? Us, as platonic roommates? Is that what you're angling for?"

"Oh, for fuck's sake. We have a little history, fine. The vast majority—the *overwhelming* majority—of that history we've spent as friends, and Simon, I need a friend. Melissa says: *Come get a nice two-bedroom in Queen Anne. With me.*"

He chuckled feebly, like he didn't want to but couldn't help it. "That's not how it works. You're not Simon. You don't get to *say*."

She shrugged bitterly. "Yes, I do. And I said what I said."

"I can't, though. You get that, right? Grandmother had pneumonia last year; she was in the hospital for almost a month. She's old, Melly. She's old and she won't be around much longer. I can't abandon her. She's..."

Melissa snorted. "What, she's all you have?" She hopped down off the log. "You know, if you'd leave the damn island sometimes for something that isn't school, you might have more people in your stupid little circle."

"If you didn't get nasty with everyone when your feelings are hurt, you'd have more friends."

"Fine. We're both terrible people and we don't deserve anything better."

"Speak for yourself," he said, dropping down onto the sand beside her. "And even if I don't, my grandmother deserves better. I can't just abandon her out here—with no cops, no firefighters, not even regular mail service, for crying out loud. She's lost everyone except me."

Melissa turned to walk away, back to the house or maybe back to the beater Dodge she'd gotten for a song—but it'd still been a stretch. It was the same shade of silver-blue as the hair of the old lady who'd driven it before her.

Simon grabbed her by the arm to stop her. "She won't be able to drive much longer," he said. "When she can't drive, what happens? What would she do? She's healthy, she doesn't need to go into a home. She deserves her independence. She deserves her family."

"More than you deserve a life?"

"That's not fair."

"Growing up isn't fair, Simon. Getting old isn't fair either, apparently."

"Don't be like this," he begged. "Come on. Let's go get dinner or something. Let's...let's go into Port Townsend and make fun of the tourists. Let's email Leo and tell him hello—I set him up with a Yahoo address when he came by for Christmas."

"Why don't you ask Leo to stay on the island, then? If he's around so much. He'd do it, you know. If you asked him. He'd do anything you asked him." Just like her, except that she couldn't stay there, no matter how much Simon said he wanted her to. She didn't quite trust it. If she was that kind of important to him, he wouldn't ask her to stay. He'd ask to join her.

That slowed him down. But he rallied. "Don't be mean to him. I can't stand it when you're mean to him."

"I'm mean to everybody, I can't help it." She darted out of his reach, knowing he'd try to stop her again. "I'm shitty at being a person. If you ever left the island, if you ever made any other friends...you'd have figured that out sooner." She was about to cry, and she hated them both for it. Herself for being weak. Him for knowing where her buttons were, and for knowing that she didn't mean any of this as hard as she pretended to.

"God, you're such a drama queen when you're sad."

"Same as it ever was."

He snorted. "David Byrne will never love you."

And neither would Simon. Not the way she wanted, as hard as it was to accept. Maybe if she refused to accept it, that would mean something. She stopped and turned around. "You won't even think about coming into the city with me?"

Simon took a deep breath. "How about this?" he tried. "What if, after Grandmother dies, we talk about this again?"

"She could live another twenty years."

"She won't, though. She's almost eighty. It won't be long, and it'll suck for me, but then, sure. I'll sell her house. I'll move to the city with you, if you still want me to by then."

"That's a bullshit promise. You just hope it won't matter anymore, by the time she dies. You hope I change my mind, or forget, or stop caring. Shit, we could be in our thirties by the time she actually kicks it!"

"Keep your voice down!" he urged. "When she turns her hearing aid up, she can pick up radio signals in Bremerton."

It was Melissa's turn to snort. "Sorry. You're right, sorry. I'm sorry. I suck, but you knew that already." Her snort led to some sniffles, and she almost wanted to go ahead and start crying full tilt. Everything was changing, and everything was awful. Especially her.

He slung an arm over her shoulder and started walking back to the house, drawing her along with him in a half hug that made walking awkward. "Everybody sucks, Mel," he assured her with a little squeeze. "You. Me. *Everybody.*"

18

WEDNESDAY

LEO

Leo watched Melissa disappear into the guest room, and he felt suddenly quite alone. During the day, the Culpepper house was fresh and bright, full of windows and stone, warm lights and expensive alcohol. At night, it had always felt like something else entirely.

Or maybe it was just him.

Quietly, if clumsily, he collected his own dirtied barware and put it in the sink. He turned on the tap and picked up a soap wand, cleaned up the mess both he and Melissa had left behind, and left everything to dry on the rack beside the sink. Then he spent a minute hunting for the fireplace remote before finding it between the couch cushions, and he turned off the flames. When the last of the gas line hiss had faded away, the house felt infinitely darker and colder, despite the fact that all the usual lamps were still lit.

Mrs. Culpepper never could abide overhead lighting. Every room had at least one old-fashioned lamp, standing alone or sitting on a table, and you were expected to use those lamps in her house—whether or not you thought it made the shadows darker, and the corners were already crowded with things worse than spiders.

Leo worked hard to think about other things—like how Simon was probably safe somewhere, shell-shocked from the loss of his grandmother and taking some time to himself. He definitely wasn't wounded and wet, lying in the woods beyond the house.

Definitely not.

One by one, Leo turned off the lights.

Only a few were still on; he and Melissa had mostly stayed in the living room, with brief forays to the bathroom and kitchen—but there was a night-light plugged into an outlet in the hall, no need for the overhead glare. There were small lights like that all over the house, most of them on sensors so they'd stay dark in the daytime and draw precious little power. Simon had bought them, after Mrs. Culpepper had fallen in the dark and broken her hip.

Leo thought about the go-bag in his trunk, and wished he'd brought it with him.

He could live for a night without fresh underwear or shirts, but he was overdressed for anything but a house showing or a funeral.

Would Mrs. Culpepper have a funeral? Would she be buried or cremated? Would they put her in the Sound View Cemetery? That's where most of the island residents went, unless they had family elsewhere who wished to bring them home.

Without meaning to, Leo looked back down the hall to the living room, and to the corner beside the fireplace—between the laminate wood turntable cabinet and the rack for decorative firewood that didn't fool anybody. The nook was blacker than it should have been. If Leo stared at it long enough, it seemed to move.

He looked away. "Not tonight," he told the house and everything in it. "I can't do this tonight."

It was better to think about Simon and turn all that magical thinking toward bringing Simon home safely. They would find him tomorrow, for sure. Even if it turned out that he was hurt out there, Melissa and Leo would carry him home together. They'd clean him up and get him to a doctor. He'd be fine.

Of course he'd be fine.

They could talk about Mrs. Culpepper and her remarkable life and discuss what to do with the house. If it wasn't too soon. If it didn't come off as greedy or opportunistic, because Leo surely would not mean it that way. But eventually, he'd bring it up.

And now, in the quiet of evening, Leo couldn't forget—not for lack of trying—the frantic note in Melissa's voice in the voicemail she'd left for him that morning. Her naked fear had come through the line as clear as day. In the quiet of evening, the best-case scenario looked less and less likely.

In the morning, he could walk back to his aunt and uncle's place.

He could get his go-bag out of the trunk and come back with fresh clothes and his own toiletries. Maybe, in the morning, Simon would be back. He might even sneak inside, realize his bedroom was occupied, and take the couch. Leo could find him there in the morning; his shoes would be on the floor, and he'd be snoring toward the ceiling.

The thought made Leo smile. It gave him the strength to keep walking into Simon's room and to prop the door open a few inches before he turned on the bedside lamp—chasing all the shadows out of all four corners and the closet too.

Leo stripped down to his boxers and plugged in his phone with the charger he kept on his person at all times, like a goddamn closer. Despite its velour finish, the duvet was crisp and cool; he shivered when he slipped beneath it and propped himself up with one of Simon's extra pillows.

The house was quiet.

The heater would stay off for a while, given the residual warmth of the fireplace. The rain outside was just firm enough to provide a pleasant, distant white noise—but only if he listened hard. He could blame any number of peculiar sounds on the weather, even if he knew where they were coming from. Lying to himself was easy when he didn't want to think about dark corners.

But there was something, just beyond the edge of his hearing. He mostly just sensed its presence...that soft, terrible noise. The crying of something young and lost and dead.

He hadn't heard it in a while, because he hadn't been around the Culpepper house in a while—and he didn't often hear or see anything so peculiar anywhere else. Every now and again, maybe while showing a house, there'd be something or someone left behind. Usually they only watched, but sometimes they followed. He never knew whether he should or shouldn't say anything to prospective buyers. The disclosure laws in Washington didn't require a seller to mention any hauntings.

On second thought, maybe he heard and saw lost dead people more often than he cared to think. But except for when he spent time at the Culpepper house, he never saw them when he was with Simon.

Most of the time when they got together, Leo and Simon met in Bremerton, or maybe Tacoma. Once in a while, Port Townsend. Sometimes Vancouver. When Simon began working in nonprofit fundraising, he left the island more frequently—despite technically working from home so he could keep one eye on the nearly (but not quite) immortal Mrs. Culpepper.

Leo could think about those times with a smile and ignore the strange sound in the living room corners.

Until he couldn't. It was different now. The longer he sat there in bed, light turned on, phone charging up, rain pattering on the gabled roof above, the more confident he was that the mournful noise had changed.

Was it the pitch, or was it the volume? The location was hard to pinpoint, not that he was trying to pinpoint it (yes, he was), and not because it mattered anyway (even though it might).

He did not want to think about it. He could not stop thinking about it.

He could not stop worrying about it and being afraid of it.

"Fine," he grumbled. "I give up."

He slung his legs over the side of the bed and wished for his slippers. He opened the closet and reached behind the door to the hook where Simon's fluffy oversized terrycloth bathrobe lurked. It was oversized enough that Leo could close it around himself and tie its belt in a small snug knot. It smelled faintly like Simon, or like his aftershave and preferred soap. It felt like armor enough to face the night, even barefoot.

Leo left Simon's room and set out into the hall.

He closed his eyes and immediately pictured that spot beside the fireplace. Warm and dark. Perfect for hiding in comfort, if that's what you needed. Yes, there. Just a quick look. Just to make sure it was only his imagination, and not something that needed his attention or his anxiety.

In the living room, the gas fireplace was nearly cool, and its glass was safe to touch. Beside it, Leo saw twin patches of black fog. Previously they'd been static, unmoving and unmoved by much of anything. They had been still and mostly quiet, except when they cried.

This was different.

This thing roiled and billowed, for all its small size. It writhed and raged, and Leo felt a sense of panic that didn't belong to him. Whatever it was, it was no longer stationary and sad. It was terrified.

It did not cry. It screamed.

Horrified, Leo stumbled back away from it—nearly toppling the bar cart and hitting his thigh on the side of the couch. The shadow flickered, black on black, but different shades in different moments, from different angles as it spun and rocked. It wailed. And then it was gone.

19

THURSDAY

MELISSA

Melissa awoke confused and somewhat hungover. In a few seconds, she remembered where she was—and that she'd forgotten to shut the curtains. The light outside wasn't bright, but it was technically daylight, and it had technically alerted her to the prospect of *morning* as a concept.

Technically.

Outside, the rain had retreated to an early winter drizzle. Unlike the spring quasi storms that soaked everything in short order, the mist could take hours to get you good and wet.

She yawned and rolled over to check her phone. Its charge was down to 34 percent.

"Ugh," she groaned. She rolled over and flopped out of bed, slapping her feet onto the low-shag rug and rubbing her bleary eyes. Fuck that brandy. Tonight she'd stick to cider or vodka. Or nothing. She pulled her jeans on underneath the T-shirt she'd slept in. Her socks and boots were still in the living room, laid out before the fireplace to dry.

Out in the hall, her toes squeaked softly on the parquet. She rubbed her eyes and staggered out into the foyer, then changed her mind and went to the kitchen. She'd never had cottonmouth so badly in her life. Or not since college, at least.

The kitchen was clean. The dishes were washed. So that's what Leo'd been doing when she hadn't heard him go straight to bed. She loved him for it, in an idle, admiring way.

From the top left cabinet above the sink, she retrieved a plastic tumbler and filled it up with tap water. While she drank, she stared out into the living room, and through the great glass windows that faced the ocean but mostly showed the trees.

And between the house and the water, that terrible shape on the beach.

Jesus, how had she almost forgotten about the housewreck? By bedtime it had slipped her mind, for all of its impressive awfulness. It was almost as if once it was out of sight, it vanished from existence—and how weird was that? Sure, the whole thing was weird, but even so.

She shuddered to consider it now, and tried not to remember climbing around inside it, choosing each step carefully, getting her feet soaked anyway. The smell of rust. The sticky grit of salt on every surface. The stairs peeling away from the wall. Loud pops overhead, as ceiling joists settled and threatened to split.

She carried her water into the living room, where her boots and socks were dry. Morning had dawned and everything was reset, wasn't it? Everything was fine. Sure, the housewreck was still out there, silent, empty, and alone. No sign of tourists or lookie-loos.

Melissa went to the front door and cracked it open.

Not only was Simon still missing, but the rain was back in earnest. Great. Just great.

She plugged in her phone and left it charging beside the now empty tumbler on the kitchen counter, then piled all her necessary stuff into the hall bathroom and took another, more thorough shower to make up for last night's quickie. Being wet with hot, soapy water and being wet with cold, salty water were such wildly different experiences that she stayed in there longer than she should have, letting the space fill up with steam.

When she was clean, refreshed, and smelling like her own body wash, she got dressed and went to the kitchen again. She stood there blankly, a thoughtful frown on her face.

Melissa started opening cupboards and poking through them because Simon's coffeemaker looked like it belonged in a NASA break room and she had no idea how to work it. Finally, she found a metal tin of General Foods International. It had probably belonged to Mrs. Culpepper, who never had much of a taste for coffee—but could be persuaded to sip a little instant mocha, once in a while.

A tea kettle rested on the stove. Melissa filled it up and turned on a burner. While she waited for the water to boil, she stared out the living room windows, squinting through the trees at the house on the beach.

You'd think half the island would have come to check the thing out.

Or maybe not.

This part of the beach was visually sheltered by a short promontory to the north, and most of the folks to the south had already left for their summer houses in warmer places. The island's population was at its lowest that time of year.

But Jesus, where did Simon *go*? There was no sign of him to the north, and no reason on earth he'd head south—not that they wouldn't look. Beyond that…today they'd need to take their search farther afield.

The kettle began to hum ahead of its full rolling boil.

It was a funny sound, tinny and low and rumbling. She looked back at the kettle. Is that what she was hearing? But it seemed to be coming from the living room, not the kitchen.

She'd already picked out a mug, but now she set it down and wandered, following her ears, trying to pinpoint the source. Not the living room. Maybe the hall? Still keeping quiet for Leo's sake, she followed the hall to the rear of the house, past Mrs. Culpepper's bedroom, a storage closet, and the basement door.

She tried the door.

It was unlocked, so she opened it; she stood at the top of the landing and listened. Yes. There it was, an odd, gurgling mumble that sounded like a cranky furnace. There *was* a furnace down there, though the temperature upstairs suggested it was working just fine.

But that sound.

She should probably check it out.

She stayed where she was. It was only a basement, and she'd only just looked around down there the night before. It shouldn't be hard. It should be as simple as going down to her apartment basement to do laundry, except *this* basement never smelled like Tide and fabric softener. It always smelled like something had died.

The noise was louder, there at the top of the stairs. She was too deep in the house to hear the rain outside, but she felt like she was hearing it anyway. It was white noise, several layers of it. The low rumble, the irritating patter, the foggy roar at the farthest edge of her hearing.

She held out one foot over the top step and let it hover there. She leaned forward.

But when the tea kettle screamed in the kitchen, she started to fall.

She caught herself on the doorframe and threw herself back away from the basement stairs, frazzled and confused and desperate to make the screaming stop. It was loud and long, the scream of something that doesn't need to take a breath.

She scrambled back down the hallway, fleeing toward the kitchen. "Fuck, fuck, fuck," she swore, stopping the whistle and pouring a big slug of water into the dollops of instant coffee powder. Her hands were shaking, and she wasn't sure why. She wasn't sure what she'd heard. She didn't know why it was so upsetting.

"You okay?" Leo was behind her, wearing one of Simon's bathrobes. It barely fit him, but the maroon color suited him. He adjusted the belt tied at his waist.

"Yeah, I'm sorry about that. Really, I swear—I thought I lifted the, the...thingy"—she wiggled her fingers at the nozzle—"so it wouldn't shriek when the water boiled. I didn't mean to wake you up."

He shrugged and turned to the cabinet to grab his own mug. "Don't worry about it. We should probably get this day started, anyway."

She slid the tin of instant coffee across the counter.

He picked up the tin and grimaced at it. "Is this all we've got?"

"Unless you want to try your luck with Hal," she said, cocking her head toward the coffeemaker. "But I don't know how to make him open the pod bay doors."

"No, this is…fine. I don't know how to use that thing either." He used the last of her kettle water and stirred with the spoon she'd left beside the sink. He took a short sip and made a face.

Melissa asked, "So what do we do…now? Check the rest of the island on foot?"

"We looked everywhere within a mile of the house yesterday," he noted.

She sighed. "Should we look even farther? Out past your aunt and uncle's place? Or do we…I don't know, drive around the island with our heads hanging out the window, calling for him like a lost dog?"

"Neither the best nor worst ideas you've ever floated." He blew across the top of his drink. "How about this: let's swing by the sheriff's office in Port Hadlock. If they don't have anything useful to tell us, we can start looking around the island hot spots. Flagler, the winery, the old military batteries. Nordy's too, even though it's mostly gone now."

"You knew Nordy's burned?"

"Yeah, Simon told me, last time we got together. What a loss, right?"

"Yeah." She sighed, wondering why she was always the last to know everything. But that wasn't Leo's fault, and she didn't take it out on him. "So that's pretty much everyplace, right?"

He thought about it for a second. "Nordy's is gone, but we can still poke around Mystery Bay across the street."

Now she nodded, warming up to this plan. She wasn't a great planner herself. Never had been. "That works for me. Okay, let's get moving."

"First, I need to clean up. Would you do me a little favor?" he asked. He disappeared down the hall and reappeared a moment later, holding his car keys. "Would you go over to my aunt and uncle's place and get my bag out of the trunk of my car? Simon and I are um, not the same size, and I need a change of clothes."

"Yeah, sure," she said.

He tossed her the keys, and she caught them with one hand.

"Thanks," he said. "I appreciate it. I'll wash up in the Mamie pink wonderland when I'm finished with this...coffee-esque beverage, and then we can get back to our quest."

"Great. This house was starting to freak me out, anyway."

20

2017

LEO

"She's wonderful, but Grandmother doesn't like her." Simon took a sip of the straight old-fashioned he'd ordered, considered it thoughtfully for two or three seconds, and set his glass down in the dead center of the tiny square napkin it came with. "I'm not sure why, exactly. Maybe she wouldn't like any girlfriend, ever."

Leo's own drink—a Manhattan with no garnish—sat half finished in his hand, which rested atop his knee. "It's been just the two of you for so long...maybe your grandmother isn't ready to have another woman in your life."

"I think Grandmother's just worried about women coming for the family money. Grandfather's inventions are falling out of use as elevator and escalator technology evolves, but my dad's stuff for the Department of Defense, um..." He hesitated.

"I know you have a fortune," Leo said. "You know I've never cared."

"It's…not all the money in the world. Maybe Grandmother honestly thinks Amy isn't good enough for me."

A waitress came by to pick up the basket that once held fried mushrooms and onion rings. She asked if they needed anything else. Leo asked for another round. Simon agreed.

When she was gone, Leo said with a grin, "Your grandmother never struck me as such a snob. She put up with me and Melissa for years, and we were filthy street urchins compared to you."

"Oh come on," Simon said with a laugh. "We were all nasty little rugrats. Honestly, I think she wants to protect me. But I just…"

The ellipsis hung in the air.

Something about Simon's tone made Leo both curious and concerned. "What is it? Is something rotten in Marrowstone? Is something wrong with your grandmother?" They were sitting in a bar that was just barely too nice to call a dive, huddled in a red pleather booth beside a picture window. It was Seattle, and it was wet outside, and the bar smelled like fried food and alcohol. The island felt a million miles away. So did the summers.

Simon sighed, and he sagged in his seat. He downed the last of his drink in a couple of swallows. "She turned ninety last year."

"Holy shit."

"I know, right? She's in good physical health, now that she's recovered from the hip break, but in the last few months her mind has really started slipping."

"I noticed last year that she was getting forgetful."

"Forgetful isn't the problem." Simon glanced at the bar, as

if he'd like that next round sooner rather than later. "Forgetful is almost funny, sometimes."

"Funny...how?" Leo asked, though his chest tightened.

Simon shook his head like he wasn't sure where to begin. "The other day she called me Charles and started asking about whether or not we should swap out the gas heat for electric. It took me five minutes to successfully remind her that I'm not my grandfather, and the house has been on electric heat for years. The fireplace is the only thing that still runs on gas."

"Damn."

Simon let out half a bitter chuckle. "Last week she asked when the kids were coming around again, since it's almost summer."

"Oh no." It was October. Simon and Melissa were in their early forties, and Leo was only a few years behind them.

"Oh, yes. She caught herself at the last second and laughed, and said that she knew we were all adults now, but she'd be happy to have us together again, regardless."

A lump swelled in Leo's throat. He used another swig of the drink to force it down. "That would be nice. We should make a point to do that, when summer rolls around again. Even if it's just for a couple of weeks. I'll see if Melissa wants to crash with my aunt and uncle. Or I guess she could stay with you."

"The guest room is always open, for either one of you," Simon said diplomatically. "Or both of you, if you don't mind sharing like you used to when we were kids."

"It wasn't our fault your fireworks parties ran long."

"Only on the Fourth!" he insisted.

"We both know that's not true."

"It's mostly true." Simon leaned out of the way as the waitress returned with their fresh drinks.

Leo still nursed the first one. He let the second one rest on the table between them. "I'm sorry you're starting to lose her."

"The little things, the momentary confusion, the forgetfulness…that's not so bad. But I keep finding her standing alone, muttering to herself, or to someone who isn't there. Whoever it is, she hates them. I've never heard her talk that way to anyone, ever, and when she turned around, she was holding a big knife from the block in the kitchen."

"Good God. Who is it? Or who does she *think* it is?"

"I have no idea. I read somewhere that some forms of dementia—especially when it's age-related, or something like Alzheimer's—can cause bad nightmares, but the nightmares happen while they're awake. Delusions? Maybe that's a better word? I think that's what's happening."

"Well, it sounds dangerous."

"Tell me about it. She's starting to wander too. I found her by the driftwood tree, out in the rain. She was staring at the water, or Whidbey Island, or…the rocks that lead out into the surf, whatever."

"Standing there? Staring?"

Simon nodded. "And muttering. Always muttering. I didn't catch most of it, but it was like listening to half of a conversation—eavesdropping while someone's on the phone. All I caught was something about how she was sorry, and it'd seemed like a good idea at the time, and she couldn't do anything about it now."

"Huh." Leo finished his first drink and reached for the second. This was definitely a two-drink conversation.

"She looked..." Simon frowned. "Wild. Her hair was loose, and it's almost to her waist, for chrissake. She had this streak of red paint or makeup or something, right across her eyes. She looked at me like she didn't know me, and then she started babbling at me, saying something like, 'We couldn't match him by ourselves, so we looked for help.' And then all the way back to the house—she was barefoot, I don't think I mentioned that part—she was crying and going on about how she had no choice, and what else could she do. She wanted someone to forgive her."

"And you don't know who?"

"No idea." Simon leaned back into the booth's overstuffed seating. Pleather squeaked around his shoulders. "It must have been a flash of senility. Some random firing of synapses, remixed with old memories and maybe even some soaps."

Leo's eyes watered. "She's always loved those soaps. God help us, if we ever interrupted her daytime stories."

"For real." Now Simon laughed, suddenly and too loudly. "Last spring, I had pinkeye. I must have scratched myself in my sleep, because one morning I woke up and couldn't open my left one—it was swollen completely shut. Went to the doctor, got some antibiotics." He rolled his hand like he was summing up a longer tale. "And I had to wear an eye patch for a week. One day, Grandmother couldn't stop calling me 'Steve' and I finally stopped her, and asked her why. She looked startled, then cracked up. Apparently there was a character on *Days of Our Lives* named Steve."

"And he wears an eye patch?"

"Yup. My point is, everything is getting scrambled up in her head. Time, memories, reality. She's losing her grip on all of them."

Leo blew his nose on the cocktail napkin. It wasn't really big enough for the task, but he made it work. "Being an adult sucks. It's an infinite state of losing things: jobs, pets. People."

Simon cleared his throat and looked away. "Businesses close. Restaurants shut down. Movie theaters get rebranded as 'event centers.' Actors and musicians you liked when you were a kid start dying off. Yeah, what you said. The passage of time really sucks."

"Amen to that." Leo hoisted his Manhattan in a toast. "To absent friends. And family, and places."

"To all of those things." Then Simon sat forward again and said, "*Anyway*," in a very pointed fashion. "Please tell me you have something good going on in your life. Please tell me something nice. I need to hear something nice."

"Okay...did I tell you I'm moving to Bremerton?"

"What? Really?"

Leo nodded. "I'm joining a Windemere office as an agent, and I'm moving next month."

"Oh wow!" Simon's eyes lit up, delighted on his behalf. "That's amazing, I'm glad you've settled on a course of action, and even gladder you sound happy about it. Do you need any help moving? I can come out to Tacoma, help you pack, whatever you need."

Leo shook his head. "That's all right, I've hired a company to do most of the work. I don't have that much stuff, so it's not that big of a deal. I picked a little cottage."

"Near the water?"

"Nah. In the woods," he said. He did not add that he didn't especially want to live near the water and that he wasn't a great fan of the naval base and its accompanying hassles—but the location was too convenient to pass up.

He didn't say a lot of things. He had a feeling that Simon wasn't saying a lot of things too.

Didn't they used to tell each other everything? When did that stop? It must have been just one more thing they were losing as they hit middle age.

The rest of their evening hangout was friendly and familiar and less intense, and they stayed away from the subject of Mrs. Culpepper's failing mind. They stuck to career changes and girlfriends, and the boyfriend Leo was hoping to make out of a guy he'd met on the internet. Internet romance was the next subject. That one lasted awhile.

When it was finally time to call it a night, Simon and Leo hugged and parted ways.

But on the Uber ride home, Leo couldn't drag his thoughts away from the old woman, past ninety, and the strange things she used to say and do when he was small—grown stranger in her old age. He thought about rocks on a window ledge, rolling and clattering together. Untouched.

Moved by the sound of a song.

21

THURSDAY

MELISSA

After a quick breakfast at a mom-and-pop place in Port Hadlock, Melissa and Leo swung by the sheriff's office. Melissa was driving. Her beat-up Subaru was better suited to the weather and the terrain, or that was her argument. The truth was, she thought Leo drove like a grandma and it annoyed her. She was well aware that he thought she drove like a bat out of hell—and it annoyed him in return. But apparently he was more annoyed by the idea of his shiny electric car rough-riding down the muddy access road.

Therefore he took shotgun and was gracious enough to keep his mouth shut about the takeout bags, wadded up napkins, and paper straw wrappers on the floor.

Through a pair of sunglasses so big they covered half her face, she kept one eye on the road and the other one on the lookout for the sheriff's office building. She knew it was somewhere on the main drag of the tiny town which was, nonetheless, technically a town—and that was more than Marrowstone could say.

She hit the brakes too fast. "Shit, there it is."

Leo snapped forward. His seat belt locked. "There *what* is?"

"The sheriff's office, hang on. I just need to..." She did not say, "Cross a lane or two of traffic and make a left turn," but that part was implied.

He didn't say anything, but his death grip on the armrest suggested he had opinions.

She parked in one of a handful of visitor spots, and they headed inside to a reception desk with a good-looking Asian guy in a sheriff's office T-shirt and khakis. He was just hanging up the phone when they walked in. He looked at them and said, "Hello, how can I help you?"

Leo took the lead so quickly that if Melissa hadn't already known he was gay, she would've figured it out on the spot. "Hello, Officer...?" He read the name tag beside the JCS logo in a flash. "Tanaka. I'm Leonard Torres, and this is Melissa Toft. My friend here"—he cocked his head at Melissa—"talked to one of your deputies on the phone yesterday about Simon Culpepper and his grandmother, Charlotte."

Deputy Tanaka's eyes widened with familiarity. "Oh right. The elderly woman on the beach, over on Marrowstone."

Leo said, "That's right. When will you know for certain how she died? Will there be an autopsy?"

Officer Tanaka started to answer, then changed his mind. Instead, he said, "I don't think we have that information yet, but I hope you're here with news about the grandson."

Melissa shook her head. "The opposite, actually. But I guess you've pretty much answered our question."

"Hang on, give me a minute," he said, picking up the phone

receiver. He held it against his chest and asked her, "You spoke to Svenson yesterday, isn't that right?"

"It sounds right. I remember his name was Scandinavian."

He mumbled, "Doesn't narrow it down very much around here," and dialed an extension. "Svenson? Hey, I've got a couple of folks out here wanting to talk about Simon Culpepper. You got a minute?" He paused, then said, "Great," and hung up. To Melissa and Leo, he said, "He'll be out in a second. Make yourselves comfortable."

Within thirty seconds a corn-fed-looking white guy appeared from somewhere in the back. His hair was blond to the point of being white, and a faint blush of rosacea highlighted his nose and the top of his cheeks.

"I'm Deputy Svenson," he greeted them, and everyone exchanged handshakes before sitting back down in the waiting area. "You're the woman I spoke to on the phone yesterday?"

"That's me," Melissa confirmed. "I was trying to call Simon back."

"He'd left you a message overnight, correct? Sent you an email too, if I remember correctly."

Melissa pulled out her phone and pulled up the email while she answered. "Yeah, but the voicemail was just static. The email is short and sweet, but here you go." She handed him the phone and he read it silently. "I'd ask what you think might've scared Mrs. Culpepper to death, but I'm guessing you saw what washed up on the beach."

"Yeah, that house on the sand, wow." The deputy shook his head in wonder and returned Melissa's phone to her outstretched hand. "The crazy thing is, we didn't even notice it until we were right on top of it. It's like that thing was cloaked, like some kind of spaceship. It's a hell of a sight though, once you wrap your head around it. I took a look inside, myself—thinking maybe the grandson had gone to check it out. Me and an EMT searched the first floor and skipped the second. Didn't want to try those stairs. They looked like a broken neck waiting to happen."

Leo said, "That's basically what we did. No one in their right mind would try the stairs."

"You got that right, and I wouldn't recommend that you go inside again. Hell, that place has already killed one old lady," Svenson concluded. Then he shifted the subject. "So you two are friends of Mr. Culpepper's, but you're not local. You said you were in Seattle, ma'am, do I remember that right? And your grandparents lived on Marrowstone, the Tofts."

"That's right." She nodded. "Leo lives in Bremerton. We all grew up together in the summers out here."

"Then you must have been pretty close," Svenson said, settling against the seat. "And I guess you still are, if he called you the night his grandmother died. Do you know of any other friends he might have reached out to? Somebody more local, someplace on the island he might have gone?"

They shook their heads in tandem. Melissa said, "Simon knew everyone on Marrowstone, but he was just... Well, he worked a lot, and he didn't have any family except for his grandmother. Most of his other friends were people he talked to regularly online, but only saw twice a year at conventions."

Leo added, "And he wasn't dating anyone."

"All right, well, I listened to his 911 call when I got into work this morning," the deputy said. "It was short and to the point, and he sounded pretty freaked out—like a guy who was barely holding himself together. The truth is, Mrs. Culpepper was probably dead before she hit the ground, and I think he knew it."

Melissa shook her head. "Sure, but I still can't imagine him leaving her there like that. It must've been a snap decision, made out of fear or panic."

"The real question is, where did that snap decision take him?" Svenson sat forward again, resting his elbows atop his thighs. "The tide line was pretty far away from where we found his grandmother's body, so we don't think he got swept out to sea."

Leo gasped. "I hadn't thought of that!"

Melissa hadn't either. A wave of muted terror swamped her stomach, but she forced herself to push it away. She silently reassured herself that Svenson was right. If the tide was out, it didn't take Simon. A long-ago summer flashed through her head. A little boy. An undertow. She shot Leo a look, but she didn't think he saw it.

The deputy continued. "Then the house was open, so we went inside to see if he'd—"

"Open?" she interrupted him. "The front door was open?"

"In the 911 call, he said he'd chased her outside. Either he didn't shut the door behind himself, or he didn't shut it very well and the wind took it."

"Or someone else opened it," Leo offered.

The deputy's expression said he did not find that probable. "We're acting on the assumption that Simon and his grandmother were the only two people present."

Melissa said, "We thought maybe he went for help."

"Maybe, but why? He'd already reached the county dispatch, and we were sending an ambulance. I know power was out on most of the island, but the cell towers were working just fine. Why didn't he stay with her? Where did he go?" Svenson asked with an exasperated sigh that said these questions were all rhetorical.

Melissa was getting frustrated. "What about Simon's phone? Didn't you take it with you, when you left?"

"Yeah, I brought it in—in case it turned out to be evidence. It's not like we could track him through the GPS, if he didn't have it on him. If he ever turns up and wants it back, tell him to come down here to the station."

"What *did* you do to track him?" she demanded.

Svenson sighed. "After the ambulance left with the body, I called another deputy and we searched the woods all morning. We didn't find footprints, blood, or anything else, but that doesn't mean much, considering the rain."

Leo asked, "What about helicopters? Search dogs?"

The deputy snorted. "Son, I don't know where you *think* you are, but we don't have resources like that out here. We have one K9 officer and he's a real good boy, but some days I swear to God he's mostly for show. I don't know if you've noticed or not, but this ain't Seattle."

"No," Melissa countered, "this is Jefferson County and you're supposed to take care of…of…Jefferson County. The *whole* county and everybody in it."

"Yes, this is Jefferson County," he said dryly. "Not *King* County. We don't have helicopters, we don't have SWAT teams, and we don't have search-and-rescue dogs, plural. We don't even have a spare officer to dedicate to the effort, at this time."

"Jesus Christ, what *do* you have?" she asked.

"At this particular station? We have half a dozen uniforms, one dog, and four patrol cars between us. We looked for your friend, and we couldn't find him. I'm sorry, but I don't know what else to tell you."

"That's it? That's all you plan to do? You can't be serious," Melissa marveled.

"You can file a missing person report if you want, but I wouldn't recommend it just yet. Your friend hasn't even been gone for a day, and the fact is, we have every reason to believe he's still on the island somewhere."

"Did you try—" Melissa began.

But he was ahead of her. "The Coast Guard's been alerted, and they're keeping an eye out, in case we're wrong about the whole 'washing out to sea' thing."

Melissa was just about to stand up, declare the whole thing a waste of time, and bitchily thank the deputy for his feeble-ass efforts when Leo asked a better question. "What about the house on the beach?"

Svenson frowned. "What about it?"

"Do you know where it came from? What are you going to do about it?"

Now the deputy shrugged. "No, I don't know where it came from, and it's on private property. That part of the beach is owned by the Culpepper family. If they want it removed, they'll have to do it themselves."

"But there *isn't* any other Culpepper family," Melissa insisted. "Until Simon turns up, I don't even know who's going to claim Mrs. Culpepper's body. Who will inherit the house? Or the money?"

Another shrug. "The estate is a private civil matter. But if you get any bright ideas, whether it's about the family or the house, feel free to come back and let us know."

After dispensing another round of handshakes, a business card with the deputy's email address on it, and a reminder to forward him Simon's message, Svenson disappeared back into the building's far depths.

On Leo's way out of the precinct, he slipped Deputy Tanaka his own business card and said, "If Simon should turn up, or if you think of anything else you can tell me about what happened, please give me a call."

Back at the car, Melissa said, "That deputy was an asshole, but your card trick was pretty slick. You think the desk officer will call you?"

"About Simon? No. It's obvious that the sheriff's office knows less about the Culpeppers than we do." Leo opened the passenger door and let himself inside. Once she'd settled in behind the wheel, he added, "About anything else? Who knows, but it never hurts to ask."

22

THURSDAY

MELISSA

The weather had almost cleared by the time they made it back to the island. Streaks of blue peeked through the southern sky, and the rain was back to its customary winter drizzle. "Could be worse," Melissa said, though the words still sounded like a complaint. "It could still be pouring, and at least it's not that cold. I can barely even see my breath."

"That's more about the humidity than the temperature," Leo mumbled. He had just finished answering a quick client email on his phone, and now he was setting an "out of office" message to head off future inquiries.

She glanced over at him and at the phone that was basically in his lap. "Why don't you just tell everyone, 'I've had a family emergency and will not be available until Monday'? The end. No further follow-ups."

"That's what I'm doing, but I have to do it carefully. Prospective home buyers are a pushy, needy bunch. I've already put off one couple, and I have two other people who expect another showing or two from me by Saturday."

"Call it a long weekend and forget about it. Don't you have any partners or coworkers who can pick up the slack?"

"Yeah, and they'll pick up the commission too."

"Sounds like a cutthroat business," she concluded. She drew the Subaru to a stop right at the split where the two main roadways went their different paths up the island. No one was behind her to be annoyed by it.

"What are you doing?"

"Deciding where to go next. We've searched the relevant parts of the island on foot, we've talked to the cops... Now unless you have any other ideas, I guess we need to check around the usual haunts. Should we start at Nordy's? I know it burned, but Mystery Bay is right there, and after that we could go to..." She stopped. He obviously wasn't paying attention to a word she was saying. "Leo? You still with me?"

He sat there a few seconds, staring out through the windshield while the car idled at the end of the bridge. "Yeah, I was just thinking. Nordy's is as good a place as any."

A glance at the rearview mirror told her that a couple of cars were coming up behind her. She put her foot on the gas and chose the western path to the north end of the island. When Leo neither protested nor approved, she said, "You're getting weird on me. Did you see something last night?" She asked as gently and quietly as she could. She hoped it didn't sound frightened, but it probably did. "Did you hear something?"

"Yeah, but you won't get it."

"Try me."

He sighed, like this was a useless retread of a topic that should've been left behind in their childhoods—but even so, he wasn't quite ready to let it go. "The...fine, call them the 'boys in the corners,' I don't care. I used to hear them crying, that's what I tried to tell you when we were little."

She remembered the boys in the corners. She never saw or heard them herself, but she resolved to take his concerns seriously. She could break an old habit. They were adults now, right? "Okay, last night you heard the boys crying in the corners again."

He shook his head. "That's the thing: they weren't crying. This time, they were screaming...just...*wailing*, when I got close."

"Jesus, dude," she said. "That's...awful. I didn't hear it, but if you say it happened—"

"It's fine. You don't believe me, but I'm used to it."

"I'm *trying*."

Now he sighed. "I know, and I appreciate your effort. Hey, slow down. Nordy's is coming up."

She pulled off to the side of the road into the short row of parking spaces that once served the island's general store. The building was only a single story and it sprawled, having been added on to half a dozen times over the decades. It looked like exactly what it was: a burned-out, hundred-year-old shop that had once carried everything from tampons and soap to tourist tchotchkes and fishing gear. Now it was closed, with boarded windows and black streaks of smoke muddying the sign on the roof. Someone had parked a trailer with a beat-up boat in one of the parking spaces, next to a heating oil truck and a rusty Vespa.

At first, no one spoke. Then Melissa said, "Well, goddamn. That's a shame."

"It's the end of an era. Simon told me everyone was looking forward to the hundred-year anniversary of the place. People were planning parties and..." Leo ran out of steam. "It would have been great."

"God, we must've ridden our bikes down here a thousand times."

"At least."

She set the parking brake and climbed out of the car, pulling up her hood to keep the mist off her hair. She stepped around to the front and squeezed between the oil truck and the scooter, then stepped up to the door stoop to read the sign someone had posted there. It'd been set inside a plastic sleeve to keep it from warping in the persistent damp. "Looks like they don't know if they'll ever reopen."

"The owners are getting older, and it would cost a fortune to rebuild—but I still hope somebody swoops in and saves it. I mean, it was a tourist trap...but it still meant something. It meant a lot to the island." He stayed down in the parking lot. He'd probably read the sign before, having been here more recently than Melissa.

She turned to ask him, "Was everything inside destroyed?"

"As far as I know. It's a miracle they even saved the building."

"Fat lot of good that did, if it never reopens." She tried to see inside the one store window that wasn't boarded, but it was too smoked up and filthy. She smiled. "Remember when we used to bring bottles here for deposit? What did we get, like, a nickel each?"

"Something like that. If we had a full trash bag, it was usually enough for a couple of sodas. Last time I was there, I picked up this." He reached into a pocket and pulled out a cheap Zippo knockoff. It had "Marrowstone Island, Washington" written on the side.

"Ironic."

"Yeah. I don't even smoke anymore, I just thought it was cute that they were branching out with their tourist merch, and I wanted to be supportive." Leo stared across the street at the water and a few rickety boats that were tied there. The pier looked like it must've been older than Nordy's, and probably a strong wind would knock it down—but it'd survived the storm two nights ago, hadn't it? Sometimes looks could be deceiving. "Man, the fishing guys and the camping tourists always left so much trash behind."

"*So* much trash." She lifted her sunglasses up and stuck them on her forehead, just under her raincoat hood.

The whole island was not a state park, but bits and pieces were run by the park service, or through Fort Flagler, or... Melissa wasn't perfectly clear on who exactly was in charge of which facilities. She suspected there was a lot of overlap.

But across the street from Nordy's there was a quiet open spot on the ominously named Mystery Bay. There, the park service had set up a small pavilion, bathroom facilities, and some maps—along with instructions for how to properly pay for your day pass, which was valid at all park locations, all over the island.

Leo led the way to the pavilion. He adjusted his big black raincoat, pulling up the hood and swiping at the mist on his glasses.

The small park area was made mostly of mud and gravel, with vegetation growing between the rocks and moss crawling all over the gazebo-like structures, the signs, and the plexiglass-covered bulletin boards with their bus-stop-style tiny roofs. The water beyond it shimmered in the rain, flat and sprawling between tree-covered outcroppings and the heavily forested coast of Indian Island next door. The sky was the same dull silver from horizon to horizon now, no friendly hints of blue in any direction. Fog hung low over the scene in wandering patches, swirling and diffusing around the docks, the piers, the boulders, and the boats.

"Pretty," she said, without sounding entirely serious.

"It's prettier in the summer." He nudged her with his elbow. "I see a couple of tourists over there. They won't know shit about shit, but *that* guy on the pier, he's a local. I think he works at the winery."

"Do you know his name?"

"Can't remember it," he admitted.

"Oh well, let's try him. The worst he can do is tell us to get lost."

The local guy wore a navy-blue raincoat and matching hat with a neck guard to keep water from running down his back. He was older, like many of the residents—with a salty beard and a pair of black Hunters that went up to his knees. He was tossing equipment into a small rowboat that might've been vintage or might have merely been old.

"Excuse me," Melissa began.

Leo swooped to her side. "Excuse *us*."

The guy looked up, looked confused, then looked idly happy to see them. "Hello, wait—I know you." He flipped his index finger toward Leo. "You're the Alvarez boy, isn't that right?"

"Technically I'm the Torres man, but yes," Leo said with a friendly grin. "My aunt and uncle still have that place over on the east side. I'm Leo, and this is Melissa Toft. You might recognize her too, but it's been awhile."

"Looks vaguely familiar, but I apologize for my foggy old brain—and it's nice to meet you now. I'm Ed Nelson. What can I do for you?" He sat up straight on the stumpy bollard he was using for a stool.

"We're looking for Simon Culpepper," Melissa told him. "We were wondering if you'd seen him recently."

"Simon? No, not in a few days. Last I saw him was...Sunday, maybe. Yeah, it was Sunday. He was driving his grandmother to church; I passed them on the way off the island. Is he all right? How's his grandmother doing?"

They exchanged glances that were loaded with uncertainty, but Leo took the lead. "I'm sorry to report that Mrs. Culpepper died the other night. The night of the big storm," he clarified.

"Holy smokes, you don't say! I'm sorry to hear it, I don't mind telling you, but she must've been a hundred years old—may she rest in peace. How's Simon holding up?" he asked. Then he shook his head. "I'm sorry, you said you were looking for him."

Melissa said, "We know he was with her the night she died, because he called for help—but we haven't heard from him since. We talked to the Jefferson County guys already and they don't know where he is either. There's no sign of a struggle out at the house, but it's like he vanished into thin air. We're afraid something might have happened to him."

"Speaking of houses." Leo leaned in, a touch of conspiracy in his voice when he asked, "Not the Culpepper house, but the *other* one. The one on the beach. I don't suppose you know anything about that, do you?"

The absolutely blank look on Ed's face was either a masterful acting job or true confusion. "Son, I do not know what you're talking about. We've got a lot of houses around here that overlook the beach; you'll have to be more specific."

Melissa crossed her arms and settled down deeper into her raincoat. It might've been her imagination, that the day was going colder and just a hair windier. "The night Mrs. Culpepper died, the night of the storm, you know—"

"It *was* one hell of a storm, I tell you what."

"No kidding," Leo took over. "It washed a whole house onto shore, over on the east side." He cocked a thumb toward the stretch of beach in question.

"You've *got* to be shitting me."

Leo shook his head. "Can't figure out where it came from, can't figure out what it's doing there."

"What's it look like?" Ed asked.

Melissa and Leo hemmed and hawed, trying to think of an accurate description. Why hadn't they taken any pictures? Leo had his phone in a bag and everything, so she felt silly for the oversight now—and a glance at Leo said that he was thinking the same thing. It'd just been so shocking, so unexpected, and so...something else. Sinister, perhaps. The house resisted scrutiny in a way she couldn't explain, to herself or anyone else.

It was almost like there was a fog around the structure,

preventing it from being observed too closely or seen too clearly—even in their own memories.

But since someone had to answer Ed, she took the first swing. "It's two stories, and some kind of solid construction, maybe poured concrete? It's stuck in the sand at the edge of the high-water line, so the first level is half flooded when the tide comes in."

"Huh."

Leo pushed for a little more detail. "I don't suppose there's any chance you know where it might have come from? Any stories of houses washing out to sea, either here or around the Sound?"

Ed was quiet. Then he nodded slowly. "I've been on the island since 1964. That's the year my wife and I moved out here, God rest her soul. Back then, yeah. I heard stories."

Melissa and Leo looked at each other, both sets of eyebrows raised. "Stories?" she prompted.

"Supposedly there used to be a *different* house over there, near the Culpepper's place. And then one day..." He turned up his hands in a gesture of apology. "There wasn't. I don't know why, I don't know how, and I don't know why more folks didn't gossip about it. Hell," he said, scratching the back of his neck, and then returning his hand to his lap. "If you'd asked me about some random old house a week ago, I'd have told you to talk to Mrs. Culpepper, since she is—or she *was*—the oldest person on the island. I'm real sorry to hear about her passing, though. I know I said that already, but I mean it. And I'll keep an eye out for Simon. I'll pass the word around, and maybe we can scare up a search party or something."

He wished them luck and they thanked him for his time. Then they piled back into the car and left, and as she drove, Melissa kept picking at that spot in her brain that said something was even stranger about the house than they suspected. There'd been another house on the same spot that vanished one day, and no one talked about that one either? Was it the same house? The same...fog that kept it from sticking in people's heads?

She gave Leo a side glance and asked, "It's bizarre, right? The way the house is so...slippery. Just slides right out of your mind, the moment you're not looking at it."

He was staring out the window, and he nodded, but didn't look at her when he replied. "Yeah. It sure as hell *is*."

23

2018

MELISSA

Melissa and Simon sat on a bench, facing a famous round sculpture in Volunteer Park. Gray, enormous, and shaped like a donut, it framed the Space Needle. They had large to-go cups of coffee from someplace that looked local but was a Starbucks in disguise. Everyone knew, but what could you do?

She'd asked him to meet her at her end of town. She'd just gotten an apartment up on Capitol Hill, and when she told people that, they often got excited. *What a nice part of town, sure. What a lovely area, of course. Rather pricey, isn't it?* Yes, but less pricey if you settled for the last crappy building before the really nice houses started on the next block over.

It'd been built in the sixties, as a hotel to serve the World's Fair. It was yellow and angular and drafty, with windows that were always wet with condensation.

But Volunteer Park was three blocks away, and it was lovely.

Simon said, "Your apartment is great. I don't know why you're so embarrassed by it."

"Because it's not great at all, you're just being kind. It's passing fair at best. Did you see that parquet?"

"Yes. It's vintage."

"It's literally eaten up with black mold and rotting away beneath every window. It's awful." She sucked down a little mocha. The steam was nice on her face.

"It's fine. If you hate it that much, you can always save up some money and find something better."

She rolled her eyes. "Spoken like someone who's never had to navigate the Seattle residential market with a tight budget."

"You should talk to Leo. You know he's a Realtor now, right?"

"I remember he was talking about it. He passed the exam or whatever?"

He nodded. "With flying colors. Last year."

That "last year" part felt a little damning, but she shook it off. "I hope it sticks. He's bounced around a lot since college."

"Said the pot to the kettle," Simon observed with a discreet sip of coffee, which allowed him to raise an eyebrow over the cup.

She pretended to be aghast. "Sir! I finished my associates degree, and I've been working in my field ever since!"

"Across *how* many companies now? Since college? Don't lie."

She had to think about it. "Only six, Jesus. I don't actually job-hop that often, and I really like this place. I think it might stick. They don't treat me like a child, they appreciate my expertise, and they don't watch over my shoulder every waking moment. I might have actually found my employment unicorn."

"In that case, I am very happy for you."

They sat in silence for a few seconds. Then Simon asked suddenly, "Have you ever heard the word *alaytha*?"

"What? No, I don't think so. What does it mean? Spell it for me."

"I thought it might be a name or something, but it's an old Norse word for like, a calamity or an accident. Such a weird word."

She asked, "Where'd you hear it?"

"Grandmother," he said with a sigh.

"Oh no. She's still wandering and ranting?"

"A few nights ago I found her in the basement. She was staring at the shelves, and she had her hands up, like..." He held up his own and started moving them in circles. "Almost like she was conducting an orchestra. When I came up to her, trying to stay calm—in case she was sleepwalking, or whatever—she seemed...oddly clear."

"How so?"

He frowned thoughtfully, as if he were trying to remember. "She told me that some people, when they're hungry, they eat and get full. Some people, they eat and want more. They won't be satisfied until they've eaten the whole world."

"That's grim, dude."

"She's getting grimmer and grimmer. I tried to put her back in bed but she wasn't having it. She kept saying, 'He'll start with the house, and then he'll take the island.'"

"He *who*?" Melissa asked. "Who's this 'he' she's talking about?"

Simon let his head fall back, so he was gazing up at the cloudy gray sky. "I wish I knew. Whoever he is, she's looking for him. Waiting for him? I don't know. But I can tell you this much: she's scared to death of him."

"Do you think he really exists at all? Anywhere except in her head?"

He shrugged. "It could be anyone she's ever known, at any time. Or anyone she read about, or anyone she saw on TV. There's literally no telling."

"How old is she now?"

"She turned ninety last year."

Melissa whistled, low and impressed. "That we all should be so lucky."

He didn't answer at first. He made a show of drinking more coffee, but it looked like stalling for time. "I don't know how lucky it is—her body living so long, leaving her mind behind."

Diplomatically, she said, "She's lucky she has you."

Now he nodded. "That's true. She has me."

24

THURSDAY

MELISSA

Melissa pulled her sunglasses off her face and wiped them on her right boob.

"Why are you even wearing those?" Leo asked. "You couldn't see the sun if your life depended on it—there's too much cloud cover."

"I don't like the mist, and besides, I have very sensitive eyes. These help with the glare. Now where to next? I say we go up to Flagler and ask around. I don't know how much of the park is open, this time of year, but if he went to the lighthouse or the old base, someone might have seen him."

"Flagler? Why would he go there?"

"I don't know, but do you have any better ideas?"

"Yeah," he said, then continued as if he was mostly winging the rest. "We should brainstorm, pool our knowledge, figure out what he might've done—where he might've gone. We probably know him better than anyone else in the world, so we probably have the best chance of finding him if we just, if we examine what we already know and, and draw some logical conclusions…"

"Pool our knowledge? Know him better than anyone? We didn't even know he'd taken up fragrances and bowling, man. He has a life out here, or a life somewhere nearby. He built one for himself in this utter fucking wasteland, which is frankly impressive, if you ask me."

"It's not a wasteland, it's just rural. Don't be a snob." He sat back in the seat and adjusted the belt. "And we *do* know him best. No, he doesn't tell us every stupid little thing he did all day, and we never tell him our stupid little things either."

"I tell him mine. He tells me most of his."

"Oh yeah?"

"Yeah," she confirmed stubbornly. "I told him about every dipshit I dated, and we laughed about how hard it is to meet people online. I told him about the kidney infection I had last year, and the weird old man who looks like a fisherman on the bus, that guy I see almost every damn day. He knew when I switched shampoo because it turned out I was allergic to some ingredient in it. He—"

"That's all shit about *you*. He knows *you* better than anybody, maybe. Not the other way around."

"I know him very well, thank you very much."

"What's his favorite movie?" Leo demanded.

"*The Godfather Part II*. And he hated avocados until he tried some really good guac at some function he had to attend in Texas. But he doesn't like spicy food."

"He likes those hot Cheetos. He ate them with plastic gloves, like a pretty-pretty princess."

She rolled her eyes. "Fine, he has a taste for spicy junk food. He loves westerns—"

"He loved westerns a few years ago, when he found his grandfather's VHS stash. Once he finished those, he never watched any others, except maybe *Unforgiven*. I think he liked that one."

"Jesus, Leo. It's not a competition."

"You make everything a competition, and I don't think you even mean to."

"I do not!" she protested. "You're just being an asshole."

"And you're just saying that because I know him better than you do, and you know it."

She groaned dramatically. "Would you just let it go? Please? I don't want to fight with you. We both know him really well, okay? You win. When it comes to Simon, we're totally friend equals. A veritable encyclopedia of all things Simon, that's us."

"Now *you're* the one being an asshole."

"Oh, so you admit you *were* being one before?"

"You're putting words in my mouth."

"I'm just listening to what you're saying. If you don't like that, maybe just shut up until we hit Flagler, okay?"

"Fine."

"Fine," she agreed, or concluded, or gave up. "We'll never get anywhere if we can't get along."

"You're the one still talking."

"Fuck me," she murmured, and she directed all of her irritation and attention to the road in front of them.

A couple miles later, they came to another split—one way had a park service kiosk, and the other went straight up to the northern point to the old military base, or what remained of it.

Around the final bend, she slowed the car precipitously because she remembered all the damn deer that were bound to await her, just in case some things never changed. Sure enough, a herd of about thirty lounged in the grass on either side of the road, and in the middle of the road, and at the edge of the trees, and beside the first row of buildings. If any of them cared about the car coming through, none of them showed it. Even the half grown fawns ignored the slow-rolling vehicle as it curved up toward the heart of the former fort.

The remaining buildings almost looked like an aborted effort at a Wild West town.

They faced one another across a street that was less than a city block long; their architecture all shared the bland uniformity of military style, for everything was built to be practical, not pretty. All was brown, and all the signs that identified them bore the same font and style. No decoration. No frills. No flair. Just boxy, pragmatic places without much to distinguish them from one another.

On the left they passed the park headquarters—which did not appear to be open. To the right, there was a museum that looked more like a post office than Nordy's general store ever did. Beyond lay a smattering of dull buildings; the old barracks, hospital, mess hall, and others had all been renovated for vacation rentals.

Melissa said, "I see some RVs and a couple of SUVs, so it looks like they've rented out some space, but...these are all tourist folks. I don't see anybody who—"

"Park here."

"What?"

Leo pointed at a spot beside the museum entrance, where a small gazebo hosted a series of historic maps and infographics. "Park. Here. I know those people are all tourists, but I want to ask at the museum. If Mrs. Hansen is working today, she might know something."

"Oh hey, fair point. She's still around?"

"Yeah. Sometimes she works the counter during the off-season." As soon as Melissa had cut the engine, he was out of the car and heading for the front door.

Melissa hustled to catch up to him. "Jeez, what's the rush?"

He didn't answer, but he held the door for her. He came inside behind her and moseyed up to the front counter. No one was there, but a little sign with a clock on it said, "We will be right back!" and the clock hands indicated that whoever "we" was, they'd return in ten minutes.

Leo swore under his breath and turned away to wander the shelves.

Melissa followed him. There was no one else in the small museum, and it somehow felt both too crowded and too empty all at once. "Wasn't Mrs. Hansen the one who kept horses?"

"That's her. She still has a couple of her own, and she boards a few others. Her nephew runs the stables." He wasn't really paying attention to Melissa's questions. He was running his hands along the cabinets, tickling the glass displays with his fingertips and scanning the scene for something in particular—she could tell.

"Leo, what are you looking for?"

He shrugged softly, tilting his head to the side to read the sign on an exhibit of vintage glass. "I haven't been in here in ages, but the shop used to keep old files, old newspapers, things like that."

She sighed, perhaps more dramatically than was necessary. "We aren't here to look for Simon, are we? You're only interested in the housewreck."

"Don't be gauche, of *course* I want to find Simon—and I'll ask about him as soon as the cashier returns. But learning about houses is...kind of my business." He turned away from the cabinets to face her. "I've been thinking about it a lot, and I don't think Simon was exaggerating in his email—when he said something on the beach killed his grandmother. She obviously saw the housewreck, and it obviously scared her to death. If Mr. Nelson was right, and that house washed away prior to 1964...then it might not have been the pure novelty of seeing a house wash up on shore that shocked her; it might have been *recognition*. If there used to be another house over there, she might have known about it or remembered it; and if something like that really *did* happen, we might learn more about it here, in the local history museum."

"Okay, you've got me there. Where do you think they keep the old newspaper articles? Is there, like, microfilm? Micro... fiche? I can't possibly be the only person alive who remembers microfiche."

"I also remember it," he said with a faint grin. "But the archives here are mostly just a bunch of folders with newspaper clippings and things like that, broken down by category. We'll need permission to go looking through it."

He stopped in front of a framed picture of Fort Flagler's early officers and staff, squinting to read the names that had been handwritten across the figures. It reminded Melissa of a high school yearbook, and maybe that wasn't a coincidence.

Behind them, someone spoke. "Permission for what?"

Melissa and Leo both whipped around guiltily, as if they'd been caught doing something naughty. Melissa blurted, "To see the microfiche!"

"I told you, they don't have any," Leo said to her. Then he walked back toward the counter and flashed a little wave. "Hello, Mrs. Hansen, how are you today?"

"Leonard!" she declared happily. Mrs. Hansen was a small round white woman who bore a pleasant and passing resemblance to Mrs. Claus. She darted around the counter and squeezed him in a bear hug, even though she barely came up to his shoulders. "Oh, it's so nice to see you, especially at this dreary time of year. I hope your aunt and uncle are doing well?"

"Yes, ma'am, they are taking a cruise and having a wonderful time. This month is their fiftieth anniversary. I thought they deserved a treat."

She gave him a knowing, delighted smile, and then a soft whap on the chest. "Listen to you and your big gifts. Heavens, *look* at you! This is...a lot of black you're wearing, if I'm honest, but you do look wonderful. You grew up so nicely."

He blushed, and Melissa almost joined him. She recognized Mrs. Hansen, but she wasn't sure that the woman would remember her—until she took a step back from Leo and looked Melissa up and down. "Now, I know you too, don't I? You're one of Leonard's friends, from the summers."

"I'm Melissa Toft. My grandparents used to live on the island, but they've been gone for years and I haven't been around as much as Leo. You're right, though; we used to play together as kids. Me and Leo, and Simon Culpepper."

Mrs. Hansen snapped her fingers. "That's right, yes. The Culpepper boy, poor fellow. I remember when his parents died, such a pity. And such a strange accident, I remember. The ferry, in the storm? Oh, it was just terrible. I was so glad he finally had some other children to play with when you two came along. This island can be a lonely place for little ones."

Melissa had a bad feeling that if Mrs. Hansen had seen Simon lately, she would've mentioned it by now. But just in case, she asked, "I don't suppose there's any chance you've seen Simon... recently? Or that you've heard about his grandmother?"

"His grandmother?" she asked. "What happened?"

Leo was kind enough to take the bad news off Melissa's hands. "Mrs. Culpepper died early yesterday morning. Simon was there with her when she passed and he called us right after it happened, but when we arrived..." He shrugged. "He was gone."

The older woman put her hand over her mouth. After a few seconds, she put it down again and said, "Oh, that's *terrible*. I had no idea! I heard sirens the other night, yes—maybe half an hour after the power went out."

"Simon called 911, and the Jefferson County people came out to handle the situation," Melissa added. "But we've been looking for him since yesterday and we're very worried. We don't know if he left the island or if he got lost in the woods."

"I understand, yes, yes. Poor Simon," Mrs. Hansen said with a distracted note that said her mind was wandering. "When someone has been around as long as Mrs. Culpepper, you start to think they'll be here forever. It's almost unimaginable that she's dead." She shook her head and took a deep breath. "But no, I'm so sorry. I haven't seen Simon in the last week or two. I'll start mentioning it to the tourists who pass through and make sure all the campers know he's out there. They can help keep a lookout around the inlet for a tall skinny ginger who might be dazed or lost. I wish I could do more to help."

"Actually," said Leo, "there's a chance you can help us with something that...might be related; we're not sure yet. Do you still have those local archives? I remember there was a room with some filing cabinets and a small card catalog." To Melissa, he said, "I did a summer school project, between eighth and ninth grade. It was about the history of fishing and hunting on Marrowstone, and I got almost all of my information right here."

Proudly, Mrs. Hansen said, "I remember that project and I'm glad we could help. After all, it's not as if we have a library. Let me take you into the back room. Hold on just a second; let me get my keys." She pressed a button on the register. The drawer popped open, and her keys were sitting on top of a couple of twenties.

Together, they wound back through the narrow aisles and cluttered shelves to a door that had a frosted glass window with the ghostly outline of old letters that once read, "Officers Only."

Mrs. Hansen tapped the glass and said, "This was an administrative building when the fort was still in operation."

"Why do you keep the archives locked up?" Melissa asked her.

"Oh, we have the whole building locked down better than we used to, not just the archives. Out back, we keep maybe a couple dozen propane tanks for campers and RV folks—and every once in a while, those tanks were going missing at night, if you know what I mean. Then, a couple of years ago, some tourist kids—teenagers, really—smoked too much weed, drank too much beer, and thought it'd be funny to break in and make a mess. We never have much money on hand, except maybe in the middle of summer; but some of these museum items are old and fragile, and I *won't* stand to have them defaced."

"Fair enough," Leo declared as he followed her inside. "We really appreciate you letting us take a look."

"Do you mind if I ask what you're looking for? I might be able to help you find it more quickly."

"A house," he said quickly, like he thought Melissa might answer first and do so incorrectly. She tried not to let it annoy her. "One that might have disappeared from Marrowstone—or from someplace nearby—back in the 1950s. Give or take."

Her eyes widened. "A whole house? Disappeared? From Marrowstone?" She barely got the island's name out of her mouth when she caught herself. "Wait, I think I know what you're talking about. I found some clippings maybe a decade ago, when Port Hadlock's little newspaper closed. They offered me their stash of island-related archives, and I read something about it then." She turned around and made for the far wall.

Melissa elbowed Leo, and he elbowed her back.

They followed Mrs. Hansen back to a row of filing cabinets, lined up like the soldiers who once might've stood there at attention. She tried one cabinet, opened a drawer, then changed her mind. She did it a second time, didn't see what she wanted, and tried the bottom drawer of the fourth cabinet. Her fingers tripped across the folders, chose one, and pulled it out with a flourish.

"It'll be somewhere in here, I think. I want to say the year you're looking for is right around 1950, and this is everything Marrowstone related from the newspaper between 1948 and 1953. If I'm wrong, just grab the folders on either side, because I know it's in there someplace. I remember it now, yes." She put one finger on her bottom lip and tapped it thoughtfully. "It was such a peculiar tidbit, and I wanted to know more about what happened...but I only saw a couple of short pieces about it. That was the strangest thing of all. It should've been a huge story, out here where not much ever happens. But somehow, I don't know. After a while, I suppose it just slipped everyone's mind."

On a nearby desk, she dropped the folder and opened it up—revealing a stack of newspaper clippings, bundled together. "It's funny how that happens sometimes. Isn't it?"

Melissa didn't think it was funny. She thought it was suspicious.

25

THURSDAY

MELISSA

The museum door chime was only a couple of jingle bells on a ribbon, but they could be heard all the way at the back of the building where the archives were kept, and where Melissa and Leo stared down at the folder. Mrs. Hansen said, "I'd better go see to that! You two enjoy yourselves." And she exited the room, leaving them alone.

A rickety office chair rested against the wall. Leo pulled it forward and offered it to Melissa, who said, "Don't mind if I do."

A metal folding chair was a lateral move; he chose one from a small stack, popped it open, and pulled up beside her. "All right, what have we got?"

"Stuff about the park service, stuff about the fort. A couple of things about the ammunition batteries, before they cleaned them up and opened them to tourists. Looks like there was some federal grant money…" She flipped through page after page. "And a kid who went missing. I wonder if they ever found him."

Leo took half the stack and started flipping too. "And in this pile we have...a few things about decommissioning more buildings here at the fort. A piece or two about the winery. Another story about the lost kid."

"I think that's a different kid. Wait a minute, look." Melissa pulled out a single yellowed paper fragment. A grainy photo at the top showed a large midcentury house. It had two stories and a sloped roof with two chimneys poking through it.

Leo adjusted his glasses. "Holy shit, I think that's it. *That's* the house on the beach."

He held one side of the scrap between two fingers, and Melissa held the other. They read at the same quick pace.

Lorentzen Home Complete in Time for Wedding

Despite construction and weather delays, Gunnar Lorentzen's beautiful and unique house is finally completed on Marrowstone Island—just in time to serve as the backdrop for his pending oceanside nuptials to Alcesta Ellingboe, daughter of Phillip and Caroline, sister of Otelia. The house, which has been christened "Tidebury" by its architect, Mr. Lorentzen himself, is almost 3,500 square feet, making it the largest private dwelling on the island. It boasts all the most modern features, with state-of-the-art heating and appliances.

Tidebury House is located on the east side of the island, facing the sunrise at the edge of the beach. Nestled just within the tree line, it enjoys an exquisite view of Puget

Sound and the shipping lanes. Mr. Lorentzen has declined to confess how much it cost to build, but for such a unique and outstanding property, can any price be too high?

“Tidebury House,” Melissa said quietly.

“Otelia? What kind of name is that?”

“Or Alcesta, for that matter. No idea.” Then she took the article from Leo and turned it over. “When was this? Okay, here’s the date: April 19, 1950. Mrs. Hansen was spot-on.”

Leo reached for it, wiggling his fingers. She gave it back. He reread it, double-checked the date, and pushed his glasses up onto his forehead. He brought the clipping up close, within a few inches of his eyes. “Thirty-five hundred square feet is a big-ass mid-century modern. An early one too—the design isn’t Craftsman inspired at all, or anything like that. It’s all modern, all the way. Daylight basement.” He pointed out a low long window near the ground. “Told you so. Right now it looks like it’s missing a chunk of its…” He made a face like he was doing math. “Northern side in this picture? Yeah, the north side. The house on the beach is maybe two thousand square feet in its present state, and most of that is probably not accessible, given the condition of the floors and ceilings and…and the roof, and everything else.”

He handed it back and she took it in for a closer look.

“The way it’s flipped around now, facing the island, not the water…it’s like someone drove it back onshore to look for its old lot,” she said with half a laugh. But the more she thought about it, the less funny it was. “Leo, this is creepy as shit. I wonder where it was built in the first place? This doesn’t say anything about the address, just that it's on the east side. More than half the houses on the island are on the east side; that's not helpful."

"No, it's not." He reached back into his pile of clippings.

Melissa took her phone out of her bag and snapped a picture of the scrap in her hand.

"Good idea," he said. "I should've thought of that."

"You work in houses; I work in images. Let's each play to our strengths, eh?"

"Teamwork!" Leo declared. Smiling, he kept scanning. Ten minutes later, he said, "Here we go. 1953." He slapped the article down on the desk between them.

Storm Wreaks Havoc on Marrowstone

Four Dead, Two Missing after Night of Devastation

Marrowstone Island remains without power twenty-four hours after a terrible storm surge pushed onto shore. Trees are down by the dozens, debris of every shape and size litters the beach, and both main roads remain blocked to traffic. Power and cleaning crews have been deployed to the area, but the causeway is presently washed out. Merely reaching the island is proving difficult. The military is likely to intervene, given that Fort Flagler has reportedly sustained significant damage as well.

At least four people are confirmed dead: a fisherman who was found drowned on shore, two people in a houseboat that broke its moorings, and a man who died when a tree fell on his house. None of these victims has yet been identified. Two others have been reported missing, though their names are also unknown at this time.

Without waiting to see if Melissa had finished reading, he flipped through a few more stories and then said, "Here it is. Here's the money shot—or the journalistic equivalent, thereof. Three days later," he noted, and he handed it over.

Missing Victims of Storm Identified

Mr. and Mrs. Gunnar Lorentzen Washed Out to Sea with Their House

The largest modern home on Marrowstone Island was utterly destroyed in last week's storm, and its residents appear to have been inside. Authorities on Marrowstone have confirmed that Tidebury House, as it was locally known, is no longer standing—and indeed no longer exists on the island at all. The lot where it was built has been scoured by the ocean, leaving nothing behind but a basement and some of its contents. No sign of the young couple has been found, and both are presumed dead at this time, but Jefferson County officers and soldiers from Fort Flagler have joined the search to recover their bodies.

Melissa frowned down at the small document fragment. "That's it? That's the whole story?"

"That's all they printed. There's a byline at the bottom, and no indication that it carried over to another page. Mrs. Hansen *did* say details were thin on the ground."

"She wasn't kidding." Melissa kept flipping through her stack, eyes peeled for anything else about the house or its occupants. "You'd think something like that would be front page news for weeks. Remember when that old shipping container washed up?"

"It was barely half a shipping container, and there was nothing inside. It was still the hottest news all summer. If it happened today, it'd be the hottest Instagram spot for miles. I'm just surprised the house isn't already swarmed by people. Nobody seems to know about it but us."

"And the people we tell."

He nodded and said, "Sure, but we've told one old guy who was trying to do some fishing, and Mrs. Hansen. Don't get me wrong, Mrs. Hansen is basically the town crier, but she's only known about the situation for half an hour. It's not like we took out an ad online or wrote it up for *The Stranger*."

"I don't know about you, but I'm getting a real weird feeling that we're not supposed to see the house, or remember the house. I don't think anybody is. Does that sound nuts?"

"Yes. It sounds nuts. Which doesn't mean you're wrong." Then he stopped skimming the piece as he spoke. "Whoa."

"Whoa?" She set her clips aside.

"Whoa." This time he simply read aloud. "'One week after the storm that washed her house into Puget Sound, Alcesta Lorentzen was found wandering the shoreline. She was dazed and injured, and according to police, she has not spoken a word since she was spotted by lighthouse workers. She has been transferred to Jefferson Healthcare in Port Townsend for evaluation. No other word on her condition is available at this time.' That's it. That's the whole update, except this time there's a picture." He handed it to Melissa, who eyed it curiously.

"One of her wedding photos, or so the dress would suggest. She was pretty. The poor woman, I wonder what happened to her."

"Unless she stayed as hale and hardy as Mrs. Culpepper, she's almost certainly dead by now." He was nearly at the end of his newspaper clippings; he fanned out the remaining few like a hand of cards, then tucked them all back into a pile again, disappointed. "That's all I've got. Is there anything else about her in your pile?"

"I don't think so." Melissa held up her phone again and took a picture of the grainy black-and-white photo. When she'd finished, she thumbed through the rest of the folder's contents. "Nope. Nothing else over here. If there were any further updates on her condition, they happened after 1953."

He eyed the filing cabinets like he was weighing the possibilities of going through every damn one of them. "We can always come back," he concluded. "Mrs. Hansen will let us look again later, and we only have a few more hours of daylight. Let's make the rounds while we still can."

"You're right. Let's get back out there. All we can do is keep looking."

Once they'd put everything back where it belonged, they said their goodbyes to Mrs. Hansen and got back into the car. They drove out past Flagler to the RV camping spot at the point, where they found mostly tourists, though Melissa and Leo were desperate enough to start asking them about Simon too.

They each picked a favorite photo of their missing friend and queued it up in their phones. Then they chose a section of the RV lot and went around to all the people who were out and about—building campfires, hooking up propane tanks, and smoking weed in folding Adirondack chairs.

But no one had seen him.

They tried the same tactic over by the artillery battery on the way back to the Culpepper place, where three SUVs and a truck towing a small camper were parked across the road. No dice there either. Everyone they found was just passing through.

At the lighthouse, there were many "NO TRESPASSING" signs but also a couple of scientists in protective gear who were willing to look at Melissa's phone and sadly shake their heads. No, they hadn't seen Simon.

It was the same story at the winery, where Mr. Carson and his daughter greeted Leo as warmly as Mrs. Hansen had, with a similar level of polite confusion mixed with welcome directed at Melissa. No one had seen or heard from Simon since a week or two before. Everyone was so very sad to hear about his grandmother. What do they mean, there's a house washed up on the beach?

"We're getting nowhere," Melissa complained as she put the car back into gear.

Leo was quiet for a few seconds, looking out the window. "He could've washed out to sea in the storm."

"No. No," she said again with a shake of her head. "You heard the deputy, the tide wasn't anywhere close to where they found Mrs. Culpepper. Wherever Simon went, it wasn't toward the water. Not in that weather."

"He was in shock. It was dark. A rogue wave could've surprised him, knocked him down. Dragged him into the surf."

"Stop it. Stop saying that. Simon *didn't* drown. He *didn't* get kidnapped by a rogue wave."

Leo didn't argue. Maybe he didn't want to believe it either. Maybe he didn't want to waste his time. Finally, he asked, "Then what do we do now? Go door-to-door? We've hit every logical spot on the island."

"Now...now we leave the island, but only temporarily. We haven't eaten in hours."

"Oh yeah." He checked his watch. "It'll be dark soon, anyway. All right, let's get some food, then go back to the Culpepper place and see if Simon magically showed up while we were gone."

Glumly, they headed back to Port Hadlock.

26

THURSDAY

LEO

Leo and Melissa picked up some questionable Chinese takeout from a gas station and drove back to the Culpepper place shortly after sunset. Between them, they tried to muster some optimism, still struggling to hope that Simon had simply walked away to clear his head after witnessing his grandmother's demise.

"He'll be there when we get back. He'll turn up covered in dirt and leaves, scratched up from head to toe," Leo proposed from the passenger seat, happy to distract himself from the thought of Simon washing out to sea. Leo had washed out to sea once. It was all too easy for him to imagine it. "And he'll have a great story about how he got turned around in the dark and the storm, and..."

They pulled up to the Culpepper house. It was dark and dead.

His heart sank.

Melissa grabbed one of the takeout bags and climbed out of the car. She kicked the door shut without a word.

They let themselves inside and turned on the lights.

Leo scanned the foyer for any sign that anyone else had come or gone since they'd left that morning. No such luck. He sat down in the living room's leather easy chair, glancing over at the corner to see if anything untoward lurked there. He neither saw nor sensed anything, so the boys were being quiet. Good.

Melissa said, "If Mrs. Culpepper was alive—"

"She'd never let me eat here, on this chair. I know. But she's no longer with us, and Simon never gave a damn. It's his house now." He used the chopsticks to scarf down a big bite, being careful to keep from splattering any sauce. It's not that he was *afraid* of the prim and proper ghost of Mrs. Culpepper...but the superstitious prospect of her presence kept him tidy.

Melissa swallowed half an egg roll in a single bite. "I wonder what they'll do with her body, if no one claims it."

He thought about it, chewing slowly. He swallowed and said, "She has a plot already paid for, over in Sound View. Maybe the county will put her there."

Sound View Cemetery was only a few lots away—a small, essentially private place that was only technically open to the public. Not everyone who died on the island was buried there, but it had become the default final destination for many residents.

Melissa said, "Maybe?" and went back to eating.

When they were finished, Melissa collected her pajamas and clean underwear and left them beside the bathroom sink, then shut the door and said she was taking a shower, but she'd be done in a few minutes.

Leo knew what that meant. *A few minutes* could mean closer to thirty, or as long as the hot water would hold out.

Mrs. Culpepper had been a fan of showers that could boil pasta, and she used to brag about having a water heater the size of a Volkswagen.

He wouldn't have told Melissa, but he was glad that she'd be occupied for a bit because he wanted a little alone time. More specifically, he wanted to go to Tidebury House without her.

He didn't want to answer her endless questions, or keep one eye out for her, or entertain her nervous nature. Jesus, she'd been downright cowardly on their first foray inside. Sure, it was dangerous and scary in there, but it wasn't exactly a...

A what? A haunted house?

He shook off the thought and steeled himself, then headed out to the garage. There, he retrieved the orange emergency flashlight. It flared to life when he pressed the button, casting a wide yellow light in the dim, cool space, which smelled like gasoline and mulch. "Perfect." He went back inside to get his raincoat off the rack, tucked his arms into the sleeves, and quietly left—shutting the door with the gentlest of all possible clicks.

The porch light was burning bright; it was the first thing they'd turned on when they got back to the house.

"Fuck it, we should go ahead and file a missing person's report, whether that deputy thinks it's too soon or not." Leo grumbled to himself as he walked the long pathway to the beach, his light bobbing in front of him. At least then, Simon's absence would be noted on some record somewhere. "I know the FBI gets involved in missing person cases sometimes. Maybe we can make that happen."

In the morning, Leo would do a little research and maybe make some phone calls.

For now, he paused by the big driftwood log that had been everything to everyone when they were kids: a couch, a fort, a pirate ship. Home base.

"Simon, where are you? What happened?" he asked the night.

The rain was back, a soft patter that was not as bad as the day before, but the temperature had dropped and it felt unfairly brutal all the same.

Leo tightened the strings on his hood to draw it tighter around his face. He pointed the light straight ahead, where it illuminated the side and corner of the beached building lodged at the high-tide line. It was very white in the beam's light, paler than the sand and brighter than the light itself. Surely it was only his imagination, but the thing seemed to glow.

"It's a trick of the darkness. Nothing unnatural about it," he told himself. No lightning, no thunder. Only a cold, wet wind that blasted off the water.

He approached the house, leading with the light. The porch was right there, broken into chunks, but climbable. It was even easier now than before, since Leo had pulled his sneakers out of the trunk of the Tesla. He held on to one of the squared columns with the rough rock overlay and hoisted himself up with one hand.

The light was too big to hold in his mouth. He had to juggle it between hands—and sometimes his front raincoat pocket—when he needed both arms.

He should've done this in the day. He should've just told Melissa to wait for him and stay put. He could've sent her on some silly errand; she was easily enough distracted, and she was prone to making her own busywork when she was stressed about something. It wouldn't have been hard to chase her out for an hour. Why had he been so impatient? Why?

This was an activity best suited to the light of day and he damn well knew it.

Regardless, he stepped over the front doorjamb, letting the light fill the interior. He stood still and listened. Rain chattered against what was left of the roof, and the wind gusted strangely through the broken windows. It made a wheezing noise, like soft, difficult breathing. It sounded like the house needed an inhaler.

Leo continued inside anyway. He let his Realtor brain churn. It provided exactly the level of distraction he needed to take the edge off his fear.

The tide was somewhere between in and out, far enough down the sand that the main level was mostly dry—except for the tide pools in the sunken spots on the floor. Was there any floor left, or was it all sand? The thick upended board that ran the length of the entry was likely a floor joist. The surface...it might've been early for parquet. Could've been tile, once upon a time. Could've been ordinary plank floors. White oak? That was still popular in the fifties, wasn't it?

He ran the light across the spaces he'd seen before, quickly and lightly, seeing nothing new. Pressing onward, deeper into the house, he reached the entrance to a dark hall. Now he pointed the light back there and watched the beam cut through it. He could see doors on either side, though he still could not see the far wall or anything beyond it.

He could not shake the feeling that someone else had been inside. Recently. On this trip through the house, he found even more signs.

In the first room on the left, a bedroom with a bed still inside. A nightstand with two of its three drawers missing. The ruins of a rug, soggy and blackened, pushed up into a pile against a wall.

The next room was a bathroom, its door split down the middle. The sink was stained with red streaks from spigot to drain, where the ocean had corrupted the enamel over steel.

"Wild," he whispered.

Something whispered back.

He started and stood up straight, whipping around and aiming his light back into the hall. It was the wind, surely. Nothing else whistled and gasped like that. Did it?

A loud crack sounded somewhere to his right, back toward the porch. "It's only settling," he said too loud, too fast. "Every old house makes noise." He crept back into the hall and checked the next two doors. The first revealed a hall closet that still held a row of coats, their hangers clinging to a bowed wooden rod. They were soaked and swollen together into one giant lump that was held in place by a thick crust of barnacles.

The last door didn't open. When he tried it, a low, gusting moan blew through the hall.

Leo looked around and saw nothing. He heard only the wind, because it *must* have been the wind. It only sounded like the house was breathing. Nothing of the sort was happening at all.

He retreated to the main entrance and looked out the window again. He aimed the light down at the wet sand, along the bottom of the wall as far back as he could. Unless he was wrong about the house's layout and general dimensions—and he was quite confident that he was not wrong—then the securely locked door at the end of the hall on the right led down to that daylight basement he'd noticed before.

Or it once did. Now it led to nowhere but a wet drift of sand, deposited by the tide as it'd come and gone.

The other side of the door was hard to see from Leo's angle, but he could detect the ghosts of dead bolts and chains running the length of the frame. "What did you keep in the basement, Mr. Lorentzen?" he asked very quietly.

Only the soft, rhythmic gasps of the wind replied.

Leo checked his watch. It'd only been ten minutes. Melissa would still be in the shower, singing something ridiculous from the late nineties, whether or not she thought anyone could hear. Her voice was okay at best, in Leo's opinion. She didn't care, and he liked that about her.

He turned his attention to the stairs. They leaned away from the wall at an angle. There was no rail. They were slick with seaweed both fresh and decayed, and they crawled with small crabs that scuttled away from the flashlight beam.

Leo took a deep breath. He took the first step.

It held. He gave his foot a wiggle. The stair didn't move.

Encouraged, he tried the next one, first clearing a spot in the coating of critters and slime with the side of his shoe. It felt more secure than he'd expected. Two more steps. He reached out to the wall to steady himself; each stair was invisible despite the light, for each one was buried in the same opaque muck.

By the time he reached the top, he had to stretch to reach the wall. The stairs had fallen out of position by a couple of feet, and the upstairs landing had sagged loose. With an undignified hop, he made it onto the second floor—and it had cost him nothing more than muddy shins and dirty palms.

He wiped his hands on his jeans. He didn't wear jeans often, but when he did, that's what they were for: wiping things on. If Melissa knew him as well as she thought, she would've noticed he was up to something as soon as she'd seen what he was wearing that morning. But Melissa wasn't always as observant as she fancied herself.

The second story was as crooked as everything else, but not quite as dark. Much of the roof was gone and though the sky was absolutely starless, the lighthouse to the north offered an ambient, sometimes sweeping glow. Leo could see that where the roof was present, it had partly fallen inward—but here and there, it was held aloft by the bowed, cracking walls.

"Flat, sloped roof," he remembered from the newspaper picture. "What else is up here?" he asked the empty night as he carefully wandered. The floor beneath him was as slick as the stairs. It'd once been covered with carpet; now it wore a combination of mud and ocean flora, and the slant of the floor was almost too much to let him walk upright. He hugged the wall, his feet slipping and sliding as he went. He passed another bathroom, or maybe a laundry room? Were those common in houses like these…or would laundry have gone on the first floor, or in the garage? "Probably the garage," he guessed. The words echoed back, bouncing off the slick, wet walls. "Like Mrs. Culpepper's place."

His real estate brain buzzed while his hands shook and his feet struggled for purchase. The light was wild in his hands. He dropped it. Picked it up again. Shook off a small angry crab.

Kept going.

The hallway terminated in a large room with half a roof and only three walls. It was the end of the upstairs—or the end of what Leo could reach without a ladder or a grappling hook. A quick swipe of the light revealed exposed studs, traces of peeling wallpaper, the skeletal remains of either a couch or a chaise… and some graffiti that was hard to read from where he stood.

"Somebody *has* been inside here," he said to himself. "I wondered when the locals would find it."

Deeper into the room he shuffled, over something that once might have been a piece of furniture. He found a stable-feeling spot and planted himself there.

One hand, held out for balance. One hand, shining his light on the wall.

I HAVE WHAT I NEED AND I'LL
TAKE WHAT I WANT

Leo recoiled, and the slight cringe was enough to send him sliding. He caught himself on the far wall and climbed to his feet again, aiming the light again, reading the message again. It didn't look like spray paint, and he couldn't figure out what else it might be, or even what color it was for certain. The letters were dark enough to look black, and the light bleached everything around them. They could've been dark red or dark blue.

Were they made of paint? Had they been there long?

The wind wheezed, too loud and too close. The sound came from behind him. In the hall. He turned around with the light and saw nothing, heard only the back-and-forth rush of air that wasn't really wind, was it? No, not wind.

Behind him again. In the room with three walls.

He spun around light first.

The light settled upon a boy. Seven or eight years old. White, with eyes that were too light, and lips that were too blue, and skin that was almost translucent. Light passed through him like a pane of glass.

Leo did not notice that he'd stopped breathing until he gasped so hard that he coughed. He stumbled backward and fell, scooting back into the hall on his ass.

The light was on the floor with his hand.

The light was up, and it was shining through the boy.

"Who—who—who—what? What is happening? Who are you?"

The boy's hair and clothes were dry. What a silly thing to notice, in such a frantic moment. His little body swelled and contracted, dragging air into his chest with tremendous effort and squeezing it out again. He looked at Leo with something between sorrow and fear and determination.

"Go," the child mouthed. Only the broken sound of his breathing came out.

Went in. Came out. Went in.

It was louder than thunder in Leo's ears, and he couldn't stand it. He couldn't stand. Wait. He didn't need to stand. He scuttled, backward and crab-like until he could pivot at the waist and crawl on all fours. Until he dropped off the landing onto the butter-slick stairs.

His tailbone banged against the next two steps as he rode

them down. He pulled himself to his feet but only for a moment. There was no friction, no grip, nothing firm to hold. He toppled off the side where a rail ought to be and down to the floor below.

Stunned but not especially harmed, he collected himself. Or he tried to.

One sneaker was gone. It must've come off when he fell, or he must've left it in the mud, his foot sucked free against its will. The wheezing was a buzz saw between his ears, but he was almost out, almost free, almost away from Tidebury House.

He flung himself over the broken front door, which still lay in the foyer, and almost rolled down the porch to the sand—where he scurried upright and ran back to the Culpepper place as fast as he could, as if it could save him.

27

THURSDAY

MELISSA

Taking a shower at Mrs. Culpepper's place had always been An Experience; Melissa had considered it the very height of indulgence as a kid, because Mrs. Culpepper never once fussed at her about using too much hot water. After a strange, stressful week, here was a chance to relax. Alone in a big beautiful house, except for Leo—and God knew he wouldn't barge in on her.

Alone without Simon, who could be anywhere.

And Mrs. Culpepper was dead.

The shower came on cool, and then warmed up fast—with enough water pressure to take the chrome off a bumper. As Mrs. Culpepper had gotten older, it probably hadn't been safe to leave the water heater turned up so high, but bless her and Simon forever for leaving it that way.

Melissa stripped down and stepped in, drawing the curtain shut. It was a ridiculous curtain, a maroon shade straight out of the late 1980s with more ruffles and tiebacks than the average flower girl's dress, and it smelled faintly of mildew like everything else that time of year.

She stood with her face in the stream, letting the full blast of the warmth and water strip off most of her makeup and leave her cheeks pink. It felt amazing.

It felt terrible.

Only for an instant, the tea-steeping water temperature shifted to "colder than a witch's tit in a brass bra." By the time Melissa had finished yelping and getting out of the way, it was already back to "hotter than a Phoenix tarmac." Relieved, she stepped back into the flow and lathered up.

Another flash of ice hit her like a slap.

She stumbled out of the stream and glared at the shower head, feeling like it simply could not be trusted, even though steam rapidly filled the room. Slowly she dipped one foot at a time back into the gloriously hot water, and since it held, she finished rinsing off. "Old pipes," she explained to herself.

A white flash filled the room as one of the bulbs over the vanity flared and burned out with a vivid pop. It startled her, but not as much as the frigid water that followed.

"Fuck!" she shouted, staggering out of the tub, nearly bringing down the shower curtain with her. She grabbed the nearest towel and wiped her face.

With a sigh of surrender, she reached back in to turn the water off. "I give up," she informed the hardware, but neither of the knobs moved. They were stuck as thoroughly as if they'd been welded into position, which was ridiculous. She's only spun them on a few minutes before.

Steam floated up into her face when she disturbed the curtain to get a better look. She coughed, rubbed her eyes, and used both hands to try to wrench the "hot" knob into the off position.

"This is insane. I don't... What the fuck, seriously. Mrs. Culpepper, are you mad at me for something?" Under her breath, she added to herself: "I'm talking to a dead woman. What the hell is wrong with me?"

A soft murmur fluttered through the room, chattering words she couldn't quite parse. Then as clear as day, she heard the phrase, *"Got your attention."*

Melissa took a step backward, slipped on the bathmat, and crashed into the remaining towels that hung on the rack. "Who said that? Leo?" No. She knew it wasn't Leo.

More soft, indistinguishable sounds that were words, weren't they? She just couldn't understand them, like they were spoken very quietly in another language. Then a few lined up, loud and strong enough to understand: *"If you know what's good for you."*

It was Mrs. Culpepper's voice. She'd know it anywhere.

"Where are you? Mrs. C? I'm sorry, I...I know you hate it when I call you that," she said to the blisteringly steamy room. "Mrs. Culpepper? Oh God, what the hell is happening?"

"Stay inside! Don't let him..."

"Don't let who what?" she asked desperately. "Leo? I shouldn't let Leo do what?"

"Not Leonard, you little fool."

Gasping, barely able to breathe, Melissa slid down to the floor, where the steam was not quite so thick. "Is it Simon? Do you know where he is? We can't find him," she confessed, and her eyes filled with tears. "I'm so sorry, we're trying so hard. We looked everywhere, and the police won't help at all, and I just..."

Very close this time, so close that if the woman were alive and standing in front of her, Melissa could have kissed her wrinkled cheek. Not whispered this time, but shouted: *"Simon is here, and he won't stop screaming!"*

Melissa pulled her hands over her mouth to keep herself from screaming too. She was thinking of Leo, and the boys who once cried in the corner but now they were screaming, and Simon was screaming, and did that mean he was dead? "Where?" she begged. "Where is he, just tell me!"

"...here..."

Melissa flailed on the floor, but the tile was slippery and the rug was small—she'd kicked it when she fell, and it was shoved up against the tub. The surface beneath her was as slick as ice. On her knees, she pulled down a towel and tried to kneel on it, to stand on it. To reach the doorknob, even though she couldn't see a damn thing. She could find a doorknob, couldn't she?

There it was.

She got a grip and lost it, and grabbed the knob again. It didn't turn. She used it to pull herself up and she wrapped the towel around her torso. Now she was standing, shaky and soaked and terrified. Now she could see the mirror; though it was nearly blank with steam, she could see a shape standing behind her.

She turned around and saw nothing.

The whispers came again, not quite hissed and not quite mumbled: *"...keep him out..."* Then she caught two syllables, a single name. *"Gunnar."*

"Gunnar? The guy who built…who built the other…the other house?" she repeated. "I saw his name in the, on the, there was…" Her head was throbbing and she couldn't breathe. The bathroom had never felt so small, or so tight. Why couldn't she open the door? What was wrong with…with everything? The shower, the knobs, the lock, the curtain. Static sparkled across her vision.

Finally, clear as day: *"He seeks Alaytha, and he will find it."*

The knob clicked. The door swung open, and steam billowed into the hallway; Melissa followed it, coughing and gasping.

Her brain raced in a thousand directions, but all those rampaging thoughts clattered against each other, arriving nowhere. The cooler air of the hall on her face, in her lungs, sharpened her. Her fever fell by degrees, and her sweat-covered skin prickled to gooseflesh.

Suddenly she was freezing.

She leaned on the wall to catch her breath and get her bearings. Her vision was clearing and now she was only cold; she wasn't dying. She wasn't trapped. "What do you mean, Mrs. Culpepper?" she asked the house in her too-loud outside voice. It was stupid, she assumed, to yell at ghosts. She wasn't an American tourist trying to make herself understood; she was standing in a dead woman's house, buck naked except for a towel and a sheen of sweat, and apparently there were dead boys screaming in the corners—and maybe Simon too.

No one replied, living or dead, and she heard no screaming anywhere.

Except. That wasn't true.

She *did* hear screaming, but it wasn't coming from inside

the house. It was happening outside, and getting closer by the second.

She scrambled down the hall.

Where was Leo? He was supposed to be there; she'd expected to find him snoring on the couch, one glass of brandy too many down the hatch while she was occupied in the bathroom. But if that were true, he would've heard her, wouldn't he? He would've come to help. Leo always tried to help, even when he probably shouldn't.

She reached the front door. She opened it.

The screaming came right for her, nails on a chalkboard in her ears.

Hollering all the way, Leo shoved past her into the foyer then turned around and yelled, "Shut the door!" and when she hesitated long enough to look outside, just for a peek, just wondering what was chasing him, he decided she was moving too slow. He flung himself at the door and slammed it for her.

With that loud and final crash, they were sealed together inside the Culpepper house.

Both of them panted like they'd run a marathon, and both of them dripped water where they stood. Melissa in her towel. Leo in his rain-soaked garb. Silence inside, except for the white-noise rush of water being wasted in the hall bathroom, because she hadn't turned off the taps. Silence on the other side of the door, except for the pattering rain.

"Leo?" she squeaked.

"Melissa?" he squeaked back, then coughed.

"Do you hear anything?"

He was doubled over, his hands atop his knees while he

gasped heavily, trying to catch his breath. Now he swiveled his head to look at her. "What?"

She ran a hand across her forehead, sweeping wet hair out of her eyes. "Do you hear anything? Anybody—" It was her turn to cough. "Anybody in the corners?"

"*Fuck* the corners," he said.

"I'm sorry?"

He shook his head. "They're full of, of cobwebs. Nothing that's really aware anymore. Dark little..." He hunted for a word. "Leftovers. The ghosts of ghosts."

"Don't say that." Melissa sniffled and her eyes were burning. "I think Simon is one of them."

"What?" he asked sharply. "No, he's not. Simon's not dead."

"But I think he *is*," she insisted, and now she was crying outright, not trying to hold it back or hide it. She clutched her towel and slid to the floor, cross-legged and too miserable to even feel weird about the chill of the tiles on her bare ass. "Mrs. Culpepper, she said Simon was with her, and he wouldn't stop screaming," she sobbed.

"Shut up, just shut up." He stood up straight now, and he pulled off his raincoat—tossing it onto the hat rack so hard, he knocked it over. He did not go pick it up. He let it drip freely onto the parquet. "Simon isn't *dead*, Melissa. Mrs. Culpepper isn't talking to you."

"Where the hell *were* you?" she demanded. "I didn't even know you'd left the house! What were you doing out there, and why is everything screaming, everywhere—"

Almost angrily, he kneeled before her and took her by the shoulders, forcing her to look at him. "I went to the Tidebury house, okay? There's a message upstairs, somebody wrote it on the wall and it's…it's just words, but I don't think it's graffiti; I think somebody left it there for *us* to read. And then I saw a ghost. It tried to talk to me, and it was a ghost, a real live ghost."

She gurgled a laugh despite the circumstances.

He let go of her shoulders. "You know what I mean. Pull yourself together. We have to…we *have* to pull ourselves together."

"I'm trying, I swear. But Mrs. Culpepper locked me in the bathroom, and she fucked with the water to get my attention," Melissa explained. "She was so insistent, and so…*scary*, Leo. She was scary. I never thought she was scary before, not even when we were kids and she'd get pissed at us; I never"—she gulped—"I was never afraid of her like this."

"Well, I'm afraid of whoever left that… Jesus, you should see it. It's a message, written on the back wall, on the second floor. It says something like, 'I have what I need to take what I want.' I'm afraid of *that guy*, and I'm afraid of the kid who chased me out of that house, wheezing like a punctured tire even though… You know what?" He paused his frantic rambling. "I think he was trying to help. He was trying to warn me about *that guy*."

Now he pointed at the door, or whoever he believed waited on the other side of it.

Melissa tugged her towel a little tighter; she'd left wet footprints everywhere she went, and the tiles were already slick enough to wipe her out with one wrong step. Standing, and then on careful tiptoes, she went to the window to see what had him so rattled.

Out past the porch, down the stairs and walkway, at the bend where the path curved toward the beach...a man stood—unmoving. The darkness of the tree canopy and the night beyond it left him little more than an impression, a shadow.

She had a sudden flash of memory, of a conversation several years before. Simon, and his grandmother's deteriorating mind. Someone she watched for. Someone who frightened her. But the recollection flared and burned out, eclipsed by her terror.

"Who the hell is *that*?"

Leo's jaw was locked as tightly as the bathroom door had been. He reached for the curtains and yanked them shut. "If you made me guess, and you didn't care if my answer was completely deranged...I'd say it's Gunnar Lorentzen."

28

THURSDAY

LEO

Melissa turned around and took a few seconds to organize her thoughts. She was wet and ragged, her hair sticking to her skin and her face so flushed that Leo was almost worried about her. She adjusted her towel and said, "Well, Mrs. Culpepper said to keep him out."

"Yeah, I'm working on it," he snapped. He made sure the door was locked, dead bolt and all. His heart pounded and his chest hurt from running and yelling. "Give me a minute. Did you leave the water on?"

"Um...I was distracted."

He walked away from her, into the hallway's cloud of steam, and ducked into the bathroom. In there, he couldn't see a damn thing, but he knew where the tap was in the tub. The curtains were open and the floor was wet, the bathmat soaked. Navigating by touch, he twisted the knobs and they went silent.

Seconds later, he heard Melissa. "Leo? You okay?"

"I'm fine." He emerged looking and feeling shiny, but

unscathed. "You really think Mrs. Culpepper locked you in the bathroom?"

Melissa nodded, sharp and tense. "She said we're safe inside here, or I think that's what she meant." When she stopped talking, her teeth chattered hard, rattling marbles in her mouth.

Leo had questions, and he would appreciate some follow-up information. He didn't ask. Instead, he said, "Okay, first. First, you need to put some clothes on."

"Shit. Yeah." She hustled back down the hall to her chosen room. Her feet slapped damply on the floor as she went.

"I'm going to..." He ran out of things to say. What had he meant? Close up the house even further? Make some phone calls? To who? Well, he could start by checking the whole house and making sure every single entry point was secured. The windows were all locked, and something inside him recoiled at the idea of moving the curtains.

What if?

No. Simon wasn't dead. The stranger wouldn't come inside. None of these things were true or real.

Thinking otherwise would send him into a panic spiral and he couldn't afford that. Better to trust the windows and check the doors. Trust Mrs. Culpepper. She said, "Keep him out," so she must believe it was possible to do so.

The Culpepper house had three main entrances: front door, back door, and the door that led inside from the garage. While Melissa got dressed, Leo checked them all. All were locked, but he felt like he was forgetting something. His brain still buzzed with the encounter in Tidebury, and the words on the wall haunted the back of his head.

So sinister and direct.

The more Leo thought about it, the more he believed that yes, the little boy had been trying to help. It was a more pleasant possibility than the alternative, and the message on the wall had been large, clearly written, and high off the ground. "A kid didn't write that," he considered aloud. Not even a dead one.

"Didn't write what?" Melissa was back, wearing not pajamas but jeans and boots and a T-shirt with a sweater over it, like she was ready to book it out of there at the drop of a hat.

"I was just thinking about the kid ghost. The one who was making that noise. He looked like maybe a first or second grader."

"So a small kid. Not like, a teenager. Do you think...?" She frowned, then went ahead and finished the thought. "Do you think he's one of the boys in the corner?"

"No. Those—they're younger or smaller. Lesser, somehow. They never looked like the ghosts of children. They looked like watery shadows. He might've been one of the missing kids in the paper archives, though. Maybe those disappearances were related to Tidebury too." It felt silly to have missed the connection before. It was obvious, wasn't it?

"Is that guy still out there?"

"No idea." He put his hands on his hips and stared around thoughtfully. "But I feel like I'm forgetting something."

"Is it your shoe?"

"What?"

"Your shoe." She pointed down at his feet.

Both of them were caked in mud and sand. Only one still had a shoe on it. "Shit," he said. "It got stuck inside the house."

She went to the window like she meant to pull back the curtain and check outside. “Don’t! Whatever he is, whatever he wants…none of it’s good.”

To his surprise, she obeyed. “All right. Did um…did Simon ever tell you about his grandmother’s dementia-related delusions? He told me she used to be afraid of someone, or was looking out for someone. But he didn’t give it too much weight, because, well. You know. Half the time she thought her grandson was her dead husband.”

“I remember something about that,” he lied. He only knew about the dementia and the confusion. He didn’t know she’d been scared of a specific presence. “But I don’t remember any details.”

“There weren’t any. God, I wish Simon was here, so we could just ask him.”

“Well, he’s not. But if Mrs. Culpepper’s ghost is determined to keep somebody out of the house, we might as well assume it’s the same somebody who spooked her in the past.”

“Sure, why not?” Then she said, “Hey, did you lock up everything?”

“I checked all the doors. Everything’s locked up tight.”

“There’s a door in the basement—you know, the one with the hatch that leads outside. Did you check that one? We should make sure it’s locked too.”

“Shit.” Leo’s stomach was still sloshing with residual fear, but they’d come this far, hadn’t they? Might as well head down there while he still had some adrenaline to propel him. “All right. We’ll look together. But first, let me do something about…” He waved down at his mismatched filthy feet. “Give me two seconds.”

He was back in a flash, wearing the dressier shoes he'd worn to show houses to clients. Upon his return, he saw Melissa creeping up to the curtains again, plotting a peek outside. He opened his mouth to tell her to leave them alone when she shrieked and tumbled backward, throwing the heavy old curtain shut as thoroughly as possible and scuttling across the living room.

She pulled herself to her feet, quivering all the way. "He's *still there*. Just...standing there, motionless. Like a photograph." She shouted at the window, or whoever was on the other side of it, "Get the fuck away from here! We're calling the cops!" To Leo, she added, "He's looking at the house like he can see through these curtains. Like he knew exactly where I'd check for him, looking like, like..."

"Please don't. Please get a grip on yourself," he begged. "We have a plan. We do what Mrs. Culpepper said. We lock up the house. We keep that guy out, whoever he is. That's where we start. Now get your shit together, because I barely have a grip on my own. I can't manage yours too."

It seemed to get through. Her shaking dropped from fifth gear down to second. "Right. You're right. We do what Mrs. Culpepper said. She knows...or she *knew*..."

"She knows," he firmly agreed. "She's still looking out for us."

Melissa took a deep, shuddering breath. "Okay. But we need to check the basement door."

He took a deep breath of his own. He hoped it wasn't as shaky as hers had sounded. "Let me get a flashlight. We don't want to get stuck down there if the power goes out, like it did the night she died."

Leo raided the garage for the Maglite, secured the door behind himself, and returned to Melissa. "Here. I dropped the other one somewhere between Tidebury House and the Culpepper porch."

She took it out of his hand. "Cool, thanks. I'll go first."

He didn't fight her. "Feminism," he said with a thumbs-up. "After you."

The steps were straight and even, and when Melissa pressed the switch on the wall, a big bright row of fluorescent lights on the ceiling lit up like a supernova. "See? Nothing to be afraid of."

Nothing about the wobble in her voice suggested this was true.

Even so, he followed her, one step after another. Side by side wouldn't have worked; the stairs were too narrow, and there was no rail to hold. It was simple caution, that's all. That's what he told himself.

Mrs. Culpepper's basement looked perfectly ordinary. It held shelves, crates, exercise equipment that hadn't been used in decades, and plastic bins with labels like "Christmas ornaments" and "Easter place settings." The floor was bare concrete and mostly clean, except for a few old paint splatters and an upside-down spider corpse. The door leading outside was on the far wall.

Melissa stopped at the bottom of the stairs. Leo joined her. She held the flashlight out, even though the light above burned steady. Neither of them moved.

Then Leo said, "Something's weird about this basement, and I don't think I ever noticed it before. The other door...it opens up into that shaft, right? The one that looks like a tornado shelter on the south end of the house?"

"The steps on the other side lead up and out. What's so weird about it?" she asked.

"Not the hatch, though that *is* a little weird I guess. I mean, this space is a lot smaller than the house's footprint." He walked away from her, scanning the walls as he went. "See that line up there, on the ceiling? It's uneven, it..." He pointed, inviting her to follow along with his finger. "The concrete is different. A different grade or something." Leo had an idea brewing, and he didn't like it. He didn't put it out there for Melissa to hear. It wouldn't help anything if he was right, but his Realtor brain was chugging along, throwing out terrible suspicions left and right.

Regardless, she was catching on. "Over there, it looks like they put in a window or something? Up real high? But then they changed their minds and filled it in."

"Daylight basement," he said, and that's all. He didn't want to chase the idea to its logical conclusion. Not while he was standing down there in the close, humid space with its cold floor and low ceiling.

"There's something behind that row of shelves. Something on the wall," she said. "I noticed it years ago, but Mrs. Culpepper made me leave it alone."

"Let's continue to do what Mrs. Culpepper says. Let's check the basement door and get the hell out of here."

She tucked the flashlight into her back pocket and said, "Do what you feel, dude. I want to see what's happening on this wall." The shelves were cheap black plastic, and the things that rested on them weren't heavy. She put her shoulder to the nearest end and started to push.

While she went to work, Leo rolled his eyes and went to check the basement door. He steeled himself, turned the knob, and pushed it open just far enough to see beyond it. A quick look. Nobody there. An empty corridor, leading up to a pair of hatch doors—secured with a bar and a padlock. Perfect. Thank you, yes.

He shut the door and locked it with prejudice. "Nothing to see here. It's secured from the inside. Padlocked and everything."

Like she hadn't heard him, she said, "Man, this is...this isn't just weird. This is *crazy*."

"What's crazy?" he asked. Then he turned around.

"I *knew* the old lady was hiding something back here."

Baffled, he came to stand beside her. "What the fuck am I looking at?"

The eastern wall of the basement was now exposed, and Melissa was right: the shelves had obscured something interesting. Behind the tubs of old clothes and shoes, forgotten board games and books, the wall was marked by an enormous black circle that grazed the floor and the ceiling. Within it, a series of runes had been written in red and yellow—concentric rings of symbols that neither Leo nor Melissa could read.

"What the fuck *indeed*." She took a step back and used her flashlight for a spotlight, even though they could both see it just fine. "I mean, they're runes, right? Viking runes or whatever." She set the light on the nearest shelf edge and pulled her phone out of her sweater pocket. She called up the camera and took a couple of pictures, with and without the flash. "People know how to read these things, right?"

"They're like Nordic hieroglyphics. We can probably find a guide online."

"Was Mrs. Culpepper Nordic?" she asked.

He shrugged. "Maybe? Probably. Almost everyone is, around here."

"Culpepper was her married name," she mused. "It sounds British, maybe—like the name of a quaint village with a lot of cozy murders and an old priest who moonlights as a detective."

"Sure, but. You don't really think Mrs. Culpepper did this, do you?" He couldn't picture it, no matter how hard he tried. The very idea of her lurking down there with a brush and a can of paint, meticulously drawing these enormous symbols... He couldn't wrap his head around it.

"Either her or Simon. One of them must have done it."

"It could've been her husband," he argued. "Before he died, he could've... I don't know. Lots of people like runes. Pasty homegrown Nazis like runes; they love all that Viking stuff."

She snorted. "I know, and it's very rude. Leave my wholesome seafaring ancestors out of it, that's what I say."

He turned away and made for the stairs. "Let's get out of here, that's what *I* say. The basement's locked up, and that means the house is locked up. We're safe inside, just like Mrs. Culpepper told you. Keep reminding yourself."

"Okay," she said, not sounding especially convinced. She collected the flashlight and followed him back toward the steps. Then she stopped at one of the shelves. It was overloaded with boxes and unused housewares like everything else, but something familiar was sticking out. She touched the tip of an old yellowed steer horn, and she thought about a near-drowning and the roar of the rocks, more than thirty years ago. When she glanced down into the box she saw a clump of feather veins and dust, for whatever else was inside had been eaten by moths years before.

She shook off a feeling like cobwebs and ice water, and climbed up the steps behind Leo.

Neither one of them saw the things written on the eastern wall begin to move. They did not see the runes shift, rearrange, and strain as if something terribly powerful was pushing against them from the other side. They did not see one of the runes crack, and brighten, then crumble off the wall's surface in a soft puff of dust.

29

FRIDAY

MELISSA

At some point in her life, Melissa had probably known a worse, longer, more frightening night…but she couldn't think of one. Maybe the time she went to the hospital thinking she was dying, and it turned out to be kidney stones; but of course, there wasn't any Tramadol in the Culpepper house to make everything feel pretty much okay again.

She and Leo had slept in the living room, in what almost looked like a blanket fort by the time they were finished with it—a stack of bedding and pillows and emergency supplies in case of a power outage.

Neither one of them expected a power outage. Collecting the emergency items had mostly been an exercise in finding something useful to do, anything helpful at all to pass the time till morning. It may or may not have been more useful to find weapons or make coordinated plans to leave, or even call the police on the off chance that the guy outside the house was an ordinary guy with ordinary motives.

But they didn't do any of those things. They couldn't, not without knowing what happened to Simon, and not with the added uncertainty of ghosts on the premises. Certainly not while filled to the brim with so much terror packed tightly in their chests.

They huddled together and took turns sleeping, mostly by accident. They listened to the rain outside, the intermittent hum of the furnace kicking on, and the big boats out in the shipping lane calling back and forth to the shore with their loud, low horns.

They barely even spoke. What was there to say?

Melissa knew she should start with an apology, but that didn't mean she was planning on it. She couldn't figure out where, exactly, she should begin—or where her apology should wander and what details it should hit.

When they were children together, Leo had often been the odd kid out. Besides being too small to keep up with her and Simon's shenanigans, he'd also been too sensitive to…everything, physical and psychological alike. Only now did it occur to Melissa that Mrs. Culpepper might have had a good reason to indulge him. She hadn't doted on Leo, not exactly. But she'd never contradicted him either, when he swore he'd seen something frightening or unexplainable. She'd always asked questions and listened carefully to his responses.

"You took him seriously," she whispered, in case the ghost was listening. "Because you knew he didn't make up the boys in the corner. You *always* knew."

Now Leo was sound asleep on the couch. Melissa's back was resting against it; she was sitting on the floor, blankets bundled around her and her phone plugged into an outlet behind the bar.

The sun was up. The house was quiet. Even the rain outside had stopped.

She didn't know if the strange man was still waiting at the property's edge, but her gut said he was gone. Daylight couldn't fix everything—maybe it couldn't fix anything, really. But the world was clearer now, and quieter, and the island sounded alive with normalcy.

Squirrels and other creatures scuttled up and down trees and ran through the grass. Ship horns still blew, out past the bay. Seagulls shrieked bloody murder over everything and nothing. Something was walking outside, near the house.

She tensed.

The footfalls tripped lightly through the leaves. The pattern was wrong. Not two legs, but four.

Crawling carefully out of her blanket-fort nest, Melissa went to the east-facing window and stood beside it, her back to the wall. With one finger, she lifted enough of the curtain to let in a sliver of watery gray light. Exposing as little of herself as possible, she peered through the glass.

She was greeted by a blank brown expanse, which she soon recognized as the flank of a very large buck. A couple of does snuffled through the underbrush a few yards away, and a gangly fawn flopped down on the ground to rest.

She thought about opening the curtains but glanced back at the snoozing Leo and decided against it. One of them might as well get some rest. She tucked back into her own little nest and picked up her phone. Almost fully charged again. Good. It'd been hovering just below 10 percent by the time she'd finally put it down the night before—but it'd held up long enough for her to do some reading, and as it turned out, Leo was right. Plenty of people knew plenty of things about runes.

Even the oldest variety had been largely translated by the end of the nineteenth century, but there was a wholly different problem with the ones they'd found on the wall downstairs: if they were letters spelling words, Melissa couldn't read them. She didn't speak whatever language they were written in. The longer she beat her head against the issue—referencing and cross-referencing the pictures she'd taken with every useful, reputable site on the subject she could find—the more confident she was that they weren't ordinary text.

"I'm coming at this from the wrong angle," she admitted to herself.

"Coming at what?" Leo yawned big and loud, then rubbed at his eyes. "Oh hey, look. We're alive."

"And Mr. Lorentzen isn't outside the house anymore. So there's that."

A scuffling of leaves on the other side of the window prompted Leo to sit up and look concerned. "You don't know that for sure."

"Don't worry about the perimeter. It's just a bunch of deer. I already checked."

"Really?"

"Yeah," she said. "I left the curtains shut so you could sleep."

"Thanks." He felt around for his glasses, then remembered he'd left them on the end table. Once he had them back on, he did not seem eager to look outside. "You're positive it's just some deer?"

"Yup." She put down her phone and stood up again,

cracking her knuckles and stretching her back. She'd been sitting in the wrong position for too long and now an assortment of odd spots ached. "Watch this." She drew back the curtains in a quick sweep.

He flinched but didn't yelp. "I don't see any deer."

She went to the east windows and did the same, startling a big-eyed doe. With a flip of her tail, the animal bounced off between the trees.

"Okay, that's a relief. I'm not actually worried about getting murdered by deer. All the same, we should..." He paused to yawn again, and to swing his legs over the side of the couch. His pants were still dirty from his adventures in Tidebury the night before. His dress shoes were untied on the floor. "Check around outside in the light of day, that's what we should do."

"Feels like all we've done for the last two days is check things."

"You're not wrong." He put on his shoes and picked up his raincoat from the foyer floor where he'd left it. He stuffed his arms into the sleeves. "But I'll feel better once I've walked the perimeter."

She sighed. "I'll come with you."

Outside, they found deer shit and hoofprints near the walkway, and a streak of muddy footprints on the bricks. "Those are mine," Leo noted. "See? One shoe-foot, one sock-foot."

"I don't see any other prints..." Melissa looked off the side of the porch. Under the windows, a series of flowering hawthorn shrubs flourished. Beyond them was only mud. She picked through it carefully, until she reached a specific spot. "Not even over here. I swear to God, Leo—that guy was standing *right the fuck here*."

"I believe you," he said, and he didn't look for himself.

They strolled past the driveway and the garage, checking for signs of trespassers—but seeing only more deer shit and evidence of raccoons having rummaged through a neighbor's recycling.

Around the side of the house, still nothing. No indication that anyone had come or gone, nefarious or otherwise...until they reached the southern wall of the house, where the hatch from the basement was set against the ground.

They stood. They stared.

Leo said the obvious out loud. "Someone tried to get in."

"Something," she corrected him. "*Something* tried to get in."

The hatch doors were covered in gouges, deep and sharp. They weren't the kind of marks that might have been left by claws or fingernails.

He whispered, "It looks like someone took a sword to the doors."

"Or a rake? Good God, how did we not hear this?"

"We were...really tired? Really freaked out?" he tried.

"Sure. Why not?" She didn't have any better answers, so she swallowed hard and walked around the hatch, staring down at it all the way. "The door held, though."

"Mrs. Culpepper did not fuck around with security measures."

"No, she did not." Melissa tore herself away and headed back toward the front door.

Back inside, they made yet another neurotic sweep of the house's interior. It did not take long to determine that they were the only people present, living or dead, so they locked themselves inside again while they made a light breakfast from whatever they could find. Toast and jam, some cereal, a bit of fruit.

"Practically a continental breakfast, right?" Leo suggested, stuffing a slice of apple into his mouth.

"Better than most of the ones I've had, to be honest." She was talking with her mouth full, and she did not care. She swallowed and said more clearly, "Maybe this is stupid, but—"

He waited. When she didn't finish her thought, he prompted her. "Go ahead, spit it out."

"What if both of us are stressed out and worried about our friend, and we're sad about Mrs. Culpepper, and it's affecting our judgment? What if that guy outside the house...what if he's some rando who knows she's dead? What if he was casing the place, because he thought nobody was living here anymore?"

Leo opened his mouth and lifted a finger like he was about to argue, but he didn't. He dropped his finger and said, "You know what? That's not a terrible idea."

"Thank you. I agree that it's not terrible. I'm not sure how *likely* it is, but it might be worth visiting Port Hadlock again. Maybe we can have a word with that cute guy at the sheriff's office desk. If nothing else, we'll get the activity on the record. Then if something happens later—"

"Something like what?"

She tried not to let the interruption derail her. "Something like...if somebody breaks in and trashes the house or if our bodies are found on the beach like Mrs. Culpepper's. We don't want to get blamed for crimes we didn't commit or let our potential murders go unsolved. We should let the authorities know there's somebody hanging around, other than us."

He considered this. "I don't enjoy the idea of my own unsolved murder, so all right. Let's file a report about the guy outside, once we clean up here. We can file a missing person report on Simon, while we're at it."

"Yes, also that. We will clean up, and we will load up, and we will go to Port Hadlock, and you can do some more flirting."

"I'm already on board. No reason to oversell it."

Deep down, she didn't really think the stranger outside was casing the place for criminal purposes. Or not even deep down—just barely below the surface, where she was furiously keeping her shit together so Leo didn't have to do it for her.

But the light of day really was magic, wasn't it? It could make her second-guess almost anything, even the things she knew in her bones.

30

FRIDAY

MELISSA

This time Melissa did the dishes while Leo changed into something clean and threw his filthy Tidebury-searching clothes into the washing machine. When he emerged, wearing a fresh shirt and his earlier dress pants, she grinned. "Gunning for Deputy Tanaka, got it."

He feigned being aghast and offended. "I would never!" Then he added, "But seriously, these are the only other clean pants I have until my jeans come out of the wash."

They cleaned up. They loaded up. They locked up.

And they headed toward Port Hadlock in Melissa's beater Subaru—but she hadn't driven a mile when she slowed down to a crawl, and then a stop. Then, since there was no one behind her, she put the vehicle into reverse. She parked in the middle of the road and let the engine idle.

Leo didn't ask what she was doing. He'd seen it too.

"Something's going down over at Sound View," she said.

"Should we...?" he asked.

Melissa was driving, so she made the call. "We should pay our respects, right?"

Neither of them knew of anyone who'd died on the island other than Mrs. Culpepper, and they both assumed her body was in a refrigerator somewhere in Port Townsend's hospital. But when Melissa turned down the short dirt road to the cemetery, she started to wonder. The island wasn't big. The cemetery was only barely open, as far as she knew, and Mrs. Culpepper had owned a plot there—she'd mentioned it a dozen times. She wanted to be buried next to her husband.

"Aw, this looks sad," Leo said, a pained expression on his face. "No seats, no minister, no mourners."

"Well, it's not pouring anymore, but the weather is still garbage. Maybe they're just digging the hole and setting up for the funeral." Melissa pointed at a small backhoe that was wrapping up its task beside a deep rectangle.

Leo indicated a coffin being unloaded from a van. "Nope. Somebody's going in the ground."

Slowly Melissa drove through a chain-link gate, and then under the sign announcing the place: "Sound View Cemetery." It had never been much to look at, though it had a nice view on the east side—if you were the kind of corpse who appreciated the ocean.

Two men were unloading the casket with a motorized lift, a woman was climbing out of the backhoe, and an old guy with a shovel sat on top of an adjacent tombstone. No one else was present at all.

There was no clear or logical place to park, so she pulled off to the side of the dirt road and got out. Leo followed her.

Together they walked up to the grave site, this sharp hole in the ground surrounded by angular stones and a few short rounded ones. This wasn't an especially old cemetery, all things considered, and it wasn't an especially fancy cemetery either. It was on the island, and that's all it needed to be.

Melissa wasn't sure where to begin, but that was fine. Leo had gotten in the habit of introducing himself to strangers. It must have been a useful side effect of his profession.

He strolled up to the woman from the backhoe and said, "Hello, excuse me. I don't mean to bother you, but we were just wondering who passed."

The woman was in her fifties, wearing overalls with a plaid flannel jacket. Her body was sturdy and her face wore an expression that was partly irritable, partly tired, and partly curious. "Do I know you?" she asked. "Or her?" she added, with a cock of her head toward Melissa. Then she changed her mind and said to him, "Actually, you look a little familiar."

He offered her his most disarming smile. "Ma'am, I've always known I stood out, here on the island. My aunt and uncle live two roads north of here. The Alvarezes? Maybe you know them."

"That's right, yeah. I know Marco. Did some work for him when they were regrading that retaining wall out back behind their house."

"Yes!" he said, happy to have found a point of commonality. "I'm Leo Torres, the little kid who stayed with them in the summers. And of course, I still check in on them. They're getting older, and they have no children of their own."

"That's good of you," she said approvingly. She pulled out

a cigarette and a lighter, sparked up, and then said, "What about *her*?"

Melissa offered a small wave. "Hi, I'm Melissa Toft. My grandparents lived here on the island until—"

The woman cut her off. "Toft, I know that name. They've been gone awhile now." Apparently satisfied that she was speaking with quasi locals and not tourists who'd wandered in from the public parks, she answered Leo's original question. "I'm Anne, and you don't need the rest. Anyway, maybe you knew the old lady," she said, aiming the lit end of her cigarette at the casket. It was a shiny black model with silver hardware. Looked expensive.

Melissa's heart started sinking, and it settled in her stomach. "Old lady?"

"Otelia Culpepper," she said. "Dropped dead of a heart attack a few nights ago. It's sad, of course, but it's hard to call it a shame. She was almost a hundred years old."

"Otelia?" Leo asked, looking suddenly and deeply confused, and more than a little shocked.

Melissa elbowed him softly.

Anne shrugged. "I never knew her as anything other than Mrs. Culpepper. I was surprised to see that name on her death certificate, myself."

From behind them, the old man on the tombstone said, "When I was a boy, people sometimes called her O'Charlotte. It took her awhile to shake it."

Now they all looked at him. He was thin and hunched, wearing clothes that were too big for him, and a hat that let strands of wild silver hair poke out around his ears.

Melissa said, "But I saw her driver's license. Sometimes, she'd tell me to get money out of her wallet for one thing or another, and I swear, her name was Charlotte."

The old man nodded and then laughed. "She must've legally changed it. Hard to blame her, really. Poor woman, her and her sister both. Can't imagine what their parents were thinking, to name them so silly."

Melissa and Leo looked at each other, wondering how to play this card they'd been dealt. She could see in Leo's eyes that he recognized the name from the news clipping, same as her.

In the end, he was the one who asked, as if he didn't already know, "Mrs. Culpepper had a sister? She never talked about one."

Now the old man cackled. "Otelia and Alcesta, those were their names. Born half an hour apart. 'Course, by the time I came along, they weren't speaking anymore."

Anne didn't notice their shock. "Hold on now. They were *twins*?"

"Not the matching kind. They didn't look alike or nothing." He waved toward Anne like he'd appreciate a cigarette, if she'd spare one. She spared one. Leo pulled his little "Marrowstone Island" lighter out of his pocket before Anne could offer hers, and the cigarette flared to life. "But she's still around. Who else do you think signed off on this burial? Nobody knows where the grandson ran off to."

Leo said, "We've been looking for him the last couple days."

The old man shrugged. "I sure as shit don't know where he is, and no one at the county did either. The funeral home got hold of Alcesta, is how I heard it. She told them where to put the body. Both of the old ladies have plots here, but I don't think the sister wants hers. Some grudges are tougher than death."

Melissa's mouth hung open. "Mrs. Culpepper has a twin sister who's still alive. I'm sorry, that's... It's hard to imagine. I knew the woman almost forty years, and I had no idea!"

He shrugged. "I'm seventy-two next month, and I never heard of them being in the same room together. Not after what happened."

Anne leaned forward. "What happened?" she asked, her voice dripping with eager conspiracy.

Melissa couldn't have asked it better herself, though she already had an idea. Leo's fierce grip on her wrist suggested he was thinking the same thing.

"Oh, that whole mess with the house, oof." The man was clearly delighted by the attention and happy to milk it. "The sister, Alcesta, she got married to this fellow and they built a house, right over there." He waved his freshly lit cigarette toward the north. "Big fancy place, cost a lot of money. Everybody was real impressed. But it hadn't been standing long, not more than a handful of years, I wouldn't think, when a storm took it."

Leo audibly gasped, then clapped his hand over his mouth. When he removed it, he said, "I'm sorry. Please, go on."

Melissa knew why he'd gasped. Puzzle pieces were falling into place left and right.

The old fellow continued, a gleam in his eye and a grin at the corner of his mouth where he kept the cigarette. It bobbed while he talked, keeping time with his patter. "Oh, it was a terrible storm—like nothing anybody'd ever seen out here, and we've seen our share. In the morning, the house was gone, and as the story goes, the young couple was gone with it. Then a week later, some folks found Alcesta wandering the beach all by herself. She wasn't all right, though. Not anymore. She wouldn't say a single word—not to the folks who found her, not to the police or the doctors, not to her sister either. Rumor has it they had a falling-out. It was almost as if Alcesta blamed her sister for what happened during the storm. After that, she went to some fancy assisted-living place, and I don't think she ever came back. I don't think she ever set eyes on the house her sister built, right on the same god-damn spot," he said, making *goddamn* into two words for emphasis.

Melissa thought she might puke. She didn't know why. She was thinking about the basement, and the different kinds of concrete, and the window that used to be there but wasn't anymore. "I'm sorry, you're saying that Mrs. Culpepper built her house... right on top of where her sister's house used to be?"

It would explain why the trees that faced the ocean were slimmer than the ones behind the house. They were younger. The original stretch of trees had been erased by the storm—scraped into the water.

Anne looked puzzled. She chewed on the end of her own cigarette, then realized that it'd burned down to a nub. She dropped it to the ground and used her shoe to snuff out the last of the cherry; it fizzled in the wet grass. "Huh. I can't decide if that's thoughtful, or rude, or just plain cheap." When everyone looked at her with questions in their eyes, she shrugged.

The old guy laughed again. "I don't know why she built her place on her sister's land, if that's what it was. I don't know why she felt the need for *some* house to go there, even though it feels like it'd come with a curse, doesn't it? Then again, if the other woman wasn't coming back, well. I suppose there wasn't any real harm in it." He threw a glance over to the casket, which was almost ready to be lowered into the grave. "And Mrs. Culpepper certainly lived there a long time, and she had a real long life. Hard to call it cursed."

Anne accepted this. "When you put it that way…I don't know. What was her maiden name, you remember?" she asked him.

"Ellingboe," Leo answered. Melissa frowned at him, but he said, "It was in the paper, remember? The clipping about the wedding. The bride's family name was Ellingboe."

"Oh yeah, that's right."

A ratcheting sound behind them suggested that Mrs. Culpepper was making her final journey. They all turned to watch, and Melissa fought the urge to salute or say a prayer. Something, to mark the fact that a woman had lived almost a century, and now she was going to ground all but alone.

She looked away, scanning the cemetery and the trees around it, and looking back down the little road that had brought her there. Simon would show up, any second now. Any moment. He couldn't let them bury his grandmother without him.

But Simon did not join them.

The casket dropped, inches at a time.

When it was in place at the bottom of the hole, the men with the van unhooked some cables and pulleys and reloaded their equipment. One of them approached Anne with a clipboard and some paperwork, breaking up the little group and freeing Melissa and Leo to approach the grave.

Together, they looked down at the shiny, bright casket. The earth around it was very wet and very sandy; pieces of the walls sloughed off, splatting onto Mrs. Culpepper's expensive resting container.

Leo said, "I wish we had some flowers or something. She should have flowers, at least. A minister, maybe. Should we say a few words?" He looked truly stricken, for the first time since he'd known the woman was gone. The hole in the ground must've brought it home for him.

"Um, I don't know? She wasn't religious, really. Was she? I know Simon took her to church sometimes, but I always got the impression it was a social thing more than a Jesus thing."

"You're probably right," Leo said, but he didn't look especially soothed by the thought. "I still think we should say something."

"You do it. I don't know what to say. You're the salesman."

He gasped a little laugh, not anything as merry as a chuckle. "I can't sell heaven on taking her, if that's what you're getting at."

She shivered and tugged her raincoat tighter. It wasn't raining, but the jacket was an excellent windbreaker and it was lined with fleece. "No, I mean. I work in pictures; you...you work in words. Right?"

He nodded now. "I get it. Um." He cleared his throat and looked around.

Anne had returned to her backhoe, checking her messages on her phone and probably waiting for everyone to get out of her way so she could throw the dirt back in. The old man had crushed out his cigarette on the tombstone and left it there. He was gone. The two guys with the van threw it into gear and drove back down the little dirt road.

Leo cleared his throat again, and it led to a brief coughing fit. Then he said, "We are gathered here today…well, a couple of us are gathered here today…missing those of us who aren't. I know if Simon was here, he'd know exactly what to say and what to do. It would be hard for him. He and Mrs. Culpepper were each other's only family—or that's what I thought until about ten minutes ago," he added, mostly under his breath. "I don't know why her sister isn't here, but if she's the same age as Mrs. Culpepper, she might not be in very good health. There's a good chance she's simply not able to travel."

"Benefit of the doubt, and all," Melissa contributed.

"Benefit of the doubt. Now, I understand that they weren't close," he said diplomatically, "but I'm sure her sister feels the loss all the same. And so do we. We knew Mrs. Culpepper most of our lives, and she was kind to us, even when we were nuisance little kids who spent too much time underfoot. She did it for Simon, who she loved so much, and would've done anything for. I wish he was here with us. I wish we knew what happened to him. I… We…we've loved him most of our lives too."

His eyes were filling up, and his voice was getting thick. He wrapped it up while he was still clear enough to do so. "Goodbye, Mrs. Culpepper. We'll try to find Simon and make sure he's okay. We'll take care of your house too. One way or another."

Silence fell between them for a few seconds, and while they stared down at the increasingly dirty casket, the rain began again. It fell in fat drops, slowly and heavily, splashing into the hole and onto the ground around it.

Finally, Melissa exhaled a long, shuddering breath. "And

don't worry, Mrs. Culpepper. Whoever that guy is, we'll do what you said. We'll keep him out."

Leo wiped his eyes, and he smoothed a dark curl of damp hair out of his face. "Well. We'll do our best."

31

FRIDAY

LEO

Back in Port Hadlock, Deputy Tanaka wasn't at the desk, and Deputy Svenson wasn't in either—so they explained the situation to a heavyset young woman who turned out to be a new hire with no knowledge of Marrowstone or its vintage gossip. She had little interest in it either, but she was very keen to take their trespassing complaint seriously, and she vowed to pass it up the chain of command. Then she took down all the relevant information for a missing person report and wished them a nice day, so Melissa and Leo set out for lunch.

Leo said, "That could've gone worse. Or better."

Melissa couldn't argue. "It went, anyway. What should we do after this?" she asked around a bulky mouthful of burger. They'd stopped at the diner on the old main drag, where the atmosphere was retro and the food was uniformly acceptable.

Leo sipped a strawberry milkshake, then pushed the straw aside. "I suggest we go looking for this mysterious twin sister. It feels a little soapy, but I think Mrs. Culpepper—of all people—would appreciate that comparison. And I don't know about you, but I'd love to meet her."

"God, yes—so would I," Melissa agreed. "But even if we find her, she might not talk to us."

"Sure, but how many visitors can she possibly get in a month? Or a year? We could probably even claim we're related to her—call her our great-aunt. Nobody would know the difference. Maybe not even her."

Melissa shrugged and picked up a fry. "Simon might have visited her every now and again, over the years."

Any warm, happy feelings Leo might have been working up to evaporated at the thought. "Simon didn't know about her. He couldn't have. He would've told us."

"Maybe. But if anyone else was aware that Mrs. Culpepper had a sister, it was him." She crammed the french fry into her mouth.

"Simon's always been a shitty liar, and he doesn't like to keep secrets," Leo insisted.

"That's your heart talking, not your brain," she argued. "Simon obviously didn't tell us everything about his life, or his family. He tried to keep secrets all the time. Remember how long it was, before he told us what really happened to his parents?"

"The ferry accident. Mrs. Culpepper is actually—"

"Right. *She's* the one who filled in the details, not him. Remember the fireworks, the first time? He totally wasn't going to tell her. Or when he got into NYU? He didn't tell her about that either."

"He told her eventually. He went there, didn't he?"

She shook her head. "Don't miss the point. He didn't even

tell her he applied for colleges that far away. He *did* want his own life, you know. He just wanted her to be safe and happy too…and that mattered more than his desire to be on his own, I guess. I don't think he had any idea she'd live so long. I sure as hell didn't."

"He loved her, and he did right by her. There's nothing wrong with that," Leo insisted.

"He loved us too. He could've run away with us, or just… started a real life, someplace else."

"Run away with *you*, you mean."

"Oh, shut up," she told him, without any real venom. Mostly, she sounded tired. "You were just jealous."

He barked a grim, unpleasant laugh. "Me. I'm the jealous one?"

"Jealous of me."

"Sometimes? Yes," he admitted. "Especially when we were small. In adulthood? Not so much. *You*, on the other hand. You stayed jealous of Mrs. Culpepper your whole life. You envied her house and her money. You envied Simon's devotion to her, and you blamed her for keeping you two apart."

"You're full of shit."

"Yeah, but I'm not wrong." He expected her to mount a vigorous defense.

But she didn't. "Okay, but at some point, it was just selfish of her. She was willing to tie him down for his entire life, when he could've been…he could've gone…" She shrugged. "Anyone. Anywhere. Instead he stayed here, looking after an old lady, living his life on the internet—or on the road. It wasn't fair to him."

"She didn't exactly hold a gun to his pretty red head. He made his choices." Then something dawned on him. "But you can't bring yourself to blame him, so you blame *her* for not dying at a more convenient time for you, personally."

Melissa looked startled. "Fuck, when you put it that way, I sound like an asshole."

Leo hadn't meant to put that fine a point on it. He tried to back off a little. "I didn't mean… Look, I'm sorry."

"No, you're right and you know it. It's fine. I know I'm an asshole. If I weren't, I'd have more friends than like…some people I know from work, a few randos from the internet, and the same two dudes I've hung around with since I was ten."

She looked so miserable and defeated that he struggled with the urge to comfort her. "You're not an asshole. Or if you are, then I'm an asshole too. Simon was too good for either one of us."

They sat there in silence for a beat. Or two. Or three.

Finally, Melissa said, "Mrs. Culpepper was an asshole too. If she and her sister stopped talking more than seventy years ago, there's no real reason for Simon to know she existed. For that matter, the late, great Mr. Culpepper may not have even known. Simon might be a shitty secret-keeper, but his grandma was an absolute *master*. Apparently."

Leo nodded. "I think he'd be every bit as surprised as we were, to hear his grandmother had a twin sister. It's just my personal opinion, and you're free to disagree. But I don't think he would've kept that to himself."

She tilted her head back and forth thoughtfully. "All right, I accept that assessment, and if we ever find him, we can ask him."

Leo knew what she was working up to, and he didn't like it.

He tried to get ahead of it. "*If* we find him? You're the one who said Simon was dead." He stabbed at the remains of his corned beef hash with a fork. "Not me. I don't believe it."

She stared down at her plate. "It felt true when I said it."

"But it probably wasn't."

Melissa looked up again, her eyes hard and serious. "Then where do you think he is? What do you think happened to him? *Please*, give me some alternatives to the obvious, awful fact that something has gone spectacularly wrong for the last heir and scion of the once-great Culpepper family. I'd love *nothing more* than to have something else to fixate on."

"What do you mean, something else?"

But when she answered, he dearly wished he hadn't asked.

"Every time I picture his fate, he's lying dead in the woods somewhere between his house and the lighthouse. I imagine him lost and dehydrated, passing out and dying in the fucking rain, where no one can hear him call for help. I think about him standing over his grandmother's corpse and wondering what to do, wondering what she was so afraid of, and—"

He held his hands above the table and waved them. "Jesus, Melissa. Lower your voice."

She did, but only enough so she could claim compliance. "I think about Simon getting chased down the beach by the man from Tidebury—only to have storm debris fall on him, or trap him and drown him when the tide rolled in. Then I think about the waves, dragging his body out to sea."

"Stop it. Stop doing that."

"I *can't*," she whispered fiercely. "I've *tried*. Last night while you were asleep, I drank the rest of that brandy and took a couple of allergy pills from my purse stash, all in the service of trying *not* to do that. But Simon hasn't come home, Leo. He hasn't come home and we can't find him, because *something happened to him*. You and I both know it. Mrs. Culpepper practically said it. It's not my fault you don't want to believe it."

"Of *course* I don't want to believe it," he whispered in return, leaning forward over the table as if to menace her—but it was only so that she could hear his emphasis without sharing it with the whole restaurant. They were already getting weird looks from nearby customers. "I don't want it to be true."

"I don't either! But I *need* to know what happened to him—even if he's not alive anymore. I want to know what's up with that house on the beach, and…and…that guy who was trying to get into Mrs. Culpepper's house." She used the back of her hand to wipe her eyes, and she sniffled. "I'm not assuming the worst, I'm assuming the most likely. If he were okay, if he were someplace safe and healthy and happy, he would've called us by now—if nothing else."

"He doesn't have his cell phone!"

"But cell phones *exist*. He could've borrowed one from somebody. Shit, *pay phones* still exist. Technically. Somewhere. If he was alive, he would have sent us a message by now."

They finished the rest of their meals in silence, then paid their check and piled back into Melissa's car. They sat there, staring straight ahead.

She didn't crank up the engine. She said, "I don't want to fight with you, Leo. You and I want the same things. We want to know more about Mrs. Culpepper's sister, and we want to find

Simon—preferably alive, safe, and well. So here's what we're gonna do: We're gonna sit here for a minute and see if we can find Alcesta Lorentzen with our phones. Then we're gonna see if there's any chance on earth that we can reach her, and talk to her, and maybe even get her to answer some questions—who knows. After that...or, if we can't track her down...we'll go back to the Culpepper house and regroup."

Leo sighed and pulled his phone out of his pocket. "I can work with that."

"Good." Now she started the engine but didn't put the car in gear. She let it idle in the parking space. Before he could ask why she'd waste the gas, she leaned forward and turned up the heat. "Because it's cold outside and this way, the windows won't fog up while we sit here."

Research wasn't especially fast-moving, since the cell signal wasn't much to speak of, and the load times were slow. The car filled with impatient grunts and groans, and they each held their phones up to the left, to the right. To the ceiling. At one point, Melissa unbuckled her belt and crawled into the back seat—not that it improved her signal strength in the slightest.

"Watch it," Leo complained when her feet whisked past his head.

"Sorry. I'm just trying to get one...more...stupid...bar."

"I know, this sucks," he agreed. "But I think I've got something."

She dropped herself back into the driver's seat with an *oof*. "Really?"

"There's a long-term care facility about fifteen miles from here. It's technically a Port Townsend zip code, and it's the only place of its kind for a hundred miles. It was built to replace a facility that burned down in the 1970s."

"Yikes, a fire at a nursing home?"

"I have deliberately chosen not to click that news link, yes. I don't need the nightmares." He swiped through another page and found a phone number, then clicked it and held up a finger to signal for quiet.

Someone answered on the third ring. "Cedar Groves Assisted Living, how can I help you?"

"Hello, my name is Leonard Torres and I'm calling on behalf of the Culpepper family—with regards to the recent passing of Otelia Charlotte Culpepper. Do I understand correctly that her sister, Alcesta Lorentzen, is a resident at your facility?"

"I...well, yes. And also no."

"I'm sorry?" He set the phone to Speaker and held it out so Melissa could hear. It'd be easier than relating the whole thing later.

"She's here, but for heaven's sake, don't call her Mrs. Lorentzen; she doesn't like it."

Smoothly, he pivoted. "Ms. Ellingboe, then. I certainly wouldn't wish to offend."

"Yeah, she's...a piece of work."

He chuckled politely. "Her sister was much the same. Are you aware that she was buried this morning, in the Sound View Cemetery on Marrowstone Island?"

A slight hesitation. It sounded like she was moving some papers around on a desk. "Um...yes. Ms. Ellingboe signed off on that yesterday, if I recall correctly. We were all frankly surprised—I don't think any of us knew she had a sister. Or that she was aware enough to understand and sign paperwork, but there you go."

"Indeed, my friend and I were surprised to learn about Ms. Ellingboe ourselves, and we'd known Mrs. Culpepper for most of our lives. That said, we were wondering if there was any chance we could have a word with Ms. Ellingboe." He fished around for a good excuse that went deeper than curiosity, but didn't sound completely insane. He steered clear of Tidebury, ghosts, and Gunnar Lorentzen. "If that's all right. We'd like to pay our respects, for one thing, and for another we have some questions about a few family items that were found in Mrs. Culpepper's home."

"Really? I'm sure that would be fine; she doesn't typically get visitors. You said you're calling on behalf of the family?"

Melissa and Leo scrunched their eyebrows at each other. He said, "Yes, ma'am. My friend and I grew up with Mrs. Culpepper and her grandson, Simon. On Marrowstone Island," he added, since a handy network of friendly locals had gotten him this far.

"I'm sorry, did you say there's a grandson? Then she has a nephew too. Goodness, that's interesting. Will he be with you?"

"I'm afraid he isn't with us right now. I hope that's not a problem?"

When she didn't immediately reply, Melissa frowned at Leo. He shrugged at her.

Finally coming to some conclusion, the woman on the other end of the line said, "If you want to come out and see her, I'm sure that'd be fine. The man from the county coroner's office was the first visitor she's had in years, so perhaps she'd enjoy the company. But fair warning: perhaps she *won't*. Ms. Ellingboe isn't much of a talker."

"Excellent, thank you, ma'am," Leo told her with a mixture of excitement and relief. "We'll be there in another half hour or so, will that be all right?"

The receptionist said it would be fine, and they exchanged parting pleasantries before hanging up.

Melissa said, "Hot damn! I can't believe you found her so quickly!"

"It was just a guess," he admitted, calling up directions to the rest home on his screen. "But like I said—it was the only place in the region."

"I'll take it. Here," Melissa reached past him and opened the glove box. "Put your phone in this, and stick it on the window. Get me some directions to this facility." She handed him a suction cup mount and put the car back into gear. "And let's go have a nice talk with an old lady who hated her sister."

32

FRIDAY

MELISSA

The Cedar Groves Assisted Living facility was a sprawling single-story building on the outskirts of Port Townsend. It was nestled in a grove of birches, pines, and alders, which Leo called "ironic" and Melissa called "who cares." She couldn't have picked a cottonwood or birch out of a lineup if her life depended on it. Leo responded to this by pointing out a few examples of each.

When she expressed dubiousness, he added, "I had to learn about trees. For my job."

"Why?" she asked, making a slow loop of the parking lot—squeezing past an ambulance and on the other side of it, a hearse. "You sell houses, not trees."

"People who buy houses want to know what kind of trees are on the property. Especially if they're very large and likely to fall on a roof."

"I guess that makes sense." She parked in a spot for visitors, and they went inside.

The floors were shiny and bright, and the walls were industrial green, the color of old scrubs. The trim was probably white once, but now it was light brown. Everything echoed, from the squeaky wheels of chairs to the soft tap of rubber-tipped canes, and the clicking of computer keys, and the murmuring of patients. In the distance, a soda machine delivered a beverage with a jarring clunk.

"Hello, are you Mr. Torres?" asked the receptionist. She was a petite woman with short blond hair and red-framed glasses.

He flashed her his best Realtor smile and approached. "Yes, that's me. You must be the woman I spoke to on the phone."

"I'm Emma, yes. And this must be the friend you mentioned?"

"Melissa Toft, hello," she said. "Thanks so much for letting us see Ms. Ellingboe on short notice."

"I just hope you haven't wasted your time, driving all this way. But visitors are visitors, and maybe she could use the company. Even if they hadn't spoken in most of a lifetime, it still must feel very strange and lonely to lose your twin sister."

Emma called for someone to mind the phones. She dropped her cell phone into her pocket and said, "Come with me, and I'll take you to see the fabulous Ms. Ellingboe."

Melissa wasn't sure what that meant until they entered a room that was larger than she expected, and very clean if rather cluttered. A plush, brocade-covered love seat rested against the wall with a small table beside it. Plump pillows in bright colors decorated the bed, scattered atop a fat silk duvet in a killer shade of purple. A blue velvet robe with furry gray trim was tossed across the foot of the bed. A feather boa lounged atop the vanity mirror.

And a tiny old lady sat in a wheelchair by the window.

Her hair was perfectly coiffed, and the pearly silver color of Mrs. Culpepper's vintage Cadillac. She wore a robe similar to the one that was lying on the bed, but in rich green and fluffy black. Two little slippers peeked out from under the hem. They were black velvet with gold thread details.

Emma knocked on the doorframe to announce herself. "Hello, Ms. Ellingboe? You have visitors. They've come all the way from…" She looked at them, waiting for an answer.

"Seattle," Melissa told her.

"Bremerton," said Leo.

"From a long way away. I'll just leave them here, if that's all right with you. If any of you need anything," she said to everyone present, "we're just down the hall. I'll come back to check on you in a few minutes."

Leo thanked her, and Melissa added her thanks before Emma could disappear.

Then they stood there, barely over the threshold. Not sure what to say. Or do.

Melissa braved the old lady first. She walked carefully, slowly inside. Leo followed behind her, staying a few feet back. "Hello, ma'am," she began. "My name is Melissa Toft. I used to spend summers on Marrowstone Island. My grandparents lived there for years and years."

She received no response. Alcesta stared through the glass, watching something else, somewhere else.

"We, um…me and my friend here, his name's Leo. We're old friends of Simon Culpepper, who would be…I mean, you would be his great-aunt? I think?"

She blinked, very slowly. But she said nothing.

"Your sister, Charlotte. Or...Otelia? Am I saying that right?" She pronounced it *oh-teel-ya* without much confidence. "As far as I knew, she was just Charlotte. Or Mrs. Culpepper. That's what I always called her. Do you mind if I...?" she asked, gesturing at the foot of the bed—the side without a robe on it. "Could I sit here, would that be...?" She thought about moving a pillow on the rocking chair that faced her, but the moment felt fragile. It felt like diffusing a bomb, and she wasn't sure why.

Still no movement. Not even another blink.

Melissa took it as permission. She sat down slowly, carefully, leading with her hand to make sure she didn't sit on anything important.

She was close enough to reach out and run her fingers across Ms. Ellingboe's fragile skin, but she was almost afraid to. It looked like a wedding veil draped over a skeleton. Dark blue veins crept beneath the pale surface, stretching along the elderly woman's arms like rivers on a map.

Melissa drew up one knee and turned to better face the room's silent resident. "I hear you don't like to talk, but perhaps you won't mind listening. You've already heard that your sister's dead, and I'm sorry about that—even if you weren't on speaking terms. We attended her burial out at Sound View Cemetery this morning," she said, exaggerating. "That's when we learned about *you*, and it really threw us for a loop. Me and Leo spent almost every day, every summer, at her house for years. We went there to play with Simon. His father was Charlotte's son, but he and Simon's mother died back in the early eighties. Charlotte wound up raising him there, in that house." She paused, wondering if she'd seen a twitch at the corner of Alcesta's eye.

Melissa looked over at Leo. He was tense, ramrod straight. Fiddling nervously with his smartwatch.

"Did anyone tell you how she died?" she asked.

Alcesta's shoulders shifted.

"She ran out of the house in the middle of the night, in the middle of a storm. She collapsed on the beach. That's where Simon found her. He told me... He sent me an email," she tried to explain without making it too fiddly. "He thought something on the beach must have scared her to death."

The old woman's eyes slid toward Melissa. Her head did not move.

In that odd moment of contact, Melissa was confident of something. So confident, she said it out loud. "But you already know what she saw on the beach, don't you?"

Now the old woman closed her eyes.

"Mrs. Cul...your sister, Charlotte, built her house where *your* house used to be. She put it right on top of the foundations that yours left behind when it washed out to sea. She even replanted the trees that used to be there, and then she sealed up the basement, but it's strange down there. She painted something crazy on the east-facing wall. We found it behind some shelves." Melissa reached into her bag and pulled out her phone. She pulled up the photo she'd taken of the basement wall, a picture that caught the full scope of the circle and the concentric ring of runes inside it. She held it out. "Could you tell us what it means? Or what it...says?"

Alcesta opened her eyes. She gazed down at the phone and said a single word, as clear as a bell: "Thornbury."

Leo jumped. Melissa almost dropped the phone, but didn't. She passed it to Alcesta, who took it in fingers so thin that Melissa thought the weight of the device might break them.

Now Leo came forward. He picked up the pillow from the window seat and left it on the bed, then sat down so they both could face her. "Ma'am," he said, awkwardly this time, not smoothly like when he was speaking with strangers. "Simon is missing. Do you know what happened to him? Do you know where he might have gone?"

She spoke again. "Tidebury."

Leo looked like he wanted to ask something else, but Melissa got ahead of him. "Wait, Tidebury or Thornbury? And what's a Thornbury?"

Ms. Ellingboe sighed and rolled her eyes like she was dealing with a couple of idiots—idiots who were annoying enough to prompt her to speak up at long last. With one bony finger, she pointed at the photo on the phone. "Thornbury," she said. She tapped a specific spot on the screen. "*Thorn.*"

Melissa leaned forward to get a better look. Alcesta had highlighted a specific rune, at the top of the circle in the twelve o'clock position. "Thorn? Is that what that rune means? Buried thorns? I'm so sorry, I don't understand at all."

Ms. Ellingboe sighed again, and then she started talking. Her words flowed quick and precise and unexpected. "*Bury*, you fools," she said, rhyming the word with *worry*. "It means *guarded by*, or *protected by*. Put *thorn* in front, and there you go: guarded by thorns. It's clever, I'll give her that."

"So...so you *can* read this?" Melissa asked.

She swung her head back and forth, like this was the wrong

question entirely. "These runes don't spell words, that isn't what they're for. This one is called *thorn*. This isn't a message to be translated; it's a spell to be cast, like...like sheet music for an instrument. But there's no one left alive who knows the tune."

Melissa closed her mouth because this time, she knew it was hanging open. "A...a spell?" she stammered. "Um...I'm pretty sure Charlotte was Lutheran?"

As if she hadn't heard, Alcesta Ellingboe continued. "*Tidebury* was mine, guarded by the ocean and the sharp pull of the moon. *Thornbury*, she must have named hers, guarded by the earth and the sun, and the things they grow together."

Her face grew flushed, and her hands started to shake. But still she squeezed the phone, though her wrist sagged low.

"Ms. Ellingboe, are you all right?" Leo asked. "Should I get someone to help you?"

She laughed and it wasn't the laugh of a woman who'd lived for a century; it was the bright mockery of a pretty young woman in a yellowed newspaper clipping. "*Help*," she scoffed. "I've had help enough already, and it almost killed me. Charlotte raised the stones, you know—she thought the earth could send us down to the bottom of the ocean and hold us there. Then she covered it up, wasn't so hard to do. A little after-spell, a little shroud... No, not so difficult at all, when so few eyes would see it anyway."

Melissa gently took the phone, and then held Alcesta's hand. "Ma'am...what happened that night, when Tidebury washed away?"

She looked down at her hand, now clasped in Melissa's. Her gaze tracked up the wrist, the arm, the elbow of the person who wanted so much from her. "My sister tried to kill me. *That's* what happened."

Leo gasped, "Oh God," like he was watching *The Real Housewives of Someplace Dramatic.*

Now Alcesta turned her laser-hot glare on him. "We both wanted my husband dead, but I thought we'd do it together. I thought she'd let me get out of the way, first."

"But why?" he pressed. "What did he do?"

Her eyes narrowed, glowering tightly at some distant memory. "He was a man of infinite appetites. He wanted more of everything: knowledge, power, respect. There wasn't enough of it in our world, so he sought another. I found him..." she said. Her voice faltered. "Writing. Collecting. Terrible things. Terrible pieces..." She shook her head sharply, like these were thoughts better off banished. "Like so many men, he wanted control and he didn't have it. He couldn't control the stock market, or his business, or reputation. His health. His standing. His *wife*," she added darkly.

Melissa was aghast but enthralled. "But..." She almost said that it wasn't possible, but she'd seen the house on the beach and now she did not know. Anything was possible, surely. "How did you plan to stop him?" she finally asked.

"My sister and I were two against one: *Vǫlva* against a man who refused to know his place and time. A madman and murderer. Yes, he was a killer. We *knew* he was a killer," she repeated, underscoring the point, or perhaps reminding herself. "We'd chosen our weapons, borrowed them from our grandmothers in the old country, but we hadn't yet chosen our time. We needed a bright, dry day. We needed sunlight."

"The best disinfectant," Leo agreed.

"What's a Vǫlva?" Melissa asked.

Alcesta didn't respond to either of them. She kept talking like if she stopped, she might never start again. "But Charlotte, when the storm came... I don't know if the storm was his making or if it was only a coincidence. But she thought...she thought we could use it to kill him. Someone had to, after what he did to those little boys. Before he did even worse."

Leo's eyes went wide. "The boys in the corners," he murmured to himself very softly, like he didn't expect anyone to hear.

Ms. Ellingboe heard him anyway. "They're a stain, that's all. He used them; he...he needed three, so he took three." She shook her hand loose from Melissa's hold. "He used them for lures. Worms on a hook. No." She changed her mind. "Dimes, for a pay phone. He tried to contact the things that lie below and beyond. Charlotte may have...she may have been right. She *did* send us away, didn't she? Back into the ocean, to the very bottom, to sink and to drown. But I'm a very good swimmer and I never minded the cold. I was always a very good swimmer. Every summer, at the lake in California..."

Melissa and Leo shared stricken glances. Ms. Ellingboe's mind was starting to wander.

With considerable caution and no small amount of fear, Melissa said, "There was a time I fully believed that Mrs. Culpepper could do anything—but I don't understand how she could drown a whole house. With people in it."

The old woman snorted. "Charlotte and her *stones*. She should have used fire, like I damn well told her. Those poor little boys. Gunnar deserved no less."

"What did he do to them, Ms. Ellingboe?" Leo asked. His skin glistened with a sheen of nervous sweat.

She frowned like the question surprised her. Then she replied like he was too stupid to sit there upright, and her answer was merely a small favor to a hopelessly slow learner. "He fed them to the machine he built, the one he named *Alaytha.*"

"Wait, what machine? Say that again," Melissa asked, very quickly, sensing that she'd both learned something useful, and that the old woman was losing the thread.

"A pay phone, yes. Three dimes, and he could make a long-distance call to a terrible place," she said with a sigh. "But he won't stop there. That was only a taste, and he's still very hungry. He'll take the whole island and everyone on it, if you let him."

33

FRIDAY

LEO

Alcesta Lorentzen, née Ellingboe, sat back in her wheelchair looking deeply unhappy, but you couldn't call it sadness. Leo thought she looked angry and disappointed, and perhaps resigned to something he hadn't figured out yet. He watched her settle down into the seat, where she looked even smaller—like a child, or even a child's doll, with a blanket across her lap and a shawl around her narrow shoulders.

For reasons he could not articulate, he was absolutely terrified of her.

She couldn't have weighed eighty pounds, and she barely had the strength to keep her eyes open, but there was something powerful about her all the same. She reminded him of Mrs. Culpepper in her relative youth, how she'd seemed sturdy and commanding even when Leo was in high school, and by then he was easily three times her size. Even then, she was shrinking into the small hard thing she'd eventually become.

He could've knocked Mrs. Culpepper aside with the back of his hand; he could've thrown her across the street with minimal effort. But never, no. He would've never crossed her, or offended her, or tried to harm her.

Mrs. Culpepper had been a force of nature to be treated with respect. She never needed to threaten or beg, bluff, or bully. She had expectations and Leo always understood that. He understood that he was in her presence by her grace alone and that she could send him away at any time. Like she sent away her sister's house.

Her sister, this venerable twin nobody knew about...she had that same authority, but hers was further concentrated by pure, distilled *rage*.

Whatever had been reliable and strong about Charlotte was stubborn and fierce in Alcesta. Where Charlotte had a genuine fondness for her grandson and even (if Leo were to flatter himself) her grandson's friends, Alcesta had no such softness about her. Leo halfway thought that if someone gave her a gun, she'd go on a spree.

But something horrifying and certain at the bottom of his stomach said that she wouldn't need a weapon, because this was no ordinary woman. Mrs. Culpepper had not been ordinary either, but she went to some trouble to hide it. Ms. Ellingboe did not bother. He knew it as surely as he knew that she was right about the little crying spirits.

Leo wanted to flee the room, but that was not an option.

Alcesta held him there by sheer force of will, and she did not soften when she looked up at him, directly, right in his face like she wanted to punch it. "*The boys in the corners*," she said with a hard harrumph that made her whole body bounce. "You must be a sensitive soul, if you call them that—if you even noticed them at all. Don't worry about them. There's nothing you can do for them. Nothing you *should* do."

"But Ms. Ellingboe," he said, though his mouth was terribly dry. "They aren't crying anymore. They're *screaming*."

Now she went a little softer. She was almost gentle, or was she only amused? It was hard to say. "They don't know much, but they know he's come back. The two he used, I mean. One boy died before he could kill him. That's why his phone call didn't work. Only two dimes. He needed three."

Leo wasn't sure what that meant, but he wasn't sure he cared. He still had one real question, and he strongly sensed that Alcesta's cooperation was running short. He'd better ask it now or risk it going unanswered forever. "Ma'am, *please*. Can you tell us what happened to Simon?"

Melissa said, "Oh for chrissake. She doesn't know."

He didn't believe Melissa. He didn't take his eyes off the old woman.

She matched his stare moment for moment, in resolve and confidence. He did not like the faint smile that tugged at the corner of her mouth. It looked almost mean. She replied carelessly, like the answer didn't matter. "The grandson? Oh, there's nothing you can do for him either. Not if Gunnar's got him. He's probably in the corners by now."

Leo stood up, breaking whatever chain had held him there. He squeezed past her and Melissa, went to the room's door and stood beside it, looking out into the hall. A pair of orderlies chatted as they strolled past. A nurse went by with a tray full of tiny paper cups full of pills. The phone rang, down at the front desk. He held out his head and took the kind of deep breath that was supposed to clear his head.

It was so hard to breathe in that room, with that woman.

Melissa handled her better, and he didn't know why. Melissa didn't seem afraid or worried. Maybe she couldn't feel it. He heard her say, "I hope you don't mean that, Ms. Ellingboe. We love our friend Simon, and we want him to come home."

The old woman shrugged. "It's not my fault you don't like the answers. It's not my fault Charlotte fucked it up with her impatience or that she was willing to force sacrifices and choices on other people. Sacrifices and choices that weren't hers to make!"

Emma from the front desk was approaching. Alcesta was getting loud.

The receptionist smiled at Leo then looked past him. They both looked into the room, where Melissa was almost knee-to-knee with the woman who hadn't willingly spoken in decades, and now seemed unable to stop.

Emma asked in the softest whisper, "What's happening? This is crazy!"

Leo couldn't argue with her, but he couldn't answer either.

Melissa asked, "Ms. Ellingboe, what do we *do*? Not for Simon, not for the boys. What do we do about Gunnar? He's there, outside the house. Outside Thornbury."

"Charlotte's wards won't keep him out forever. Now that he has his third dime—one to make up for the boy he lost to chance—he'll be strong enough to break them. My sister, she knew what was at stake. Together, we could have..." Her hands slipped slowly back down to her lap. "Together, if she'd only..."

"Ms. Ellingboe?" Melissa reached out to touch her again, but didn't. She withdrew before making contact.

"I'm tired."

Emma, still dumbfounded, rushed to the old lady's side. "I had no idea you could be such a chatterbox! Here, let's get you back into bed."

Alcesta did not resist. She allowed herself to be helped up and over, and onto the mattress. Melissa assisted, looking very unsettled by the whole thing, but taking care to make the old lady as comfortable as she could.

When they were finished, the receptionist said to Alcesta, "I'll get Teddy, and he'll bring your meds, all right?"

She didn't answer. She was back to staring straight ahead, this time at the ceiling. She didn't utter another word—not when Melissa and Leo told her goodbye and to have a good afternoon. Not to Emma, who seemed very eager to get her talking again. And not to Teddy, who arrived just as they were leaving.

Badly shaken, Leo followed Melissa to the car and climbed into the passenger seat.

She got behind the wheel and sat there with her keys in her hand. "You believe her, don't you?"

He badly wanted a beverage, any beverage. Preferably a strong one, but he'd settle for anything wet. His throat was so dry he could barely answer. "Yes, and so do you. Melissa, what do we *do*? And what kind of machine is an alaytha, anyway?"

"I don't know, but I've heard that word before. Mrs. Culpepper started muttering about it a few years ago, and she wouldn't tell Simon what it meant. He told me he looked it up online, and it was an old Norse word for some kind of minor apocalypse."

"Like Ragnarök?" he asked. "At least I've heard of that one."

"Smaller scale, or that's the impression he gave me. Hang on." She looked it up quickly on her phone. "Here it is—and it has that character in it too. The 'thorn.'" She turned the screen around and showed him. "*Aleyða*: it means *to totally lay waste, to turn into a wilderness*. Now what was that other word, something Swedish or...I don't know. It started with a *W*..."

He tried to steer her back to the original question at hand. "Look, I just want to find Simon, one way or another. I don't want him to be dead, but I need to know what happened to him, even if he's gone. Don't act like you don't need that too."

Her head popped back up again. "I'm not!"

"Everything you asked that woman had to do with the stuff in the house, not Simon," he accused. "You've already decided he's dead, and now you're more interested in that shit in the basement."

"Oh, *you're* allowed to be interested in Mrs. Culpepper's house? But I'm not? At least I'm not trying to sell it as soon as her body's cold."

"That's not fair."

"*You're* not fair," she countered. "We don't know what line of inquiry might lead us back to Simon. Everything happened at basically the same time—Mrs. Culpepper dying, the house washing up, Simon disappearing. They're obviously connected, and who the hell do you think you are, trying to imply that I don't care about him as much as you do?"

"I never said—"

But Melissa was on a roll. "Oh, there's a *lot* you never said. Did you ever tell him you were in love with him? I assume you never got up the nerve."

"Fuck you!" he said, his voice a little higher than he meant for it to be. "I told Simon I loved him a million times."

"Oh, you know *exactly* what I mean. Any idiot could see you were besotted with him by the time you were twelve."

Aggravated almost beyond words, he fired back. "It took me awhile to figure out my shit, okay? It happens to a lot of us, and you don't have any room to talk. I know about what happened between you two, the summer that the whale washed up on the beach by the fort."

The look she gave him made him want to get out of the car and walk back to his aunt and uncle's place. It made him want to get his car, then bring it back and run her over with it. "So what? Jesus, it was just the one time, and it was weird for both of us, and we never did it again."

"Yeah, right."

"Well, it's true. I can't make you believe it, if you don't want to. And frankly? I don't care enough to try." She threw the car into gear and backed out of the space, pulling out into the parking lot a little too fast. "That doesn't mean I was carrying a torch for him or anything. It was a stupid mistake. Sixteen-year-olds are allowed to make those."

"You wanted him to love you."

"He did love me," she insisted.

"Not the way you wanted him to."

She sniffed and stared over the steering wheel at the wet, slick road ahead. "You're one to talk, aren't you? What did you expect, that one day he'd choose when it was time to settle down? Because he *did*, Leo. And his choice was neither one of us."

Back on the main road, she did some of her loosest, most pissed off driving—gunning it through yellow lights and cutting people off to get the lane she wanted.

This wasn't going to work. When she was wound up like this, she was impossible. Hell, maybe he was impossible too. With this in mind, he threw her a reluctant, feeble bone. "We won't get anywhere if we keep bickering like this. Let's cool off, okay? We need to keep our heads on straight."

"My head's just fine, thanks."

"Tell me about it," he tried again. "I can't believe you actually got the old lady talking."

She relented. Very slightly. But it was a step in the right direction. She un-gritted her teeth, and it was a good sign when she said, "Me either."

He kept pushing. "You really think she hadn't talked to anybody since she got there?"

She checked her rearview mirror, decided she had enough room to get ahead of somebody, and did so—not bothering with her blinker. "No idea."

"Well, it was still pretty cool of you to jump in there, take the lead. I never know what to do with old people. Mrs. Culpepper's the only one I've ever really known. My grandparents died young. I didn't really know them."

"I know."

"How much of it do you think…? I mean, some of what she said was obviously nonsense. It'd be a miracle if she didn't have some kind of age-related dementia."

She sighed as she pulled up to a stoplight, then beat her head against the steering wheel very slowly. When she stopped, she said, "Leo, I know what you're doing. I accept your apology."

"I didn't apologize."

"Not in the direct way, no." He didn't argue, so she continued. "I'm sorry too. This is stupid, this whole thing is...stupid. Crazy. Whatever. I'm just so goddamn *tired*, and that woman she...she pushed buttons I didn't even know I had. Old people in general don't bother me, but that *particular* old lady...she was like a mean version of Mrs. Culpepper."

Leo hemmed and hawed even though he agreed. "I don't know, if I thought my sister had tried to murder me by throwing my house into the ocean, I might hold a grudge against the world too."

The light changed and Melissa kept driving; soon they hit the two-lane road that would lead them back to the island. The other cars dwindled.

Then it was just the two of them, crossing over to Indian Island, and then to Marrowstone again.

34

FRIDAY

LEO

Leo and Melissa swung by the Alvarez place so Leo could borrow some clean boots from his uncle's closet; then they trudged back to the Culpepper house. The day was running late by the time they reached the porch, but it wasn't dark yet, or it shouldn't have been, but the island was parked under the shadow of another storm, and the sky was more gray than white—and going grayer by the moment.

For a moment, they stood in Mrs. Culpepper's foyer like they didn't know what to do next.

Leo sighed heavily. "Let's lock up, huh? Not that I think a dead bolt will do much to stand in Gunnar Lorentzen's way."

"No," she agreed. "Whatever's keeping him out, it's in the basement."

Out loud, he said something he'd been thinking about all the way back from the nursing home. "I think he had some kind of office or laboratory in that daylight basement. I think that's what's behind the wall with the runes on it. Maybe it's where he kept his crazy Aleyða machine."

"Maybe." Melissa walked slowly to the living room and peeled her phone out of the plastic bag. Her charging cord was still plugged into the wall beside the couch. She hooked up the phone and sat down, looking ill or exhausted, or some combination of the two.

Leo knew the feeling. He went around the room closing curtains.

She said, "I don't understand why Mrs. Culpepper didn't just destroy it all. If she knew it was important and dangerous, why not just fill the basement with gasoline and toss in a match? The basement must have been all that was left of Tidebury after the house washed away. Right?"

"Right," he nodded, assuming she was correct. When he was finished with the curtains, he joined her on the couch. He leaned his head back and stared at the ceiling. "Maybe she couldn't, for some reason. Maybe she kept it for some kind of insurance. I don't know if it matters now. I wish we could drag Alcesta down here and ask her what she thinks."

Melissa grunted. It wasn't a laugh, not quite. "Even if we could, she wouldn't tell us."

"Yeah, no kidding." He checked the time. It was almost four o'clock. "It's probably too late to catch Mrs. Hansen at the museum, but tomorrow she might let us poke through the archives again. Remember, there were a couple of clippings about missing kids? At the time, I didn't think much about it. A missing boy, seventy years ago… It didn't occur to me that his disappearance might be related to Simon."

"Shit, you're right. Now I wish we'd looked a little closer."

He silently kicked himself. He'd skimmed the headline and

seen nothing about a house, and he'd moved on to the next clipping without another thought. "Let's see if we can find anything about them on the internet. You have good google skills. You always have."

Graciously, she said, "You're the one who found the nursing home in five minutes flat."

He was glad. She was willing to cooperate and that meant she was finished being mad at him. "You would've found it in another thirty seconds," he replied. "Let's combine our powers for good and see what shakes out of the web."

He badly wished he'd brought his laptop, but he'd left it at home. He hadn't planned to be here this long, and it wasn't like he didn't have plenty of data to burn through, but the small screen gave him a headache if he stared at it too long.

Lucky for him, Melissa was on point. She had something useful within a few minutes.

She sat up with a start and pinched her screen, scrolling around and skimming at top speed. "Okay, I've got something. It doesn't look like those old newspaper articles in the museum ever made it to the internet, so I thought I'd come at it from another angle: I went looking for *three* missing children instead of one or two, and I got a hit. This reporter did an investigative piece about twenty years ago in the *Seattle Post-Intelligencer*. Look." She handed him the phone.

He read the headline aloud. "'Three Lost Boys: What Happened on Marrowstone Island in 1953?' Holy shit, here we go." He scanned the article as fast as the connection would let him. "Three boys went missing in the span of two months, and they were never seen alive again," he summarized. "David

Burton, Jr., Andrew Jansen, and George Morrill." His heart did a little clench behind his ribs. It almost hurt to think about; the boys who cried in the corners had been real children once. They had names.

"Keep reading," she urged. "Wait until you get to the bit about George."

His lips bobbed while he silently read, until he began calling out the highlights. "David Burton, Jr. and Andrew Jansen went fishing in Mystery Bay...alone?" He shook his head. "Man, the fifties were a wild time. They were eight years old and ten years old, respectively. And first cousins."

"Their boat was found washed out into the shipping lane a week later."

He picked up the thread from there. "No signs of a struggle, and authorities thought they fell overboard and drowned. I don't see any mention of life vests or anything but, again, it was the fifties."

"Poor kids. It's a wonder anybody survived the era of lawn darts."

"I think that was the sixties." He was still reading. "But close enough, yeah. Anyway, then George Morrill went missing from his front yard. He was outside playing with some toys, and when his mother called him inside for dinner, he was gone." He lowered the phone and looked at her. "He had asthma. So *George* must be the ghost boy who's been wheezing inside Tidebury House! Oh my God," he added as his eyes tracked further down the article. "They found George..." Out of reflex, he looked toward the beach, knowing that the curtains were shut. "On the driftwood tree? *Our* driftwood tree?"

"That's what it sounds like to me. Gunnar couldn't have been too worried about getting caught," she noted. "Seems pretty lazy or stupid to dump a kid's body right at the edge of your property."

"The point is, he only had *two* murderable kids to use for his evil purposes. Two dimes, not three."

Melissa nodded eagerly, then stopped. She looked stricken when she said, "But he has three *now*. He took Simon. He took the boys because they were too small to fight back, and he took Simon because he was...because he was *there*. And *that's* why Alcesta said that Charlotte's grandson must be in the corners now."

"Don't think like that. We *can't* assume the worst."

She uncrossed her legs and stood up, leaving her phone on the couch's arm. "Honestly, we might as well. We know that Gunnar's a killer, and Alcesta said he needed three victims to... to do whatever. Make his crazy-ass phone call to hell."

He suspected she was walking away so he wouldn't see her cry, and that was fine with him. He preferred to cry alone too, given the option, and he didn't even disagree with her. He just didn't have the bandwidth to grieve right at that moment. Not when somebody or something was disappearing people and driving houses up out of the ocean and onto the beach like a dune buggy.

"Melissa?" he called.

She was halfway down the hall. He couldn't see her anymore, he could only hear her. "What?"

"You all right?"

"Not really, but we can't...we can't just sit here."

He asked, "Do you have any better ideas?"

She didn't answer right away. A door opened. "I was thinking about taking a shower. But I'll leave the door open, okay? If I yell about being locked in by ghosts, I want you for a witness. Even if you can't help."

"*Obviously* I'll help."

"Well, you'll try." She returned to the living room, where she leaned against the wall and crossed her arms. Then she started, her eyes darting from left to right, up and down. "Wait. Leo. Do you hear that? What is it?"

A loud, strange noise ratcheted through the house, like peppercorns in a grinder—but something bigger, something heavier.

"What the hell?" He climbed to his feet and stuffed his feet back into his uncle's boots. "Where's it coming from?"

Melissa stood there, her back now pressed against the wall like she was trying to hold it up. "Everywhere? Nowhere? God, what is it?"

There was something sandy about the sound, something gritty and rough. It echoed through the corridors and off the high ceilings in the living area, and through the kitchen, and down through the dining room that no one ever used because it was "formal."

Even though she'd asked the question, Melissa answered it. "Something's happening in the basement."

"We should lock the basement door. The one here, in the hall. We should, we should—" Leo desperately looked for some alternative to the obvious. He did not want to know what was making that noise. But he needed to. "We should lock the whole damn house and just go sleep at my aunt and uncle's. Nobody's trying to get inside there, except for me—and I have a key. Melissa? Where are you going, Melissa? What are you doing? Melissa, stop. Don't."

Too late.

She was already dashing toward the basement door at the end of the hall in sock-feet, sliding and stumbling.

And he was on her heels. He couldn't let her go down there alone.

The noise stopped. It started. It sputtered and almost stopped again, then continued. It reminded Leo of someone with a chainsaw trying to cut up a log that's too big for the equipment. It was the sound of a struggle.

Melissa threw the basement door open and ran down the stairs.

No time to hesitate. Yes, it was louder. Yes, the moment the door was open everything became more immediate and aggressive. Yes, it was coming from down there.

His boots did not fit well; he'd underestimated the distance between his own shoe size and his uncle's. The shoes flopped around as he flew down the stairs behind her, and he fought to stay upright—grabbing the wall as he descended. He ran to keep from falling.

When he reached the bottom Melissa was there, standing frozen and staring at the wall with the runes.

They hadn't put the shelves back. The big black circle was on full display and so were the markings inside it, those concentric rings that spelled out magic in a language he did not speak and could not read.

Melissa had her phone out, with a photo of the wall on the

screen like she'd been comparing the two when she stopped and stared slack-jawed.

Leo didn't have to follow her gaze. The runes were moving, grinding like millstones nested together. It made him think of a combination padlock on a high school locker, spinning and spinning in search of the right combination.

"You're seeing this too, right?" Melissa squeaked.

"Literally, what the fuck is happening?" He did not expect a response. He didn't expect anything except confusion and staring, but she surprised him.

"It's broken. He broke it." She fiddled with her phone and held it up facing the circle and the symbols, and that's when he realized she'd set it to record video. "Nobody will ever believe this, not even with footage," she whispered. "Nobody except for you."

She wasn't wrong, and he knew it. "These marks on the wall…they're not a 'no trespassing' sign, and they're not a warning. Put them all together, and they make a lock." He held out his hand, his finger trying to track the outer ring. "And someone's trying to figure out the combination."

"No. Someone already *did*," she insisted. "And look, just…" Melissa didn't point at the screen, but at the second row of sigils, spinning more slowly than the outer ring, and in the opposite direction. "Two are missing. Now it's just spinning and spinning, not catching and holding like it's supposed to."

"Two what? Two runes?"

"Yeah. Compare it to the pictures I took before," she said, but didn't offer him the phone.

Leo didn't want to believe it. He tried hard not to, but the whirling images on the wall wouldn't let him lie to himself. "We have to get out of here."

Melissa didn't move; she held up her phone, getting more video. "What do you think is behind it? We've got Thornbury, we've got Tidebury…which 'bury' is this? What is this lock protecting? What if it's the machine, the Aleyða? What if it's still back there?"

He took her by the arm. "I don't care, we're leaving. Now. Me and you. Come on."

"Okay," she said, but she was slow to put the phone away.

He was dragging her, but she was letting him. "Back up the stairs and lock the door. Back into the hallway and get your stuff if you have anything important. Get your charger, get your purse, get your coat. We aren't staying in here for another goddamn *minute*."

She trailed behind him, tromping heavily up the basement steps and back down the hall.

By now, night had thoroughly fallen, even though it was barely 4:30. The rain was back, louder and harder than before. When they got outside the air smelled like snow, or like ice coming off the ocean, driven by the wind. Leo pulled up his hood and Melissa copied him, her whole body shaking.

"What do we do?" she asked. "Where do we go?"

"My aunt and uncle's place. We'll spend the night there."

She was looking back toward the beach, toward Tidebury.

"Melissa!" he said, trying to snap her out of whatever distraction was making her slow. "Get your keys. Come on. You're driving. My car's still parked over there, let's go."

"That won't be far enough away," she told him, and the words sounded almost panicked, almost ready to run away screaming. "We should get off the island. We should go to Florida or something. Someplace that won't be a…a…wasteland, when he's finished with it."

"There's no such place," he said glumly. "Men like the one Alcesta described…they don't just quit when they succeed. They keep going, keep taking. If you don't stop them, they don't stop coming."

But she didn't budge. She stared back toward the ocean.

"To hell with this." Leo took her arm again and reached into her bag. It only took him a second to find her keys, so he removed them and dragged her to the driveway, to her car. He flung open the passenger door and pushed her inside, then closed it. He squeezed into the driver's side, holding the seat adjuster with one hand and sliding it back; with the other hand, he used her keys to crank the engine.

When he had enough room, he slammed the door shut and threw the Subaru into reverse.

"Put your seat belt on," he commanded.

Melissa did it without asking why and without even pointing out that he wasn't wearing his own.

He punched the gas and tore out of the driveway, down to the tiny dirt road that led to the main drag. In the rearview mirror—he tried not to look but couldn't stop himself—he saw the back of the house and the basement hatch, and a tall shadowy figure standing beside it. Even farther back, down the little walkway that led to the water, he caught a glimpse of the giant driftwood log where a little boy had died some seventy-odd years ago.

He thought about a child who couldn't breathe.

He thought of that hatch, and that wall, and those runes.

And he fishtailed the long heavy vehicle away from the Culpepper property, in an effort to leave them all behind him.

35

SATURDAY

MELISSA

Melissa awoke the next morning feeling entirely too warm and uncertain why. Her mouth was dry, her head hurt, and her body ached. She was wearing someone else's clothes. Whose? Wait. Oh, right. They belonged to Leo's aunt Anna.

Leo's aunt was shorter than Melissa by three or four inches, so the pajama bottoms were high-waters that dusted her calves. Yesterday's clothes were in the laundry. Leo was next to her, lying on his side—a big comforting bear, wearing his uncle's T-shirt and his own dress pants. His other items were also in the laundry.

It'd been silly, or that's how it felt in the light of day—the idea of sleeping huddled up together like they were little kids again. But even when they were too tired to keep their eyes open, they were still scared shitless, each one afraid to let the other out of their sight.

She rolled carefully out of bed, tucked the blanket back around his shoulders, and crept into the bathroom.

On the way out of Mrs. Culpepper's house, she'd grabbed the messenger bag that served as her purse—but she'd been too distracted and terrified to pick up her small rolling suitcase too. That meant no toothbrush and no makeup. But shit, Leo already knew what she looked like, and she found some Listerine under the sink.

In the fridge, she found no milk. In fact, she found almost nothing; it'd been cleaned out before the Alvarezes had left for their anniversary cruise. A wise course of action to be sure, but not one that was helpful to Melissa at the moment.

She pulled a glass down from the cabinet and filled it from the tap. Then she went rifling through the pantry, where she found a box of Hostess snack cakes and a bag of chips.

She sat at the table and pulled out her phone, then pulled up the footage she'd shot the night before. Her stomach turned along with the wheels. (She'd started to think of them as wheels, ever since Leo had said that thing about the locks.) Yes, it looked like a combination lock or some oddball cipher from a movie. Something Indiana Jones would squint at and subsequently solve with a pocketknife or a bag of sand.

Melissa was not Indiana Jones.

The only rune she knew for a fact was "thorn," and that was only because Ms. Ellingboe had pointed it out so forcefully. She put the video away and called up her browser. In a few minutes, she knew a few other runes, and more about "thorn."

"Thornbury," she said around a mouthful of too-sweet snack cake. What a peculiar word. "Two houses alike in dignity," she muttered. She'd started college as an English major, before she'd shifted to graphic design. "But there's no Romeo or Juliet here, is there?"

Not that she could identify. A young married couple, yes. That's where any resemblance ended.

"Futhark," she read the word. "Foo...thark. Futh-ark?" She toyed around with accented syllables and speculative pronunciation. That's what the alphabet was called, named such for the first letters identified. It was the equivalent of calling a keyboard a "Qwerty." Soon, she'd learned about "thorn," which was a north Germanic or Scandinavian import. It made the "th" sound.

"Guarded by thorns." She turned the phrase over in her head. "Guarded by tides." She played with that one too.

The rest of the runes meant little to her, even when she found a site dedicated to rune magic. Melissa had never believed in magic, not by necessity nor choice. It had simply never occurred to her that it might be a real thing and that, furthermore, she might someday encounter it. But here she was anyway, scrolling through websites that put a "k" in "magick" and painstakingly comparing her findings, rune by rune, to the photos she'd taken downstairs in the Culpepper house.

After an hour, she still didn't understand very much about the particulars or the processes—but when she double-checked the video she'd added to her queue of strange evidence, she realized that a third rune was also damaged.

"He broke two, and this one was collateral damage," she mumbled to herself. "I bet the rest will just unravel."

"What will unravel, where?" Leo was up. He was quiet for a big guy. She hadn't heard him coming up behind her.

"Oh, I was just looking at those runes, trying to use the internet to figure out what they mean."

"Any luck?" he asked. Bleary-eyed and in his borrowed clothes, he went to the kitchen and reached into a cabinet, pulling out a can of Diet Coke. He yanked the tab and it cracked open with a hissing fizz.

"Not really. Hey, I didn't know there were sodas."

"You want one?"

"God, yes."

He pulled out another one, then found a glass and got her some ice from the refrigerator door. He brought them both and set them down in front of her.

She thanked him and said, "You know me so well."

"I've known you a long time."

Melissa poured the soda over the ice and paused the video on her phone. She turned it around and pushed it across the table to Leo. "I followed Alcesta's lead and went looking for magic instead of language. It doesn't make *much* more sense that way, but it does track better as a spell than as a message. Also, look at that one, next to the spot where the other two used to be."

He squinted down at the screen, then removed his glasses, wiped them on his shirt, and squinted again. "It's fading."

"Fading, being worn away, something like that." She reached over and swiped right a couple of times until she found a picture she took the first night. "That's the first one that disappeared. It's called *nauthiz.*" She pronounced it the way the website said to, like *not this*. "Which is fitting, kind of. It's the symbol for willpower and intention. I think it was the first one she wrote, and it was probably the first component of the lock."

"I can work with that theory. If that's the case, then the others...hm." He picked up the phone and pushed his glasses up on his forehead so he could look more closely. He'd always been nearsighted as hell. "So Gunnar, in his efforts to undo or unlock something...he started at the bottom and worked his way up, counterclockwise."

"I think you're right. I mean, I also think we're crazy, but—"

He set the phone back down and restored his glasses to their usual position. "At least we're crazy together. If I'd seen it alone, I would've doubted my sanity for the rest of my life."

"Me too. Even though I got video. And pictures."

He shrugged at her and sat back in the dining room chair. "People have video and photos of Bigfoot, and nobody believes them. Likewise UFOs. Ghosts. Angels."

She sighed and settled unhappily in her chair. "We can never tell another soul about this, can we?"

They sat there rehydrating for a minute before he replied. "We could tell Alcesta. And after last night, I wouldn't mind seeing her again. I have some new questions."

"Yeah, me too. I don't know how cooperative she'll be, but we can give it a shot."

"I'll get dressed," he concluded, rising to his feet and pushing the chair back underneath the table.

While he was gone, Melissa kept reading and making notes in her phone. The next rune was called *eihwaz*. Over in the phone's notes app, she jotted, "Strength, trustworthiness. Reliability." And then *perthrow*, the rune of fate.

Did it matter what the runes meant, now that the lock had been breached? Probably not. But it beat thinking about the fact that they might have been inside the house when it'd happened, and that Gunnar Lorentzen had made himself at home down there, doing God knew what, while they slept or snacked or argued.

She hoped he'd done whatever dirty work he'd intended while they were out. It didn't make sense, but it was her hope all the same.

Eventually Leo finished getting dressed and grabbed a snack cake and another can of soda, calling it breakfast. Then they were ready to go.

It only took thirty minutes to get back to Cedar Groves.

They parked in the same little lot, with the same assortment of employee and visitor cars, minus the hearse—next to an ambulance that was parked and quiet, though its engine pinged a lingering announcement that it'd only just arrived.

Back inside, Emma was not on the desk. Today they were greeted by a youngish Black guy who had a bald head and a good beard, and a pair of light blue scrubs. He asked how he could help, and Leo launched into a charm offensive.

"Listen," said the receptionist—whose name was Bryan—as he leaned forward in a gently conspiratorial fashion. "I'd love to help you, and I'd *happily* take you to see Ms. Ellingboe. Especially seeing whereas you got her talking yesterday."

"You heard about that?" Leo asked.

"*Everybody* heard about that. She's been here since the dawn of time, and I don't think anyone ever heard her say more than two or three words—and those were in her sleep. But I'm sorry, it just won't be possible. We found her this morning in her chair by the window. She passed last night, at some point after bedtime."

"Then she...got out of bed first?" Melissa asked, shocked to hear it. "And she went to the window on her own, I assume?"

"So do I, but I'm not sure how. I've been here five years, and I wasn't aware that she could walk that far unassisted. I'm not sure where she found the strength. I really am sorry," he said again. "She was a weird one, but I never had any trouble with her, except for the one time she pinched my ass a few years back."

"Spicy old lady," said Leo, still trying to be charming, but the wind had gone out of his sails.

He shrugged. "It beats getting punched in the face, and Mr. Allman has done that twice."

Melissa's shock was wearing off, and she was starting to get angry. Not at Bryan, and not at Leo, and not even at Alcesta in particular. Or Mrs. Culpepper. Or Simon. Maybe she wasn't angry after all; if she thought about it, maybe she was only scared. "Could you, possibly...?" she started, then tried again. "Do you know where she'll be buried? Did anyone claim her body?"

He shook his head. "She didn't have any living family as far as any of us knew...up to a couple of days ago when her sister died. Her body's almost certainly going to the same place as her twin."

Leo said, "I'm not sure they wanted to spend eternity together."

Melissa shook her head. "It's too late now. They're stuck with each other on the other side."

"They probably won't bury her any time soon, though. It'll be a few days," Bryan said with a shrug. "The storm, you know. It's supposed to hit tonight or tomorrow; I doubt anybody will go to the trouble until it dries out at least a little."

"Storm?" Melissa and Leo said at the same time.

He shrugged again. "Check the forecast, because it's gonna be bad. I mean it's been raining, sure—but man, the weather's been *weird* this year. I've heard thunder twice in the last month. Twice! I've lived in the northwest for years and until last month, I *never* heard any thunder. This late in the year, it's especially strange."

Leo, no longer in flirt mode, mumbled, "Yeah, it's been... crazy. Well, thanks for your time, and um...I'm sorry we missed her." He turned to leave and Melissa was going to join him when Emma came sprinting down the hallway.

"Wait! Hello!" she called. She was waving something in her hand.

Melissa asked, "Did we leave something behind yesterday?"

Emma's sneakers squeaked on the shiny floor when she drew up to a stop in front of them. "I'm so glad you came back! I had no idea how to reach you, and I thought, I thought," she paused to lean forward for a couple of panting breaths, then stood up straight again. "I thought I'd have to throw this away."

Then she presented them with an ordinary white envelope. Melissa was closest, so she took it. Something small and hard was sealed inside it, about the size and weight of a domino. She could feel it through the paper.

She turned it over and saw a message in shaky handwriting: *For Otelia's Houseguests.*

Emma asked, "That's you...right? That was her sister's name, wasn't it?"

Leo said, "That's...that's us. And that was her name, yes." And he came closer to get a better look.

Melissa ran her finger along the seal and opened the envelope, dumping a single sheet of paper and a small white block into her palm. The note was composed in the same jagged handwriting as the directions on the outside, and it was even approximately as brief. It read, in its entirety: *Destroy them both. leave nothing behind of either house and let the Vǫlva do the rest, or else the island is lost—and so are you.*

The small white block was blank on one side.

On the other, a rune.

36

SATURDAY

MELISSA

Back in the car, Melissa left the engine running again while she looked up the new rune on her phone. Leo fidgeted in the passenger seat. He read and reread the little note; he examined and reexamined the envelope, the handwriting, and the rune itself.

Fat splashes of water hit the windshield.

She flipped the wipers on with one hand without thinking about it. "Okay. So. Oooh boy, it's this one." She turned the screen around to show him. "Right? This is the same as…as what's on the, the domino? Whatever it is? The thing that's probably carved out of illegal ivory or something."

"There are antiquity exceptions for endangered animal products," he said. "And this has to be a hundred years old, if it's a day. But that's definitely it; that's the rune. What's it called?"

Melissa reclaimed the screen and scrolled, then summarized what she read. "The rune is called *kenaz*, and it's…well, shit. Ms. Ellingboe packed a lot of meaning into a dozen words."

The look on Leo's face said his heart was sinking, just like hers had when she'd read the rest. "And? What's the message from beyond?"

"It means *torch*. It stands for fire and ancient knowledge, and in magical tradition it suggests a controlled use of power, precisely directed and concentrated. It may also imply that the student has…has…" She wasn't sure how to parse that next bit. "Become the master? I'd hardly call us masters of whatever the hell is going on."

"We don't have to be masters. We just have to be competent, and we're basically the only people left who have any idea what's happening out there." He sat back in the seat, poking the seat warmer button to crank it up.

"The meaning comes with all these other connotations, man, and all of them sound like…" She kept scrolling, reading silently.

"Sound like what?"

"Sorry. They sound like precision, and confidence, and using your intuition and esoteric knowledge to tackle big tasks successfully—even when other people don't understand them. Leo, she wants us to burn down the houses."

He immediately balked. "We can't just *assume* that. And we can't do that either."

"I'm not saying we should," she replied with exactly as much conviction as him. Which was none. "I'm saying that Ms. Ellingboe *wants* us to. Don't get me wrong. Point me to the matches, and I'll torch that awful housewreck to kingdom come." Then she paused, lowered her phone, and craned her neck to look at the sky through the windshield. "Not that matches would cut it. Look, Bryan's right. There's a big fat cloud bank rolling our way."

"And to think, we could actually see cracks of blue this morning."

"The weather lies out here." She sat back, reclining away from the steering wheel again. "But everything's too wet, even if we wanted to burn down Mrs. Culpepper's house. And I, for one, *don't*." She started to say something else but pulled up her phone again and started tapping on the screen keyboard.

"What are you doing now?"

"That other word in her note. *Vǫlva*. She said that in the nursing home too, but I didn't quite catch it—or she pronounced it with a *w* instead of a *v*. Screw it, I'm saying it with a *v*. No way I'm trying to copy that old Norse pronunciation. Now I want to see what it means, and…I bet the vowel in the middle is just an *o* for googling purposes, hmm…"

She went silent. Stayed silent. She scrolled swiftly with her finger, her eyebrows getting lower and lower, her forehead wrinkles deepening.

"And? Hey. Melissa. Hey. What did you—"

In reply, she turned the phone around and showed him an illustration that looked like it came from a book of fairy tales. She could hardly speak, but she squeaked out, "Does this…does any of this look kind of…familiar? To you?"

He leaned in close and used his hand to shield the screen from glare. "It's an old white woman with long silver hair, dressed like a shaman or something. It's not Native American, though. I don't think?"

She pulled the phone back and stared at it some more. "It's

the Scandinavian version of a lady shaman, pretty much. A Vǫlva is a...like a priestess. A magician. She's got... Look, the paint on her face? The smudge of red down her forehead? And see what she's holding? We've seen something like that before, I know we have. I know *I* have," she corrected herself.

"I have no idea what you're talking about. It looks like an animal horn. Or one of those Viking mead cups, like they sell at the Renaissance fair."

She nodded. "Yeah, kind of. But longer—this one's at least as long as the woman's arm. Mrs. Culpepper had one."

"What? No."

"She *did*." She nodded again, harder. "She had it that summer, when you, when we...when you almost drowned." Melissa did not meet Leo's gaze, even though it was practically boring a hole through her head, laser-style. "When you went under, I started running for the lighthouse, to try to get help. When I got back, you were okay. Mrs. Culpepper had pulled you out of the water, and she had, she was holding, it looked like...this. And I saw it in the basement, it's in a box by the bottom of the stairs. You can go see it for yourself."

She turned the phone around again, both eager to show him and reluctant to look away. "And her face, look, the red? The paint?"

Her brain was spinning like the runes on the basement walls. The basement. The hatch. Mrs. Culpepper in the 1980s, carrying a horn that looked just like this one, with paint still smudged on her face. "You told me once, when I asked you what happened—how you made it back to the beach—you said that Mrs. Culpepper walked on water, but I always thought that you were delirious, and it must've been the rocks. I never noticed them before that day, and now I think…I wonder. What if they weren't there before? What if she made them? Called them? Moved them, or something?"

Leo didn't answer, but she could see the gears turning in his head. When he spoke again, he said, "I wish we could ask her. Either one of them, really—but that ship has sailed."

"And now her sister says to burn it all down. But we can't do that, not even if we want to, right? Any fiery efforts would be doomed."

"There are ways around the moisture, I bet. But you're right. We can't just burn them down, or even blow them up—I don't think blowing things up counts as burning them, necessarily."

She said, more confidently than she felt, "Well, I don't care if it *was* a dying old lady's final wish. I won't…I *can't* hurt Simon's house." She put her phone away, then fastened her seat belt and urged him to do the same. "Let's um, let's…" Her head was spinning in a dozen directions at once, and she couldn't focus on any of them individually. She needed caffeine. "Let's start with coffee. There's a Starbucks with a drive-through on the main drag."

"Best idea you've had all day."

"Well, it's still early." She put the car into gear and headed out of the parking lot but pressed the brakes when a gurney came rolling out of a side door, accompanied by two orderlies bundled up against the weather. The gurney had a body on it. Melissa knew it was a body, because it was in a big black body bag. She knew it was probably Alcesta's because that was just the kind of luck that she and Leo were having.

In silence, they watched the men load the wheeled table into the back of the ambulance and shut the double doors at the rear. When the vehicle's parking lights came on, Melissa shook her head and left the Cedar Groves facility in the rearview mirror.

Fifteen minutes later, both she and Leo had sweet, caffeinated beverages that were big enough to barely fit the cup holders, and thirty minutes after that, they were served lunch at the same diner where they'd eaten the day before. When they were reduced to swabbing fries around in ketchup on their mostly empty plates, they returned to the subjects that mattered.

Leo got the ball rolling. "Since we filed a missing person report on Simon, maybe we can push the search up the food chain. We might even get the FBI involved."

"The FBI won't be able to find him either, though," she said glumly.

"No, but they're better equipped to help us than a tiny sheriff's station that somehow serves half the county. The feds might help," he insisted. "I'm not ready to give up yet."

"There's giving up, and then there's admitting that you can't succeed. You heard the old lady yesterday."

"Simon *isn't* in the corners," he protested.

"Even if he's not, he's somewhere beyond our reach and I hate it. The thought makes my head hurt, and my stomach churn."

Defiantly, he said, "That's just the burger talking."

"If you want to lie to yourself, that's your business. But I can't afford to stay away from my job too much longer, so I'm going to have to...adjust. I'm not a Culpepper, and I'm not a Realtor with a Tesla. I'm a graphic designer with a nine-to-five that pays my bills without a lot to spare, and I need to head back to Seattle in a day or two. At the very least, I have to go get my laptop and a few more clothes. Then I can come back and camp out with Simon's internet, at least until it gets shut off because nobody's paying for it."

"You *can't* stay in that house alone. You couldn't even stay there last night, with me—and I'm definitely not staying there again. But I bet you could stay over at my aunt and uncle's place. Hm."

"I don't want to impose on them. They're super sweet, but I'd only be in their way."

"They won't be back for another couple of weeks," he said thoughtfully, but she couldn't tell exactly what he was thinking about until he added, "so how about this: let's clean up our stuff, abandon Thornbury for now, and relocate to Chez Alvarez. We can use that as a new base of operations."

Something clicked in her head, two suspicions cracking together. She leaped to a conclusion. "You want me to clear out so you can stage and list the house. You'd rather sell it than burn it down."

He rolled his eyes. "Of *course* I'd rather sell it than burn it down, but don't be ridiculous. I can't do that without Simon or his grandmother's permission, or their estate's permission. I don't know how it would work, exactly. Now that you mention it," he tacked on a little too late for it to sound sincere. "But I can find out."

"Even if it's not possible for you to sell it right this second, that's where you're going with this, isn't it?"

The look on his face said he had a snappy comeback on

deck, but whatever it was, he swallowed it down. "My concern about the house is practical, not personal. Something will have to be done about it eventually, whether or not Simon ever turns up."

"Whatever lets you sleep at night."

"Crashing over at my aunt and uncle's. *That* will let me sleep at night. You'll sleep better there too. Okay?"

"Yeah, okay. You're not wrong." Then she snorted at a ridiculous thought. "But are you *sure* you want that Culpepper listing? It might be a hard sell, with a monster trying to break inside all the time—and the mess in the basement. Never mind that hunk of garbage out on the beach. You'll drive yourself crazy trying to put a positive spin on that property."

"No kidding. As for Tidebury...I guess you could call in a demo crew and have it torn down. Remove it piece-by-piece, that's probably the only way. It won't be cheap," he added with a sigh. "I just don't understand how it's survived this long. Why isn't that wreck at the bottom of the Sound?"

"Gunnar Lorentzen, I have to assume. Look." She changed pace. "I don't really want to go back to the Culpepper place even for a quick visit, but what else are we going to do? We can't just leave all our crap there, and we should probably close up the house—if for no other reason than there's a storm coming, and we aren't planning to burn the place down because that would be insane."

"That *would* be insane."

"Totally insane."

He smiled tightly. "Glad we're in agreement."

Once again, they headed across the causeway onto

Marrowstone Island, where the weather was getting worse. The sky had darkened enough that the headlights came on, despite the fact that it was early afternoon. The rain came and went, but every time it came, it was worse than before.

"If the FBI got a missing person report for Simon, what would they do with it?" Melissa asked, almost rhetorically. She had to speak up over the flapping of the windshield wipers and the splattering rain that hit the car fast and hard.

Leo crossed his arms and settled down low in the seat, looking like he'd rather be anywhere else in the world. "They'd do more than Jefferson County, I bet. The FBI has dogs, at least. Searchlights. Helicopters. I don't know. I don't know how any of this works."

"I don't either, and I'm not trying to hassle you, dude. You don't have to get so defensive. Please believe me when I tell you, I would do anything—literally *anything*—to roll up to the Culpepper place and see Simon sitting on the front porch, grinning and waving, and..." Her eyes were starting to fill up, so she abandoned that path. "But you and I both know...we know better than anybody what the odds of that are. He's *gone*, Leo. We might never know what happened to him, or where he went, or how he got there. That's the truth, and nobody hates it more than I do."

"It's *not* the truth, it's your opinion."

She hit the brakes hard, fast, suddenly enough to send both their seat belts snapping.

"What?" Leo shrieked, a tad too high and a tad too loud. "What is it? What are you doing?"

She didn't answer. She didn't have to. A pair of deer gave

her car the stink eye, then bounded off into the woods. "I'm sorry," she whispered. "I'm sorry, I didn't see them until the last second, oh God."

Her heart was hammering. The deer were gone. She took a couple of deep breaths and pressed the gas again, proceeding more slowly now.

A loud, low roll of thunder cracked up the sky from the east, or possibly the north. It was hard to pinpoint, even though it roared for nearly ten seconds before petering out. Melissa and Leo tensed up all over again.

Leo said, "That guy at Cedar Groves was right. I never hear any thunder. Or I hardly ever do."

"Me either. That was…not weird, just upsetting. It's like we're driving underneath a train."

By the time they pulled back into Mrs. Culpepper's driveway, they might as well have been driving through a biblical event. The rain was coming down sideways and at tremendous volume; the wind had kicked up and the whole island felt like it was clinging to its bedrock, lest it wash away.

Melissa didn't like that thought. She didn't like the storm, even though the worst wasn't supposed to hit for another couple of hours—or that's what the weather app on her phone said. This was plenty bad enough.

They flung themselves into the foyer as soon as the door was unlocked, and they shook like dogs—then peeled off their outerwear and left it on the hat and coat rack by the door. No one cared about water stains anymore.

Melissa eyed the bathroom as she passed it to collect her things in the guest room.

She tried not to think about the faucets and the steam, and the distant, tinny voice that she had known so well, for so many years.

Down the hall in the guest room, her things were scattered and the bed was unmade. She packed up again. She took her time sorting out the room, making the bed, folding the blanket that always rested at the foot, and tidying the nightstand. If the soft sounds from Simon's bedroom were any indication, Leo was doing the same.

Neither of them wanted to leave. Neither of them wanted to stay. But an era had ended, and there was little sense in pretending otherwise.

Melissa did not think she'd ever be back again. Simon wasn't coming home, and as hard as that fact was to swallow, she couldn't convince herself otherwise; maybe Leo would return to run the real estate listing, when the house finally went up for sale.

It occurred to her that she might have better luck asking an insurance company or a probate court officer to go looking for Simon, since they should be the ones most invested in finding him alive. Someone needed to inherit the house before anyone could sell it, right? How long would it sit empty before the county or the state seized it? And why would they? Back taxes? Probably. The house had surely been paid off for years.

She didn't intend to ask Leo to find out, because the answer wouldn't make her feel any better. She didn't know how she hadn't seen it sooner: He was gunning for that listing. He wanted the sale. Did she blame him? Yes. Was that fair? Probably not.

She blamed him anyway.

Melissa zipped up her small rolling suitcase. That was everything. Whatever they were going to do, she was ready to do it. Or as ready as she was likely to get.

37

SATURDAY

LEO

Leo did not want to leave the Culpepper House. He wanted to lie back down in Simon's bed and stare at the ceiling, soaking up all the smells, the sights, the memories, so he could carry them with him. After all, he'd been coming to visit since he was seven years old. One afternoon he'd wandered through the woods unattended, in the way that children of the 1980s so often were, and he'd found the sprawling, shiny, fancy Culpepper residence almost by accident. He'd heard there were other kids on the island, and if he just poked around a little, he'd find them.

He'd poked around. He'd found them.

At first, Simon and Melissa had acted like he was some small alien, beamed down into their midst. By then, they'd been the only kids on the island for a couple of years. They were older than him, and they were both intimidating and enthralling in their world-wise ways.

Leo had just started first grade at a rural public school outside of Tacoma. He was the biggest little kid, and the quietest;

he wore "Coke-bottle bottom" glasses that were so heavy that they left grooves on his nose and across the top of his cheeks. There had been bullies.

But in the summers, he'd had Simon and Melissa.

Even when they were too fast for him, too strong, and too mature—whatever that means, when you're all in grade school and nobody knows anything—they'd still been the three amigos, just like the movie. Kids know when it's them against the adults. Kids will form packs or communities when they need a place to belong, just like adults. Just like dogs, or deer.

Thirty-five years ago, Leo had belonged on Marrowstone. Now, if he forced himself to admit it, he did not.

He could still navigate it like a local, and it was funny in a warped kind of way—how Melissa clearly relied on him now. He'd always known that she viewed him as a bit of an albatross around their necks when he was a kid, and even if she'd gotten over it in time, he'd never shaken that quiet knowledge. But when the shit hit the fan, she'd called *him*, hadn't she? When she was afraid for Simon, and when she needed help, *he* was the one she reached for.

The truth was, Melissa didn't have that many friends either.

And honestly? Fuck Melissa, but she was probably right about Simon being dead, and Leo prayed so, so hard that she was wrong. He refused to admit that Simon wasn't coming home. It didn't make sense. Even if it was true.

A soft, strange noise pricked at the very edge of his hearing.

"What was that?" he asked the ceiling. Melissa was packing up her own things, stalling in her own ways. She'd never hear him, unless he shouted. He wasn't shouting. He heard it again, a faint grinding, and the sound of something falling. Masonry, unless he missed his guess. Stones or bricks or something.

He closed his eyes.

He heard rain on the roof, drumming hard. Wind through the trees outside. Melissa, swearing to herself. Something downstairs, moving. Not the sound of life, or something scuttling—but the sound of something gritty rubbing against something else. He tried to tell himself it might be rats. It might be raccoons. It certainly wasn't in the basement, no.

It certainly wasn't downstairs.

"It's *definitely* something downstairs," he said with a deep breath, a groan, and a terrible feeling of impending doom.

He sat up. The bed squeaked. Melissa was zipping something up back down the hall, some compartment on her small suitcase—he traveled enough to know the sound. Should he call her attention to the strange noise? He was closer to it than she was; Simon's room was farther along down the corridor. She probably couldn't hear it yet.

Quietly, he left Simon's bedroom and headed down the hallway which had always seemed so impossibly long. And at the end, on the left, the single door that was solid wood and painted white. He unlocked it.

The mechanism clicked over with the faintest *ping*, and he pushed the door open.

He stood at the top of the stairs, gazing down into a pool of darkness. He glanced over his shoulder. Melissa was still in the guest room. She hadn't heard him. All right. He turned on the light, and now he could see well enough to descend the wood slat stairs, down to the too-small basement that worried him—especially now that he knew what he knew: that the basement once belonged to another house.

Or part of it did.

The noise was brighter there, at the top of the stairs. Not louder, just easier to hear—and definitely coming from below. Leo let his real estate brain run through the details in the background while he descended. It calmed him like a mantra, as silly as that sounded. Even to him. (Especially to him.)

One step. Two steps.

The basement of the Tidebury house had remained in place after the storm, and it had been restored or reused by the Thornbury house. Mrs. Otelia Charlotte Ellingboe Culpepper had done that on purpose, even though she could've just filled it with concrete and paved over it. He did not know why. He might never know why.

Three steps. Four steps.

The present basement, into which he was descending, was considerably smaller than his general architectural knowledge suggested that it ought to be. A hasty estimate might call it four or five hundred square feet, though the upstairs house's footprint would support something considerably larger. They could've added a couple thousand feet down there, if they'd really wanted the extra room.

Five steps. Six.

Now he could see the floor surrounding the staircase landing. He saw old tools, Christmas wrapping paper, boxes of books. Probably the Gothic romances Mrs. Culpepper could never get enough of. A box with sure enough, a big horn sticking out of the end. He avoided it. Too much nostalgia. Too much power. Too much fear.

Seven. Eight. Nine. Ten.

He stood on bare concrete, gray and white with a couple of stains that looked like motor oil or laundry detergent. It was damp. Not quite wet.

Wait.

A trickle of water dribbled from a spot on the floor from behind the wall with the runes. The runes themselves were stationary, but the sound of masonry crumbling rang in Leo's ears all the same. There was a rhythm to it—almost.

Not a very good one for music. Not a bad one for the rise and fall of tides.

He was absurdly glad to see that the runes were not moving anymore. His stomach had turned with those spinning wheels, sliding around on the wall as if they weren't painted there. It was insane and impossible, but he'd seen it. He'd watched the symbols roll, left to right, back and forth. They'd made him think of the insides of a pocket watch, wheels within wheels.

Now they hummed, but they did not roll—even though they wanted to. The tension was palpable. It filled the room. Those marks wanted to spin. They *struggled* to spin. The engine was running, but the car was in neutral.

Yes, that was it.

No, that wasn't it.

They were frozen like a garbage disposal that had seized up. He remembered his aunt Anna standing in front of their kitchen sink with a broom handle, jamming it down the drain and leaning, hoping to pop something loose. He'd never forgotten the sound the motor made while it revved harder and harder but couldn't move the blades…yes. That was closer to what he was seeing and feeling.

And hearing.

The buzz burrowed into his brain while he stared at the marks, each one bigger than his open hand. Where was the water coming from? There. The bottom bricks—no, the cinder blocks, that's what they were—had cracked and crumbled, opening a hole in the wall about the size of a coffee cup. That's where the water was coming from. It trickled down and pooled at the center of the room, where once there might have been a drain and now there was only a sunken spot.

He watched the puddle grow.

Whatever had broken, had broken before. Whatever was going to happen down there, had happened already.

"Not good for the resale value," he joked to himself, but the words tasted sour and he wished he hadn't said them, even though no one had heard him. He was nervous, that's all. Afraid, even. He'd always hated that basement, and always known that it hated him back—which was madness, wasn't it? Well, it was no crazier than the boys in the corners who cried and cried, until they screamed.

It was amazing, what children could absorb and accept as normal and true.

It was amazing, how the water came faster now. It'd gone from a trickle to a fine, steady stream.

Leo crouched down low and picked at the broken wall around the hole. It flaked away in his hands—too easily. The bricks were as soft as chalk. More chunks fell away as he investigated, and the hole widened. The lock had failed. The wall was breached. The standing wall was little more than a formality.

He dropped to his hands and knees. Beyond the wall, he saw only darkness.

But his cell phone was in his pocket.

He whipped it out and turned on the flashlight app, then got back down on all fours.

Or all threes. Avoiding the water, he brought the phone low and aimed it through the hole, then lowered his face until his cheek was almost on the ground. His glasses slipped; he adjusted them with the back of his hand and tried again to see inside.

His knees were getting wet. His hands were starting to shake from holding himself and the phone steady in such an uncomfortable position—his neck twisted, his head low and turned, his other elbow acting as a kickstand. His elbow was getting wet too. The trickle was now as thick as a fat milkshake straw, not the feeble drip of a coffee stirrer.

The hole in the wall was about the size of his face. The light burning through it from his phone was wobbly and bright, throwing and sharpening shadows. It was hard to tell exactly what he was looking at.

"Some tables?" he guessed out loud. "With some stuff on them?"

His kickstand elbow slipped. He almost dropped his phone in the water but held it aloft and let his arm take the brunt of the dampness instead. With his head lower, he could listen better. Through the hole, the gravelly, sandy noise churned. It was almost like holding a shell to his ear and hearing the ocean.

But it wasn't the ocean. He couldn't tell what it was, and no matter how hard he tried, he couldn't imagine what it might be. It called to mind rocks crushed together, grinding one another into pebbles. It made him think of Aunt Anna and her mortar and pestle. Stone on stone.

He stood up straight again, rubbing at the wet spots on his elbows and knees, for they were going numb. He scanned the little basement—the *definitely* too-small basement—and spotted a bucket with some lawn-care equipment and long-handled tools sticking out of it. A pair of loppers, a rusted spade, a tire iron, a set of crusty jumper cables. A broken bird feeder. A wrench as long as his arm. A small hatchet.

He took the hatchet. "That'll work."

He returned to the wall and started swinging.

He did it almost gently at first, for no real reason except that he wasn't accustomed to breaking things on purpose. He tapped the back of the hatchet's head against the edge of the hole and more wet crumbles fell. He kicked them aside and used the hatchet as a hammer—but he met so little resistance that he flipped it around and started hacking in earnest.

Sometimes people saw a fat man and thought they were looking at a weak man, but that was a stupid misconception. A fat man is strong by design; he has mass and inertia. He has weight to throw behind physical effort, and he has the power to fling it.

Before long, the size of the hole reached the edge of the runes.

Leo tapped the tool's head against the next rune in line for destruction. He used no more force than it would take to crack a boiled egg's shell.

The metal head sank an inch into the wall. For all that the blocks around the hole were fragile, this was different. It might as well have been baby powder, or ashes.

He raised the hatchet again and swung it fast, again and again, until he had a hole big enough to not merely see through but climb through. Was that what he wanted to do?

Was it really?

Sweaty now, he paused and pulled out his phone again because there was nothing to see, yet. Everything beyond the wall was blanketed with a heavy shadow.

He turned on the light.

He shined it through the hole. He ran the beam over the tables he'd spotted before, and the cabinets, and the walls from corner to corner. Yes, here was the missing square footage. Yes, this is where the water was coming from. Yes, this was definitely part of the old house, of Tidebury, which now sat on the beach.

Yes, he started shouting for Melissa at the top of his lungs, and her name was shrill in his mouth, his voice was high with horror. Yes, now he understood.

Yes, no matter how much it hurt, or how strange it was, or what kind of betrayal it felt like.

Yes, they needed to burn it all down.

38

SATURDAY

MELISSA

Melissa finished zipping all her clothes and toiletries into the suitcase, and she sat on the foot of the bed, unsure of what to do next. Maybe Simon would turn up in the woods, years from now—his body half sunken into the earth, his bones exposed to the elements, his bright red hair bleached pale from exposure over the seasons. Actually, that wasn't the worst thought. Was it? There were worse fates, surely, than dying in the woods and becoming one with nature or whatever. It sounded peaceful, when she thought of it that way.

A quiet resting place, surrounded by trees. The occasional visit from deer, walking in silence on their spindly legs.

Or a quiet corner in an old house, where he could cry and sometimes scream.

"No." She shook her head and planted her hands on either side of her thighs. She hated the idea that she might never know. She tried to get okay with it, and failed. What if she never saw this house again? What if it sold to someone else, and she drove out to it someday—years from now—and didn't even recognize it? What if Simon *did* come back, and he was furious with her for giving up so easily?

On the other hand.

Maybe she should've given up sooner.

If she'd given up on dragging Simon out to the city, given up on the pair of them staying as thick as thieves into adulthood. Given up on any lingering thoughts in the back of her head that they might have, maybe, been able to build a life together. If she'd done all that, then what? Would she have traveled more, had more friends, been more successful?

Been happier?

She should've traded in those stupid, immature fantasies for new experiences and people years ago. If she'd been able to do that, maybe her life would be better. More.

Enough.

Even without Simon, who'd built his own life without her, hadn't he? It wasn't far removed from the same life he'd always had, but he'd grown and changed and succeeded regardless. Shit, for all she knew, he'd been happy there on the island—parked in his grandfather's office, helping charities raise money for good causes, keeping one eye on his grandmother.

He always *said* he was happy.

But. Then he was running outside in the middle of the night in a storm. Losing his grandmother. Vanishing into the dark, falling and dying. Vanishing.

"No," she said again, in case anyone was listening. In case it mattered. But the thought was welling up, clawing its way into her brain and blossoming there. She couldn't shake the image:

not his remains, poking through the earth—but his weak, soaked body too shattered by injury or illness to survive without assistance. Too frail to call for help or find it on his own.

She still had a little time, didn't she?

They could still take a few hours to check the nearby woods just one more time, couldn't they?

Another crack of thunder out over the ocean startled her. She clutched the duvet even harder. "This fucking storm," she complained. All right, so maybe this wouldn't be the best possible time to go looking, with the early sunsets and the darkness rolling across the sky, promising a driving sort of rain that would pierce the tree canopy and soak everything, everywhere.

Storms—*real* storms, not just a whole lot of rain—weren't common on Marrowstone, and they didn't tend to last very long. Whatever this was, it'd be gone by morning...or by lunchtime tomorrow at the latest. That would still give them a few hours of the cold gray daylight on Sunday to go looking before sundown.

"Melissa!"

She clutched her chest and gasped when she heard Leo scream her name. It was not a friendly, casual scream that merely summoned her attention—it was a terrified demand, and she was confident that it came from the basement.

With a trip and a scramble, she hopped off the bed and raced out into the hall.

"I'm coming! I'm coming, hang on! Leo?" she screamed back, already breathless and running toward that door. She slammed past it and flew down the stairs, where she found Leo with an ax in one hand and his cell phone in the other. His pupils were as big as buttons and his mouth hung open. He was sweaty and dusted in something light gray. He looked like he'd been digging graves.

"Are you...? Is there...?" She wasn't sure what to ask. Something was wrong—critically wrong—but she didn't know where or how to begin asking what it was or how to help.

Leo held up the ax and pointed it at the wall where the runes were painted.

Melissa slapped her hand over her mouth without even thinking about it. The wheel of runes was broken, its left half crumbled away. Or hacked away? "Leo, what did you *do*?"

Unable to speak, he shook his head and opened his mouth. Closed it. Finally said, "It wasn't even spinning anymore. All I did was make the hole big enough to see...to see what's behind it. Look," he begged. "*Look*."

She didn't want to see. But she needed to know.

He held out his cell phone, the flashlight still burning through his battery life.

She took it. She turned it over, and for an instant, the beam hit her in the eyes. She faced it away from herself and pointed it at the hole in the wall—big enough for an adult to climb through without too much crouching and ducking.

Melissa looked back at Leo.

She looked at the wall, barely sturdier than a bag of flour.

She crept toward the hole as if it would swallow her, but Leo had seen enough. He stood back with his weapon and a shell-shocked expression. If she'd snapped her fingers in his face, he might not have blinked.

That's when she noticed that he was standing in a couple inches of water.

It spilled over the lowest cinder block bricks, down at the junction of the wall and the floor—filling the basement at a steady stream.

Carefully, her heart in her throat, she stuck her arm through the hole and shined the phone's light around the room on the other side.

It was a room, yes. A big one. At least as big as the basement space she stood in, and maybe bigger. Hard to see what was in there. Water on the floor, for sure. It spilled over her boots and soaked her socks. It was cold as fuck.

Three tables, she could see that much. A set of wood shelves against a wall, beside a boarded-up window near the ceiling. But the phone light was too white, too sharp, and it was hard to see any details. She aimed the light at the wall beside the hole. She didn't see a switch, but she did see a string.

She pulled the string. By some miracle, an overhead bulb lit up with a fizzling cough and a puff of dust.

Behind her, Leo's teeth were audibly chattering. He said, "I feel so stupid. I should've thought of that."

She stepped through the hole, into the room where the water was a little deeper; it pooled against the lowest row of cinder blocks, for they hadn't eroded entirely down by her feet. Maybe it was her imagination, but the wall seemed firmer, less likely to fall right down, the farther it got from the giant wheel of runes.

The lock had broken. Someone had come inside.

But that someone was long gone now. Melissa felt a strange

sense of detachment, and she felt curiosity, and she felt her feet getting wet through her boots. She was standing in a room that had been sealed for decades—a basement space that someone had gone to a great deal of trouble to wall off and lock up, by means both analog and esoteric.

Melissa let the hand with Leo's phone fall to her side. The light overhead was not good, but it was good enough.

Three tables, yes. Slabs, really. People-sized, with a drain at the feet. Mortuary tables. Metal ones with legs that were covered in brittle rust. On top, where they must have been stainless steel, someone had scratched marks up and down them. More signs, more symbols. Different ones. Whatever language they were in, Melissa didn't recognize it. Not Greek. Not Cyrillic. Not Chinese or Japanese or Korean.

These symbols did not run in circles like the wheel of runes, they ran in lines—angles and squares. Where the runes were spare and organic, these signs were busy, cluttered, and mathematical in their precision.

So this was what Gunnar's magic looked like. It was non-Euclidean geometry, and it went up against the Ellingboe twins and their runes. They might as well have been from different planets. "A pay phone," she remembered Alcesta saying. The symbols must have been some kind of number, profound and powerful enough to reach another dimension entirely. Which part was the area code? That line of roughly written formula? That circled sum?

"Melissa, look on the shelves," Leo begged. "Tell me it's not what it looks like. I need...I *need* for you, I need for *someone* to tell me it's *not*. Just say that it's *not*."

But there it was: a pay phone, built to place calls to another reality. It was monstrous and complex, cobbled together out of loose parts from a thousand other things. An electrical panel. A body made of file cabinets, stuffed with vacuum tubes and wires, primitive circuit boards and typewriter keys. Buttons from an old adding machine. Fuses. Switches. Colored glass insulators, scraps of knob-and-tube.

It took her breath away.

"Melissa?"

"Hang on, Leo," she whispered. "Give me a minute. Let me see. I need to…look."

39

SATURDAY

MELISSA

The franken-machine squatted against the wall, rusted and crumpled. Valves and gears stuck out here, protruded there. A depression in the middle reminded her of a soda dispenser, the kind with the computer that lets you program your preference. What went in that little nook?

"Is that you, *Aleyða*?" she asked it. "Are you the machine the Ellingboe sisters were so afraid of?"

Leo didn't hear her, didn't know, or didn't feel like responding.

He'd been spooked silly by something on the shelves, but putting it that way made it sound trivial and, deep down, she knew that it wouldn't be. Leo wasn't a scaredy-cat kid anymore, and neither was Melissa. She could do this. He'd already faced whatever darkness awaited back there behind the runes. Now it was her turn.

Now.

The shelves. They were mounted beside the machine, stacked from waist height to the ceiling.

Upon them Melissa saw glass cases full of jars with faded labels, like in a museum exhibit. An especially gruesome exhibit, now that she looked at it closely. Almost without thinking, she pulled up Leo's phone. It was locked, but it was the same model she had—and she used her thumb to swipe on the lock screen. There. You didn't need a passcode to use the camera. Yes. She started taking pictures.

Everyone has a way to impose distance. To assert control and order.

It was the only thing she could do without thinking about what she was seeing, and she couldn't think about it. (She didn't want to think about it.) She couldn't understand it. (She didn't want to understand it.) She chose to record it, even though the light was low and the images were bound to be grainy. The flash wouldn't do any good. It would bleach out the shots; it would bounce off the glass surfaces of all these jars with their specimens and test tubes and yellowed labels that were foxed with mildew.

NUMBER ONE, read the closest. The words had been written with lean, tall handwriting.

Pencil, Melissa thought. Not ink. The letters reflected silver when the light hit them directly. RECOVERED SPECIMEN REMAINS. Three jars sat under the label. One held four small teeth that looked like they'd been through a fire. One held a few scraps of something charred that once was white. (Bones, reduced to shavings that were burned around their edges. No. Just take the picture.) The last held a powdery light residue that could've been cinder block dust, but wasn't. (Ashes, or something like them.)

NUMBER TWO, read the next.

More of the same—three jars lined up on the shelf above their label—but two of the teeth were grimy with something that looked like rust, but wasn't. One of the bones still had the curve of an eye socket and part of an upper jaw. A small one. The skull it came from hadn't been very big. *Couldn't* have been very big. Had to come from a child. (A little boy, but she knew that. She knew that, and she forced herself to ignore it.) The last jar looked like it held scraps of leather mixed with fireplace ashes, but that wasn't it. (Dried flesh and ashes of a different sort. Try not to think about what sort.)

"'Number three,'" she read aloud.

On these jars, there were fresh fingerprints and smudges where years of grime had been swiped away with recent handling. She could see their contents more clearly than the older jars, which appeared to have gone untouched for decades. In the first—like the other two—there were teeth. Relatively fresh teeth, no more than a few days old—with gory roots still attached. She counted six of them, still crusty with blood and saliva. Molars and cuspids. Bits of gum as pale as sashimi.

The next held bones, charred around the edges. New bones, bones that were wet before they were burned. A larger piece of skull with a larger nasal bone still attached. This one came from an adult. She reached up to touch it, to add a fingerprint to the glass or wipe someone else's away. But she drew back her hand.

Something in her gut said, *Don't.* She took a picture.

The last jar...three jars, three tables, lots of things in threes... this one didn't hold ashes and leather. This one held little bones from fingers that looked like dice, and strips of tissue drying to jerky. Scraps of hair.

She brought up Leo's phone and found the flashlight button. She shined the light directly into the glass and through it, to better see the contents inside. She saw a fingernail, whole and bloody. What looked like part of an ear. Coils of something that could've been bits of intestine, dehydrated and cracked.

She kept returning to the hair, a few stray locks, their ends singed. The rest, wavy and red.

Her brain refused to make any connections.

"Melissa?"

Leo was still outside. She did not answer him. She was too busy trying not to see what was on the shelves in front of her.

She turned her attention to the tables again. Two with dust settled into the nooks and crannies, rendering the strange engravings bright and visible. She blew on them to see them better, but still didn't understand a single line. And the third table. The third table had been used sometime in the last few days. Maybe the last few hours.

When she touched it (she shouldn't have touched it) it was damp, but that was only the ambient moisture, the water that was past her ankles now, not that she really noticed. Even though it was so cold she could barely feel her toes. Even though her shoes were heavy with it, and she was starting to shiver. Even though the hair in the jar was red and it was wavy, a little curled lock in a pile of grim, ground-up, used up, burned up body bits.

It was humid in the basement on this side of the wall. So humid that nothing dried quickly or well. The table had held something wet, not long before. She swiped a finger across it and drew up a damp smear of blood, beginning to oxidize brown.

Etched into the table she saw a series of horizontal lines, each one holding more mathematical-looking figures and symbols. Instructions? A spell? A curse? The markings were dim with grime and she could not read them, so she wiped her finger on the table again—leaving a cleaner swipe across the first line. It was right where someone's head would go, if this were an examination table. Right where a little pillow might be, if it were a casket.

The markings began to glow.

Melissa drew back her hand. A metallic cough belched from the machine against the wall. The slot that looked like a nook—no, a niche, a place for a saint's statue to go—lit up with a fast, bright glow. Then it went dark.

The red hair, burned at the ends. Curled in the jar, atop the rest of what remained.

The teeth, their nerves and roots pulled loose and collected without ceremony.

"Melissa?" Leo called again. "*Please*, Melissa?"

Her lips parted to reply. They closed again. She looked back and forth between the tables, the jars, the machine that did not look like it could possibly work—couldn't possibly do anything except sit there and rust—but it rumbled a soft, grinding hum despite its decrepit condition.

To herself (or to Leo, if he could hear her), she said, "First, you take it apart. Then you take it in pieces, from the table. You put the pieces in the machine and it…it does…something. Extracts something. Everything." Pieces of what? Pieces of who? She declined to think along those lines. Three tables, two dead boys. One dead boy found at the driftwood log. One missing adult man with red hair, surely lost to the corners by now. Three jars, full of bloody pieces and curls.

He must have been alive, until quite recently. Gunnar must have kept him somewhere, needing him alive. Unwilling to let him die too soon, not like the boy with asthma. The small corpse he'd left on a driftwood log.

No. Not going there. Not thinking about that. Her soul could not hold that much grief, not all at once.

She held up the phone and put it on burst mode, holding down the button and aiming the lens here, there. Up and down. What if it could tell her something her eyes couldn't? Why was the machine still doing something, or still able to? It leaned heavily against the wall, pure wreckage as far as she could tell.

"Someone's been inside here," she said, just echoing what Leo'd told her, except now she believed it. "Someone who can walk through walls, now that the lock is broken."

"Melissa." Her name was a choked, wet sound.

"Mrs. Culpepper kept him out, and now...now the runes are in ruins, and he goes wherever he wants. He comes inside. He does his work, he uses his tables, his machine. He slices them up like salami and feeds them to that machine and it—it does something. It's *still* doing something. Still trying to place that long-distance call."

The buzz rose up loud in her ears. The machine was thrumming, warm and electric.

Melissa was standing in water.

Somehow, that got through to her brain faster and harder than the red hair in the jar, and the teeth, and the bits of skull.

"I'm standing in water. Leo!" she hollered. "Leo, get up on the stairs! Get out of the water! Right now!"

His reply was a single syllable, and it could've been anything. A grunt, a yes, a cough.

She put his phone away and sloshed through the water, back to the hole. She climbed through it, not bothering to turn off the light.

Leo had done what she'd told him; he was standing on the wood steps, a foot or two above the water. She joined him, and pushed him, and hurried him up and out, into the hallway.

By the time she shut the door she was sobbing, and Leo looked like he was falling apart. They were both so brittle, so shaken, that thinking straight was impossible—and everything else felt that way too.

She sat down, her back against the door, her wet feet oozing dirty water on the hallway runner. She held out Leo's phone, and her arm, her hand, they were shaking so badly she nearly dropped it. "What do we do? What do we...? Who do we call? How do we...? What do we *do*?"

He took the phone. His eyes were red and his hands were no steadier than hers. His voice was so thick with tears and phlegm that he could barely squeeze out words, but he did, and he said something she knew but could not spit out to save her life. "The sisters already told us."

"But we—" A loud buzzing rose up from the basement; she could feel it through the door, almost as clearly as she could hear it. Something awful was still alive. The machine was sending out a message, fueled by rituals too terrible to speculate upon. "We can't stay here," she finished. "We have to go, we have to get out. We have to burn it down, everything. Both of them."

"*Yes!*" screamed an answer from somewhere down the hall.

Melissa and Leo screamed hard in return, loud, like they could push the horror away with their voices, but it wouldn't work—it couldn't work, and they knew it, and Melissa almost couldn't stop herself. Not even with her hand over her mouth.

Leo grabbed her hard and held her against the door, for comfort as much as protection; she felt his heart banging like a fire alarm but she clung to him as the ghostly cry echoed through the house, down the corridor, up and down the basement stairs even though the door was shut. It was a single word that dragged on for too many seconds. It moved like the rain outside, blowing all around, coming from every direction at once.

When it stopped, they were not alone. (If in fact they ever had been, inside that house.)

Mrs. Culpepper stood at the far end of the hall. She looked exactly like herself—exactly the way she'd looked the last time Melissa had seen her: ancient and frail but dressed sharply in expensive clothes that had been tailored down to her geriatric size. Her hair was perfectly pinned atop her head, and very white. Her patent leather flats glinted in the night light that was plugged into the wall by her feet.

Leo's grip on Melissa loosened. Her grip on him did not.

"*I can't do* everything *myself.*" When she spoke, her voice sounded terribly far away—as if she could either appear clearly or be heard clearly but not both at once. "*The one time I tried, I mostly failed.*"

"Tonight? Now?" Melissa asked, and she'd either started crying again or never stopped in the first place, she wasn't sure—but her nose was stuffed up and she could barely see for the tears and confusion.

Mrs. Culpepper said, "*We'll buy you what time we can.*"

Then she was gone.

40

SATURDAY

LEO

Leo and Melissa sat in Melissa's car, neither one of them knowing what to say or how to start talking. It was one thing to think that Simon might be dead, or even feel strongly that he *was* dead, and a different thing entirely to think of him sliced into pieces and processed by a terrifying machine, with whatever remained left over stashed in jars like some kind of goddamned trophy.

But Leo had known, the moment he'd seen the third set of jars. He almost understood it, in the broadest sense; he almost had an idea of what had happened, and how.

Not why.

He had a gruesome, haunted feeling that he did not *want* to know why—and even if someone told him, he certainly wouldn't understand it. Whatever was happening on Marrowstone was vast and terrible and outside the realm of human reason. Whoever was causing it was no human at all. Leo understood that part now, if nothing else.

The rest, he grasped in pieces.

Gunnar Lorentzen needed three living people. The first time, he chose children. Was it because they were easier to manipulate? Simpler to catch and kill? It couldn't have been something specific to their age, not if he'd resorted to Simon in the end. But the first time, George had died before reaching the machine. Had this procedural hiccup weakened Gunnar? Had it made him vulnerable enough that Mrs. Culpepper thought she'd shoot her shot? Something *did* fail, that was the point. And his sister-in-law had sent him away.

But not for good.

Two dead women. Two houses.

Two people—Melissa and Leo—left to finish their work.

Melissa said, "We can't walk away now." She'd backed her car out of the driveway and taken it to the edge of the road that led to the property, as if ten yards of trees and dirt might be enough to protect them from someone who didn't need doors.

The sky was the color of slate, and the sun would formally set in an hour, but it was dark enough already. Water fell in horizontal sheets, gusting hard and slapping loudly on the windows, ignoring the wipers. The Subaru's headlights had come on automatically. They shined through the trees onto the Culpepper house. Onto Thornbury.

"Do you see him? Do you see anyone?" Melissa asked anxiously. Fog collected inside on the windows, even though the heat was running. The car's engine wasn't hot enough to clear it yet.

He shrugged. "I think he can hide if he wants to. I think he can show himself, if he'd rather."

"Can he *die*, though? That might be the only thing that matters."

She reached into her bag—the only thing she'd brought from the house when they had fled. She pulled out the envelope and its cryptic contents. "Here's what Alcesta gave us."

Leo hadn't brought his go-bag. There was nothing inside it he couldn't replace more easily than he could face going back inside that house again. "I know what it is. We already looked it up. We know what it means. Give me a second, let me think." His mind raced. How could you burn down two structures in the middle of a terrible rainstorm?

Melissa was on the same page. "Whatever we do, we have to do it now. This storm..."

"Yeah. This storm. Fire can and does burn, even where it's wet. But we would need..." What? What might do the job? The gears in his brain spun wildly.

She snapped her fingers. "The propane tanks!"

"What?" He looked at her like she was insane. Maybe she was.

"The propane tanks at the museum. Mrs. Hansen. Newspaper clippings."

They were reduced to communicating in keywords now. All right. "All right, that's a start. Blow it up, burn it down. Gas will burn, one way or another. But I don't think there were more than fifteen or twenty tanks back there."

"That's a lot of propane, my dude."

"Enough for *Thornbury*, sure. But we'll have to go harder for Tidebury." Something pinged at the back of his brain, something he'd seen and idly wondered about, and now struggled to recall. "Something *more*."

"Like what? Dynamite? Nitroglycerin? Because I have no idea how to get my hands on anything like that—much less in a hurry."

"Oil!" he said, as suddenly as she'd cried, "Propane." "Heating oil. Some of the older homes around here, they still have oil tanks for the winter! Though it has a really high ignition point...hm." Then he explained, speaking so quickly that he almost tripped over the words: "Selling a house with oil heat can be tricky; these days people think it's old-fashioned, and buyers want either natural gas or an electric furnace."

"Okay, but what does a *high ignition point* mean? I have electric heat, and I don't even control the building thermostat. I don't know a damn thing about this shit."

He flapped his hands while he mentally hunted for the fastest way to convey what he meant. "People hear the *oil* part of heating oil and think it's dangerous—and it *can* be, but it's usually not. Under normal conditions, you could drop a lit match into a bucket of the stuff, and the match would just...go out, like you'd dropped it in water. That's because you have to get heating oil fairly hot before it'll catch fire: at least a hundred and forty degrees. Oil heaters are designed to do that in a controlled manner. You follow?"

She nodded. "So, something like a propane explosion would set it off, got it. But where do we get heating oil? It's not like a gas tank; we can't just siphon some off with a plastic tube and a strong stomach. Wait. We could use regular old gasoline, couldn't we?"

"Do you know how to siphon gas out of a tank? Because I don't think I could do it without poisoning myself." Suddenly he knew what had prompted the thought of heating oil. "Nordy's."

"Nordy's burned down."

"I know. But an oil truck's been parked out front since we got to the island. Everybody's using that space for parking, because they know nobody needs it anymore. Fuck me, that's what we'll do. We'll steal the truck."

Melissa was on board immediately. "Okay. Let's do it."

"All right." He swallowed hard. He spent twenty seconds trying to come up with some explanation for what they were about to do—something that wouldn't mean the end of their respective normal lives the moment anyone figured out what had happened. Something they could tell the police, the neighbors, the newspapers, if it came to that.

Nothing sprang to mind.

Then again, they might get lucky. There were no traffic lights on Marrowstone. No speed traps or cameras. Anybody who had a video doorbell system would never get a glimpse of the Culpepper property or anything near it.

"Weird things happen," Melissa said quietly, and it almost shocked him. But she wasn't reading his thoughts; she was only thinking along the same lines. "Between us, we'll figure something out."

"I wish we had more time. Look at the clouds. The storm's right on top of us." Or it would be, in a matter of minutes. A long line of curly black clouds spilled over the horizon line, coming in fast. "It's now or never. I'll take the oil tank truck."

"You will?"

He nodded. "Unless you know how to hot-wire a vehicle."

"I don't. Wait. You do?"

He nodded some more. Uncle Marco's old truck had eventually gotten to where it wouldn't start any other way, but he'd always refused to get rid of it. "Just one of my many skills. How are you with breaking locks and stealing propane? We're pressed for time, and your Outback will hold more tanks than my Tesla."

"Fair point. I'll figure something out."

"Drop me off on the way to Flagler. I'll meet you back here as soon as I can."

"Is this really the best idea? Should we *really* split up?" Her eyes were stricken, and he almost wondered if she was even capable of holding up her end of the bargain. But she rallied before he could answer. "No, you're right, we have to do it this way. We'll get it done twice as fast."

Another loud clap of thunder rolled across the island, blanketing it with noise. It ran long and low, rumbling through the trees and over the waves. Leo hadn't seen any lightning cracking the sky beforehand, but he could see it now, flickering off to the east.

More thunder.

A great cosmic flashbulb went off, brightening the woods and the Culpepper house, and the small dead child by the driftwood log, and the black-clad man who watched from the front porch. Melissa threw the car into gear and peeled out, backward all the way, down the drive and onto the main drag.

41

SATURDAY

MELISSA

The windshield wipers frantically flapped but didn't do much to clear the view as Melissa gunned it for Nordy's—an aggravating drive that required going south for a couple of miles to the causeway, then grabbing the western road back north up the island. There were only a couple of streets that ran between the two, and she'd missed the last turnoff because she couldn't see worth a damn through the rain. She prayed out loud for all the deer to stay clear of the road, because God knew she'd never spot one in time to stop for it.

"They're probably all huddled up in the woods under the trees somewhere. Hunkering down," Leo proposed. He had one hand on the "oh shit" bar above his window, and the other on the side of the seat. "Here it is, up ahead."

"I know. Been here a million times." With a shriek from her tires, she almost did a U-turn to whip into the single row of parking spaces beside the burned-out shell of a building.

Leo reached for the door handle and paused. "Meet me back

at the Culpepper property as soon as you can. If I beat you back, I'll start hosing down the Tidebury house."

She agreed. "And if I beat *you* back, I'll get cracking on Thornbury. We'll hit them both—propane to blow them up, oil to burn them down."

With that, he gave her a nod and a look that she couldn't quite read. "Now or never," he said, and he yanked the door open and flung himself out into the storm.

Melissa didn't look back, except to make sure that he wasn't right behind her when she pulled back out onto the western road and started hauling ass for Fort Flagler. She suddenly couldn't remember what the speed limit was—but it didn't matter. Nothing could've slowed her down, short of a head-on collision with another car.

There weren't any other cars.

She hit the park entrance, sliding around the sharp curve that led her out to the old military buildings that overlooked the shore. She could barely see them; a hard fog had rolled in, and the old buildings were little more than blank gray boxes.

She didn't see much in the way of RVs or campers, and only two of the buildings had even a single light burning within. She didn't feel a sense of privacy so much as a dreadful isolation.

Keenly and miserably, she wished Leo was there with her. She'd broken the law before, but not like this. Her misspent youth had featured some shoplifting, a couple of egregious parking violations, a few speeding tickets. But nothing like grand theft in the middle of an old military installation.

Would it be grand theft? She idly wondered about what charges she might eventually face as her Subaru sloshed through the half paved roads, and then left them. She hopped the spot where a curb ought to be and drove right onto the grass and gravel beside the small museum in the former army building.

Melissa didn't know how much a tank of propane cost. If anyone had been present, she would've handed over her credit card and offered to buy the whole lot, but the museum was locked with a big handwritten "CLOSED" sign hanging on the door. It swept and swayed in the wind and rain, but she caught the words *storm*, *safe*, *tomorrow*, and the phrase *weather permitting* before she hit the parking brake and ran around to the back.

Her hair slapped wetly in her face and the hood of her jacket didn't do much to stop it. She wished she had a better raincoat and that she was wearing it; she was already soaked to the bone, just from running to the car from the Culpepper house and then running around the side of this smallish outbuilding.

She wished a lot of things. She was shit out of luck on every count.

The tanks were blocked off with rusted metal grating. Melissa paced back and forth in front of the cage. It wasn't particularly sturdy—maybe twice as hardy as something assembled with chicken wire. But when she shoved her fingers through the holes and pulled, nothing budged. She tried again and still was not encouraged. The damn thing was tougher than it looked.

She checked the gate that let Mrs. Hansen come and go with the full and empty tanks. Its padlock wasn't anything special; she'd seen vastly more impressive bike locks outside Columbia Center in Seattle, but that only meant she could probably bust it if she had...any tools at all.

But she *did* have tools. Her emergency kit, in the back of the vehicle.

She ran back and popped the hatch—then yanked the levers to put her back seats down and expand the rear storage. A gust of wind threw a gallon's worth of rain right in her face, right into the car. She swore at it and swiped away as much as she could.

All her emergency supplies were stashed in a set of accordion storage boxes that usually sat ignored in the wayback. She hooked one side with her hand and yanked it forward, then fished for something useful while the rain blew and splashed around the raised rear door.

"Where the fuck is the…?"

There. A hammer/axe/prybar/heaven-knew-what-else multi-tool her dad had given her for emergencies. This was an emergency.

"Now or never," she muttered as she hefted it high.

A hard gust of cold wind drove needles of water into her face when she turned around. She flinched and ducked, shielding her eyes. She felt her way back around the building, to the cage where the precious propane tanks were stashed—locked due to vandals, or so Mrs. Hanson had said. Well, there was no time to vandalize like the present.

Melissa's fingers were wet and numb, and finding the gate was one thing, getting a solid handle on the padlock and its chain were another. She finally found them, and she tightened the chain around the nearest bars—pulling it taut, and the lock along with it. She held it in place with one hand, the lock pinned against the gate's frame.

Her right hand lifted up the emergency trucker's tool and started swinging.

One, two, three strikes. Something split and cracked, but it was hard to tell what, or if it was something useful—or merely something else breaking in the storm, which was busily smashing everything it could. Melissa kept swinging.

The sound of metal on metal rang through the storm and evaporated, like every other noise except for the harsh static of falling water and shaking trees and the occasional long, deep rumbles of thunder that nobody ever heard, that far north, that far west.

Finally the padlock split open and the chain fell away.

Melissa yanked the gate latch and hauled the whole thing open, fighting the wind to hold it. New problem. Some of these tanks were empty. She was about to completely lose her shit when she saw the sign. "Empty tanks here, full tanks there, got it."

She grabbed a full one, hauled it up, and groaned. These things were heavier than she'd expected, a good forty pounds apiece. One by one, she heaved them up onto her knee, and slid them into the back of her car. When the thing was packed full, she stood back and counted. Ten. Ten tanks, and that was all. Would it be enough? She had no idea.

"One more," she declared, having just remembered that she had an open passenger seat.

She grabbed her final selection and strapped it in with a seat belt so it wouldn't fly through the windshield if she stopped too fast. She slammed the door shut and ran around to the other side of the car, then she slipped in behind the wheel and closed herself inside.

Violently she shivered; she turned on the engine and cranked up the heater onto full blast, knowing she didn't have time to let it warm her up.

The car's wheels whipped mud in a great brown arc as Melissa fishtailed and spun on the way back to the road, cutting deep grooves in the grass and on the unpaved stretches of road that were more mud than asphalt. It'd taken her half an hour to reach Flagler and load up the car; she hadn't made bad time, considering the weather and the weight of the tanks.

She wondered how Leo was doing. His assignment had kept him closer to the Culpepper house, though if he couldn't get the oil truck hot-wired, he'd be stuck there.

Two minutes later, she blew past Nordy's and saw that the truck wasn't there anymore.

She laughed, and it was an absurd, maniacal sound, alone in the car with enough propane to blow her back to Seattle—with the hard white noise of the rain and a backbeat of the windshield wipers slamming back and forth.

Back at the island's southern point, she slowed down in order to turn left and head north again. "I'm almost there," she said, in an effort to telepathically communicate with Leo or only to reassure herself.

But something caught her eye. To the right. On the causeway, or just coming off it.

"The *hell*?"

She squinted through the rain, trying to trick her eyes into ignoring the wipers. She willed herself to see through the sheets of running rain. Whatever had come across the bridge—in the middle of a thunderous late-fall rainstorm that couldn't possibly be natural—was person-shaped and wearing a long light-colored overcoat pulled up over their head.

Whoever they were, they walked as if the weather was clear and the road was dry; they strolled with a long, smooth stride that met no resistance from the wind or rain. It was a silly thing to notice, how the person ignored the weather entirely, their overcoat billowing and blowing, whipping around them. But they weren't straining or leaning forward, bracing themselves.

Melissa slowed down.

No, that wasn't an overcoat. It was more like a robe, something with far too much fabric to call a coat. A cloak, perhaps. And it was intensely white in the dull, dimming gray of the afternoon gloom.

Melissa slowed down even more, pulling up alongside whoever the hell this was. Something was wrong.

Through the passenger window Melissa watched as the person strolled onward, unbothered, toward the eastern road that headed to the northern point of the island.

The wind ripped hard along the causeway, blasting the island and everything on it. The robe blew back and Melissa saw a flash of arm. It was thin and pale, and wearing chunky bracelets, the details of which she couldn't see.

"That cannot be good," she concluded, then sat up straight again and punched the gas to pick up the pace. She passed the traveler and glanced in the rearview mirror. They were still walking, unaffected by the maelstrom. Their white hood was oversized; it flapped around their face like wings, hiding any hint of identifying features.

Melissa tried to quit looking back. The weather in front of

her was too terrible to ignore, not if she wanted to arrive back at the Culpepper house in one piece and not run off the road into a tree. And then probably blow up, considering her cargo.

She risked another glance regardless.

The vigorously striding figure was gone.

Melissa almost hit the brakes, but didn't. Her stomach flooded with a strong, sharp feeling that said something was wrong. But she knew that already.

Melissa returned her attention to the road ahead.

There was the stranger. In front of her. In the road. Walking north.

Now Melissa slammed on the brakes and thanked heaven for all-wheel drive. The car's tires squealed and the back half of the vehicle swayed, lined up again, and slid forward another dozen yards before stopping in the middle of the thoroughfare—right where a dotted line ought to be, but wasn't.

They were in front of her. Walking away. Melissa had nearly run them down. She hadn't. Whoever it was. Whatever it was.

Vǫlva.

The word stuck in her head as she watched them retreat (watched *it* retreat). Nobody moved like that. Nobody sashayed through one of the worst storms in the last hundred years without even—now she noticed, now she understood how wrong this really was—without even getting wet. The robe swirled and flowed as light as chiffon. It should have sagged and dragged, soaked and heavy.

Melissa's headlights shined bright through the rain, through the driving mist and rolling fog, through the stranger in the middle of the road who flickered, and sparked, and vanished.

42

SATURDAY

LEO

Leo tumbled out of Melissa's car and landed in the narrow parking lot in front of Nordy's. The rain smacked him in the face; he pulled up his hood, and the wind blew it away again in an instant. He wiped his glasses. It didn't clear them at all. Every drop wiped away was replaced by several more. The storm was a hydra, and he hated it.

Melissa's car was disappearing down the road. Her taillights shrank to tiny points of red, then vanished in the rain.

"We can do this," he assured himself. He ducked over to the heating oil truck, using its bulk to shield himself from the rain. Suddenly it dawned on him that while, yes, he did know how to hot-wire a vehicle...he did not know how to jimmy one open. "Shit," he said, then shook his head. No. The cold and damp was getting to his brain. If it wasn't unlocked, he'd find a rock and break a window.

Potential problem potentially solved.

He was on the passenger side of the truck—it wasn't nearly as large as a big rig, but it was about as big as a very short school bus. He'd never driven anything that size before, but how bad could it be?

The passenger door was locked.

He gave his jacket hood one more opportunity to stay up, but it didn't cooperate. The wind wouldn't let it. Rain pelted his head, his face; it smeared his glasses and dragged them down his nose, pushing them off the edge of his cheeks. He shoved them back up. They slid back down.

The wind came from every direction at once. It wouldn't matter which way he went around the truck. It wouldn't matter if anyone came by and noticed his presence; no one could see a damn thing anyway. This is what he told himself. He wasn't sure he believed it, but it kept him moving.

Over to the driver's door, he took a deep breath and tugged the handle.

It lifted with a click, and he gasped at the sheer luck of it.

He threw open the door, crawled up the tall step, and squeezed into the seat—which had previously been occupied by an elf, or perhaps a first grader, because this was ridiculous. He found the lever under the front of the seat, yanked it, and the seat snapped back so far he could barely touch the pedals. He took two seconds to adjust it to something usable and reached for the panel under the steering wheel.

Then he paused. He'd gotten lucky once. This was Marrowstone. Nobody locked their doors. Even the tourists tended to be older folks with RVs. People routinely left their keys in their vehicles.

He took a second to pat at the cup holders, to open the glove box and lift up the floorboard mat.

Then he tugged the visor, and the keys dropped into his lap. "Oh thank God," he breathed. It'd been a decade or more since he'd tried to hot wire anything, and back then, he'd had his uncle reminding him how to do it. He might have overstated his confidence and competence in this matter, when he'd reassured Melissa that he could do it.

But keys made everything easier.

He jammed the most likely suspect into the ignition and cranked it, then remembered he was dealing with a stick shift and adjusted his approach. It'd been a minute since he'd driven a stick too.

But he could do it. He was more confident of his skills with a manual transmission than he was with the wires under the dash.

The vehicle rumbled to life. Relieved, he made himself comfortable with the pedals below. He adjusted the seat one last time, checked his mirrors, and threw the truck into reverse with more gusto than he'd meant to. It lurched and hopped, then rolled backward onto the road, where he leaned on the brakes to get control again.

No one was coming in either direction. He could take a moment and breathe. He would beat Melissa back to the Culpepper property without even trying; there was no sense in being careless. He sat up straighter, pulled on his seat belt, looked up, and shrieked. Someone was standing in the road. The windshield wipers kicked back and forth, clearing the glass for a fraction of a second at a time.

No. Not someone. Something.

He put the truck into first gear and crept forward. What the hell was *that*?

Not a person. Not an animal either. It was something larger than a bucket and smaller than a bear, very dark in color, and it was rolling. Awkwardly, roughly, like a basketball that was losing air. "Is that…?" he murmured, leaning forward over the wheel. "A rock?"

That's what it looked like. Except rocks didn't randomly roam down streets no matter how much wind and rain was driving them—they didn't turn and roll over the shoulder, then disappear over the grass and between the trees in front of Leo's eyes as if someone was piloting them with a remote control.

"I didn't see that," he forced himself to conclude. His memory flashed onto a summer afternoon and a pocketful of pebbles, laid out on a windowsill behind the kitchen sink.

He sat back. The engine had cut out. He started it again and went for first gear one more time.

Now he was ready.

Now he was driving, hugging the right shoulder because the oil truck felt like driving a cruise ship. It was top-heavy and the wind was coming in hard, making the whole thing sway back and forth so wildly that he might get carsick for the first time since he was a kid. When he took the southern curve that amounted to a wide U-turn—swinging back up to the eastern road—it felt like a scene from a cartoon; he imagined the truck leaning up on two wheels, but it hugged the road hard enough not to tip over.

When Leo slammed the brakes again, an image of the back wheels lifting off the ground and the headlights kissing the dirt flashed through his mind.

"Fuck!" he yelled, having stopped mere feet from another

large rolling rock. This one he might've mistaken for a bear, and there was no way in hell it was just cruising along under its own power, but Jesus Fucking Christ, there it went.

He panted out loud while he watched it disappear into the trees.

He'd forgotten to drive. The engine had cut out again. He turned the key, got it running, and put all the gears and pedals back where they belonged.

Honestly, the rocks felt like the least of his problems. Shit, they weren't even the weirdest of his problems.

What if something happened to Melissa? What if she couldn't get inside the propane cages? What if there weren't any full tanks? What if there wasn't enough oil in that truck to burn anything, much less everything? He had no idea how much it held or how much it would take. What if after all this trouble, this didn't work? What if the houses didn't burn? What if that didn't stop whatever the hell Gunnar Lorentzen was trying to do? What if they were just destroying evidence?

Never mind the rocks.

Wait. What if Melissa had a wreck, trying not to hit a rock? Great. One more thing to add to the pile of things he could obsess about while driving an unwieldy vehicle in the rain and trying not to crash it.

The storm line passed over the island, and everything was suddenly much darker. Not yet dusk, but Leo could see it from here. Lightning sparkled across the flat gray sky, and thunder bellowed at the same instant, which was never a good sign.

He idly wondered how to turn on the headlights, but he did not go fishing around in the unfamiliar vehicle to find them.

They wouldn't help that much, and he was almost back to Thornbury and Tidebury.

New thing to worry about: How would he get the oil truck onto the beach?

He tried to recall the paths through the trees, the side routes, the unpaved spaces where something this big could pass, and he blanked on every count. The beach sand would be wet and packed enough to drive on, if he could just get that far.

Hm.

The turnoff for the next lot. Now he remembered. The planned house had never been built, and there was a long dirt driveway leading right to the sand, if he could find it. It ought to be just past...

He whipped past the turnoff for his aunt and uncle's place, and the next one up was the Culpepper place, and the one after that...

The side road was still unmarked, but if you knew about it, and if you slowed down and paid attention, you could find it.

Leo slowed down to a crawl, down to second gear, and saw the road just in time to keep from flipping the truck in an effort to catch the turn. He pushed his legs out straight, pressed his feet down hard, and the brakes engaged just in time. He turned right, hit rough mud, and trusted the weight and power of the truck to keep moving.

It did, but it complained about it.

The truck creaked and groaned, and the axles bounced, rattling Leo's bones as he grimly forced the truck down a couple of wet ruts. Tall plants scraped along the vehicle's underside and tree branches dragged across the roof, the top of the tank, and the windshield, but he held it steady and kept a firm foot on the gas without gunning it—for fear of getting stuck.

Everything under the canopy was soaked with mud or fallen leaves or pine needles—or most likely some combination of all that and more. He could take it slow and steady, or not at all. Stuck was not an option.

Finally the way opened, and to his right he saw the lot that had never been developed. Whoever owned it had gotten as far as a naked foundation and abandoned it, either running out of money or interest in the project.

Only a few more yards.

Yes, over there. The beach. Debris coated the high-tide line, but that was normal and expected; if he had to, Leo would get out and personally drag some driftwood out of the way. Much to his relief, it didn't come to that.

He spied a clearing where a dune had eroded and the shell-seeking beachcombers had worn a path. It was narrow and it was slippery, but with a grinding of gears and a fierce belief in the righteousness of his mission, Leo rammed the truck past fallen limbs and the washed-up trunks, tires spinning fast while the truck moved slowly across the long, slick strands of seaweed and tufts of grass, and the bunches of sea pickles blooming with sour little gherkins.

The front tires hit hard sand and the truck lunged.

The farthest edge of the high-tide line was firm enough to drive on, as he knew it ought to be. He'd seen summer travelers and locals tootling around in golf carts and ATVs even when they weren't supposed to; the sand would hold bicycles and cars, and by God, it would hold a fuel oil truck.

In the back of Leo's head, he thought of Mrs. Culpepper, promising to buy them time. "Hold on, Mrs. C. We're coming." He knew he was starting to think of her like a patron saint—someone he could petition and pray to when the chips were down, but he didn't honestly think she was listening. That didn't stop him from whispering her name as he drove up onto the sand, careful and frightened, through the dunes and around the biggest bits of driftwood and debris...or crunching over it with the truck's big tires and crossing his fingers that he wouldn't get stuck.

He did not get stuck.

He gritted his teeth and pushed onward, up the beach—or down it, if he thought about it from a north-south angle. He'd gone one lot north, and now he was doubling back to the Culpepper property, heading south along the high-tide line. He ought to see Tidebury any minute. Any second.

Finally.

A squat black shape against the light gray of the sand, the midgray of the sky, and the blue-gray of the ocean with its rough white waves thrashing onto shore like they were dying. The waves did not touch Tidebury House, and indeed they were still probably several hours away from overcoming the front porch.

Mrs. Culpepper had thrown Gunnar into the ocean, house and all. She must have thought it might hold him, but she'd been wrong, hadn't she?

Wrong about her efforts banishing him for good, and wrong about him being unable to inflict further damage on them or the people she loved. Leo pushed thoughts of Simon out of his head, and then he chased away the sound of Mrs. Culpepper's ghost.

He focused on the path ahead. It took considerable concentration to drive through the howling wind and horizontal rain, especially with the sand sliding beneath the truck's wheels and Tidebury, right there, straight ahead.

Dead ahead.

He pulled up as close as he could to the front porch. How long was the hose that would send the oil spraying inside? He didn't know, but he'd rather be safe than sorry. He adjusted the truck's position, and when he was confident that he could cuddle up no closer, he put it in park and cut the engine.

For a moment, the world was quiet—if only by comparison. He sat behind the wheel and stared through the windshield at the ocean, which was either approaching or retreating, and he didn't know which.

Deep breath. Okay. Yeah. Ready to go. Except he had no idea how to crank on the oil or deploy it into the housewreck. But Leo was a problem solver and a fast reader—and he was certain of two things: one, he could not waste time screwing this up; and two, all knowledge is contained within the internet. He still had enough signal to look up a YouTube video or two, and in five minutes he'd successfully convinced himself that he understood the gist of getting oil from inside the truck to inside something else.

He squinted out through the rain. No sign of Melissa yet. No headlights through the trees out by Thornbury.

Might as well get a jump on things, like he'd said he would.

He threw the door open—or he tried to. It strained against him, but he forced it open and let it slam shut behind him, hard enough to take off a finger.

His glasses slipped. He adjusted them, jamming them onto his ears and willing them to stay put.

He pulled up his hood, knowing it wouldn't stay but hoping it'd shield his eyes long enough to hook things up and get things rolling. *There was the connection, yes. There was the valve, yes. The hose, right. Looks long enough to go in through the front door.* It might be a stretch, but he'd make it work. *There were the gauges, all right.*

He cracked his knuckles.

He took one more swipe at his glasses with his free hand, and he got to work.

43

SATURDAY

MELISSA

The apparition reappeared ten yards down the road. Melissa's headlights cut right through it, giving it a wild yellow glow that looked almost heavenly—like this was an angel, dry as a bone and strolling down the middle of a road. The phantom shifted again, skipping farther and farther away. Another hop. A moment of sudden darkness and more sudden brightness. The ghost was beyond the headlights. Its exuberant robes billowed, a bright white spot in a low gray world.

Then it was gone.

Melissa tried to calm her heart, but it wasn't even beating, it was vibrating. She felt like she was about to have a stroke. She couldn't afford a stroke. She had to get back to Thornbury, to the awful laboratory in the basement. She had to get ready to burn it all down.

The Vǫlva needed her.

Leo would be there already. She fully expected to find him pulled up with the fuel truck's contents emptied into Tidebury, ready to kick some ass. Melissa had never been fair to him, not once, and she knew it now and all she could do was be the support staff he required.

Now was the time to have each other's backs. Now was the time to be literal partners in crime, God help them both.

She pushed the gas again and her propane-stuffed Subaru rumbled forward. Almost there. She passed the turnoff to the Alvarez place. Now she just needed the next one. She looked one last time for the ghost in the road but didn't see it.

Then the correct turnoff came into view. She took it hard and fast, and did her best to make the long unpaved drive to the Culpepper house without any further bumping, bumbling, or rattling.

What would it take to set off some propane tanks? More than a rough car ride, surely. But she didn't know it for a fact and she didn't want to hit the skids and blow sky high, so she kept it careful.

The house appeared at the end of the muddy road.

Its empty driveway was an inviting target but Melissa had a better idea. She pulled off onto the leaves, mud, and pine needles, and plowed through some flowering hawthorn that Mrs. Culpepper would've murdered her for destroying, even a month ago. The sharp branches and thorny ends scraped along her paint job, and she couldn't have cared less. She only cringed because she could hear the high-pitched squeal of it, dragging along the driver's side door.

She stopped just past them, a few feet beyond the basement hatch.

On the one hand, her plan meant eradicating every earthly

trace of Simon, which seemed cruel and unfair and hard-hearted. On the other, maybe it would free him or give him peace. Him, and the boys who cried in the corners, without even knowing they were dead.

If destroying the last of their mortal remains wouldn't do it, probably nothing would.

Through the trees and toward the beach she looked for headlights, but didn't see them, and couldn't see Tidebury at all. The low clouds and thick fog obscured everything past the edge of the property where the trees screened the ocean view.

"Simon is dead," she reminded herself, for all that it hurt. "All I can do now is put him to rest."

Or give it her best shot. She'd likely never know if it worked or not, and she had to come to peace with that.

She zipped up her coat, pulled up the hood, and drew the strings tight to hold it around her face. She flung open the door and climbed out into the darkening, soaking storm.

Staying close to the body of her vehicle, she shuffled around to the rear and fought to open the back door, but the wind had a better grip than she did. It swung up so hard and fast that it almost clapped her in the forehead; she ducked just in time. The door bobbed, then stayed up where it was supposed to be.

Melissa reached past the first row of tanks and grabbed her multi-tool again.

Now it was time to get past the hatch.

She knew it was locked from inside, a couple of times over—but she had broken one gate, and she was ready to break the rest of the world. Hoisting the tool up high, she brought it down directly on the hatch handles, again and again. The wood splintered and cracked; the hardware held.

It couldn't hold forever. She wouldn't let it.

Melissa was too angry and too happy to hit something as hard as she could, and soon there was a hole where she could see the chain that held everything shut. Half a dozen more whacks, and the metal latch collapsed—dropping the chain inside. It clattered down to the stairs with a tinny crash.

"Victory!" she declared. Prematurely.

Opening the hatch doors proved easier said than done. The wind fought her every step of the way, and her hands were eaten up with splinters by the time she had one side open and lying flat on the ground beside the hole.

"Fuck it!" she announced. The other side could stay shut.

She stomped down the stairs to the landing, where water was already collecting in shallow puddles at the corners. Now the basement door.

Her hands hurt and she was already winded from battling the hatch, but she wasn't finished yet. She flipped the tool over to use the hammer end as a battering ram. A few good whacks knocked the knob and its lock through the wood and into the basement's interior.

Melissa put her hand through the hole, pulled out the last of the hardware that clung to the frame, and stood back—then kicked it open. It smacked back against the wall.

The path was clear.

But she was alone in the basement, and the water in there was half a foot deep. It spilled over her shoes and into the hatch landing.

She swallowed hard and looked at the hole in the wall where the circle of runes used to be. She already knew what was back there, and she didn't want to see it again—but she couldn't ignore the epicenter of everything terrible that was happening…and everything that was likely to happen, if she and Leo couldn't stop it.

She didn't know what that would look like.

She hated having only the most half formed idea of what was happening. She hated how she and Leo were the only two people left alive who knew even *this* much. She hated the thought of destroying Mrs. Culpepper's house—though the prospect of blowing Tidebury to smithereens almost put a smile on her face.

Mostly, she hated that Simon was dead, but there wasn't anything she could do about that except follow his grandmother's instructions—however bizarre and frightening and vague they might be.

She ran back out, up the stairs, through the hatch. She returned to her car.

The tanks were slick and wet from rain blowing into the car. Melissa gripped the nearest one with both hands and hauled it over the bumper, setting it down gently on the ground. One more. She set it down beside the first. Might as well grab the third, get the whole first row out of the car and ready to blow.

She heaved the closest one into her arms and headed down into the basement, watching her feet as much as she could over the bulky propane canister. Her shoes squished and slipped when she hit the concrete basement floor, but she'd made it in one piece—and now all she had to do was duck back through the hole, deposit the tank, and do it all over again a few times.

She wanted to close her eyes, even though that didn't sound like a good idea.

Through the wall she went, taking care to keep her eyes low. She did not want to get a good look at anything the room held and hid, but she couldn't help stealing a glance at the tables, the shelves, the jars. Three all in a row, the last one clear and new, filled with bloody bits.

Hastily, she looked away.

She put that first tank on the third table, the one that still wore smudges of gore. She couldn't *not* think about who the gore had come from. It made her want to take her little emergency hatchet to the tank right then and there. Sure, it was crazy thinking and she knew it, but crazy thinking was all she had going for her. A sane person would've been having a drink and some early dinner, and talking about the impossible weather while lounging someplace warm and dry.

Back up the stairs. Next tank.

When she was finally finished, she'd left tanks on each of the tables and on the floor in front of the enormous, mysterious, rusted-out machine of ill-intent. It did not protest this promise of destruction; it didn't do anything, even crackle or groan. It appeared entirely dead.

"Sorry, Simon," she said. "I wish we'd gotten here faster. I wish we could've helped before it was too late. I'm so, so sorry."

With that, she went back up the stairs. She dropped the open hatch door shut, because there was no sense in letting in the rain. It was wet enough down there already.

She slammed the car's rear door shut and got back behind the wheel, bringing half the sky with her—or that's how it felt.

Everything was soaked, and everything dripped, and she found it oddly tiring to move so much through the storm. Running through water was always bad; running through wind made it even worse.

Running through wind and water while carrying forty-pound gas tanks was a whole different kind of misery. Her hands and shoulders ached from the effort, and she was only halfway finished.

She pulled her keys out of her pocket and wiped them on her jeans. She started the car and backed out of her spot behind the house, then did a three-point turn, and pulled out past the driveway—at which point she hesitated. There was no path wide enough for the vehicle between her and the beach.

"Shit."

She drew up as close to the dunes as she could without risking getting stuck, and then she could see the fuel oil truck. Leo had parked it on the far side, presumably with the intent of running the hose through the front door.

She asked herself, *Where'd he turn, to get the truck onto the beach*? Without an answer, she concluded, *Fuck it. I'll carry these over there by hand.*

Even if she ran up to Leo and asked him, it'd take more time to find out and drive around than it would to just haul the damn things herself.

Melissa cut the engine.

She unhooked the seat belt on the passenger side and ran around the back of the car to grab that lone tank first. Once she had a good grip, she started running in a shuffling stumble—through the path between the dunes, past the driftwood log where a little boy's body was left decades ago, and onto the beach.

As soon as she hit the sand, a bright streak of lightning cracked the sky—accompanied by thunder. It startled her badly enough that she lost her grip and dropped the tank. It started rolling, then stopped, but it'd given her an idea. The sand was firm and packed. Her back ached and her fingers were stiff from the cold and the strain, and that was okay. She could roll these bad boys around.

"Leo!" she yelled as she got close. "Where are you?"

His voice yelled back over the roar of the surf and the storm.

She couldn't make out what he was saying, but she could loosely gauge where he was coming from—so she pushed the tank around the front of the house, barely registering the odd rich stink in the air that was surely the oil from the truck. "Leo?"

"Right here," he announced. He was holding a nozzle connected to an enormous accordion-style hose, pulling it down the front steps. "You got the tanks?" he asked, then lowered the nozzle and got a better look. "You got the tanks. More than that one, I hope?"

"There's more in the car. How'd you get the truck onto the beach?"

He waved his hand like this question was irrelevant—or more likely, he didn't feel like he had the time to explain. Then he asked, "Where'd you park? Other side of the dune?" She nodded and he said, "Good, that's good. We can carry these over. Did you already do the Culpepper house?"

She nodded again. "Yeah, I put them in the basement. In the mad scientist's laboratory."

"Good call, yeah. I'm almost done here. Help me with this? It's heavier than it looks. I can hold it but it's hard to move it around."

She left the tank beside the front porch and helped him with the fat blue hose; it was as big around as her upper thigh, and he was right—it was heavy as hell. "How much oil is left in the tank?"

"A couple hundred gallons, if I'm reading the gauges right." He grunted, pulling the hose down onto the sand and dragging it back toward the truck.

Melissa lifted her section of the hose as high as she could while he reattached the nozzle to the tank. "God, I hope this works."

"It'll work. You ever try to put out a grease fire?"

She frowned, trying to figure out where he was going with that question. "I know you're not supposed to use water to put one out?"

He grinned wildly, and without any humor. "This stuff burns hot and stubborn by design. It'll be almost impossible to extinguish. It'll have to burn out on its own."

"Right on. Let's hope this one burns a hole to the center of the earth."

"Your lips to God's ears." When the hose was secured, he began to help with the rest of the tanks, much to Melissa's relief.

They stuck the tanks in the foyer and living room of Tidebury—floating and soaking in all that heating oil. It took some doing; they formed a very short chain between them, with Leo on the sand passing tanks up, and Melissa on the porch, half chucking them and half rolling them as deep into the house as she could send them without disappearing inside herself.

They finished, and the house was as doomed as it was going to get.

Melissa said, "Let's pull the truck back, before we set this off."

"Excellent plan, yes. Then we can, we can..."

She saw the wall he'd hit and was struck with a sudden solution. "Fireworks!"

"What?"

Excited now, she smacked at his shoulder. "We can set these off with Simon's fireworks—he still has a stash in the closet, remember?"

"Holy shit, *yes*. You're right. That's perfect, and those big M80s have long fuses, yes, yes, *yes*. We can grab some when we dump the oil, then come back." Then his enthusiasm flagged. "It won't be very hard, burning down the Culpepper place. We can probably set a regular fire on the basement stairs and let it take its course. It'll hit the propane tanks and heating oil eventually." He was speculating. She could hear it in his voice. "If this doesn't work..."

"It *will* work. Failure is not an option."

"Clichés won't save us now," he protested. "Come on, hop in the truck and let's get moving."

44

SATURDAY

LEO

Leo cranked the ignition, twisting the key until the engine turned over. "There's a little road over here. Kind of a service road, but..." He paused to look down at the gear shift, put it in reverse, and gave it some gas. The wheels spun, then caught, and the truck started crawling backward. "Sorry, I meant to say, there was supposed to be a new build on the next lot up—but they never got farther than the foundations and the access drive. We'll have to go back up the beach, but—"

"Turn on the headlights," Melissa suggested anxiously. Her hands felt around over her shoulder, then down by her hip, seeking a seat belt, Leo suspected.

For all he knew the truck didn't have any. "I don't know how," he admitted.

She stopped hunting for the belt or fastener and leaned forward, feeling around on the dash. Finding a knob, she pulled it—and the lights kicked on, shining straight ahead.

"How did you...?"

She shrugged. "I helped a friend move in a truck this size. I thought maybe they were similar."

"A good guess." He made an awkward turn with too many stopping points, stalling out once and swearing considerably more times than that. "Maybe you should drive."

"Nuh-uh. I can't drive a stick."

"You couldn't possibly do much worse than I am," he said. "Shit, I can't even tell…where's the…?"

Melissa gasped and grabbed his arm.

He quit fighting the stick and looked up, following the headlights.

The truck was pointed at an angle between Tidebury house and the ocean, and there, just beyond the edge of the doubled glare, a shadow stood. It was man-sized and man-shaped in the fog and mist.

"Leo…"

"I see him."

"Run. Gun it. Get us out of here, you have to get us out of here!" She was starting to panic, and her panic was not helping him control his own rising hysteria. It was also not helping him drive an unwieldy and unfamiliar vehicle.

"Shut up!" he told her. It snapped out of his mouth too hard, too fast, but he couldn't take it back and he didn't especially want to. "You have to…give me a second; I'm just…" He struggled with the gear shift, got it back into first, and got the truck moving forward. He veered hard to the left, back toward the tree line and the side road that wasn't far away, not even a quarter of a mile. An eighth, maybe. If that.

But he couldn't see it.

"Faster!" she screeched.

"I'm doing the best I can!"

Second gear felt like a leisurely crawl. Leo did not want to look back at the man, at Gunnar Lorentzen, because who else could it be? But he looked up anyway and saw that the shadowy silhouette was walking—slowly, carelessly, with a casual swing to his step. He strolled toward Tidebury and Leo couldn't shake the feeling that it was a victory stroll, the stroll of a man who'd gotten what he wanted at last, and no one had stopped him.

Third gear.

No. A grinding of wheels and a stall-out.

Once more, Leo got the pedals where he needed them and started the engine. Before Melissa could screech anything new and useless, he preemptively screeched at her instead. "I'm trying!"

"I know!" she screeched back.

Gunnar Lorentzen raised one hand and made a small flipping gesture. It was the kind of motion Leo might make if he was telling a client not to worry about a roof, because it's only two years old. No, that smell isn't something worrying, it's just new paint. A tiny tossing of the fingers.

"What? What was that? What did he just do?" Melissa babbled, surely knowing that Leo didn't have the faintest fucking idea, any more than she did.

"Nothing. It was nothing," he said to fill the cabin with something other than the fog of their breathing and the stink of fear. But he was wrong, and he knew it as soon as the words were out of his mouth.

A fresh roar rose up, louder than the engine, louder than the storm—but sounding like a combination of both. Leo saw the tremendous shadow looming first.

Something as tall as the sky itself was rising out of the ocean. Not a creature, not another house, not a ship or a driftwood forest of cedar and pine.

But a wave.

"Fuck," he whispered.

"Fuck!" Melissa screamed, loudly enough to bust an eardrum or blow out a window.

They grabbed each other and clung tight, and when the wave swamped the truck, it tossed it like a toy. The cabin spun like a washing machine, over and under and up and down as the truck twisted, slipped, and skidded hard into a dune—where it collapsed onto its side, wheels spinning in the air.

The windshield split inward. Water gushed into the interior, then receded almost as quickly—leaving the occupants wet and freezing and stunned, battered and confused. Wind and rain blew through the broken window, washing tiny shards of tempered glass into their laps.

"Are you okay?" Melissa asked from underneath him. The truck had landed on the passenger side, with the driver's door facing the sky.

"Yes," he said, unsure if it was true. He tried to climb up off Melissa; neither one of them wanted him lying across her lap, but there was nowhere to brace himself and he struggled to get up without hurting her. He tried the gearshift but the knob snapped off in his hand; he put one foot on the glove box door, but it slipped off and he kicked her shoulder.

Finally he found purchase by pulling himself up with the steering wheel column. He got one hand on the door latch and jumped, pushed, and shoved. The door popped open a hair and the wind caught it, whipping it all the way back with a loud slap.

"Out. We have to get out."

"Working on it," he told her with a grunt.

Leo got one leg braced on the seat's headrest and worked the other one up to the dashboard, where it lodged next to the speedometer. Now he had enough purchase to get his head and shoulders up and out, and all of his weight off Melissa, so she could follow him.

Rain slapped his face and the wind was cold enough to cut. By some miracle his glasses were still on his face, but it was very hard to see.

Where was the water? Which direction? Everything was topsy-turvy, and if he hadn't been so scared, he might've thrown up.

His eyes landed on Tidebury. He carefully turned his torso, making sure to keep his footing. Something was happening at the house. Inside, there was a light, cold and so white that it was almost blue. The shadowy man who haunted them stood beside it. He hadn't moved, as if throwing a wave at a truck and flipping it into a sand dune wasn't even worth watching.

"Leo? Do you smell that?"

"It's just the engine," he said. It was a lie. He could smell it too, and he could easily detect the stink of gasoline in the mix. The fuel tank must've cracked. All the more reason to get out as fast as possible.

One leg, over and out. Next leg. It was difficult, slippery work but soon he was crouched on the chassis. He put a hand back down inside. "Come on. I'll get you up."

She climbed out like he did, carefully and with a few slips before she got her head and shoulders over the side. Then she wormed the rest of the way out and fell down to the sand with a soggy thump.

Leo came down behind her, landing with no more grace at all. He hauled her up by her elbow and said, "Come on, we have to get away from this truck."

"It's making weird noises…"

She wasn't okay. He was confident enough that he didn't ask. At best, she was in shock. At worst, she was injured in some way that wasn't immediately obvious.

He pulled her along the side of the dune, trying to put distance between them and the truck and the man on the beach too. "We have to move."

"I'm coming; it's fine; I've got this."

"Okay, but I've got *you*." He ducked his head under her armpit so he could hold her closer and more firmly, because it looked like they were going to have to run.

Melissa yelped when he put his other arm around her waist to steady her, but she didn't push him away and she tried to fall into step. "We can't just…we can't leave *now*."

"We *have* to leave now," he argued. "We can, we will, we should…not be right here next to something that might explode."

Melissa looked back at Tidebury and for a brief maniacal second Leo halfway expected her to turn into a pillar of salt, but she didn't. She only gasped and said, "No…"

Because Gunnar had seen them. He knew they were still alive and out of the truck. He turned his attention from Tidebury and its sinister white glare and faced them once more.

"Melissa? We have to run."

"Where?" she asked, and the single word sounded desperate.

He shifted his grip on her waist and started to hustle toward the dune—maybe over the dune? Is that what he was thinking? As if a dune would stop a wave of water that was taller than a house. He could already see trees cracked and broken along the shoreline where the first one had knocked them nearly flat.

It was hard to breathe. It was hard to walk in the wet sand. It was hard to feel anything, he was so cold and so wet. It was hard to think.

Lorentzen raised his hand and a fresh rumbling came from the ocean; it was a loud and cluttered sound, the rushing howl of water gathering, and rising, and rearing up to crash down on the shore from a terrible height.

Melissa stumbled. Leo held her up.

His mind scrambled, seeking something that looked like safety—something that could be reached in a matter of seconds while toting a fellow adult along for the ride. But there was nothing. No place. A fleeting thought suggested Tidebury itself, since Gunnar wasn't likely to smash it to bits, but even that terrifying prospect was too far away to make for a plausible plan.

A great wall of water cast darkness on the beach, a hard line of shadow that was as dark as the dead of night.

Melissa buried her face against him and squeezed him hard.

Leo grabbed her close and held onto her as tightly as he could. Maybe he could shield her. Maybe she could use him for a life raft or a safety bubble, maybe one of them could walk away from Marrowstone alive, and that would be better than nothing, maybe.

He closed his eyes. He took the deepest breath he could.

But the wave didn't fall.

It hovered above the beach, dropping fish and shells and seaweed and industrial wreckage that had fallen or been thrown into the ocean. Something was holding it up.

Someone.

Leo opened his eyes. Someone stood between them and the water, between them, and Gunnar and Tidebury. This someone wore something flowing and white, and they glowed with a warm white light that burned in contrast to the sickly illumination inside the housewreck.

Their arms were raised. Then one arm came down slowly and swung forward—flinging the wave back from whence it came. It splatted back down into the tide with a crash, and the water seemed to boil in its wake.

Melissa looked up just in time to watch it fall, and to watch the waves scatter and rock. "Oh shit, it's you again..."

"You again?"

She released Leo and stood on her own. "I saw...whoever that is. On the way back with the propane tanks. Ouch."

"Ouch?"

"I'm fine."

He didn't want to argue with her. It was easier for everyone if she was, in fact, fine—or willing to pretend for the sake of escape. "We have to get back to Mrs. Culpepper's house."

"But the truck? The oil?"

"It's a regular old house," he said firmly enough that he almost believed it. "It'll burn like any other, and the basement is full of propane. We'll torch it and then see what we can do about that guy. That *thing*."

Gunnar was furious; Leo could see it in his posture, in the sweep of his arms when he tried to call the water again—but the stranger on the shore stood firm. Then they looked over their shoulder, back at Leo and Melissa, and suddenly it was not a stranger anymore.

"Holy…" Leo began and did not know how to finish.

Melissa said, "Is that…? No. That's not…"

Alcesta Ellingboe Lorentzen had planted herself on the sand, standing between them and certain destruction. She threw back her hood, revealing a headdress made from an animal skull over a great mass of long, tangled, wavy hair that was silver-white with tips of gold. Her eyes were smudged with a stripe of black paint, and a streak of red splashed her chin. In the hand that held the waves back where they belonged, she grasped a long thin staff made of something dark. Her arms were heavy with scraps of fur and bangles made of bone or wood.

She looked every moment of the century she'd survived, but she no longer appeared frail and small; now she was strong and angry in equal measure, and she was fully prepared to take it out on the man she'd once vowed to honor and obey.

She waved the staff in a circle, and a soft orange light appeared. Her other hand rose and opened, all five fingers splayed beneath the ball of light—and it grew brighter, harder, and sharper around its edges.

When it was the size of a beach ball, she threw it like she'd thrown the wave—with a thrust of her arm. It hit Gunnar in the chest; he staggered but stayed upright.

He reached for the ocean. Alcesta reached for the air around her. She called it to come in, closer, and she shaped it with her staff, with her hands.

Leo looked to the woods, looked to the Culpepper property. Looked at the ocean, the sand, and the ongoing duel.

Then he saw the boy.

"George," he said, as if the ghost could hear him.

George nodded as if indeed, he could. He waved to them, gesturing that they should come over the dune and go back to Thornbury.

"Okay," Leo said. He'd take any help he could get.

Melissa didn't seem to need so much support now; she'd either shaken off being stunned or the adrenaline was kicking in, overriding any debilitating pain. Leo took her arm anyway and helped her over the dune—where they had only the slightest protection from what was happening on the shore beside Tidebury. "What are we doing?" she asked.

"Thornbury. This way. George."

It wasn't enough of an explanation. Melissa accepted it anyway and kept up with him as they rushed through the late afternoon that was swiftly turning to night.

Behind the dune, the terrain was mostly soft, wet sand and tall grass, with a minefield of driftwood logs and branches instead of an easy path.

They crawled and scurried, tripped and rallied.

When they reached the great driftwood tree at the edge of the property, George was gone.

Back on shore, a battle was underway—but that meant no one was watching Leo and Melissa as they ran down the path and up to the house. The front door was open. No, the front door was absent. It'd been ripped right off the hinges and tossed into the bushes.

Inside the house, something had changed. Maybe everything had.

Mrs. Culpepper's foyer and living room now looked like the housewreck on the beach, wet and ruined. The rot hadn't reached every place, every corner—not yet. But it was creeping before their eyes, crawling across the floor and soaking it, turning it black with mold. It slipped up the walls, peeling the paint and rusting the fixtures as it oozed down the hall; it sneaked along the ceiling and cracked the glass lampshades, and it warped the chandelier over the dining room table, turning it green with tarnish.

They stared at the scene with absolute horror, neither one of them knowing what was happening or how to stop it.

Out in the front yard, something laughed.

45

SATURDAY

MELISSA

Melissa did not turn around to look. It wouldn't matter who was standing there, if anyone stood there at all. No helpful ghost would laugh like that, and no wily old lady ghost either. No powerful Vǫlva, no helpful god. The laugh came from a man, and it wasn't Leo.

The Culpepper house was being swamped before her eyes.

She could not shake the sudden awful impression that its life was being siphoned off and given to the house on the beach for purposes she had no hope of understanding. But she *did* understand that wet things don't burn easy, and there was no chance of getting the heating oil truck back upright. They'd never get it to the house in time to beat the living, crawling damp.

Melissa started to run toward the hall.

Leo called her name, but all she said in response was "Fireworks!"

Then he started running too.

They tore down the corridor to Simon's bedroom. Melissa ripped open the closet door and ransacked the interior, throwing the closet contents onto the bed.

"Got 'em!" she announced with relief, glee, and a tentative note of hope. The box was full and ready for next year's Fourth of July. She saw roman candles, sparklers, cherry bombs, and a fistful of M-80s. "Shit. I thought there'd be more. *Shit*, Leo. Will this be enough? I don't know; I can't tell..."

While she'd been looking through the box, Leo'd been following up behind her, searching the nooks and crannies she'd missed, and now his ass was hanging out of the closet while he rooted around. "It doesn't have to be!"

"You haven't even seen what's in this box?"

He backed out of the closet with another box of the same size. "No, but I found the big guns," he said, and he dropped the box onto the bed beside a pile of summer clothes. "They're blockbusters, and they'll absolutely do the job, if we hurry."

The explosives in question were enormous and red, a little thicker than a can of soda. "Oh my God, those look like they'll take off a few fingers."

"Quarter-sticks will take off your head, and I'm ninety-nine percent sure they're illegal, which raises a question or two about Simon's internet shopping. Man, these fuses are...not long enough to make me feel good about getting clear before they blow, but..." Even as he spoke, the soaking black wet curled along the doorframe, swelling the wood and rusting the hinges.

She finished the thought for him. "But we need to hurry."

She picked up the box of smaller fireworks and her ribs screamed. She was confident she'd bruised a few and maybe even broken a couple, but that wasn't all. The right side of her head had hit the window when the truck flipped, and then Leo had landed on top of her when he fell out of his seat. Now a goose egg was blowing up behind her ear, and when she stood up straight too quickly, the whole world went fuzzy...but adrenaline kept her upright.

"You're not okay," he said flatly. "Let me do it; I'll run them down there."

"I'm fine. I *will* be fine," she corrected herself. "But if you want to take the basement, I won't stop you."

"I think I've got a plan." He took the big box and sprinted for the basement stairs.

"Thank God."

Melissa did not have a plan. She had a box filled with maybe twenty pounds of fireworks. Firecrackers, really, though the roman candles could pack a punch as she'd once learned the hard way, and she still had a scar on her shoulder to remind her. But she had no time to assess or analyze, pursue best practices, or even figure out what those might be. A singular thought bounced around in her head, and all it said was *fire*. She could leave a breadcrumb trail, couldn't she? Yes. Scatter the damn things like confetti, starting in the hallway and working her way around to the living room, the foyer, the kitchen.

By the time she got to the kitchen, the box was pretty light, and that's when she realized it contained more than just fireworks. A handmade slingshot had been left in the bottom, and the sight of it almost stopped her heart with grief.

The summer she and Simon were thirteen flashed through her mind—every warm, salty moment of climbing on rocks and firing bottle caps and cherry bombs at seagulls, and waving little American flags on sticks and bright sparklers, and the red-white-and-blue trifle Mrs. Culpepper had made with strawberries and blueberries and a little too much whipped cream, but it was delicious, and Melissa sobbed out loud because it was gone now, all of it was gone, and it was never coming back.

She grabbed the slingshot anyway and stuffed it into her jacket pocket. She couldn't leave *everything* behind. Her suitcase, yes. Her travel clothes, certainly. Any random earrings or socks or toiletries could burn with the rest of it. But *something* should escape with her. She deserved some piece of comfort, and the house was decomposing around her.

She opened the microwave and threw in the last of the M-80s. She could hear Leo bounding up the basement stairs.

When he did not immediately appear, she went looking for him. She found him in the hallway, crouched over and carefully spilling something on the floor. "The hell are you doing? Let's get out of here while that's still an option."

He did not look up. "I cracked open some of the quartersticks, and I'm following your breadcrumb trail with gunpowder."

"Oh my God, you're a *genius*."

When he'd run out of the gritty black dust, he stood up and wiped his hands on his pants. "Yes, I am. Now let's get the fuck out of here."

She ran back to the kitchen, and it was Leo's turn to ask: "What the hell are *you* doing?"

"Starting the microwave." She grinned to herself when he didn't ask any follow-up questions. "Here goes nothing, okay? Get ready to run..."

With a deep breath and a quiet, brief prayer that amounted to "God help me," she pressed the microwave button that said, "Five minutes," and shouted, "Go! Run for my car!" as she rounded the kitchen peninsula and slipped on the living room floor, which was slick with cold water and seaweed slime.

"One second." He pulled his Marrowstone Island lighter out of his pocket and struck it once, twice. A third time. A flame kicked in on the fourth attempt, and the look on his face said it almost surprised him, but he was willing to take it. He touched the flame to the edge of the gunpowder line, and it sparked to fierce, hot, sparkling life.

He stood up straight, stuffed the lighter into his pocket, and started running. "Where's your car?" he asked on the way out the door.

"By the driftwood tree!" she reminded him.

Down the porch steps they charged, then down the path that led to the driftwood tree and the path that broke through the dunes. Her Subaru was still there, and the back hatch was still open, goddammit, so everything inside was even more soaked than it'd been before—which in retrospect felt almost impossible, but there it was.

She whipped out her keys and started the car while Leo piled into the passenger seat. From force of habit she reached for the seat belt then yelped when she drew it across her chest and belly. She plugged it in anyway.

"Are you *sure* you're okay?"

"Yes, and stop asking." She hit the gas hard enough to make the wheels spin, but she was on firmer turf than mere sand, and the vehicle leaped up and forward, back toward the access drive.

But when she hit the edge of the dirt road, Leo grabbed her arm and told her to stop.

"What? Why?" she asked.

"Nothing's happening. I don't think it worked—but I have an idea." He opened the door and spilled out, slipping when he landed. They were both frozen to the bone and half drowned, and everything felt like a frictionless surface when their extremities were so cold and stiff.

She wanted to shout his name, call him back, tell him to be patient. She didn't want him to leave her alone—she couldn't stand the thought of being alone out there on Marrowstone without him, and it was so terrible that she'd rather run back to the house and blow up with him than be the sole survivor of whatever the hell was happening.

But she stayed where she was, gripping the wheel so hard that her knuckles were white. The engine was running but the vents weren't blowing hot yet. She was cold and wet and in a profound sort of pain that told her something was broken, badly broken, someplace deep inside.

She'd have to deal with it at some point soon. But not yet. Not now. Not while the adrenaline was holding her upright, and she could still breathe through the hot, spreading pain in her chest.

Melissa wiped her wet hair out of her face; it felt slimy and limp, like leftovers sitting too long in the fridge. Her breath fogged around her, and she shivered hard enough to hurt her damaged ribs, but she watched through the back window as Leo ran around the garage to the back of the house. Then she knew it in an instant: he'd gone to the basement hatch.

She turned around and faced forward again, too afraid to watch, too afraid to get out and join him—and afraid that she'd only screw something up if she tried. "Deep breath," she reminded herself. "Trust Leo, he knows what he's doing."

Thirteen-year-old Melissa would've laughed at the thought, but thirteen-year-old Melissa had been a real asshole.

The seconds ticked by and Melissa could hear her heart protesting every aspect of the situation, but it probably hadn't been ninety seconds when Leo came barreling around the corner of the house.

He yanked open the door and yelled, "Drive! Drive! Drive!"

He didn't have to tell her twice, or three times either. She went down the only road that came or went, narrow and dark and clogged with mud though it might have been.

"What did you do?" she asked, and it sounded hysterical even in her own ears.

"Took me a second to get the lighter to spark. Everything's wet and I can barely feel my fingers—then when it finally caught, it burned the shit out of my finger and I dropped it."

"You dropped it down the hatch?"

He shook his head. "No, I went downstairs and lit the fuse on one of the—" An explosion finished his sentence for him.

The initial blast was followed so quickly by a second, and third, and fourth fifth sixth, and they all ran together in the timespan of a cough. The Culpepper basement belched fire and the whole house bounced—the roof popped up and caved in, and dozens of smaller blasts sizzled and barked before a final, larger explosion went off in the kitchen.

Oh right. The microwave.

The windows went orange and warm as the curtains caught fire. The windows that hadn't broken yet started breaking now, cracking from the flames or the recreational explosives.

Leo and Melissa watched it through the back of the Subaru, from a spot thirty yards back in the trees. They couldn't see any details, but they didn't need them. They could see enough to know that the house was going up in flames. It was burning down to the ground.

Leo whispered, "The boys in the corners."

She wanted to say something about them, ask questions about them. She wanted to mourn for them, but she hadn't known them like Leo had, and her soul was all full up on misery. Even if he had any real answers, Melissa might not want them.

Instead, she said, "Tidebury."

"How?" he asked. "I only have a couple of M-80s left. They're loud as hell, but they're not that much bigger than cherry bombs. I doubt they're hot enough to blow a propane tank—and I dropped the Zippo. I can't light anything now."

She thought about her emergency kit in the trunk. "I have matches, the waterproof kind that are dipped in wax for camping and stuff. Maybe I can go inside, open the propane valves, let the gas leak..."

"That's crazy talk, no."

She continued anyway. "*Then* you can throw in some of those M-80s."

"That idea is...less bad. Still not great, but less bad. I refuse to agree to anything that ends up with you dead, though. You need to know that."

A bright yellow light flared on the beach and shot like a comet across the dunes—followed by another towering wave rising out of the ocean. A long shadow rose into the sky on the other side of the burning house, the woods, the path, and the driftwood tree.

Melissa and Leo watched as it smashed into the ground closer to Tidebury. The ground shook and the trees rattled; a swell of water rushed through them and dissipated through the forest.

"Fuck this," Melissa said. She cut the engine and got out of the car, letting the wind take the door and shut it behind her.

She splashed down into the last of the tsunami and let it spill over her ankles. Her shoes were already soaked and there wasn't any current to yank her off her feet, so who cared?

Leo got out too. "Melissa, we can't just—"

"We can't just sit here, no." She cut him off and opened the rear door. "I have matches, and I have...rags; I have a quart of 10W30." She started taking inventory. "Does motor oil have to get extra-hot to burn, like heating oil?"

"Probably?" he guessed.

"Okay, what else do I have in here...?"

Thunder and lightning teamed up to shake the island and light it up even brighter than the scuffle on the beach ever could. Melissa cringed until the sound passed, then wiped more rain away from her face and went back to work. "Paper towels, all soaked by now; jumper cables... Could we set off something with a real big spark? Maybe the oil truck's battery?"

"It's leaking gasoline; we'll just blow ourselves up!"

"Don't care, I'm taking these cables anyway." They were stashed as a tight coil in a plastic holding case. She grabbed it and slung her arm through the short handle strap. "First aid kit," she muttered. "Flashlight, emergency flares...fuck, they're soaked. Everything is *soaked.*"

"Shit, flares would've been great."

She shut the car's back door and juggled the motor oil, the box of waterproof matches, and the cables. "A lot of things would've been great, but we'll work with what we've got. One house down, one to go. Now or never." She held out her fist.

Leo held out his own fist and gave her a bump. "Now or never."

Together they raced to the beach.

46

SATURDAY

LEO

Melissa had given Leo the jumper cables and the quart of oil, but she carried the rest of it without his assistance. Without even watching her closely, he could see that she'd done some damage, possibly to her ribs or collarbone, and a bruise was spreading out from her hairline, across her right temple. She kept shooting him down when he asked if she was all right, so he'd resolved not to do it anymore.

Knowing that she wasn't just hurt, but badly injured...it wouldn't help or change anything. It didn't matter if she was hurt. It didn't matter if he was hurt either.

As things stood, he was battered enough from head to toe. He was pretty sure he'd sprained his left wrist when he'd wrenched himself over the side of the truck, and his knee was bleeding through his pants—but he didn't dare roll up the hem to take a look. If he needed stitches, if he needed a brace or even a cast, there was nothing he could do about it right then and there. If Melissa could power through whatever was wrong with her, then Leo could power through whatever was wrong with him.

He hoped.

So he helped carry the cables and the oil, and they raced back into danger with aching bones, torn muscles, and throbbing heads...back to the beach.

They arrived just in time to see Alcesta Ellingboe flung onto her back with not a wave, but a spray—a sideways waterspout that spun her and knocked her to the ground.

Encouraged, Gunnar approached her, though he knew better than to come too close. "*The years have changed you, darling.*"

From her spot on the sand, she snarled, "*They haven't changed you.*" She pointed her staff at the sky and called down lightning this time; it struck the staff and rocked her—she braced herself with her free hand on the ground and directed the electricity at his face.

It hit him between the eyes and he staggered back, then laughed—the same laugh Leo had heard by the house, nasty and victorious. But Gunnar's voice sizzled now, and sparked. The bolt had hurt him. Not so badly that he couldn't shake it off, but the halo and the fizzing pixels of light reminded Leo of why you don't throw a toaster in the bathtub.

Alcesta used the staff to pull herself to her feet, dazed but angry enough to fight through it. "*You can't have the house.*"

"*I* do *have the house,*" he countered. "*It's almost ready to welcome Him.*"

Leo could hear the capital *H* and it worried him.

His widow said, "*My sister's home is gone already. There's nothing left to feed Tidebury.*"

"*I need nothing else.*"

Leo's stomach sank. It sounded so true and so final.

Melissa caught it too. "Fuck him. He can't have *shit.*" With that, she started running toward Tidebury—a little too carelessly, a little too slow. The sand was hard to run on, no longer just wet and packed but soaked to a sludge by wave after wave; it was quicksand and she was breathing too hard and leaning to the right like she had a stitch in her side.

He started after her. "No, let me do it."

She stumbled, and he caught up to her. "If I'd known she had fucking *lightning* at her disposal..." she muttered, like she'd barely noticed he was beside her.

From what he'd seen so far, whatever Alcesta and Gunnar were doing involved whatever was available in the moment, and neither one could generate anything new. "Let's just get inside," he said, but that was easy to say while they were still a couple hundred feet away from the house—and the path would take them right behind Ms. Ellingboe, who might not see them, and Gunnar, who almost certainly would.

Gunnar, who immediately did.

He saw them. He opened his mouth and started to scream something low and something angry. There were words, but the storm was loud too, and Leo couldn't make out what he was saying.

"Melissa...?"

"Way ahead of you!" she said, and she started to sprint.

Leo shouted, "No!" and with a few long strides, he got her by the back of the coat and pulled her back—just in time to keep her from catching a very focused jet of water upside the head.

The blast came hard and fast, and it wasn't empty; it was full of small shelled animals and big pieces of flotsam and jetsam. When the last of it splashed against the dune behind them, it almost blew a hole straight through it.

"We have to get to the house!" she objected, tearing herself free and scrambling forward again.

He grabbed her by the foot and pulled her down again. "You can't help anyone if you're dead!"

She face-planted in the sand, and then kicked herself loose and flashed a look at Alcesta. "Apparently that's not true!"

Gunnar was incoming, and now Leo could see his face clearly with every fork of lightning that split the clouds above and the cold light that spilled out from Tidebury. He looked like a man—like the same man he'd been in an old photo in a yellowed scrap of newspaper. He had not grown old like his wife but remained young and vigorous and filled with fury; it radiated from his body like heat from desert asphalt.

"Don't watch, just *run*," Leo begged Melissa. "He'll kill us both, and then nothing we've done matters, none of it!"

He had to get her away from this. She was too easily distracted, too determined to see what happened, even if it'd get her killed. He didn't know how hard she'd fight if he tried to physically remove her from the scene.

He could do it, if he had to. He was bigger and stronger.

He'd go first. He'd hit the valves on the propane tanks and get the gas flowing. She had the matches, but he could take them away from her if he had to.

He did not have to.

A new noise blew through the cusp between night and day,

there on the shore. It was resonant and deep and bigger than the thunder that crashed above them, wider than the coastline itself. At first it was a single note, something in a minor key that sounded like it came from an enormous horn. It rose half a note higher and became even louder, even larger, and Melissa buried her head between her forearms like the volume might kill her.

Leo dropped to his knees and tried to cover his ears, but the sound was inescapable. It called out from the center of the earth itself, and it would be heard by everyone, everywhere.

Everything.

The sand began to shake. It started with a rumble and became much rougher, much more like an earthquake—a bad one, the kind that don't come too often but wreak absolute destruction when they do.

The long, unnatural note dimmed and faded, but the shaking did not.

Then came the stones.

Leo pulled Melissa toward him across the sand, and this time she didn't fight. She let him drag her. She grabbed his hands and used him to climb back to a standing position though he was still on his knees. He joined her. He looked for Tidebury, the only thing big enough to orient himself, but it was gone.

No. Not gone.

Hidden.

Something larger than Gunnar Lorentzen, larger than the house, was coming together between them. Loudly. Leo heard the sound of grinding and stacking and assembly, the sound of something building itself on the fly with the parts at hand.

"*Rise, goddamn you. I haven't got all day.*"

"Jesus fucking *Christ*!" Melissa gasped.

Leo couldn't even get that much out. Not when he saw Mrs. Culpepper.

She was still positively ancient in appearance—but now she wore robes like her sister's. Her hair flowed full and wild in the lashing wind, and she wore a headdress of antlers and thorns. Her forehead was powdered white, and a streak of red paint ran from her hairline to her chin, giving her a look that was both feral and primal.

She held a horn that was half her own size, gotten perhaps from some paleolithic beast—a lumbering and northern creature, covered in hair, maybe the same hair from the pelt she wore across her shoulders, over the robe. Long striped feathers spilled from her antler crown and billowed from her shoulders.

Leo saw it all when her sister stood upright again and called for more light, more heat, and shaped it into a ball she could wield like a lamp or a weapon. The glow was large enough and bright enough that it lit up the whole beach.

But not Tidebury.

The thing that stood between Leo and Melissa and the housewreck on the sand was massive and made of rock—the same black boulders that had rolled across the road, and the boulders that pocked the beach. It was lumpy and uneven, cobbled together loosely and without much care for form.

But it had form.

Leo could see it, when the assembly of rock rose to its knees and hauled its tremendous bulk upright, and suddenly, he understood why he hadn't drowned that one summer so many years ago. The rocks made legs. Arms. A head. A shoulder for

Mrs. Culpepper to stand upon as it rose, perfectly steady, as if she were on solid ground and not...

"What *is* it?" Melissa was upright now too. Looking up in disbelief, just like Leo was.

Two words knocked together in his head. "A golem? A troll?"

Alcesta asked her sister, "*What took you so long? Did you swim here, or crawl?*"

"*I was never as good a swimmer as you. I had to get my gear, then attend to the boys.*" She cocked her head toward her own house. "*Had to wait for the fire.*" She looked down at Melissa and Leo, and she frowned. "*Took you long enough.*"

"Sorry?" Melissa said. "We're sorry?"

Leo wasn't sorry. "We got it done, didn't we?"

Now the ghost's frown slipped into a lopsided grin he'd never seen before, and she aimed it at him. "*That you did, I suppose.*"

Her sister felt less accommodating. "*Finish off the job. We can't hold him forever.*"

The rock giant lurched to the side, and Mrs. Culpepper's attention shot back to the man who wasn't a man anymore.

Alcesta waved her staff at them. "*Go!*"

And the battle raged once again. A sister with a staff. A sister with a horn. A pile of rocks that had shaped itself just so.

"It's a troll," Leo marveled.

But the anthropomorphic pile of boulders was in front of them, and they had to run around it in the soft soaked sand that fell away under their feet. It was like running through mud, and it sucked at their shoes, and another blast of water hit the creature hard enough to knock one arm free.

Melissa shrieked and Leo ducked and weaved. Boulders and bits of broken rock crashed around them, beside them, in front of them. A chunk landed on Leo's foot and he yelped. Something pummeled his back and rolled to the ground. Chips of jagged black detritus blew past his head, cutting his ear.

He took a step. Or two. And collapsed.

The rocks had stopped falling from the sky, but Melissa was down. Her coat was ripped and she was pulling herself up, but she wasn't getting all the way back to her feet. She was stopped in a seated position and breathing very heavily.

He crawled over to her, cutting his hands on shells, on bits of volcanic basalt that rained down on everything, everywhere—the joints of the giant having ground them down to pebbles. When he reached her, he realized she was struggling with something, maybe stuck, maybe hurt too badly this time to keep moving forward.

But no. She was digging around in her pocket. She pulled out an envelope folded in half. It was so wet that the paper fell away in pieces.

"What are you doing?" he asked her.

She reached into her other pocket and pulled out a slingshot.

"Where did you get that? Where did you find it?" He'd seen it before. A summer flashed through his head. Coke bottles lined up on the driftwood tree. Pennies and tiny pine cones for bullets. Simon breaking a window. Melissa breaking Mrs. Culpepper's taillight. Leo accidentally winging a seagull and subsequently getting attacked by it.

But mostly he remembered Melissa, knocking one bottle cap off the driftwood tree with a second bottle cap at twenty paces.

She was more than twenty paces away from Tidebury, but now that the stone creature was coming apart, they had a clear sightline.

Not a safe one. More rocks dropped down on them, with larger ones to come, he was sure of it.

She shook the wet envelope, and it came apart in her hand. The rune for fire fell into her palm. She loaded it into the slingshot and said, "Cover me, Leo."

"What? *How?*"

"Let me know if anything's about to fall on me. Try to stop it if it does." She pulled back on the elastic strap and held it, even though it clearly hurt her to do so. Even through the dark and the rain he could see the strain on her face, but she closed one eye and drew the sling of the old-fashioned toy up to her cheekbone.

The rock creature was rumbling and shuffling; it wasn't very mobile, and it did not seem capable of picking its feet up off the sand, which was just as well. If it took a step back, it would crush them both. Gunnar Lorentzen was shouting and swearing, and great gushes of water splashed past it, around it, and through its cracks, dousing them and the mighty Mrs. Culpepper—who blew the horn again, nearly popping Leo's eardrums. He was already sitting down, but now he doubled over and tried to bury his head under his arms while still keeping one eye on his friend.

Melissa cringed too, but she did not lower the weapon.

Would this even work? Why did she think it might? What happened to propane tanks and waterproof matches? Not that they had a prayer of getting close enough to Tidebury to use them, not now.

"What are you waiting for?" he asked desperately.

As if in answer, a long flash of lightning cracked the sky, illuminating every corner of everything on the whole goddamn island.

Melissa said, "That." And she released the rubber strap.

It fired the rune with a snap—flinging it mostly straight and mostly true, flat like a frisbee, narrow end first. A bullet shaped like a biscuit, a tiny piece of otherworldly magic that Leo would never understand, not if he tried for the rest of his life. He liked to think that the tiny projectile whistled as it flew, as it arced and shot straight through the nearest broken window into Tidebury House.

A moment of quiet dropped across the beach. Total quiet. Even the storm held its thunder.

Then the world went white with an explosion that made the Culpepper's inferno look like a tea light. It was followed by heat that was almost fierce enough to burn hair, even at that distance—a radiant, miserable, melting hotness that spread out in a circle and throbbed in waves.

Gunnar shrieked and the troll swayed, blown back like everything else—but strong enough to hold its ground. Leo couldn't see Alcesta and didn't know where she was, what she was doing. But Mrs. Culpepper was descending slowly, in a controlled fashion, as the rock monster dropped to one knee. To both knees. To all fours. To the sand. She raised her right hand, the one that held the horn…and she brought it down in a smashing gesture that the troll copied, smashing through the roof of Tidebury House and collapsing the walls into the lavalike interior, where nothing could live and nothing could find safety.

Tidebury House fell into fire, and the storm waned to halve its previous power—to something that felt ordinary for all its misery. The rest of the giant crumbled and settled into a long line of great black rocks, stretching out from the high-tide line to the ocean's edge.

47

SATURDAY

MELISSA

Melissa and Leo sat on the hood of Melissa's car. It was still parked in the trees, on the access drive that once led to the Culpepper house, and now led to a charred heap that smoldered and sizzled; it threw up hissing mist as the rain dripped into the nooks and crannies that hadn't yet cooled to ashes. Smoke drifted up from the beach, but they could only see it in the split-second flashes of lightning that still kicked across the sky—though more infrequently now. The storm was retreating, and the remains of Tidebury House were obscured by the trees and the dunes beyond Thornbury.

Night had only fallen a couple of hours before, but it felt like midnight. The sky was as black as ink and the clouds obscured every star.

There was no moon.

Deputy Svenson and an EMT whose name Melissa hadn't caught were taking notes and rendering first aid, respectively.

The medic said, "Ma'am, we really need to get you some

X-rays. You've got one broken rib for sure, maybe two or three—and probably a concussion. Maybe even a transorbital fracture. Like, around your eye socket." He pointed at the corner of his own eye.

It wouldn't shock her. She did not reach up to feel the goose egg, and she did not pull out a mirror to look at the bruise that had probably spread up her forehead and down her cheek. "I'll go to the hospital if you want. I can walk to the ambulance."

The EMT looked back and forth between her car and the muddy road. The ambulance had been left at the main road turnoff. It would've only gotten bogged down and needed a tow if they'd tried to come closer.

Leo added, "I can too. Don't worry. You won't have to carry a fat man through the mud—just give me a crutch or something. My foot isn't broken. My knee will be okay."

Melissa put her hand on his unhurt knee and gave it a squeeze. Rain on the disposable rain ponchos they wore hammered loudly in her ears, and probably Leo's too. She didn't know why the emergency pros had insisted on the gear; she was already so soaked that she might never feel dry again, not for the rest of her life. But it felt impolite to refuse, so she'd donned the clear plastic anyway.

Leo had done the same. He looked as thrilled about it as she felt. He'd hurt both of his legs. One knee had a gash that would need some stitches, and the other leg had been hit by a falling boulder. It'd left the kind of abrasion that wouldn't heal soon or easily, but eventually.

Deputy Svenson had a voice recorder visible but protected by his own, more official-looking rain poncho. He asked them both, apparently not caring who answered, "Did you actually *see* the lightning strike that hit the Culpepper house?"

They both nodded, without even glancing at each other first.

Leo said, "We were on the beach when it happened. It was *so loud...*"

"You were on the beach in a thunderstorm, because you thought you'd heard someone calling for help."

Melissa took that one. "Inside the housewreck, yes. We thought it might be Simon, or...or somebody else, I don't know. It was hard to hear. The storm was...loud. We went out to look, to see if we could help."

"I still don't understand what you were doing in the Culpepper house in the first place with the grandson missing. Why did you hang around?"

Leo's turn. "We were holding out hope that he'd come home. He begged us to come out to the island, and we did. We couldn't just turn around and leave. Besides, it's not like we broke in."

"Yeah, you said. Stayed there all the time as kids, and you knew about the key under the mat. And your aunt and uncle"—he cocked a thumb to the south—"they live in the next house over, right? The Alvarez family. Neighbors already confirmed that for us."

"I have no reason to lie, sir. If you'll recall, your office was our first stop when we came out here."

"I know. I'm not trying to grill you; I'm trying to figure out what happened."

"That makes three of us," Melissa said, more earnestly than a lie might have called for. "All I can tell you is we heard someone calling for help, and we ran out to the housewreck. We were trying to look inside, but it was getting dark and we were still deciding what to do when, when…" She gestured at the sky, then used her index finger to make a zigzag motion. "Crack. Boom. And the whole Culpepper house just…went up like a bomb hit it."

"I can't believe it's gone," Leo sighed. "I really, *really* wanted to find out if Simon wanted to live there or if he might want to sell it."

"That's right, you're a Realtor."

He nodded. "That place was worth a fortune. Not even a small fortune, but an *actual* fortune. It could've put me over the top at our brokerage."

Melissa thought he was playing it up because he didn't want the cop to think they'd burned it down. Blown it up. Whatever. That was fine. Leo was a good liar, especially when he wasn't completely lying.

She was pretty good herself. "When the lightning hit and the Culpepper house just…" She made a noise like a cartoon explosion. "You know. We ran back there, freaking out."

"And by pure coincidence, the house on the beach also somehow…was destroyed."

"Not at the same time, no." Leo chose his next words carefully. "We realized there was nothing we could do for Mrs. Culpepper's house, so we went back to the beach. Simon had a collection of fireworks that…look, between you and me? Fireworks aren't my thing. But Simon had some that weren't strictly legal. He loved to put on shows for the Fourth, every year. Ask anybody on the island—everybody came out for them."

"Everybody," Melissa echoed, nodding.

The deputy sighed. "Yeah, I heard about those."

"We were afraid we'd get shot with a stray M-80 or something, so we ran back to the beach in order to get clear of the blast zone. Melissa had brought her phone. We were trying to call 911, but it was really wet and we barely had a signal."

"It took me three tries before the call even went through."

"While we were out there, that's when the earthquake hit. We were right beside the housewreck on the beach, hanging out against the back wall," he explained earnestly.

"Trying to keep out of the rain," Melissa added.

"But we didn't want to go inside. I mean, come on."

The deputy nodded.

Leo continued. "We kept calling in through the windows, and we didn't hear anything. I don't think anyone was actually in there. Could've been a cat or something. There was so much noise, so much thunder...we could've misheard it."

"A cat," the deputy said flatly.

Melissa jumped in. "Obviously I *hope* not. I hope some poor cat wasn't trapped in there, and didn't get...crushed, or washed out to sea, or something. I hope it wasn't a person either. But I don't think it was. I think we were just hearing things. The wind sounded strange when it blew through that place. All the windows were broken, you know," she added with a tired shrug.

The deputy snorted. "Yeah, okay. Then...the earthquake. They felt it as far away as Bremerton."

Leo gasped. "I hope my plants are okay!"

Melissa and the deputy both gave him a look. He shrugged. "I have a ficus that keeps trying to fall over and break the pot.

If it fell the wrong direction, it could take out a window. It's… um. It's gotten out of hand."

"But the earthquake. It happened while you were on the beach, by the house," Svenson prompted.

Melissa rallied and took point. "Yes, and it was *wild*. The sand it went…it went like water. It was like quicksand." She'd seen a Discovery Channel thing about a city that sank in the Caribbean. An earthquake hit, and the sand had liquefied beneath it. "Everything rolled and the house it just, the walls folded in on one side, and these rocks that were down the beach—farther north than they are now—they rolled right over it."

"That's when you got hurt?"

"It was all kind of a blur. Everything happened at once—and it was getting dark. I fell at some point…" She felt it was all right to be vague. Vague was more or less true, for one thing, and for another, she probably had a concussion. The EMT had said so.

Leo backed her up. "It happened in waves. The first one threw us up in the air, and when we landed the ground was moving underneath us. I don't know exactly how I got hurt, or what I hit, or what hit me. All I know is that when everything stopped shaking, I thought I had a broken leg, and I thought Melissa was dead."

The deputy looked at the medic. The medic shrugged.

"All right," Deputy Svenson said. "The place was barely standing, so I guess it's no great shock that it fell apart. We can look over the scene in the light of day later. Let's get you two to a hospital."

The EMT said, "I'll go see about a crutch."

The cop and the medic left, and then, for a minute, Melissa and Leo were alone.

Quietly, Melissa asked, "What about the fuel oil truck?"

"What about it?"

"They'll notice it eventually."

He nodded. "I'll um...I'll tell them I stole it. If anybody asks. I'll say I was stuck in the storm because my Tesla...no. I'll tell them that me and you got in a fight, and you threw me out of the car over by Mystery Bay."

"Ooh, I get to be the villain. I love it."

"Oh good, I was afraid you'd be upset." He leaned over and tapped his shoulder to hers. He finished the rest of his story on the fly, she was pretty sure. "You dumped me there, and I got freaked out by the storm. The truck was parked at Nordy's, so I took it—but I...I took the wrong turn because I couldn't see through the rain; the windshield wipers are shit or something. I ended up on the beach by accident."

"What were we fighting about?" she asked.

"Hm."

Then she said, "Wait, I know. We were fighting about Simon. The fight we had earlier, about...who loved him more, I guess that's what the root of it was. The truth is always easier to remember, okay? When they ask about the truck, that's what we'll do. We'll change our stories, so that we didn't hear someone crying in Tidebury. We'll say we were fighting, and I walked away, and you followed me. That's how we ended up on the beach."

He perked up. "I like it. I get to be a villain too."

"We're both terrible, you know."

"Damn straight. Hey, how did you know what the rune would do?"

She smiled off into space. "I didn't. I thought..." She cleared her throat. "I thought I heard Simon. I heard his voice, like he was very close, whispering in my ear. He said to try it."

Leo's eyes went red and he looked away. "You really think it was him?"

"I hope it was. I hope the fire did something to let them all go. Mrs. Culpepper, she said—"

"You think she set them free?"

She nodded with more confidence than she felt. "I do," she continued to fib. "How else would I have known to give it a shot? So to speak."

"So to speak," he repeated. "Okay. I'll choose to believe that."

"We might as well. There's no telling what really happened. Literally or figuratively."

He laughed, a deep belly bark that ended with a snort. "No shit. Hey. I'm glad I'm not the only one who knows. I'm glad you were here."

"I'm glad *you* were here. I *literally* couldn't have done it without you. And you couldn't have done it without me either," she said, sparing him the compliment and knocking her shoulder against his. "Look at us, working together like adults. Simon would be proud."

"I hope so. I think Mrs. Culpepper was, a little bit. In the end."

"You know what? I think so too. Not Alcesta, though. She didn't care if we fucked right off into the sun."

"She would've tossed us into the Sound as soon as give us a hand. But they needed us," he pointed out. "They couldn't have done it without us. When you think about it...they were very lucky to have us."

"Damn right they were."

The EMT was coming back with an aluminum crutch. He sloshed through the mud, lifting his feet too high with every step, trying to avoid splashing. The fire at Thornbury still simmered in the basement, and with the road all but washed out, there was no way to bring a fire truck. The county firefighters had a guy monitoring the scene and had otherwise decided to let it go.

So long as it didn't spread to the trees around it, it could burn down to cinders.

And it probably would.

Epilogue

1953

Otelia Charlotte Ellingboe stood alone, milling about in her sister's living room. It was a nice living room in a nice house. The fanciest on the island, if you believed the tiny rag of a newspaper from the next community over...not that there was much competition. Though most of the island's handful of residents had money—you needed to have money to live so remotely—few had bothered to create a place so permanent and so grand.

Until recently no one had bothered to build there at all, save the military, and even so, the fort at Marrowstone's northern point had never served much of a purpose, if you asked Otelia.

She checked her watch. Checked a clock that hung on the wall above a television the size of a space capsule. Tapped one foot. Tapped the other foot. Alcesta was almost forty-five minutes late, and time was not on their side—or so they suspected, though it was difficult to say for certain.

In a gold-tone frame on the fireplace mantle, there was a

wedding photo: it was Alcesta and her husband, Gunnar. Otelia scowled at it, but she understood why her sister left it up. They wouldn't want to arouse any suspicion.

So far, they were reasonably confident that there wasn't any suspicion.

Gunnar was perhaps the most solipsistic man she'd ever met—exactly the sort to ignore everything that failed to serve his purposes, up to and including his own wife and her family. He was an infuriating fellow and always had been; Otelia had never seen the appeal of marrying him, but twins are not a single unit with singular preferences, any more than any other two siblings—full, half, or step.

These two in particular did not look any more alike than two sisters born in different years: both were petite and slender, but Otelia was a platinum blond with curls, and Alcesta's hair was a darker honey, as smooth and flat as a tide pool, much to her aggravation. Otelia preferred leisure and lounging, reading and radio. Alcesta was fond of volleyball, and she was an excellent swimmer—though she didn't do much of that, so far north.

Swimming was best reserved for vacations in warmer climates.

Otelia scowled at the photo again, then reached out and smacked it facedown on the mantel. She winced to hear a soft *crack* that said the glass had split. Well, Gunnar would never notice. Maybe Alcesta wouldn't either.

If she ever showed up.

Otelia had no husband, and she was not especially interested in finding one. Maybe that would change someday; maybe it wouldn't—but she had bigger problems than spinsterhood right that moment. Maybe one day she'd decide to embrace routine and domesticity, maybe even succeed where her sister had failed at finding a suitable mate...after their plan came to fruition. If they could pull it off and subsequently get away with it.

They'd already decided: they would blame an earthquake.

Certainly, the quakes had become a source of local chatter, occurring lately with increased frequency—even for an island situated on the Ring of Fire. The sisters' first experiments with their grandmother's heirlooms had been erratic and messy, so it was just as well that they lived so far out in the middle of nowhere.

Fewer witnesses. Fewer complaints. Fewer questions, less speculation about what, exactly, was happening on Marrowstone Island.

The military base hosted only a skeleton crew, and other than that, there were no more than a few dozen year-round residents.

"But they'll complain," Alcesta had said.

"Complain to who?" Otelia had asked. "About what? Seismic activity? Tell them to take it up with God," she said. "See if they pick the right one."

Their learning curve was steep, but they had ancient notes, scribbled on scraps and stashed inside the trumpet that had come from the old family, in the old world.

Alcesta sometimes talked like she'd like to see the homeland one day. Otelia did not see the point. "It's the same as here, but colder and darker and wetter. What on earth would possess anyone to live there, much less to choose it—having known more pleasant places?"

"Don't you want to know where you came from?" her sister had countered.

"I know where I came from, and it only had so much to offer. The best of it came in the box from Great-Aunt Klara. The rest can stay where it is."

Otelia was on the verge of walking out, of giving up for now, of concluding that Alcesta was not fully committed to the proceedings, when she finally heard the grinding wheels of a vehicle coming down the driveway—a lengthy unpaved strip that turned into a river of mud over each winter.

"Finally," she muttered.

Two minutes later, her sister came hustling into the house. "Sorry I'm late; it took longer to peel myself away than anticipated. He's in a mood today; it's hard to explain." She dropped an armload of miscellany on the round table in the grand entryway. "But I'm here now, and he's off to the train station, so we have all afternoon and most of tomorrow without him, so we can practice and...and plan, I suppose."

Otelia eyed the pile of random items that her sister had left behind. She saw fresh flowers wrapped in cellophane, some magazines, and a box with a ribbon untied. She folded her arms and raised an eyebrow. "Are those going-away presents?"

"Like I said, he's in a weird mood. Did you make any progress on the basement door?"

"None. He might as well have welded it shut," she admitted, turning away from the gifted detritus. "Or painted it on a wall, for all the luck I've had getting it open. I don't know what's keeping it closed, but it's beyond my ken. We may have to forget about it and—"

"Forget about it? He spends half his waking life down there; it must be important!" Alcesta protested.

"Nothing in your basement is more important than getting rid of this man."

"Yes, I'm well aware," she replied, and the words sounded like acid. "But there's always the chance that something down there might prevent our efforts."

"There's a better chance that you're stalling again."

Alcesta scowled. "Oh, drop dead already."

Lightly, Otelia said, "Wrong target, dear. I'm not the one who's making children disappear in the name of bad magic."

"No, you're just the one borrowing it from overseas. At least Gun's is homegrown magic, and I'm not wholly convinced that ours isn't just as bad. Or worse."

"Don't be ridiculous. We aren't hurting anyone but ourselves, and this is our birthright, if you listen to the old ladies. We're born to ours. He's chasing someone else's, and whoever that someone else may be, their price of entry is much, much steeper than ours. His wants blood. Ours wants..." She hesitated.

"Yes? *Do* go on. What do you think this magic wants from us? What will it cost us, if we use it?"

Otelia shrugged off her uncertainty. "It doesn't matter."

"It'll matter eventually," her sister pressed.

She shook her head. "First things first. We eliminate the known, pressing problem—and sort out the rest later, from a place of safety on an island where little boys don't disappear and don't turn up dead when they're of no more use to a monster." Surely they could agree on this much. Surely nothing good could be summoned or called or used when this was the price of entry. "Whatever his end goal might be, we cannot let him achieve it. You saw the thing in the storm. I know you did."

"I saw it."

"He wants to bring it closer."

"I know," Alcesta said, some of the acid leaving her voice. "I…I saw it. It's like he's trying to feed a stray cat, lure it into the garage so he can tame it and let it catch mice."

Otelia snorted. "Yes, he's exactly the sort to believe himself capable of training, or managing, or controlling…something like that. But another storm will come. The bad kind, the kind you can smell when you open the front door." The kind you could see in the clouds and watch in the waves as they frothed against the shore, creeping toward the tree line at high tide.

"You're undoubtedly correct." Alcesta wandered to the fireplace, as if thinking something was different or wrong; she saw the fallen photo in its frame and reached for it—then changed her mind and left it lying facedown. "Did you do that, or would you blame it on seismic activity?"

"I did it," her sister confessed without the slightest sense of guilt.

"You couldn't even have him looking at you from a photo?"

"Pick it back up, if you'd like to gaze wistfully into his eyes."

"Stop it," Alcesta snapped. But even so, she walked away. She exhaled heavily and ran her hands through her hair, working herself up, or down, or only trying to shake off some extra nervous energy. "If we can't act like civilized adults, and cooperate, and, and behave ourselves, Good Lord Almighty. This will never work."

"Fine. You're right," Otelia said. "We can do this. We don't have to walk in lockstep or achieve perfect agreement. We already agree on the goal. We only have to nail down the plan." She tried to make it sound more confident than she felt.

She was only moderately successful. Her sister heard some note in the words, some implication—or else she only imagined it and amplified it. Otelia didn't know which, but Alcesta said, "I'm not really in the mood for your self-righteousness right now."

"What self-righteousness? I said you were right. I thought that's what you wanted."

"You didn't mean it," Alcesta said darkly. "You *never* mean it. You think if you use the right words, say the right thing, go through all the right motions—then anything you do is fair and correct, and must be forgiven as a matter of course."

"If I'm right about these tools from Great-Aunt Klara, then a little precision is important for success, so I'm not sure I see the problem. If we aren't going to do this right, then we'd better not risk it at all."

"You know that's not what I meant."

Otelia sighed. "I wish you were right about that. I wish I knew what you meant." Even when her sister tried to be direct, she talked in circles and side tangents. "But I can live without knowing everything if you can. I can live with just about anything, if you'll help me with this. It was your idea, after all."

Alcesta faltered, then folded her arms and leaned back against the wall beside the fireplace. "Of course it was my idea. I saw him first, for what he is."

Otelia almost said something hasty in response, but restrained herself. Too much was at stake. "It stands to reason. You're the one who's closest to him."

Alcesta shook her head very slightly. "I thought I was," she said, softened just a hair by her own misreading of the man. Or that's what Otelia thought. "I'm not sure anyone's truly close to him, though. He keeps it that way by design." She stepped away from the wall and headed toward the kitchen.

Otelia caught up with her there. "We can do this. We just have to stay focused, and be clear with our intentions and firm in our resolve."

"And our cooperation. We have to do this together. We can't do it alone."

She nodded. "Obviously," she said, while thinking something else entirely. What if? What if Alcesta didn't pull her weight, or worse yet, what if she pulled her punches? What if she faltered, changed her mind, or hesitated at the last moment? What would Otelia do?

Could she do this without her twin?

Should she?

Alcesta echoed, "Obviously, yes. Neither one of us is strong enough alone, or I would've done this myself."

"Would you have?" Otelia asked before she could stop herself.

"What? What are you implying?"

"Nothing! I only wondered if...if you'd go through with an ordinary murder, if that were all it'd take to stop him from hurting anyone else, or calling upon any further forces of evil, or—"

"Forces of evil? You give him too much credit. He's only

trying to make a call to a place where no one wholesome will pick up the phone."

"No good operators running the switchboard?" Otelia joked weakly.

It only irritated Alcesta. "Very funny. You're always so funny."

"I'm not trying to be..." she began, then gave up. "Never mind. I'm sorry. Can we get to work?"

"See, there you go again. Saying you're sorry, picking the right words, just to move things forward so you can get what you want."

"I thought this was what we both wanted?" Otelia was losing the thread, but that happened all the time, when it came to her sister. Sometimes she felt like the woman was a minefield of unknown dangers, easy to trip and quick to harm. If she was careful about choosing her words, well, she had reason to be. The wrong one could turn into a supernova.

"Don't be ridiculous, nobody *wants* this," Alcesta said. "But we have to do it. Stop trying to make a virtue out of a necessity."

"All right. We'll do it your way." Were those the right words?

Not quite.

"Damn right we will, and we'll do it on my terms; he's *my* husband. I'm the one who stands to lose the most. I deserve to run the show."

"Then run it, for Christ's sake! Get your staff; I've already got the trumpet. The beach is right over there through the trees, and the weather is calling for violence. Lead the way, if that's how you want it. Show me how to do this to your satisfaction."

Alcesta snorted and turned away, but she did in fact open the cabinet doors beneath the kitchen sink. She reached inside, underneath, and felt around until she'd retrieved a worn wooden staff wrapped in a towel. "Don't be obsequious. It doesn't suit you." She went to the back door and pushed it open; it slapped back and forth in the wind until she got a better grip and held it steady.

"I can't argue with that." It was always her phrase of last resort, and it rarely worked. But it sometimes did. Never for very long, but perhaps for long enough. She took a deep breath, collected the trumpet she'd left on the dining table, followed her sister down the winding path to the ocean—past the venerable old driftwood tree and onto the shifting sands left behind by the receding tide.

ACKNOWLEDGMENTS

I always hate writing these segments, because I live in mortal terror of accidentally leaving someone out—but I'll keep this brief, and here goes nothing. Starting with the usual suspects: Thanks to my amazing agent Stacia Decker, my exceptional editor Rachel Gilmer, and all the fine folks at Sourcebooks who've been part of bringing this book across the finish line. Many grateful waves of appreciation also must be directed toward my husband, Aric—who keeps the bills paid while I ride the inconstant waves of a writing career—and likewise, to my tipsy ladies in the clubhouse at the end of the universe (they know who they are). That we all should be so lucky to have such a team in our corner.

ABOUT THE AUTHOR

Cherie Priest is the Philip K. Dick–, Hugo-, and Nebula-nominated author of over two dozen science fiction, fantasy, mystery, and horror novels and novellas, including *Boneshaker*, which won the PNBA Award and the Locus Award for Best Science Fiction Novel, and the critically acclaimed *I Am Princess X*, which was a YALSA Quick Pick for Reluctant Young Adult Readers. Her books have been translated into nine languages in eleven countries.

Born in Tampa, Florida, she currently lives in Seattle, Washington, with a menagerie of exceedingly photogenic animals.